Children of Andalon - Book 1

Andalon Legacy

T. B. Phillips

Andalon Legacy
Children of Andalon, Book One

Published by Andalon Press
Copyright © 2022 by T.B. Phillips

Cover design by Lynnette Bonner of Indie Cover Design, images ©
  depositphotos.com, File: # 39270889
  depositphotos.com, File: # 58942251
  depositphotos.com, File: # 61370153
  depositphotos.com, File: # 71958319
  depositphotos.com, File: # 77111675
  depositphotos.com, File: # 101144436
  depositphotos.com, File: # 166767036
  depositphotos.com, File: # 545892330
Book interior design by Stewart Design, https://StewartDesign.studio

ISBN 978-1-7331805-6-6

Part 1
Seventeenth Summer

Robert sprawled on soft grass, bathing in warm sun and watching lumbering clouds pass slowly overhead. He listened as summer wind whistled through high branches, rattling pines as a reminder of its strength. The creaking in their sway informed the wind of their resolve, intent on bending as much as possible before eventually succumbing. High atop one, broad wings unfolded and slowly gathered that summer wind while carrying a solitary eagle upward. The boy marveled at the gracefulness with which it flew, yearning to join the voyage and leave the valley and the mountains behind.

He ignored the splashing of water and joyful shouts of teens playing in the river not far from his meadow. They were happy sounds, but Robert felt almost to have outgrown them, thinking again of the eagle and how it too ignored the goings-on of those cursed to walk the ground. That was his fate, tied to the dirt of the world and doomed to live forever upon its back. If only the boy could soar like a bird.

Though his heart craved journey, he would never leave his mother's home until ready to make one for himself. That was the reason for the worry and why he clung to boyhood on this day, his heart brimmed with wanderlust but his mind overflowed with logic. This was his seventeenth summer, the marker of adulthood and harbinger of freedom to blaze new paths. His logical side won the brief battle over the boy within, and he thought again how leaving would affect his mother.

Eusari wasn't truly his mother, but that fact never mattered to the boy. Robert loved her dearly and bore her name of Thorinson. Shortly after his own parents met death during the Brother's War, she claimed Robert as her own. She loved him and nurtured him, even after bearing two children of her own a half year later. Those twins splashing in the river were his younger brothers, born too late in the season to claim this summer as their seventeenth, but were almost men of their own by size if not maturity. Their merriment worked to lure him into momentary boyhood, drawing him to frolic and play in the water.

Strangers found the twins nearly impossible to tell apart, tall and broad of shoulders, well-muscled for their age, with strong chins and flowing yellow hair. Their eyes shone from beaming faces like sapphires burning with internal light. They, unlike Robert who preferred to remain clean shaven, wore patchy facial hair with pride, each hell-bent on growing a full beard before the other.

"Come on!" Franque called. "Quit dreaming about Tara and give me a challenge. I've already tossed Krist so many times, I'm afraid he'll drown if he goes under one more!"

Robert smiled as the older twin's words incensed the younger and rolled over to watch them wrestle.

Though born only a few minutes apart and equal in every other way, there was no mistaking Franque's superior confidence over Krist's. The twins stood a full head taller than Robert and seemed to have room to grow more as summer wore on. The broadness of their shoulders had always been noticeable but last spring had witnessed a thickening of each. Soon these boys would be mountains of men in both stature and purpose. He doubted either would remain to tend the farm, choosing instead a life of soldiering or maybe even as constables.

Krist lunged at Franque and was easily pushed away, forgetting as always to set his feet properly. This infuriated the boy, who sputtered and spit water while righting himself to try again.

"Were you really dreaming of me?" a soft voice asked from behind.

Robert turned to see a Pescari girl standing a few feet away, her moccasins having muffled any sound of approach. He smiled up at her, a beautiful sight in the traditional buckskins worn by her people. The fringes and tassels swayed in the breeze, and her hair seemed to tease him as it fluttered about.

"Or were you staring at Felicima," she asked dryly, indicating the sun high above, "letting her burn madness into your mind and choosing instead to bond with that eagle and fly away to the city?" She added while kneeling beside him, "I think you want to run away and join the Dreamers."

"I would never leave any of you," he admitted. "Mother needs help with the farm and I promised to give her one more summer before I venture off. I don't want her to have to hire hands until after Franque and Krist make their own choices. Besides, you know how she feels about the Dreamers. She doesn't want any of us to go near them whenever they're around."

"Don't wait for your brothers," the girl protested, wiping raven locks from her face and revealing worried eyes and a furrowed forehead. Something bothered her deeply. "They're spoiled selfish brats most of the time, not at all like you. As for the Dreamers, it's your life to live now as a man, not Eusari's to rule over."

Only then did Robert notice the redness around the girl's eyes, no doubt raw from tears. "What's wrong?" he asked. "Did you and Flaya fight again?"

She nodded. Lately it seemed the girl and her own mother had been at odds over everything, their raised voices sometimes carrying on the night winds and through his window.

"She threatened to take me away for my seventeenth year," Tara admitted, "so that I may have my ritual among our own people."

Robert sat abruptly, his pulse racing at the thought of his best friend leaving, even for a year. The possibility brought pangs of loss as if she'd already gone. "But you don't want to?" Robert asked.

"No. I am not like my people, and I'm not like *her*. I may be Pescari, but only because of blood." She pulled uncomfortably at the buckskins. "These, especially, have grown unbearable. They serve no purpose except to draw unwanted attention in town."

"But your father was shappan. Don't you want to honor him?" Her father had also died in the Brother's War. Robert envied the details she knew of him, the chieftain of his Pescari clan.

"I do not believe in the ways of my father, for they are not mine. I've never even met another except those who bring news to mother. I cannot honor his memory."

These words shocked Robert. Spoken during daylight, they amounted to blasphemy. He pointed to the sun and said, "You say these things under the eye of Felicima. Do you reject her as well?"

Tara tugged once more at her buckskins. "I don't believe Felicima is anything but a ball of fire like the headmaster said."

Robert fell silent. Only a few days before, their teacher had ranted against her people's beliefs, using Tara as an example of the need for science over religion. He had wondered why she remained silent instead of defending her culture and finally understood. She leaned toward agreement. Quietly he said, "Don't listen to that man. He's a jerk, and so is most of the class."

"Especially that new girl from Fjorik," Tara agreed.

"Greta?"

"Yes, her. She's turned many of the girls away from me, even those I thought were friends."

"Well, she's a jerk, too. Maybe we should tell Franque and Krist and let them thump a few heads to leave a message."

"No!" Tara replied sharply. "No violence. I'm angry with them, but not angry enough to involve the twins."

Another splash in the water caused them both to turn. This time, Krist had figured out a way to toss his brother and Franque floundered on his back. The younger of the two flexed triumphantly until a leg caught his own and toppled him also into the river. The resulting flurry of punches informed Robert that playtime was over. They'd both have black eyes if he didn't intervene.

"I've got to go," he said, scrambling down to pull off whichever had the advantage before one of them drowned. By the time he'd dragged Franque off their brother, Tara had left the meadow as silently as she'd arrived. Robert scanned the tree line for a last glimpse but found none. "Come on," he said to the shirtless twins, "let's get back to the farm. We've got school tomorrow."

"*You've* got school," Krist sneered. "You're the only one who likes it."

"I *do* like school," Robert agreed. "It's my ticket to something better in life."

"I don't need school to better myself," Franque said, gingerly touching a split lip. "I'm gonna sail away from here someday. I don't need math or science to work on boats."

"Actually you do," Robert explained. "Every sailor knows the stars and the best can sail by them. They can estimate elevation and range too, and you'll need math for that."

"Yeah, dummy," Krist said to his twin as he pulled on his shirt. "You're too stupid to be a sailor, so you'd better learn to plow a straighter line."

Franque waited till the shirt covered his brother's eyes then popped him one in the mouth, marking their lips to match. With a grunt and a growl the younger twin tossed the garment aside, eyes burning with fury. Franque laughed and took off running full speed toward the farm with an angry Krist hot on his heels.

Robert shook his head, watching them go. He glanced once more toward the meadow, wishing to spend a few moments longer with Tara. After a deep sigh, he walked slowly after his brothers. Somewhere, high overhead, an eagle screeched triumphantly as it spied prey upon the ground, but the young man never looked up. He knew better than to wish to soar on the winds. If he truly was becoming a man, he had to put aside boyish fancies.

CHAPTER TWO

Robert Thorinson scratched chalk against slate, scribbling his answer then eagerly holding it up. The headmaster looked up from the fire warming his pot of tea and gave an approving nod before returning to his stoking. Pleased with the speed of his own wit, the boy beamed with pride. The problem had been a difficult one, forcing several calculations before arriving at an accurate conclusion. Groans from the other children let him know not everyone enjoyed his victory, but he ignored their protests. He was nearly always the first student to finish assignments.

A pair of felt erasers collided with the back of his head and he spun in his seat, scanning the room and meeting the frowning faces of his twin brothers. Both shook their blonde heads, irritated at being beaten, especially on a day when the winner of the contest would receive an afternoon without chores. As he turned around a piece of chalk struck his ear. Whirling he locked eyes with Krist who mouthed a threat. Beside him, Franque silently pounded a fist into his palm as if letting Robert know what trouble he'd face when they returned home to the farm.

Robert ignored their taunts. He knew they were only teasing, for that was their way. He watched the pair slip from their chairs, taking advantage of the headmaster looking away to reach below the desk for a textbook. Robert mouthed for them to sit down, but they only smiled back and waved their goodbyes before sneaking out the door. No doubt they were headed to the river for an afternoon of fun.

Tara leaned close to his ear. "We should go with them," she whispered. "I don't want to stay."

He shook his head. He never cut class or shared in his brothers' trouble; it wasn't his way. Even talking during class was something he refused to do.

"Come on," she urged, a long lock of dark hair falling across her face and making her somehow prettier than she already was.

He hated that he found her so attractive. She was, after all, like a sister to him and the twins. Besides, she may be leaving soon.

"I can't," he finally said. "I have to meet with Mr. Yurik later and help with his new project. He's close to another breakthrough."

"Master Thorinson! You and Miss Tara may cease your chatter at any time," the headmaster commanded. Looking around and noticing Franque and Krist's absence, he asked accusingly, "Where are your brothers?"

"I don't know," Robert replied, "they were just here."

"They said they were going to paint graffiti on your barn," Tara lied, "and leave a bucket of flaming crap on your doorstep. If you hurry you could catch them."

"Of course *you* would know, your kind are usually the source of such mischief." The man became a flurry of dark robes as he darted to the door, turning only to remind the class they had chores—all except Robert who had won the contest. "And you can haul the trash, Miss Tara, since a little dirt won't hurt your filthy buckskins." Then he darted the opposite way the boys had gone, racing toward his homestead.

"There's your answer," Tara said with sudden anger, grabbing Robert's hand and dragging him toward the door. "I want to go *now*."

A girl's voice froze the pair before they even stepped outside. "Mr. Genius may not have chores to do, but you do, Pescari. Go haul the trash, Tara, and toss in your smelly buckskins while you're at it."

The other children laughed, especially Sam Rawlins, the butcher's son, and Peta Grenwich whose father was the blacksmith.

Robert felt the angry way Tara's hand squeezed his tighter. "Don't do it," he said. "Ignore her."

"I can't *ignore* her," she whispered. "I've been listening to her prattle on for weeks. The headmaster lets her do it and I'm sick of them both!" She whirled around to face Greta Greenbriar, whose family had recently moved upriver from Fjorik via Logan City. "You have a problem with my heritage?" she demanded.

"I don't have a problem with your heritage," Greta said, rising from her chair. She stood several heads taller and was set heavier than Tara, the sign of her northern blood. "I have a problem with your filthy presence in *our* school and *our* town."

"*Your* town?" Tara balked. "I've lived here my entire life and I don't remember inviting *you* to live in it!"

As Greta stepped forward, Robert urged his friend to back down. "Don't do it," he pleaded. "It won't end well for you. You know how Flaya gets, especially regarding violence."

"I don't care *what* my mother thinks," she said, "and forget what I said about it yesterday. I've been listening to this one talk behind my back ever since she got here, and I've had enough."

"That's right. I *do*." Greta said with a smirk, "I'm always complaining about the stench of your buckskins and greasy Pescari hair."

Tara stood taller, straightening the garb of her people. "The only stench here," she replied, slowly tying back her hair with a string of Pescari beads, "carries along the wind as it passes between your legs."

Greta charged in anger and Robert moved to step between the girls. Strong hands grabbed him as two boys intervened. Sam and Peta stood on each side, both holding an arm and laughing as the larger girl tackled Tara to the ground. The resulting flurry of hair-pulling and fingernail-scratching erupted with screaming, and Robert struggled to get free to pull them apart.

"Let 'em fight, genius boy," Peta growled. "Every Pescari deserves a beating at least once in their lives."

"Yeah," Sam agreed with a devilish smile, "Even the girls."

Robert boiled inside, burning with anger at the treatment of his friend. Then he remembered the words of old Cedric when teaching the boys self-defense. *Fight dirty and take out the big one first,* he had said. Robert clenched his jaw and brought his foot up high into the air, stomping hard against the outside of Peta's knee. It snapped awkwardly and the boy crumpled, crying out in agony. Now, with his right arm free, Robert smashed a fist upward into Sam's nose, breaking it cleanly as blood poured down the boy's chin.

By now Tara had the upper hand, her own face bloodied but determined as she pounded the girl cowering beneath her.

"Call me filthy again!" she demanded, but Greta only sobbed.

Robert shivered against the sudden cold in the room. He grabbed her waist and heaved upward, dragging his friend toward the door while the other children stared, dumbfounded by the sudden ferocity with which each had fought. As they turned, they met the headmaster's wide-eyed stare from the doorway.

"You're both expelled," he said matter-of-factly. "And tell your no-good brothers they're not welcome back, either! I *will* be reporting this to the constable!" The man turned his attention to the warming stove. "Sam, re-light that fire while I attend to Peta."

Tara pushed past the headmaster, pausing only briefly to kick him in the knee. "Report *that!*" she snarled, then dragged Robert at a full run down the road toward the river. They never stopped until reaching its banks. There, they collapsed panting and laughing into a heap on the grass.

After a while, Robert admitted, "She deserved it. They all did, but you shouldn't have kicked the headmaster."

"Of course I shouldn't have," Tara agreed, "but it felt good. What do we do now? We can't go to the river or your brothers will see my bloody face and go after them all."

"Yeah," he agreed, getting to his feet, "the river's out of the question." He reached a hand and she took it, letting him pull her into a warm embrace. Something in her changed then, collapsing into his arms and letting out the emotion bottled within. He hugged her like that for a while, letting her sob into his chest until all the anger had passed. Eventually, all that remained was an exhausted girl. "Let's go see Mr. Yurik," he offered. "He's close by, and I was supposed to help him today. Plus, he knows medicine and can treat your wounds."

She nodded, wet tears smearing against his shirt before taking his hand to be lead away. She abruptly froze and Robert turned.

A pair of riders sat upon horseback with sky blue robes and cloaks worn high upon their heads, mostly covering the faces of strangers. The matching symbols on their robes, however, were easily recognized from a distance. They were both autumn emotants.

"What are Dreamers doing here?" Tara asked quietly.

"I don't know," he admitted, shivering as their watchful eyes chilled his spine. "Let's go," he urged and led her away down the lane toward Sippen's workshop. Every so often he stole a glance over his shoulder to see if the riders followed. Thankfully they hadn't, but he held his breath until he and Tara had rounded the bend.

Sippen Yurik was another longtime friend of Robert's mother and had been among her travelling companions when she and Flaya settled the area. But, unlike Old Cedric and Sebastian, Sippen had chosen to live apart from the others, setting up his shop along the river. There was no town in those days, only a few homesteads and a trading post, and he had served many years as the closest thing to a blacksmith. But the little man seemed to age differently than other men, and swinging a hammer quickly became too difficult to sustain his career. He only tinkered now, selling lamps and useful items in the market square.

He was a small man, barely taller than a ten-year-old child and with a head too large for his shoulders. His crooked spine helped his appearance seem prematurely aged, and his skin was deeply scored with lines. The wisps of hair clinging to his head were completely white. What he lacked in stature the man clearly made up with keen intellect though, and was a clever inventor. But without the thick glass in his spectacles the man was nearly blind, and he depended upon Robert for finer detailed work in his shop.

He was bent over a magnifying glass when the children entered. Without looking up, he said with his usual stammer, "Yuh... you're here uh... early, Robert. Wuh... what's wrong?"

"We got into a fight, Mr. Yurik, at school."

"Yuh... *you* did? Uh... or Krist and Fuh... Franque did?"

"Tara and I did," Robert admitted quietly.

This caused the little man to look up from his work, adjusting his lenses to better see the girl and boy standing in his workshop. He frowned at the blood on Tara's face. "Thuh... that's suh... surprising. Tuh... tell me uh... about it."

And Robert did. He told him how Greta and the others had been picking on Tara, demeaning her for being Pescari and how even the headmaster had stirred the pot. Sippen listened quietly, taking in every detail without flinching and nodded his heavy head at times.

"Suh... so Krist and Fuh... Franque weren't involved?"

"No, sir."

"Then it cuh... can be ruh... remedied. "Heh... here. Puh... pull up stools."

"What are you making?" Tara asked, picking up a long copper tube polished to a shine.

Robert looked to Sippen and the older man nodded, letting him explain. "It's an engine," he said.

"What's an *engine*?" Tara asked

"Something that creates kinetic energy to accomplish work."

Her face revealed confusion, and Tara commanded, "Speak in Andalonian, Robert, not like a genius."

"It moves things... any direction you'd like and does the work for you."

"Thuh... this one is fuh... for a cuh... carriage," Sippen added, beaming proudly.

"Instead of horses?"

"Exactly!" Robert exclaimed. "After we iron out some of the issues, this steam engine will use water to move the carriage instead of horses. Water's cheaper than hay and doesn't throw a shoe or break a leg."

The look on Tara's face was disbelieving, as if they described something too good to be true, so Robert showed her. He picked up a tiny boat with coiled copper tubing and a candle, placing it in a tub of water. Striking a match, he lit the candle and stepped back and waited.

"What's supposed to happen?" she asked.

"Just wait," he said with a grin.

Soon, the little vessel began to sputter and spin, then move in the water, racing faster and faster around the edge of the tub.

Tara's eyes grew large. "How's it work?" she asked.

"The candle is the source of heat, and the heated copper draws water up into the coil where it's made even hotter and pushed out the back—hot water moves faster than cold. It just keeps pulling it in and pushing it out the back, just like that! The engine we put in the carriage is similar, but different. It keeps the water sealed inside the engine and uses it to drive pistons up and down, making the energy and turning the wheels." He stepped back to let her poke at and play with the little toy, amazed by its simplicity and power.

"Robert," she said, "you really are a genius."

He blushed, "I'm not, Mr. Sippen is. He's a really good teacher."

"Yuh... you are tuh... too, Robert. Smart as yuh... your mother and father."

Robert felt his legs wobble and head go a little fuzzy. Sippen had never mentioned knowing his parents. "Tell me about them," he suddenly demanded. "Please."

"I'm suh... sorry. I shouldn't have. Thuh... that's you... Eusari's job."

"She won't," Robert complained. "She always says I'll learn more when I'm older, like she's avoiding telling me a horrible secret."

Sippen moved to an overstuffed chair near the hearth and collapsed wearily into it. "Wuh... well, you uh... are older, but thuh... that's still her story to tuh... tell."

"If you don't mind," Tara said, placing a hand on the tired old man's arm. "It would mean a lot to him."

"Uh... okay, but nuh... not all of it. Suh... some things I leave fuh... for Eusari."

"Agreed," said Robert, pulling up chairs for both him and Tara.

His parents, it turned out, had been only a few years older than him when he was born. His father had fought in the Brother's War, just as Eusari had told him, but with a twist—he'd been an officer who commanded men despite having a learning disability that affected his ability to read. The letters twisted and changed places on the page whenever he tried, so he'd relied upon his wife to help him study tactics and maneuvers. That was how they'd bonded as friends, and that friendship grew into love.

"So she was smart but he wasn't?"

"Nuh... no! Not at uh... all. They were buh... both smart. She huh... helped him to work around the reading, buh... but his muh... mind wuh...

was sharp." The old man's eyes fogged over a bit as if remembering a dark memory of the boy's parents. "And his huh... heart wuh... was good. Buh... Braen luh... liked him, even if they didn't guh... get along."

Robert paused. "Who was Braen?"

"Huh?" Sippen seemed startled at the question. "Whuh... what did I suh... say?" The little man's eyes suddenly filled with a deep sadness, as if they'd stirred up a memory best forgotten.

"You said 'Braen liked him, even if they didn't get along.' Who's Braen?"

"Nuh... no one. Juh... just an old fuh... friend." Sippen suddenly lit up. "Shuh... show her thuh... the steam carriage!"

"Oh, yeah!" Robert had nearly forgotten the reason for bringing Tara along. He grabbed her hand and led her outside to the barn. "You're going to love this!"

And she did, marveling at the smooth curves of the tubing and the copper stove in the center for boiling water and making steam. It was less of an invention as it was a work of art, but innovative, nonetheless.

"Can you take me for a ride?" she asked.

"Not yet," Robert admitted, "but soon. We need to set the drive shaft."

"Wuh... why don't you huh... help, Tara?" Sippen urged from the doorway. "I'm nuh... not feeling wuh...well and need to luh... lie down."

Suddenly forgetting her worries and the fight at school, Tara smiled broadly. "Yes, Robert. Let me help. I'm not ready to go home."

"Okay," he said, pulling down a cylindrical piece of metal from a shelf. "Grab the other end and help me slide it underneath."

"Who do you think he meant earlier?" Robert asked, holding the shaft in place while Tara inserted the pins. "I don't know of any Braen except Braen Braston. Surely he didn't mean him?"

"I remember Headmaster talking about him with Greta. Wasn't he a pirate from Fjorik?" She slid the final fastener in place, but the pair remained beneath the carriage with heads very close. Her hair brushed Robert's cheek.

He lay perfectly still. If she knew the effect her closeness was having on him, she hadn't let on. He hoped the moment would never end. "He wasn't just a pirate," he explained. "He was the exiled prince of Fjorik and a revolutionary. He founded the Dreamers and they and his army attempted to topple the Esterling Empire."

"That's right," Tara remembered, laying just as still as he. "Braston did horrible things in every city he conquered. Didn't he also go mad?"

"That's how the story's told. He went so mad they called him the Demon from the North. He was awful and forced the Dreamers to fight despite only being children."

"I don't understand. If the Dreamers fought alongside him, then why do they serve King Esterling now?"

"This king isn't the same one. There were two princes who fought a civil war. They destroyed each other, but a third son of King Charles emerged from hiding and saved the city from Braston's army. It was *his* rifle shot that killed the demon in the end. After that, the leader of the Dreamers agreed to a truce and now they serve the king."

"I heard our mothers talking," Tara whispered, her check inching closer to Robert's. "They said the Dreamers are as bad as the Falconers of old." .

"Falconers don't exist," Robert replied just as quietly. He could barely breathe with her mouth so close. All he could think about was touching her lips with his own. *But that would end our friendship,* his rational mind cautioned. "They disappeared during the war."

"There are rumors," she said, nearly as out of breath as he, "they've come back."

"From the stories Mother has told, I hope that's not..." Robert's words were suddenly cut off by Tara's soft mouth against his own. Though startled at first, he gave in and turned his body as much as he could while lying beneath the carriage. He kissed her gently, afraid and excited at the same time, but she responded by a passionate flick of her tongue that brushed against his.

"Where's Sippen?" a gruff voice suddenly asked from the doorway. It boomed into the barn and startled both Robert and Tara. Each tried to sit up, suddenly embarrassed by the state in which they were caught, striking their foreheads against the cold steel of the under carriage. "Robert! Is that you under there?" the voice demanded.

The boy slid out from beneath the vehicle and stared up at an older man with more years on him than Eusari and Sippen. Robert had once guessed him around fifty-five summers, but it was difficult to tell with the extra pounds he carried around the midsection and along his neck. He rested his weight atop a wooden peg strapped to his upper thigh. Both middle fingers were missing from the man, as he often reminded the neighbors with his raised fists.

"It's me, Cedric," the boy replied, blushing bright red as Tara joined him in staring up at Eusari's foreman.

"What're you two up to beneath that wagon?" the man demanded, eyeing them suspiciously, but then turned before they could answer. "Where's Sippen? I need to get all three of you back to the farm." As quick as he had spoken the man ambled away, hurrying to the workshop as fast as he could wobble atop the pegleg. "Sippen! Get out here! Eusari demands it!"

Robert and Tara exchanged a look then broke out into laughter. Before either could say anything, the girl pulled him close and they kissed again.

"I liked that," she said slightly out of breath while pulling away.

"So did I," he answered truthfully.

"Then don't wait so long before the next time, and stop daydreaming of flying away," she commanded, jumping to her feet just as Sippen entered the barn with Cedric Krull.

"We've guh... got to guh... go," he stammered. "There's truh... trouble."

"A whole heap of it!" Cedric agreed. "And it's all you two lovebirds' fault! I was in town and heard the constables say they're riding out to the farm to arrest the pair of you. They said something about assaulting your teacher and some students?"

Robert swallowed hard. "I'll get the horses," he said with worry racing through his heart.

"There's no tuh... time. Let's tuh... take the carriage!"

"That blasted thing better not blow off me other leg," Cedric protested.

"Don't wuh... worry. It's suh... safe," his old friend promised. "Geh... get in."

The adults climbed in the front seat and Robert helped Tara into the back, then dashed to the front to light the pilot lamp. With the turn of a handle the copper pot began to hiss, building up pressure like a tea kettle. He watched Sippen tap a gauge before nodding and pulling a large lever toward him. All at once the wheels started to turn slowly toward the barn doors which the boy opened wide. Once the carriage rolled free he shut the doors and hopped aboard, sliding next to Tara. She instantly grabbed his arm and hugged him tight. He tenderly whispered, "It will be okay."

But as they rolled through town toward the setting sun, he noticed two hooded figures perched atop horseback. Their heads turned as Sippen drove past, leaning closely in a private conversation but with eyes locked on Robert. He could make out the symbols on their sky blue robes with more distinction from this distance and stared with awe at the crest. The woman whispered something and the man nodded but they again held back and did not follow.

CHAPTER THREE

Eusari sat across from Flaya, snapping beans and removing the strings. It was easy work, except when your hands throbbed from fifty summers. Though she felt young inside, a hard life had aged her body. Sometimes her hands ached but other times her hips and knees cried out with creaks and pops reminding her to slow down. She eyed her friend doing the same, though defter and with less pain. It was a Pescari trait, it seemed, to enjoy longevity free from aches.

Flaya still wore her hair long and in the traditional braid, though what had once been pitch black had long turned to silver. Eusari touched her own, worn no longer than her shoulders, and only then so she could tie it back in summer as it was now. Her raven hair was streaked with grey, appearing far less regal than her friend. They'd both seen some years, these women, and this was their life of choice.

Flaya let out a heavy sigh and looked up from her work.

"What is it?" Eusari asked dryly.

"I'm concerned about our children," she said matter of fact. She also somehow never lost her Pescari accent.

"There's no need to worry," Eusari insisted. "I'm sure they'll be home soon. Robert usually stops at Sippen's after school, and I'm sure she went with him. Or she's with Franque and Krist"

"My Andalonian is not very good," Flaya corrected, "but I did not say I was worried. I am *concerned* she is out with the boys."

"The boys are like brothers to her, I'm sure it's still innocent."

"She's nearly a woman, and it's time I take her to find a Pescari husband. Brothers or not, eventually boys turn into men and notice the woman close at hand."

Eusari chuckled, though she hadn't meant to. "There's nothing wrong with your Andalonian, Flaya, so stop claiming there is. I get your point."

Collette snickered from the kitchen where she stirred a pot of stew. Always stew it seemed, an easy way to feed so many grown men in the household.

"Mind your business," Eusari told the maid, but then regretted it. The woman had been in their household as long as the others and had proven quite useful.

"You could cook it yourself if you wish, ma'am," the woman retorted with a smile. She knew, of all tasks Eusari loathed, the mistress of the house hated cooking the most.

"You're doing fine."

Collette tapped the spoon against the cauldron with satisfaction, pleased she'd won the sparring match.

Eusari allowed her this one victory and turned toward Flaya. "Are you certain taking her to New Weston is the correct path? She's grown less Pescari each year and seems more at home here."

"That's exactly *why* I must take her to New Weston. The Pescari there live the way we had always hoped—under the eye of Felicima and with respect for tradition."

"Tara is a spirited girl and won't adapt well to tradition, especially in a culture where women are subservient."

"She will learn to obey."

"She's sixteen summers and, if she hasn't yet learned obedience, then she never will."

"You would know," Flaya snapped, signaling she was done discussing her daughter.

But Eusari persisted. "If you take her now to New Weston, you'll lose her completely in another year. Take more time and consider if this is really for her, or for *you*."

Flaya grunted and stared down at the bowl of beans in her lap. "I see fire in her eyes, Eusari, an unquenchable one I've seen before."

At this, the Andalonian woman paused. She and her friend were kindred in so many ways, and they had agreed many years before to assist each other in raising the children. This sudden urge to immerse Tara in their culture had indeed stemmed from a deeper worry. Eusari opened her mouth to speak when the front door burst open. Sebastian hurried inside, out of breath as if he'd run from the outermost fields.

"There are constables riding to speak to you, ma'am!"

"*Constables*? Not a single lawman, but more than one?" she asked and Sebastian nodded.

"Finn Olsen brought some out-of-towners along as deputies," he said with large eyes filled with worry. In times like this he acted like the terrified child she'd taken in years ago. He was a sweet boy and did grow into a strong man, but one with a wounded mind that never quite healed.

Eusari exchanged a look with Flaya and rose, setting her bowl aside to finish later. "Where's Cedric?" she asked the farmhand.

"He rode into town hours ago in search of extra labor," he replied. "He said we wouldn't be able to plow properly without extra hands."

She nodded. Though the foreman never ran it by her, she fully trusted his decisions. "Stay here, Flaya. I'm sure this has only to do with Krist and Franque and nothing to do with the others."

"Actually," Sebastian said with averted eyes, "Constable Olsen said it has to do with Robert and Tara."

Flaya rose abruptly, setting her bowl of beans on the chair. In a flash she had pushed past them both and darted outside to face the constables.

Eusari followed close behind. As she emerged, she noticed right away Constable Olsen and the others had dismounted. *So this is more serious after all,* she realized, not at all like his previous visits. Usually he returned with her boys, leading them by the ears.

"What brings you to my farm, Finn? Have our children irritated your constituency?"

"If only it were that simple, Miss Thorinson," he replied with hat in hand.

She watched his body language and that of the others. She did not know these men, but the fact he brought them meant he would leave more than a warning this time. Someone would be arrested before the sun completely fell.

Flaya anxiously eyed Felicima nearing the horizon, willing her to drop. The Pescari woman would not hold back anger once the sun was out of sight.

"Why *can't* it be simple, Finn?" Eusari demanded. "They're children, not yet of legal age to be held accountable. What crime do you allege they committed?"

Movement by the barn caught her eye and that of the constables. Everyone turned to watch as Franque and Krist approached. The constables all settled when they realized it wasn't the two children they sought.

"Robert is nearly of age, Miss Thorinson, and will be by the time the trial rolls around."

"But he *isn't*, yet, is he?" she demanded, her voice suddenly fierce enough to cause the other men to jump. "And I'm not letting you take him into custody until he is!"

"Assault, ma'am. He dislocated the knee of the blacksmith's boy, Peta Grenwich, and broke the nose of Sam Rawlins."

Krist laughed out loud at this and all eyes shot the boy a quieting glare. But he hadn't noticed. "You hear that, Franque? Robert's got some spunk to him after all. I kinda regret skipping school now, don't you?"

Eusari cut him off angrily. "Skipping school? I'll deal with *you* later. Get inside the house!" Turing to Constable Olsen she added, "Two on one sounds like a fair fight, not an assault. Who's the witness?"

"All their classmates and the headmaster, but he's enough since he's an adult and claims to have witnessed the entire event."

Felicima had finally disappeared into a soft glow.

"What of Tara?" Flaya asked abruptly. "What role did she play?"

"Your daughter bloodied Greta Greenbriar pretty bad and assaulted the headmaster. He claims she kicked him in the groin."

Franque and Krist, who hadn't yet heeded their mother's command, laughed in unison.

Without turning, Eusari addressed them. "Get in the house *now!*" Her tone sent them scurrying inside.

"That doesn't sound like my Tara," Flaya said shaking her head. "She is Pescari, and our people shun violence unless provoked. I'm certain there's more to the story."

One of the out-of-towner constables let out a chiding laugh and said, "Ma'am, I was *there* in Old Weston when your people destroyed it. Don't repeat your lies about nonviolence around me. There isn't a Pescari around who wouldn't pick up a sword or bow out of anger."

Flaya stepped forward to argue but Eusari moved between them. "You haven't answered my question, Finn Olsen. They're underage so why are you here with deputies?"

"There are enough witnesses in that schoolhouse, and each is willing to testify in front of the magistrate that your children started it. I *have* to bring them in."

"You can't have Tara," Flaya insisted. "She is Pescari, and we try our own under Felicima's law! Your king decreed it so!"

Eusari agreed. "That's right! The law clearly states that, in crimes against the person, a Pescari citizen can only be tried in front of a jury of peers. A *tribal* jury of peers."

"Up here that isn't possible," Constable Olsen argued, "and the law is clear that in the absence of a tribal jury the magistrate can take jurisdiction."

"That's why we're returning to Weston," Flaya abruptly answered. "Her ritual approaches, and I am taking her back to our people in the morning."

"That's too late, I'm afraid. You'll need to leave tonight," Constable Olsen said with a sigh. "If she's still in this province come sunup, the girl's father will be looking for blood. And you know how angry those northerners can be!"

"We're not afraid," Eusari growled. "Let him come."

"They're refugees from Fjorik, Miss Thorinson, and a whole pack of them. They'll burn this town down and then move on to another if justice isn't served."

"And by running off a girl, they'll view justice as served?" Eusari demanded.

The constable from Weston sneered and replied, "By running off *Pescari* they'll view justice as served."

"That settles it," Flaya stated. "We're leaving tonight."

A rumble suddenly became audible from down the road, a cross between a tea kettle boiling over and a hissing cat. All eyes turned toward the noise.

"What in Cinder's Crack is that?" asked Constable Olsen.

"It's a horseless carriage," one of the other constables replied in awe.

"There's Robert and Tara now," Eusari pointed out. She could make out Cedric and Sippen in the front seat and the children just beyond them in the rear of the vehicle. "We'll let them answer to this nonsense for themselves."

"Why does it take four constables to talk to a pair of kids?" Cedric demanded as they drove up the lane. Then, before waiting for an answer, he stood in the carriage and loudly asked the constables the same question. Shaking his fists and imaginary middle fingers, he added, "Come and take them!"

"Be quiet, Cedric!" Eusari shouted and the one-legged man sat back down abruptly.

"I know that voice," he said, smiling to those riding in the carriage. "The *old* Eusari's showing through!" His remark made both him and Sippen laugh.

Robert and Tara exchanged confused glances. They only ever knew the calm and doting Eusari, slow to anger and never cruel. Whatever bothered her now had hissed out angrily.

Once Sippen pulled to a stop and shut off the engine, the constables stepped forward and surrounded the vehicle.

Once again Eusari showed a darker, more assertive side and challenged all four men. The sharpened edge of her voice caused Robert to cringe. He'd never seen his mother this angry.

"I'm his guardian," she growled, "and I'll do the questioning!"

The men stepped back and she approached the carriage.

"What happened at school today, Robert?" she asked with a quieter tone, the loving and supportive mother returning. Even her face appeared more serene and in control, whereas earlier she'd seemed nearly rabid.

"One of the girls attacked Tara, and two boys held me back from breaking up the fight."

"So it was self-defense?" Eusari asked, "For both of you?"

He nodded and heard Tara whisper, "Yes," beside him.

"What about the headmaster? Why is he saying otherwise?"

"That scrawny little bigot wasn't even there," Tara hissed. "He's a liar and only arrived after the fight was over!"

"He says you struck him," Eusari asked gently. "Did you kick the man?"

"I did," Tara replied without remorse, "and I'd do it again."

"There you have it, an admission of guilt," Constable Olsen said stepping forward. "Only the magistrate can determine self-defense, so I'm afraid I'll have to take them both into custody unless Flaya keeps her word. Take her and leave tonight." Constable Olsen commanded. "If there's a trace of you in the morning, we'll arrest her on sight."

Two deputies grabbed Robert by the arms while Constable Olsen brought out a pair of iron shackles.

"What *is* this?" Robert demanded. "I don't reach my seventeenth summer for a few weeks. Surely you won't try me as an adult for self-defense?"

"No," Eusari exclaimed loudly and definitively, "they won't."

"We have to, Miss Thorinson."

"No, you'll take *me* into custody instead as his guardian. I will stand against these charges."

"That won't work," Finn argued.

"Yes, it will," she insisted, "you said it yourself. He'll be eighteen by the time the magistrate hears the trial, but he's not old enough to be charged today. No, if you want justice served, you'll have to serve it against *me*."

Olsen turned to the others who shrugged indifferently. As he'd said, *someone* was getting arrested on this night, and he just wanted the matter resolved and closed. He stepped behind the woman, clamping the shackles loosely around her wrists.

Eusari complied willingly, despite her face screaming defiance.

"We'll be taking you to Loganshire for the hearing, so you're allowed a few personal items for the journey."

"Sippen," she said without emotion.

"Yuh... yes, ma'am?" the little man stammered.

"Pack me a bag of things I'll need."

"I can do it, ma'am," Sebastian offered.

"No! Sippen knows what I'll need. Also, include Amash Horslei's letter. I may need that after all, it seems."

"Are you shuh... sure, Eusari?" Sippen asked. "Thuh... that will chuh... change everything. He will nuh... know and send for him."

"I've no other choice, Mr. Yurik," she said sadly. "No matter what we do or don't do, it's too late to stop change, because it *will* be different soon. For *all* of us."

The little man nodded and went inside. By the time he returned with an overnight bag, the constables had already lifted Eusari onto a horse. They searched the bag for contraband and weapons. Finding none, they strapped it to the saddle.

"Sippen," she said, "don't let Cedric or the boys interfere. I'll be home in a few days or a couple of weeks."

Constable Olsen spurred his horse forward, leading Eusari's and the other constables away.

As they turned onto the main road, Franque and Krist emerged from the house and stood next to Robert.

"Okay, boys," Cedric said with excitement, "we know where they're keeping her tonight and which road they'll take in the morning. I say we catch them by surprise as they're leading her out of town, bust her free and head south across the Steppes of Cinder. By the time we reach New Weston, Flaya's people will grant us asylum."

"No." Sippen said without stammering. "We'll do no such thing."

Robert turned to watch as Flaya pulled Tara onto her horse. "Please don't take her away," he begged the woman.

She looked right through the boy about to become a man, spurring forward at a gallop and toward their home to pack.

Robert waited, watching for Tara to turn back even a single glance, but she was either too afraid or unwilling to do so. In no time at all, they disappeared into the forest.

"What do we do, Sippen?" he asked the little man.

"We wuh... wait for yuh... your mother to ruh... return," he said, then led Cedric and the boys inside.

CHAPTER FOUR

Robert awoke to banging of shutters. A tempest raged outside his open window, threatening to rip the home apart or collapse it upon its foundation. He scrambled to pull them shut, but fierce flapping bruised several knuckles in the attempt. As he cradled the wounded hand and cursed, two hooded forms caught his eye. Standing on the edge of the pasture, they waved their hands to an invisible orchestra, conducting a maelstrom of violence with their wind.

"No!" he muttered. "They must be following me!" Tearing his eyes away, he sprinted to the next room. The twins were out of bed as well.

"What is it?" Franque asked.

"Dreamers," Robert explained.

"Why would Dreamers attack *us*?" Krist demanded. "We're not a threat to the crown!"

"He's right," Franque agreed, his usually jovial demeanor replaced by a rarely seen serious side. "The Dreamers wouldn't attack us unless we've been plotting against the king or his empire. They don't bother with farms like ours. That's the job of constables."

This gave Robert pause.

"The constables hauled Mother away and are on their way to Logan."

"They didn't need four men to handle Mother," Franque said with steely soberness.

Robert let his brother's wisdom sink in, surprised by both his calmness and wisdom. The last time he'd seen this Franque was when Krist had fallen through ice and Robert nearly dove into the pond save him. It was the older twin whose calm prevailed in the situation, preventing both their deaths. He had quickly found a fallen limb and fished his brother out.

This was the man Franque could be, the one with boundless potential if he finally decided to grow up.

"Boys!" screamed Cedric from the living area, sending them running downstairs to his side. Both he and Sippen held long black weapons. The boys skidded to a halt, shocked to see rifles in the house.

"Those are forbidden!" Robert pointed out.

"Suh... so is using uh... emotancy, but thuh... *they* are," Sippen said as he pointed out the window at the figures.

"Where did you get those?" the boy demanded.

"Not now!" Sippen yelled, and Robert fell silent, exchanging a worried glance with Franque.

Cedric knelt by a closed window, unhinging a smaller shutter within the larger. As the air rushed in, he pointed his rifle and took aim. "They're too far for me," he said, stepping back and turning to Sippen. "You're the better shot."

The little man nodded, wiped his spectacles and knelt, poking the muzzle through the hatch and taking in a deep breath. As he let it out, he paused and the room seemed to go eerily quiet as Robert watched. In the next moment, Sippen's finger twitched ever so slightly and a concussive blast rang out.

"Guh... got one," the little man said with a smile.

"Damn good blasting, mate!" Cedric praised, a broad smile filling his face. "It feels like the good old times again!"

"Uh... almost," Sippen agreed.

"What is going on?" Robert demanded. "Why do you have guns, and what do you mean by *good old times*?"

Before anyone could answer, Franque called out from the next window where he'd been watching the Dreamers. "You dropped him good, Mr. Sippen!" But just then, the house shook as the winds gusted.

"Wuh... we've got to run!" Sippen ordered the others, but before anyone could move, the front doors blew open. Cedric and Sippen both raised their rifles toward the dark figure standing in the door.

"Don't point those at me!" Sebastian screamed and the barrels dropped to point at the floor.

"What the devil are you doing, barging in and scaring us like that!" Cedric demanded.

"I heard the shot and came to help."

"What were you doing before?" demanded Cedric, and he and Sippen exchanged a knowing glance. Everyone knew Sebastian had a habit of flinching in the face of danger.

"Searching the bunkhouse."

"Of course you were," Cedric muttered. He was odd, this farmhand, and Robert and his brothers had never fully understood why.

"Where's Collette?" Sebastian suddenly demanded, looking around the room.

"Duh… don't know. She wuh… wasn't here when I wuh… woke up."

"That's why I was in the bunkhouse," Sebastian explained. "I was looking for her, but she wasn't there. I thought the Falconers were defeated. Why are they attacking?" the young man asked.

"Those are Dreamers," Robert corrected, and all eyes turned to him.

"Can't be," Cedric insisted.

"Wouldn't be," Sebastian said dryly, shaking his head but staring toward the window with worried eyes.

"Nuh… no. Those are Fuh… Falconers," Sippen corrected. "I nuh… know, because I shuh… shot one. And druh… dreamers wouldn't attack uh… *us*."

"There's no such thing as Falconers," Krist said with a tremor in his voice. "What's going on?"

"There *are* such things," Cedric explained, suddenly very serious. "And we've seen worse things still. But outside there's one Falconer left and the lot of us, with Sebastian's help, we can take him!"

"Or her," the farmhand said with a tremor, reliving some distant memory.

Sippen placed a hand on Sebastian's shoulder speaking plainly and without his usual stammer. "Forget the past for moment, Sebastian. Krill's right and we need a shield."

"Who's Krill?" Krist asked and the other boys shrugged.

"I can't," the young man protested, "you know that!"

"How long has it been since you tried, son?" Cedric asked. "How long since you dabbled?"

"Not since Braen... Not since then."

"We nuh... need you to muh... make one, nuh... now," Sippen stressed. He reached into a dusty crate on the floor and drew out another gun, shorter than the others and with two barrels. He tossed it to Robert.

"What's this?" Robert asked, suddenly afraid and very confused. Nothing made sense, not the attack, nor the presence of Falconers, but especially not this odd behavior by men he'd known his entire life.

"It's called a shotgun," Cedric said with a wink. "Good for close quarters when you wanna rip someone to pieces!" He reached into a bag and pulled out several cylindrical rounds with wadding on the end. He showed the boys how to load and ready the weapon.

"But firearms are illegal," Krist protested. "If you get caught with them..."

"Yeah, yeah," Cedric said with a laugh. "The king sends his constables to lock you up." Turning serious he added, "But King Esterling ain't here, and what he doesn't know won't hurt him."

"How'd you get these?" Robert demanded. "I thought they were outlawed for civilian use after the war."

"I muh... made them," Sippen admitted. "I in... vuh.... invented them a long tuh... time ago. Duh... don't worry, I have a luh... license," he said with a wink, tossing two more to Franque and Krist. "Stay close behind Suh... Sebastian's shield and fuh... fire when Cedric tuh... tells you."

"Where will you be?" Robert asked.

"Snuh... sniping," he replied with a grin.

"This way, boys," Cedric commanded, ushering them out into the windstorm.

Franque eyed the little man holding the rifle. "But he's nearly blind, isn't he?"

"Trust me," Cedric said with a grin, "Sippen can shoot the balls off a gnat at one hundred paces."

Once they gathered, Sebastian closed his eyes and waved his hands. All at once the winds formed a circular pattern encircling the man and boys. They found themselves standing within a shimmering bubble of air.

Franque turned to Robert, mouthing a question and using language Eusari would have boxed his ears over.

Krist poked at the firm outline of the bubble and Cedric let out a laugh.

"Still got it in you, boy!" he said, slapping Sebastian on the back. "This way!" he called. "Stay close while we bum-rush him! Once I start blasting, you boys keep an eye out for his bird."

They all took off at a run, rushing toward the solitary figure standing on the edge of the farm.

"This is insane!" Robert yelled to Cedric, who was doing his best to keep up despite his wooden leg.

A bit out of breath, the older man replied, "I know! Isn't it great? Your mother's first night away and it's already like old times! Yessir, definitely like old times!"

"What in Cinder's hells is going on?" Robert pressed, still in shock over the weapon in his hands.

"We're charging a Falconer!" Cedric said as if it were clear. He panted, slowing just a bit, but gasped a deep breath of air then sprinted ahead.

The hooded figure was close now, seemingly unaware of their approach and intent on his goal of knocking down the house with his windstorm.

"Something's wrong, Krill!" Sebastian observed. "It's not right! They don't usually stand there and wait for us."

Robert looked back and forth between the two men, but kept up the pace they led within the bubble. Finally, he found he could no longer stand any more of the mystique surrounding the night. "What do you mean *usually*? Have you guys really done this before? And why do you guys keep calling him Krill?"

"Duck!" Sebastian suddenly shouted and the squad screeched to a halt, crouching to the ground as two large falcons attacked the bubble. Their large talons scratched at the layer of air while they screeched and squawked.

Cedric stood, plainly showing his irritation and shooting Sebastian a dry stare. "Why'd we duck if they can't get in?"

"Because," the timid man explained, "There's *two* of them and only *one* Falconer."

"Two…" Cedric turned slowly, eyeing the Falconer standing alone on the edge of the farm. "Cinder's Crack," he cursed aloud. "We've been hornswoggled! Drop the shield!" Abruptly, the bubble around them dissipated and the birds lunged. Cedric pulled his trigger and the explosion of feathers scattered all around.

"Look out!" Sebastian yelled.

Cedric turned, but a solid tendril of air ripped the weapon from his hands. It lurched into the night, flying quickly away as if grabbed by an invisible hand.

Franque was the first of the boys to understand. "He was the bait?" he asked Sebastian who nodded.

"We've got to find the other," the foreman said as a new bubble formed overhead. "Give me your gun," he said to Krist. The boy handed it over willingly, the fear in his eyes matching the feeling in Robert's gut.

"We can't stay in this bubble all night," Robert suggested. "Why don't we fan out?"

"Because," Sebastian explained quietly, with fear slipping uncomfortably into his voice. "Falconers can each split their mind five times, meaning we're outnumbered two to one—more if there's a third hiding nearby."

"Or a Jaguar to raise the dead one," Cedric added with a grin.

"What's a Jaguar?" Krist demanded.

"Something you don't want raisin' the dead one," Cedric said. "Now we're stuck here until he shows himself."

Robert thought of the trick the Falconer had played, luring them close and distracting them with birds. "They're testing us," he reasoned.

"They are," Cedric agreed. "They must've been testing us to see if any of us were emotants."

"And we fell for it," Sebastian whispered. "Krill, you know *why* I don't like to use it, and now they know I can. They'll come back."

Robert stared at the man with a new admiration. Never in his life would he have suspected the farmhand held power over the wind. "Why aren't you a Dreamer?"

"Because he's a coward," a woman's voice said from behind.

Robert recognized her at once. "A Dreamer!" he exclaimed. "One of the pair I saw in town!"

"Hello, Caroline," Sebastian said. "Who else is here?"

"Bearnard," a deep voice rumbled from their left side, and a large man dressed in Dreamer's robes stepped out of the darkness. He nodded at Caroline and the pair emitted several strands of air, fashioning a long, shimmering whip. With a crack as loud as thunder it lashed out at the Falconer, sending him flying backward. The windstorm abruptly ceased, replaced by an eerie calm.

"Relax, Sebastian," the woman said to the farmhand, "they weren't looking for you, they were testing the child."

Robert felt his belly tighten into knots. Somehow, he knew they meant him. The pair approached the ground where the Falconer had once stood, and the others followed. Though still protected by Sebastian's bubble of air, Robert felt the night grow colder with endless worries. This day had quickly become the strangest and most troubling in his life—with Tara gone and Eusari in the custody of constables.

Both Falconer bodies were gone.

"You need to leave this place," Bearnard said to Robert, his deep voice booming.

"Nuh... no. *You* do!" Sippen said from behind, his rifle cradled across a skinny arm. "Cuh... Cuyler promised us suh... solitude. Luh... leave us alone!"

"Where's Eusari?" Caroline demanded, ignoring the little man.

"Constables took her," Robert said. "She's to stand trial for something I did."

"Nothing *you* did," Bearnard said with a laugh. "But you *are* coming with us."

"Over my dead body!" Cedric growled, stepping between him and Robert.

"You can't have him," Franque said defiantly, stepping in front of Cedric. "He's the best hope of a kid Mother has. He's smart, destined for greatness! Take me instead!"

"Or me," Krist demanded, moving beside his brother. The twins made their best show of strength against the Dreamers, standing shoulder to shoulder.

Caroline laughed. "You've each got a bit of your father in you, which would mean something if either of you were *half* the man he was." With the flick of her wrist, tendrils of air grabbed both boys around the arms and tugged them out of the way. "But the king wants Robert, not you. We're charged with bringing your brother to Eston."

"Wuh... wait." Sippen begged. "Heh... he'll go, but first I nuh... need to talk to him. To explain."

"Make it quick," Caroline said. "We've got strict orders. He's been called and must stand before the king."

"Suh... Sebastian, come with us to the house. Heh... he'll need your help to puh... pack."

The farmhand nodded and followed as Sippen Yurik led Robert away.

Once they were out of earshot, Robert demanded, "Why are they taking me?"

"Duh... don't worry. They wuh... won't take you. Guh... go into the huh... house with Sebastian, then uh... out the back. Puh... play some huh... hide and seek," he said to the farmhand with a wink.

Sebastian smiled big, understanding what was needed.

"But why?" Robert asked again. "What's special about me?"

"It's nuh... not my puh... place to say. Get to you... Eusari and muh... make her tuh... tell you. It's time."

"Why aren't *you* coming?"

"Buh... because I'm uh... old, and a trip like thuh... that would kill me. And I huh... have to stay with the twins." Sippen held the door to the house open and slipped a piece of folded parchment into Robert's pocket. "Luh... leave the shuh.... shotgun here."

"I need a weapon."

"You huh... have one," the little man replied. "There's a buh... bag of supplies by the back duh.... door. Take it with you." He shut the door behind them with a click, leaving the two alone in the house.

"What did he mean, I have a weapon?" Robert asked Sebastian. "Did he mean *you*?"

The farmhand shrugged and said, "Maybe. We'll see." With a wave of his hand, the air around the pair glistened. "Hurry, let's get out the back like he said."

"What did you do?"

"We're invisible to everyone now, even the Dreamers."

"How?" Robert demanded.

"That's my strongest power—the ability to hide from danger. Come on!"

CHAPTER FIVE

Franque watched with wonder as Sippen Yurik led Robert and Sebastian toward the house. The night had been a pleasant surprise for the teen, full of unexpected action and promise of adventure. The man inside of him fought the child screaming caution.

Look at Cedric, that responsible voice inside Franque warned, *and watch him closely. Do what he says!*

The Dreamers had finished scouring the area for threats and concluded the Falconers had left. They, like the boy, returned their attention to the one-legged foreman.

"Been a long time since I've lain my eye upon one of you," Cedric said with a grin, fully unafraid and not caring at all they were private agents to the king.

"Been a long time since we thought we'd actually *find* you pirates," Caroline replied with an upturned nose. "Where's Eusari?"

Pirates? Franque exchanged a look with his brother, who'd also heard, and both watched Cedric and waited for his response.

"She loved you like a daughter once," Cedric said simply, his grin gone and face betraying mournful thoughts.

"There was a time I loved her like a mother," Caroline retorted without emotion, "but she abandoned us, left without warning or word. Where is she?"

"What do you want with *her,*" Sippen asked from behind, slipping into the group unnoticed.

"Where's the coward and the boy?" demanded Bearnard, suddenly agitated and shifting stance as if ready for a fight.

"*Sebastian* and Ruh... Robert are coming," promised the little man. "Wuh... what do you want with you... Eusari and her son?" he asked again.

"So he *is* still called Robert? Amash wasn't sure it hadn't changed. Have abilities awakened within him yet? Is he an emotant like his father?" Caroline asked with a sly smile.

Franque felt his mind go woozy as her words washed over him. *An emotant? Like his* father?

"Who was his father?" Krist demanded. "Eusari never said."

"A dead man," Caroline replied. "Where *are* they, Sippen? Don't force me to finish the work the Falconers started. I'll tear this farm down timber and stone if I must. Why do you defy the king?"

"Buh... because Amash muh... made a pruh... promise to us all. Huh... has he changed his muh... mind then? Duh... does he intend the boy harm?"

"We're only tasked with finding and bringing them before him," Bearnard explained. Wisps of air suddenly formed in the air as the man stepped forward, tendrils woven as strong as rope. It wrapped tightly around Sippen and raised him into the air. "But he said nothing about what we can do with you."

"Where is Eusari?" Caroline demanded as Bearnard squeezed the tendrils tighter.

"Tuh... taken by cuh... constables last evening."

"To where?"

"To Luh... Logan."

"And the boy? Where is Sebastian taking him?"

A concussive blast filled the night and Franque looked down at the smoking hot gun in his hands. He hadn't expected the kick of it, and the pain in his shoulder dulled the anger he'd previously felt—*no, not anger, a need to protect this man I respect as one of my mother's best friends.* He had expected the Dreamer to fall, but instead a bubble of shimmering air had formed around him, catching the tiny ball bearings in midflight. They floated in air, only a foot away from his skin.

Before Franque could fire a second time, Krist had charged forward. Having seen the way Bearnard had stopped the shot, he had drawn a knife and plunged the blade into the bubble with intent to strike the Dreamer dead. But, before his blade found flesh, Caroline wrapped tendrils around both boys and Cedric, binding them as tightly as Sippen.

A mixture of anger and fear filled Franque, replacing his youthful confidence with anxiety. Compelled by burning hatred, he roared rage into the night. He fought against his bonds, succeeding only in wriggling like a hooked worm about to dip into the river. The air felt wrong against his skin, a foreign substance reeking of arrogance. He desperately searched for a way to free himself and the others.

"I was correct before when I said you have your father in you," Caroline whispered into his ear, "but it seems I've underestimated how hotly the madness burns in his offspring."

"Who was my father?" Franque demanded through clenched teeth.

Caroline laughed and looked at Sippen. "She didn't tell any of them anything, did she? Eusari believed this fight was over and thought she could raise all three children, protecting them better than she did us?"

"Thuh... the Dreamers wuh... weren't her children," the little man replied. "Yuh... you weren't as important tuh... to her."

"Perhaps that only occurred to me now," Caroline said mournfully. Turning to Franque, she added, "Turn that rage into something productive and till your soil, son of Braston. We're leaving, but don't consider pursuing. We are not the evil spreading across Andalon. Those Falconers, returned from oblivion, are your foe. Them and whatever drives them. I'm certain Robert will seek out Eusari. When he does, we'll take them before the king as ordered and let *him* decide their fate." In an instant the tendrils of air vaporized, dropping the men and boys to the ground. As the Dreamers turned to leave, Caroline turned once more and added, "Just pray you twins are spared the madness of your father. It nearly killed your mother and both of *you* in her womb."

"Eusari wuh... won't let you tuh... take Robert away." Sippen warned.

"Eusari no longer has a choice," Caroline said, and she and Bearnard disappeared into the night.

Franque waited until the Dreamers had gone. "Sippen," he asked, the anger within greatly subsiding. "Who *was* our father? Was it the pirate Braen Braston?"

Sippen nodded with tears rolling down his cheeks. With the back of his hand, he wiped them and sniffed slightly. "It's been eighteen years since we lost him. Cedric and I lost our best friend, a champion for the weak and misunderstood. Your mother lost more than that, she lost the only man who ever deserved her love."

"I remember Headmaster teaching about him," Krist said quietly. "He's more notorious than Devil Jacque! He committed all kinds of atrocities during the Brother's War and ravaged many coastal villages and the southern cities."

"That wasn't Braen," Cedric muttered. "It was someone else entirely. It was called the Brother's War for many reasons, but Andalon won't ever accept it were waged by any except the Esterlings. Your father fought against his own brother Skander."

"I've never heard of *him*," Franque said. Krist shrugged, he hadn't either. "So, what she said, about Braen going mad and trying to kill us and mother? That wasn't true?"

"Caroline wuh... wasn't there, duh... doesn't know the truth," was Sippen's only reply.

"But you both were?"

"I huh... had other muh... matters to attend to, thuh... that day," the little man admitted. "I wuh... was close, but nuh... not there when it huh... happened."

The twins turned to Cedric.

"Don't look at me," he said. "I was attending to business on the ramparts and was... um, looking the other direction."

"So neither of you know? Who *was* there? Who saw him die?" Franque demanded.

"Eusari and Flaya were there and also a girl named Marita, one of the Dreamers at the time, but she left Andalon right after the war," Cedric said.

"Duh.. don't forget Amash," Sippen reminded, wiping another tear. "He puh... pulled the trigger and fuh... fired the killing shot."

Franque felt rage rise up, rumbling like a roar just inside his throat. He found it difficult to hold inside. When he finally spoke, he could barely control the growl. "Where can I find this Amash now? Who *is* he?"

"Amash is *not* the enemy," Cedric cautioned. "Your mother insisted he had his reasons."

"He's an ally and no one but Eusari and Flaya know why he did what he did," Sippen agreed without a stutter. "Eusari forgave him and so did we."

"I didn't ask what he *isn't*," Franque finally yelled, causing even his brother to flinch. "I asked who *is* he?"

"Thuh... the king of uh.... Estonia," Sippen stammered.

"The king..." Franque could not believe his ears. The king of Estonia killed his father. "And now he plans to kill Robert? Why would he send Dreamers to carry out the task?"

"I tuh... truly don't nuh... know."

"Why did you send Robert away if you didn't trust them?" Krist demanded.

"I suh.. sent him to you... Eusari, so she cuh... can tell him the truth and duh... decide. If uh... Amash wants him, it could be for suh... several reasons."

"Well," Franque said angrily, "I've *decided* on my own. I'm going to kill the king!"

"Duh.. don't be foolish," Sippen pleaded.

"Don't be a *coward!*" Franque screamed into the night, finally putting the boy aside and embracing the man within. In that moment he vowed to learn all he could about his father and embody the part of him these men admired and others feared.

In all his summers, Krist had never been inside his mother's bedroom without her. More importantly, he'd never searched through her things like a thief on a mission for answers. But he had so many questions after his encounter with the Dreamers. Foremost being the fact that Braen Braston, the scourge of Andalon and once leader of Pirate's Cove, was his father. He'd never imagined. So far, his search had only turned up evidence of his mother's life as a farmer.

He had almost given up when he spotted an old trunk in the far corner of a forgotten closet. Further inspection revealed it was a seafarer's footlocker. On its lid was a single marking of an engraved wolf's head. He hated to force it open, but by the time his mother returned, he and Franque would be gone in search of their father's killer. He shoved his blade into the lock and pressed hard with his entire weight, snapping both the lock and his knife in a single heave. Krist had loved that blade and losing it had better be worth the sacrifice.

The lid lifted with a groan. Suddenly afraid he had awakened Sippen and Cedric with his noise, he rushed from the room to check. He found them sleeping deeply at the kitchen table—their heads on the crook of their arms and hands wrapped around wine glasses. A single bottle sat between them, covered with dust except where someone had wiped away the numbers painted on the side. These read *754*. He shrugged. It must not have been a good vintage the way the men had run through it.

He returned to his mother's room and the waiting chest. Inside was a treasure trove of her memories—hidden from the light of day as if buried in a tomb. Of course she would hide her past, she'd been running from it and took great pains to hide the truth from each of her children. But for him and Franque to be the sons of the legendary Braen Braston? He wondered, was she even their mother at all, or a thief who gathered the most important children born in her generation? Either way, she hid them away like this dusty old box. He was glad they were about to sneak away. But first, he wanted to find something of his father's.

He found it right away, even if he hadn't recognized it at first, bundled beneath a jacket of black leather. He tossed the jerkin aside and it landed with a heavy thump. Confused by its weight he retrieved it, turning it over in his hands. More than a jacket, he'd found a fitted suit of leather armor, filled with dozens of sheaths to hide all kinds of knives. He drew out one of these, replacing the one he'd broken while opening the chest. The rest he set aside in a heap.

He pushed aside a fur cloak, smiling at what lay beneath. He had uncovered a northern forged broadsword. He held it up to the moonlight flooding in from the single window, marveling at the craftmanship and swirling patterns in the steel. On the pommel he discovered a northern saber cat devouring a wolf. He hugged it to his breast. Krist Thorinson had finally held something once belonging to his father.

"What are you doing?" Franque demanded from the doorway.

Krist jumped, his excitement replacing any guilt for digging through his mother's privacy.

"It was his," he said, holding up the broadsword, "I'm certain."

Franque strolled over, bending down to look inside the chest. Moonlight glistened on something else within, and his timid hand reached inside. He drew forth two items, a northern warrior's axe as intricately carved as the sword in Krist's hands. He slid this immediately inside his belt. The second item he found was a battle worn cutlass, weathered smooth but obviously well used. He put the latter back into the box.

"Come on," Franque said. "They'll wake soon, and I want to be far away from here when they do." As quickly as he had entered, he left his brother alone.

Krist paused. With guilt weighing heavy, he closed the chest and compared the markings on the lid and the hilt in his hands. His mother's symbol and his father's clashed wildly with what he knew of history. Braen Braston's people of Fjorik had built their lives preying on hers from Loganshire, just as his saber cat devoured her wolf.

No wonder, he realized, *she kept their love hidden from both her children and the people of this region.*

Eusari Thorinson was a traitor who once loved a pirate from the north.

CHAPTER SIX

King Esterling was heavyset but not horribly out of shape for his age. He blamed the rich foods and lack of exercise that came with the job. Overall he should have felt healthy, even if his knees felt as old as they did. Considering the active life he'd lived before, full of adventure and thrills, he resented the pain and the extra pounds. He swayed as one leg buckled, popping in protest over his desire to move swiftly and end this tortuous day filled with duty.

"Your Majesty?" the chancellor asked, stepping forward, fearful his king would topple over. "Are you ill, sire? Shall I fetch your physician?"

"No, Percy," Amash replied, but he lied. Illness lurked in every shadow, mocking his former youth. Recently, the headaches had worsened, growing so distracting he could barely endure the ringing. He took this moment to rub his thigh muscle just to distract his hands. They yearned to rub away the greater pain throbbing between his temples.

You never were a liar, the voice said, *but politics have made you into one. I'm disappointed in you, old friend.* Amusement lined the words, and the king detected a hint of laughter.

Be quiet, the king demanded, *and leave me.*

The first time he had heard the voice he found it familiar, a reminder of a person he'd known many years before. *Friend,* as the voice called him, was not the word he'd choose to describe this master of deceit.

He looked around at his entourage. Each pair of eyes pointedly avoided meeting his. It was undignified to witness their ruler in pain. Even worse, Percy Roan offered a shoulder on which to lean. The king waved him off, stepping gingerly the rest of the way. His quarters weren't much farther down the long corridor, just past a row of painted arches and endless vases with cut roses. These were his family's symbol, and scores of them filled the palace. He had grown to despise the smell. It reminded him of loneliness and obligation—nothing of home and family.

They reached the door to his quarters, gilded and reflecting sunlight from the open windows high above. Though splendidly carved with twisted vines and budding roses, he had tired of the beauty in this entire place.

Wasteful and overdone, he thought, *a sign of extravagance from a time when our people starved.*

None starve now, because you've done well, the voice encouraged. *Thanks to the leader you proved to be.*

I'm not a leader, King Esterling argued. *Not like* Braen *was. I'll never be as great as Braston.*

Percy pushed the door open.

The king sighed. Inside waited several body servants, each ready to strip him of robes and adorn his body with sleeping attire.

Sleep.

How had he ever found time to sleep during his seventeen-year reign? There had been so much to do, rebuilding the kingdom out of scraps of the fallen empire. The Brother's War had demanded so much of Eston's people. This city stood, but so many more had met ruin. He especially lamented the fate of his own Old Weston—buried forever beneath volcanic rock and a deep lake. The rebuilding efforts in each location had bled his coffers dry, leaving him to pass the cost on to his people. Even now, they grumbled his name for giving the city over to the Pescari.

"We must discuss the topic of succession, my lord," the chancellor said without hesitation. He had pressed this same issue many times over the past seventeen years, but the king never allowed it resolved.

"That matter is closed, Percy. I have a will, and you shall unseal it upon my death."

That time is sooner than you know, the voice cautioned.

"But the witan, my lord, may not agree with your choice. You must reveal him now. Tell me and I will vet his background and smooth his transition."

"Smooth his... You mean bribe the witan to comply? No, Percy, I won't allow that."

It's what I would have done, the voice urged. *This politician is correct—you must make back room deals to ensure transition.*

The king ignored both the man and the voice, holding his arms out while the servants removed first his outer garments and then the silkier layers underneath. He shivered as he turned, as if entering a layer of cooler air. Had he not been in a state of undress he would never have felt it. Irritated at the draft of indignity, the king waiting patiently until the attendants finished and he was once more covered.

"Will you desire anything else tonight, Your Highness?" his chancellor asked.

"No, Percy, that will be all."

"Very well, my lord. I will greet you again in the morning." The man bowed his leave, holding his spectacles to his face as he did. Only once he'd departed did the king sigh with relief.

He turned to a chair near the fireplace and spoke to its empty cushions.

"I know you're there. I felt your aura. Show yourself," he commanded. "I want a full status report."

The image of a man slowly appeared, solidifying as if born of the misty air molecules in which he'd hidden. He looked to be in his mid-thirties and sat upon the chair with legs crossed and hands resting patiently atop his lap. His robes were a richly dyed blue, and the crest upon their center identified him as a Dreamer. The golden trim around the fringes revealed him to be Cuyler, the leader of their sect. The voice liked this man, and so did the king.

"I apologize for arriving in secret," Cuyler said. "But I'd followed the chancellor closely and had to maintain the connection until after he departed. Otherwise he would have noticed."

"Wonderful," the king muttered. "What of it? Am I correct in my worries?"

"I don't know yet. He's been in your service as long as any of us but very difficult to read. All his conversations seem in order and related to your best interest. I believe he is indeed loyal to your position, at least while you're alive."

The king grunted. "But he *may* turn against my wishes after I'm gone?"

"He may," Cuyler agreed, "but what you demand won't sit well with many. Your choice of heir won't be easily understood among your kingdom, but especially not the nobles."

"I think it will, in time."

"Even the Dreamers won't understand. To those who fought it, this will remind them of the Brother's War—times best forgotten."

"Perhaps, but they should remember those who brought this peace to Andalon, and that his father was part of it," the king replied solemnly. Those were the best times of his life, when he had a purpose and a clear direction. The king paused, then asked, "What have the seers among you prophesied?"

"Another war is coming and it begins with and hinges upon *him*."

"We cannot allow another war," the king declared. "Does he cause it? Or is it a civil war waged by those who oppose him?"

"We've not reasoned that out," Cuyler admitted. "But it involves Falconers and most certainly the Fjorikans."

The king paused. "What *about* Falconers?" he asked.

Those beastly specters had been destroyed during the Brother's War, their hive mind severed and bodies allowed eternal rest.

"Some must have survived the war, and several Dreamers have reported clashes in each city," the Dreamer explained. "We can only assume they farm latents as in past times."

If the Falconers have returned, the voice suggested, *they are led by a single mind, not a hive. Find the source and destroy it.*

"There's a source," the king said. "A single mind controlling them all. Find it and sever their connection."

The lead Dreamer nodded, but his face suggested more troubling news.

"There's more?"

"It pertains to the boy," Cuyler explained. "He was attacked by Falconers. Caroline and Bearnard chased them off but were forced to reveal their presence."

"His mother and I have an agreement," the king said. "Did she turn him over to them? He'd be safer if she did."

"They did not elaborate, only reported he fled and went into hiding."

That is unacceptable, the voice cautioned.

"Find him and bring him before me." The pain between his temples pounded with worry. What if no one in Andalon understood his decision? "I must have him found, and soon."

"We will not fail," the lead Dreamer promised, then cloaked himself with a shimmering cloak of air—invisible except for a vibration against the far wall.

The door to his chambers opened and closed, and King Esterling let out the breath he held.

"Am I mad?" he asked the empty room.

Not yet, thankfully. And it's good *the madness hasn't begun to set in,* the voice said, or *we'll never succeed in what's to come.*

"You speak like you know it intimately," the king said with a laugh. Surely the madness in his chambers was his own for talking to voices.

I know it and fight against it daily. But know for certain you are not mad, King Esterling.

"What did you mean earlier when you suggested my death is sooner than I know?" King Esterling asked. "How much time do I have if I'm truly dying?"

I did not say you are dying, King Esterling. But my own time is ending, and so then, will yours.

"I don't understand," the king admitted.

He waited, but the voice had fallen silent. Climbing into bed he closed his eyes, ignoring the heavy issues of state weighing on his mind. After a while, Amash Esterling fell into a deep sleep.

CHAPTER SEVEN

The buckboard bounced along the road, shaking Tara free of the gripping fear controlling her evening. It all happened so fast, and she had clung to her mother without protest, allowing herself to be whisked away. They had gone without even a goodbye, two women alone in the night. Her eyes took in eerie moonlight and shadows along the road. Any or all could hide trouble, the worst kind even, awaiting them alone on the road. It was foolish to travel in darkness.

She yearned for Robert to protect them, riding by her side, knowing his presence would ease her fears. Even in his youth she found him strong, only to grow stronger into manhood. She loved him, maybe, but was too lost in her own youth to know for certain. But the sobering reality revealed Robert was gone from her life.

Their kiss.

She had worked up courage for many years to make the move, always knowing it was hers to make. But the events of the evening robbed her of a proper goodbye, perhaps even more than a kiss, and she wondered if he missed her as much as she did him. She wished they had never parted.

Tara yearned to jump free of the wagon and race to the warm safety of his arms.

Breaking the silence, Flaya said, "Thank you for leaving without question. I know this departure is not easy, but the Pescari woman inside you remained calm."

"The Andalonian woman inside me yearns to return," Tara replied flatly.

"That feeling is petulance, found only in children," her mother explained. "Pescari women obey, as you did tonight."

"I don't want to obey. I want things the way they were."

"Pescari are plagued with change. Our only constants are the awakening of Felicima, her trip across the sky, and our goddess' eventual slumber after descending into the western caldera."

"That's why we flee into the dangers of the night?" Tara demanded, hot anger rising within as emotion grew. She could barely contain her true feelings, and decorum meant risking burning up from within. "Anything could happen to us alone on this road. A worse fate could await us in Weston, yet we flee like cowards from the only life I've known."

"We had to leave, and you know it," Flaya patiently explained. "They would have arrested you and placed you before their laws. This *was* our only option."

"I'm not afraid to stand before a magistrate. I did nothing wrong."

"In the eyes of the Andalonians you did *everything* wrong. Worse, you showed violence beneath the eye of Felicima. There is no justice for Pescari in Andalon, and we belong in New Weston with our own kind."

"I'm Pescari by birth only," Tara replied softly, "they are *your* kind, not mine."

"You don't *know* your kind!" Flaya snapped, her voice startling the night. Nearby wings flapped and tiny feat scurried into underbrush. Only the largest and bravest animals would venture near the road now, predators seeking a meal or men hoping to feast upon a woman's fear.

Tara stared closely at her mother, observing the hidden terror beneath the woman's usually calm surface. She trembled, something the girl never thought she'd see her mother do.

"*You* are afraid," Tara said, realizing now why they fled. "But of what? It wasn't the magistrate or the constables. They were merely your excuse to leave. What is it you fear if we remain?"

"I'm afraid you will never know your father, and that ignorance may cause greater harm later."

"How, Mother?" Tara demanded. "How will I ever know a man who is gone? What knowledge can the dead provide the living?"

But Flaya had finished talking and fell quiet behind her reins. They faced a long journey, and changing her mind along the way would prove impossible.

Tara stole a glance westward toward the direction of home. She *would* find her way back eventually, and if not to home then to *him*. Her Robert was like the eagle who yearned to spread wings. He would know where to seek, should his heart desire hers.

The wind chilled the night and the crunching leaves underfoot caused Robert to worry. Were they followed by the Dreamers? Would their footsteps give them away? Where had the Falconers gone? Every sound he and Sebastian made could draw either or all threats to their woods. The plentiful shadows hid dangers, and each step could be into a hazard.

The night, which had so far been a blur, slowly cleared as if fog had lifted. He headed the wrong direction.

"I need to go after her," Robert suddenly demanded. He'd stood idly by when Flaya whisked Tara away without giving him a chance to say goodbye.

"No, you need to get to Eusari," Sebastian corrected. "It's important you see her first. Tara can wait."

Robert found himself once more torn between clinging to his childhood and becoming a man. Either he pursued Tara and confronted her mother, insisting she turn over her daughter so they may start a life together, or he sought his mother's explanation.

Eusari offered answers.

"What will she tell me?" he demanded of the farmhand. "You knew those Dreamers, and they knew Eusari. That means *you* knew my parents. Who were they?"

"It's not my place to…"

"Stop it!" Robert demanded. "You sound like Sippen! It *is* your place because I demand to know. Who were my parents?"

He had gone too far, terrifying the farmhand. Sebastian stared downward at trembling hands. Robert felt immediately sorry. This man was good, with a decent heart. But the female Dreamer was right, his cowardice was known to all. He wasn't a fighter and avoided any and all conflict with practiced skill.

"I'm sorry for yelling," Robert said softly. "You don't deserve my anger. But I *need* to know why the Falconers attacked the farm and why the Dreamers demand I stand before the king! Why is he interested in me?"

"I knew Amash... not as well as the others, but I knew him. He's a good man. I trust him because Braen did."

"Braen," Robert said thoughtfully. "That's twice I've heard that name today. Tell me about him."

"Braen Braston was my captain. I sailed under him as a boy."

"Braen Braston was a pirate! Are you telling me you sailed with *pirates*?"

Sebastian nodded. "He was also the Prince of Fjorik, a kind man, even if he had an awful temper. I was with him the day he took Pirate's Cove, and he regretted that day the rest of his life... just as I do. It was the most awful thing I've ever seen and..." The farmhand broke off, saying no more about it. The tears brimming in his eyes suggested he was finished speaking but not remembering.

"Sippen too? And Cedric?" Robert asked. "Were they part of his crew?"

Sebastian nodded.

"What does he have to do with my mother?"

"He loved Eusari and she loved him."

"So the twins?"

"Are his."

Robert felt the ground beneath him sway as his mind caught up. "What does he have to do with the Dreamers?"

"He rescued us."

"Us? So you really were one of them?"

"Never fully. I guess I never fit in," Sebastian said sadly.

"I'd say not. Those two were awful, mean even."

"I don't think they meant you harm. Caroline and Bearnard aren't bad, but they've always been bit of bullies. I think you should stand before Amash, but Sippen's right. You need to speak to Eusari before you go."

"Tell me about my parents," Robert demanded.

"I didn't know them. All I know is you were barely a newborn when Eusari arrived in Logan after the war. Collette was your wetnurse then. I only guessed whose child you were because it was never discussed openly.

Eusari gave me a choice then, to go with the Dreamers to Eston or with her, Sippen and Cedric. She took us westward and made everyone vow never to tell any of you children about the old days. Your mother wanted a new life for us all."

"I will go to my mother," Robert decided. "I'll hear what she has to say and find Tara after."

"It really is your best choice," the farmhand agreed.

The outskirts of town felt odd to the pair, watching from the forest at night, and the duo crept carefully despite their cloak of shimmering air. Sebastian had explained that there were Dreamers who could see through the shield, but neither Caroline nor Bearnard had that ability when they were younger. They paused not far from the jailhouse, watching the constables milling about the doorway.

"What do we do?" Robert asked. "Do we walk in and find her?"

"I don't know," Sebastian admitted. He hadn't thought about the final bits of the plan. "But I guess we do need to get closer."

After looking both ways down main street, the pair inched their way toward the front doors.

"Took her already, he did," one of the constables said.

"During the night?" another asked. "Why the rush?"

"Olsen said he didn't trust the others not to attempt a breakout. That little one's smart, and the fat one's unpredictable. Together they'd be stupid enough to try."

"Makes sense," said the second. "But what about the Dreamers? Why'd they say to stand watch like she's here? That makes no sense at all, not a bit, no sir!"

Robert froze, gripping Sebastian's shoulder. "It's a trap," he mouthed silently, and Sebastian's eyes grew wide with fear. The farmhand nodded and the pair turned to leave.

"He said her trial will be moved up. The Logan magistrate will preside over the case by week's end," the first guard said.

"Pity for that woman, then. It means Constable Thorinson will have jurisdiction. That woman has no mercy whatsoever!" the second replied.

Thorinson? The name baffled Robert's mind and had to hear more. Motioning to Sebastian he crept forward into the middle of the street.

Abruptly, the swirling air hiding them from view began to pick up dust from the road. The fine particles caught the current and swept up and around. At first the pair were confused. Normal dirt shouldn't have been picked up so easily, and this resin was whitish in color.

Robert sniffed. Chalk. Someone had coated the road with a fine covering of white chalk all around the jailhouse. The sound of cracking whips froze him in place as tendrils of air raced down the street. Their cover had failed.

The farmhand pushed past Robert, dropping their invisibility and raising a more solid shield. The whisps deflected, but they were the diversion. A concussive blast sent both man and boy sprawling backward onto the cobblestones. Six more tendrils reached out. Two caught Sebastian by the arms and pulled him forward, up onto his feet and then facedown hard against the pavement. He landed with a splat and Robert cringed.

He eyed the four remaining tendrils, woven like ropes that found his ankles. He felt them tug, dragging him feet first toward two shadowy figures behind an apothecary. Even with hooded cloaks covering their heads, he recognized the two Dreamers. He kept his head up as he was dragged, eyes locked onto the shimmering bonds around his legs. Even in the dark Robert could make out their pattern, braided like the rawhide they used on the farm. Cedric had spent many an hour teaching the boys knotwork, and this splicing resembled the sailor's ropes they learned.

The night suddenly plunged into wintery cold, despite being summer. The wind blew with a shivering chill and Robert watched his breath fog before him. He was suddenly afraid, not for himself but all at once for his mother and Tara. He had to get free. Both woman and girl depended upon his success. His icy breath brushed against his shimmering bonds, then joined the currents of air as if unable to escape the current.

Mother, he thought, *I've failed you. I should've expected a trap, and now I've no way to save you. They've got me,* he worried, *and I've no way to fight them!*

Robert shivered and the air immediately touching his skin vibrated off his body as he shook. This too flowed toward his bonds, but he reached out a hand, catching just enough to pull it like wet potter's clay toward him. With his other hand he gathered more and more, until he worked a ball of it before him. The boy's eyes grew wide with surprise as he crafted the air around him.

This must be another trick, he worried, but it seemed to flow like a river only he controlled. *Sailor's knots,* he suddenly realized. *They once sailed with pirates and know knots as well as I.* He worked the air then, tying and knotting it the way Cedric had always hated—indiscriminately and without reason.

"You'll never untie that easily when you most need to," the foreman had corrected. "When time is of the essence you have to trust your hands and the knot tied by another. Do it right, we tie knots easily untied and used again later."

The web Robert wove was one of his own creation, and he cast it the way he'd been taught. As soon as it left his hands, his eyes returned to the braids around his ankles. These unraveled as easily has he'd hoped. Free of his bonds, he jumped to his feet, glancing briefly to ensure the net held the Dreamers. It wouldn't for long. He raced toward Sebastian who had also found his footing. Grabbing his arm, Robert hauled him down an alleyway and hopefully toward freedom.

Around several bends they came across an older man loading a final box into his covered wagon. They skidded to a stop before him, as startled as he to have nearly collided. High up above a falcon screeched, then dove toward the man.

Robert suddenly worried they'd encountered a foe worse than Dreamers. "Falconer!" he cried and turned to flee.

"Wait," Sebastian urged. "Look at his eyes."

"What about them?" he asked, turning wildly and staring down the old man. The eyes smiling back were jovial and warm.

"Falconer's eyes are different because they're dead inside."

A large hawk spread its wings, slowing its decent and landing on the man's arm with a settling beat against air.

"Now, now, Reaver," the man said reassuringly. "These appear to be friends."

"We would be indebted, sir, if you could give us a ride out of town."

"Hmm," the man considered. "I wonder what kind of trouble you're in, to be running in the streets at night... *away* from the constable's office."

"We were attacked, sir," Robert pleaded, "and the Dreamers confused us with the thugs," he lied. "Please help get us out of town."

"Well," the man said, settling Reaver on a perch near the driver's bench. "I'm headed to Logan, myself. Are you certain these attackers are still chasing you?"

Looking around, Robert saw no one. They must still be caught in his net. *My net... of air.* What had he done? With a trembling voice he said, "I believe so... I'm not sure."

"Then you'd better climb aboard but keep low. There's a hidden compartment behind the sacks of flour. The two of you will be cramped but should fit."

Robert and Sebastian wasted no time scrambling aboard. The man's words proved correct. They barely fit but somehow were thankful for the hiding place. Soon, the wheels beneath them rolled against cobblestone, and they began their trek toward Logan.

CHAPTER EIGHT

Anne Thorinson despised crime of any fashion and felt the criminals, however petty, deserved whatever thumping they earned. The boy she watched in Logan's market square was no exception, part of the Wolfpack Gang. He was older, about twelve summers, and served as the distraction. Engaged in a loud argument with a fruit vendor, his job was to create a scene and several patrons, rich and poor, had gathered to watch the spectacle.

All eyes were on the boy except hers. Anne scanned the crowd for movement.

"I wasn't stealing!" the boy screamed. "You'll be bringin' const'bles down on me," his gutter speech accused, "for nutin!"

"I *know* you!" the vendor accused. "You've stolen from me before!"

"I ain't nevah!" the boy protested, raising a fist.

The man grabbed it straight away, a mistake because the boy created the real distraction by kicking and writhing wildly. His leg caught that of the table, toppling it over and sending a cascade of various fruits into the crowd. On cue, a half dozen street urchins descended, scooping up as much as they could carry in their shirttails before darting down Main Street. When they reached the first intersection they scrambled in all directions and abruptly disappeared.

Nice change to an old trick, the constable nodded, admiring their ingenuity. With eyes locked on the crowd she searched for the real threat.

"Let go of me!" the boy screamed again.

"Constable!" the vendor called over the laughter of the crowd. "Constable! Come quick, I've been robbed!"

The boy finally twisted just enough his shirt broke away. *Theatrical stitches,* Anne realized, as he darted ten steps toward freedom.

He could have kept running but seized upon one final opportunity by turning and offering a hand gesture. "Your mother's a tavern-turner!" he shouted to the vendor, then sprinted away.

Anne finally spotted her quarry. A skinny girl, about ten years old, deftly snipped a purse from a seemly gentleman watching the ruckus. As quick as her hand moved, the satchel fell into her basket of withering flowers, each offered for a penny. As soon as it landed, she buried it beneath the foliage into what the constable assumed was a hidden compartment.

The girl was close, and Anne was quick. Her hand grabbed the arm holding the basket and struck the space between her shoulder blades with the other. As the child gasped, the constable shoved her to the ground and slipped on shackles before her wind had returned.

"Be easy with that child!" the uppity gentleman warned.

Anne brushed away the flowers and drew forth the man's purse, tossing it toward his chest. "No need to press charges," she informed him. "I watched the little demon take it, so my word's all we need for the magistrate."

"She's just a child!" the man argued, staring dumfounded at his purse and feeling the cut leather ties dangling from his belt.

"She's a criminal," Anne said, hoisting the girl to her feet and hauling her away, "and criminals deserve punishment." She half dragged the child to the constabulary station. If she moved fast enough, she could still make it to the Wolf Den and bust the leaders of the gang sorting the stolen fruit.

The stench of the Logan docks putrefied the air, mixing smells that should never combine. Innards and carcasses lay discarded hither and thither along the fishery, and dung from various sources—human included—smoldered in dark corners between every building. Barrels piled high with rotting food and waste sat behind every door, the worst of which rested behind a tavern. The *Mangy Dog,* the sign on the front door identified it, and the inside reeked worse than the rear.

On its steps sat an old man, himself a blend of piss and rum, rubbing the bit of his leg exposed beneath leather straps. Attached to this bruised and infected stump he awkwardly carried a wooden peg, the best remnant of his sorry life and the only piece of him worth any brass. None of Pete was worthy of copper, silver, or gold.

"Spare a penny for a glass, mate?" he asked a sailor walking by. The man turned his eyes and pretended not to hear.

"You, dearies?" he asked a group of prostitutes who hurried their steps. "Have a penny to spare?" Even the bilge scum of Logan were above this man.

His life had not always been this wretched. He sailed every sea in Andalon, rising to serve as first mate under the finest captain the ocean had produced. That was his proud moment, right before the fall. He wasn't yet sure the abyss he fell into offered a bottom.

You're a coward, his mind accused. *A coward and a traitor, unworthy of remembering better times.*

He felt around for a bottle that wasn't completely empty. Only a drop would silence his accuser.

Of course, that voice belonged to the hangings-on of what used to be his conscience. Peter Longshanks, once a pious and upright fellow, had slowly shaved off pieces of that morality, replacing it with grief and loss with every decision he ever made.

You never deserved her in your life, his accuser whispered. *Like every woman you ever loved or tried to honor, they placed their faith in the wrong man. The sea should have taken you,* he lamented, *or even a sword.*

In the end though, or perhaps the beginning when viewing his life's spiraling descent, the business end of a musket had literally pushed him over the ledge. He had fled like a coward when faced with mutiny, losing his captain's ship to another.

Finding no trace of any liquor, he pulled himself up onto a salt bleached crutch. It would snap beneath his weight someday and hopefully land him face first into a puddle. Then he would finally drown like the sorry wretch he was.

"Well now," a voice said mockingly, "if it ain't Peg-legged Pete!"

He ambled around to find two sailors watching from the next porch over.

"Tell him no," Pete said defiantly. "I won't be bought with none of his pieces of silver."

"Silver?" the men laughed. "What he wants from you will earn the finest *gold* from the southern continent."

"I won't," Pete promised, but his stomach rumbled loudly and his head spun as he stared up at the pair. *Gold would mean food and a bath,* he mused.

But you'd spend the bulk of it on rum, his accuser pointed out.

Hopefully enough to drown me for good, he prayed.

One of the men tossed a small purse at his feet. "Wash up and feed that belly," the sailor commanded. "You start work tonight."

Had Pete a shred of dignity left, or even perhaps a bit of self-respect, he would have ambled off and left the money lie. As he bent down to pick it up, he toppled over. The sailors roared with laughter as his yearning for rum and death won out. Peter Longshanks was, after all, a shadow of the man he ever had a chance to be. Tears wet his cheeks as he realized he'd destroyed his body with rum, but sold his soul for gold.

After the sailors had gone, a woman's voice asked from the shadows, "What've you got there, Peter Longshanks?"

Pete scrambled to a sitting position, palming the purse and slipping it under his rags. "Nothing," he lied.

"Public begging's a crime, Pete. Haven't we been over that?"

He drew out his hand, holding the purse where the woman could see. "I wasn't begging... well, I was, but this is payment for a job. I've got a job to do, Constable!"

Anne approached the beggar, kneeling beside him casually. She held out her hand and waited. After a few breaths, Pete placed the purse in her palm. She weighed it with a shake.

"That's a lot of coin for a man like you, Mr. Longshanks. What is it those men would have you do?"

"I was to get a shower and a meal, they said."

"And?"

"And I'm to help them find a crew."

"What kind of crew, Pete?"

He became agitated, heart fluttering and beating fast. He couldn't lie to this constable, and she would never accept a piece of the purse to look the other way. Above reproach this woman was, and all of Loganshire knew it.

"Fisherman," he lied.

Anne shook her head sadly. "I recognize those men from their posters, Pete. They're known pirates and part of Devil Jacque's crew." Leaning in closer she whispered, "I hate pirates and won't be having any of their kind around my docks."

"I swear!" he lied again. "I didn't know!" He pointed to the purse. "In that case, take their gold!" He'd bathe in Lake Norton if he had to, and food could be found in time. "I don't want it, nor do I want anything to do with a man like Devil Jacque."

"Keep it, Pete," she said, slapping it into his palm. "But you work for me now."

"I... I can't! His crew will kill me if I turn him over!"

Anne smiled slyly and gestured toward their surroundings. Her green eyes and red hair seemed to dance in the sunlight as she asked, "And this? You call *this* living, Mr. Longshanks?"

His stomach dropped as a tiny part of forgotten conscience made an appearance. "What would you have me do, Constable?"

"Set him up. I want to take him down and burn that cursed ship of his. I'll send it, him, and his entire crew to the bottom of the lake before allowing a man like him to walk freely in Andalon. Get close and tell me where to find him."

The purse again felt heavy in his hand and grimy fingers closed around the sum within. He watched the woman leave, never taking his eyes from her back until she disappeared down the street.

You won't help her though, the accuser in his mind pointed out.

"No. I'm more afraid of *him*." For the first time in eighteen years, Peter Longshanks spoke the truth.

CHAPTER NINE

Robert's muscles had moved beyond cramping, and his toes and fingers tingled from lack of movement. The smuggler's compartment offered little relief, except to move from flat on his back to partially on one side or the other. He breathed in slowly, relieving some of the anxiety but little of the worry, and added more concerns along with the dank staleness of the air. If the old man driving the cart did not stop soon for the night, he worried the wagon would become his coffin.

"Sebastian," he finally whispered, mostly to ensure the farmhand still lived.

"What?" the man muttered, letting out a slight groan as he too shifted weight.

"Perhaps this wasn't a wise choice of transportation."

The farmhand stifled a laugh.

"Back there," Robert added, finally ready to face events from the evening, "I did that. I'm not sure what it was, but I did it. The air... it *obeyed* my mind!"

"Shh..." Sebastian warned. "We shouldn't talk about it openly."

"I need to," the young man admitted. "I'm scared. Does that make me a Dreamer? I don't know if I trust them enough to become one!"

"I said be quiet!" Sebastian snapped.

"I need to know now. We have no idea what lies ahead after the old man lets us out. I want to be ready."

The farmhand did not answer straight away, and so Robert waited. Finally, after several long breaths to settle his own nerves, Sebastian offered a solution.

"There's a way now," he said, "we can speak openly. I... I don't like to do it and haven't in a long time—since before you were born."

"How?" Robert demanded.

"Close your eyes and focus on the darkness. Ignore the pattern of stars you will see, looking between them and beyond."

Robert did as instructed, finding the exercise calmed his racing heart as well as his previous worries. It was difficult, to see beyond the tiny specks of light and nearly opened his mouth to demand more clarity. But then he did.

Once fully focused, the lights rushed forward into the forefront of his vision. The sensation caused his stomach to drop, the movement both unexpected and dizzying.

Good, Sebastian's voice suddenly spoke in his mind. *I can see with you now and will guide your journey. Find the cluster in the upper right. Good. Now focus on the fifth star down.*

Everything was just as promised, exactly where Sebastian said it would be. The fifth star down, he learned later, was not an address to their destination, merely a focal point they could both share. It sucked his mind forward with a rush, and Robert travelled as if flying. The sensation, he marveled, felt exactly like he expected.

You may see shapes and faces, Sebastian warned. *Ignore those. They're not real, merely distractions conjured by your mind. It yearns to remain attached to your body.*

Robert flinched with fear. "I'm leaving my body?" he asked aloud.

Not fully, but a part of you detaches whenever you enter the ether. It remains there, imprinted until you return. Right now, there is a young boy version of me, terrified and fearful in the dream world, and I'll have to face those fears when we rejoin.

They're wrong about you, Sebastian, Robert said. *You're not a coward. I think something happened to you as a child, but you don't act cowardly. Earlier tonight you protected me, and during the Falconer attack you ran to protect Collette. Even now you are overcoming your fears to take care of me. Thank you.*

Sebastian did not respond, but Robert sensed he still led the journey through his mind. The end of it neared and the passing stars slowed. Soon a world appeared before them.

Is it like ours? Robert asked, amazed by the spherical shape and clouds swirling over oceans of blue and greenish land masses.

I don't know, Sebastian admitted, *but in my heart, I always feel it is.* He led them downward, toward a continent. If it was their world, there would have been a large crack extending from a burning caldera. There was neither, only majestic mountains standing in their place. *It was like this when we found it,* Sebastian explained, *though not all of it was completed. The Dreamers have been busy since I last visited, and it's nearly complete.* After a brilliant flash of light forced them both to cover their faces, he said, "We're here. Look around."

Robert opened his eyes. The Dream World was more beautiful than home.

They stood in a meadow surrounded on all sides by dense forest. All around them tall flowers and grasses swayed on a soft breeze. The temperature was perfect, not too hot nor too cooled by the wind. Their noses filled with pleasant scents of rose, lavender, and honeysuckle. This world was a dream in which one could touch and interact.

"It's gorgeous," Robert exclaimed.

"Just wait! It gets better!" Sebastian said with a grin. Whatever he had feared before was gone, and he actually seemed giddy to explore.

Off in the distance rose a large hill topped with a gray stone castle. The moat encircling its base reflected stark blue that contrasted the perfect shades of greens all around. Even the sky appeared less pale than home, as white clouds moved slowly across.

"That belongs to the Dreamers," Sebastian explained the structure, "and it's where they meet to talk in private." He led Robert a different direction, into the forest to find a private place for their own conversation. He placed a hand atop a strange mushroom. It was out of place, and the way he gazed down upon it seemed forlorn and full of sadness.

"Caroline used to sit upon this very spot when we were friends. We were close, then, all of us were. Even Marita wasn't bullied or put out yet."

Leaves rustled nearby, and a luminescent salamander emerged. At first Robert jumped, but realized at once the creature would not harm either of them.

Sebastian laughed and rubbed its head like an old friend. It closed its eyes and settled for a nap at his feet.

"You created him?" Robert asked of the creature.

"I did, though he turned out lazier than I'd hoped as a child. Seeing him here gives me..." He paused, frowning a bit to find the correct words. "I don't know *what* it gives me, but I want to say hope. Maybe by returning I can finally move past some of the terrors I experienced as a child."

"So, I'm like you?" Robert asked gently. "I'm a Dreamer?"

Sebastian shook his head. "No, the Dreamers choose who they include, like an exclusive club you have to know their password to fit in. But you *are* an emotant. Early on I discovered you had latency, which made sense considering your father."

Robert stepped back in shock. "You lied to me?"

"Yes. I've always known who your parents were, even if Eusari and the others never told me directly. Your mother, due to deliver, was with them when they entered Eston, but they only returned with you."

"So she died in childbirth?"

"It would be easier to think of it that way," Sebastian said sadly. "Your father had already died, and you were destined to be born alone into the world. After the battle, Eusari took you as her own. Collette was your wetnurse. That's how I met her, brought by Eusari on her return to Logan."

"Sebastian," Robert demanded, "who were my parents? Why does Mother work so hard to keep it a secret from me?"

"To protect you, but telling you now will do more in that regard."

"Who am I? Why do I need protection?"

"You're Robert Esterling, son of Prince Robert and the Lady Sarai Horslei."

Robert's eyes grew big, the news catching in his throat and choking back any reply. *This is too much,* he thought. *First these powers? Now my parents?* The world around him moved and he staggered as if to fall. With swimming vision, he reached behind and felt something soft but supportive. He turned and watched as a purple toadstool spread out to bear his weight.

"Thank you," he muttered to Sebastian, the farmhand. No... no longer a mere farmhand, but a hero of the Brother's War. The one-time Dreamer and friend to pirates smiled back. "For everything, thank you. For bringing me here and for telling me the truth. Thank you, Sebastian."

"You're welcome. Eusari should have been the one to tell you, but I think she'll understand."

"So the king knows I'm alive? He wants to kill me before I make a claim against him?"

"I don't think so. I know Amash very well, and he's a kind man. Eusari said she was keeping you safe until of age. I think he means to proclaim you now, as his heir."

"So the Dreamers? They aren't trying to kill me?"

"No," Sebastian shook his head, "I don't think they are, merely focused on finishing their task by bringing you before Amash. But, like Sippen said, it was important to know the truth about your lineage. I just wish it was Eusari who told you instead of me."

"Then I should go back and face them... go before the king."

"No, Logan is along the way. You should see Eusari as planned. Let her answer whatever questions you have first."

Robert nodded, staring at the salamander at his friend's feet and taking it all in.

Suddenly, Sebastian sat up. "We have to go," he said. "The wagon stopped and the driver dismounted. He'll free us soon, and we must be fully awake."

Without warning, Robert felt his mind zoom into the clouds, retracing the dark journey home.

Robert awoke with a gasp, heart pounding and ears ringing as light flooded their secret compartment. He tried to rise, but his muscles again cramped. A wrinkled hand reached out to grab his, pulling him free of his imprisonment. Sebastian was already sitting up.

"I'm sorry you had to stay hidden so long," the old man said to both. "I wanted to get down the main road before circling back to ensure we weren't followed. Whatever you two are running from isn't anywhere to be found, but I felt it best we stayed off the main road to Logan the rest of the way."

Robert looked around. They sat in a well-hidden part of the forest, protected from above by dense canopy. If the Dreamers had bonded birds, none would find them easily.

"I think it's best if we keep only a small fire, so as not to draw attention, don't you?" the old man asked.

Robert nodded. "Yes," he said slowly, as if awakening from a dream. Only, the dreamy fog clouding his brain had only just begun to murk his thoughts. *Prince. Emotant.*

"Thank you," Sebastian said, "but my friend and I must be getting along. We're sorry to have brought you into it and should leave you now to travel on our own."

"Nonsense." The old man's eyes smiled. They were kind, as one would expect from a loving grandfather. "Reaver, you met," he said, gesturing to the Falcon. It sat hooded quietly on its perch. "We haven't properly introduced," the man said. "My name's Campton, but my friends call me Camp. You may do the same." He bowed deeply before the young men. "I'm a tinker by trade, a merchant's friend and worker of finer tools."

"I'm Robert, and this is Sebastian," Robert said, ignoring a warning glance from his friend. He took Camp's hand and shook it firmly. "A small fire is wise, but do you have any food? We're famished after a difficult night."

Camp's eyes lit up once more. "I do! I brought along perpetual soup!"

Both young men raised their eyebrows. Neither had heard of it.

Camp moved to the driver's bench and pointed at a copper pot hanging from a hook. At its base was a small compartment smoking softly with hot coals.

"The trick is to keep it forever warm, changing out the coals whenever you make a fire. It'll simmer all day long, and you add to it as you go along your journey. Small game fits best, so do roots and vegetables you find along the way. Just keep it warm and it never goes bad!"

Robert stepped closer to examine the contraption, smiling big and wishing Sippen could see it, too. This was the kind of invention the little man loved, and Robert couldn't wait to tell him. Only, he wasn't going to see him for a long time, possibly never again. Sadness overtook him, and he stepped away with a feigned smile. "Thank you," he said. "It smells wonderful."

Sebastian tended the fire while Camp dished out the soup. It tasted wonderful, and the younger men laughed quietly at his stories. He was well travelled, it seemed, and claimed to have visited every part of Andalon.

"Even Pirate's Cove?" Robert asked with shock.

"Even The Cove," Camp bragged. He yawned. "It's getting late, and I'm an old man. I think I should be getting to sleep." He stretched and stood, making his way toward the woods. "But I've got nature business to attend to first. You can't hold it as long at my age," he said with a laugh.

The boys waited till he had gone, watching him make his way deep into the denser trees for privacy.

Robert glanced at Reaver, still hooded and perched quietly on the wagon. The falcon had only moved when Camp had earlier fed him a mouse. He kept a few in a pouch around his waist.

"I think we can trust him," Robert said. "He's a kind fellow, and riding would be faster than walking to Logan. We could be there in a day or two."

Sebastian stole a timid glance toward the woods. "I don't know. He's still a stranger, and we don't know who or what he'd sell for a price. That includes information about two young men travelling this night toward Logan."

Robert found arguing pointless, his friend had a point. "Let's talk it over in the morning, I'm exhausted and think we should rest."

Sebastian agreed, but neither men moved. They couldn't douse the fire until Camp returned. He may need the light to guide his way back. Both men shifted their weight uncomfortably.

"He's taking a very long time," Robert remarked.

Sebastian shrugged and smiled. "Well," he said pointing a thumb the way the old man had walked, "he *is* old! Cedric always complains his business takes longer the older he gets!"

Robert grinned. "Cedric's takes longer because he's stuck it in so many nasty places over the years. You should hear the things he's bragged about doing!"

"Oh, I've heard. I've known that man since I was a boy, so believe me I know he has no shame!"

They both laughed aloud at this but was cut off by a sudden shrieking overhead.

Sebastian moved fast, snuffing out the fire by kicking dirt then stomping it dark.

Robert strained his eyes to see, but the falcons overhead were hidden above the branches and leaves. "Falconers?" he asked Sebastian, who nodded violently. A roar from behind caused him to jump, and he turned just in time to see two large forest cats had emerged. On the cart, Reaver squawked then rose into the air, his hood still covering his eyes. Robert's were still locked on the animals and wished the fire still burned. He picked up a uselessly smoking branch and waved it, hoping the heat would be enough.

"Jaguars," whispered Sebastian, with eyes rounded and very much afraid.

"What are those?" demanded Robert.

"Worse than Falconers!"

The big cats lunged, just as several falcons dove from above.

Sebastian moved quickly, stepping between Robert and the cats, and a dome of shimmering air formed around him. The Falcons screeched as their talons scratched against the surface and the jaguars bounced harmlessly off, pacing and circling their prey trapped within.

Robert watched the animals closely, shivering as their eyes reflected cool patience.

"It's really better if you don't resist," Camp's voice said from the tree line. Behind him stood four specters.

"How many can you fight?" Robert asked Sebastian.

But the farmhand's instinctive courage had faded, replaced by gripping fear. His weight crumbled and he slid to his knees. Along with his composure, the shimmering shield fell. Wisps of air securely wrapped around both their bodies, strangely braided ropes the pattern of which Robert had never seen. Around their feet, roots slithered like snakes rising from the ground, coiling around their legs.

"Yes," Camp said, "it's best you come along without a fight." He reached out a wrinkled hand holding four wriggling caterpillars. Holding them close to Sebastian's ears, the larvae slipped into his ears as he wept with fear. Then camp brought two toward Robert. The creatures hissed as they slid into his ears, muffling the world around him.

Robert struggled, trying desperately to loosen his bonds. Each time he connected with the wisps of air, the caterpillars screeched horribly and his connection failed. Then he passed out.

CHAPTER TEN

Sippen groaned, he was too old to drink like he used to and blamed Cedric, as usual, for the rhythmic pounding between his ears. The bottle had been their last, locked away for a special occasion or, in the actual case, a brief reminder of the good ol' days. The arrival of Falconers and Dreamers on the same night provided more than enough reason for drinking, and they mourned Braen through the night along with their younger selves. He groaned again.

His eyes opened to Cedric's voice.

"Collette! Collette!" the portly man called. "We need breakfast!"

"Where is she?" Sippen groaned, his voice barely audible. "I haven't seen her all night."

"Demon's nipples!" cried Cedric. "I forgot she'd gone and disappeared before they arrived."

"Pruh… probably still huh… hiding," Sippen argued. She was an intelligent girl, wise enough to stay hidden till danger passes.

"Smells fishier than a brothel on a Wednesday," Cedric muttered. He'd become more and more his old self since the encounter the night before, and his vocabulary nearly as vulgar. "I think she had somethin' to do with it!" he accused. "Franque!" he called. "Krist! You boys get down here!"

Neither replied.

Sippen looked up at the clock above the mantel. It was late morning, and they would surely have roused themselves already for chores. "I'm shuh… sure they're outside," he insisted.

"Boys!" Cedric called again. "By Cinder's Crack!" he cursed, then stood and stormed up the stairs, exaggerating footsteps to announced his pending arrival.

Sippen thought about the night before, praying to the gods of Fjorik for Robert's swift and safe reunion with Eusari. Then, just to be certain they were heard, he added a quick request the father and son of Eston, and to Felicima, goddess of the Pescari. You can never be too certain in matters like these, especially when Robert's safety was paramount. Everything hinged on whether Amash would keep his word to Eusari, or seek to elevate his own heir. Though true he was a good man, eighteen years could change a man.

"Cinder's Crack!" Cedric shouted upstairs, followed by, "Demon's nipples!" After that he added, "Bilge rats in me corn flour, Sippen! The turd chasers left in the bloody night!" Followed then with thump, step, thump, step, as he hurried downstairs on his pegged leg. "Wake your liver-bellied sod stompers! We've got to go!" Without waiting he added, "Kraken's balls, First Mate! Did ya hear me or not?"

Sippen stared at him and blinked. "Huh… holy shit!" he said. "I buh… believe suh… Sergeant Krill's back!"

"He never left, matey, we just ain't been need'n him! Now heave ho and let's grab the wind while the boys be close!"

Both men exploded in a flurry of preparations, hurrying here and there and sobering quickly. Amidst the panic, Sippen raced upstairs to Eusari's quarters. There were certain things she'd need, especially if something happened to the boys. He shoved everything into a satchel, frowning at the leather suit laying on the floor, then hurried outside just in time to see Krill tossing rifles and ammunition into the back seat.

"Hurry, matey! We be losing the current if we don't skedaddle straight away!"

Sippen strolled casually, tossing the satchel onto the weapons. He lit the pilot light then opened the door and slid slowly into the driver's seat. Without starting the engine, he placed both hands on the steering apparatus and said flatly, "You fuh… forgot your eyepatch, Sergeant Krill."

"Tarnation, blazes and reefs, mate!" In a flash, Krill tore off toward the house.

Sippen smiled after him. He somehow knew the boys would be fine. They were, after all, nearly seventeen summers. Then another thought entered his massive brain and he frowned. They were Braen Braston's boys, and that meant they were headed for a heap of trouble.

"Huh… hurry your cruh… crippled ass, Krill!" he shouted. They would have to drive fast to get to Logan in time.

The city of Logan loomed ahead and Franque beamed with excitement. He and Krist had thought of everything, sitting atop horses loaded with all the supplies they would need. Their food satchels dangled from their saddles, brimmed with dried meats, fresh fruit, and trail mixes to sustain the journey. They had loaded bedrolls, tin pots and pans, and even a fire starter to ease their efforts—that had been another invention by Sippen. The brothers had forgotten nothing.

He tapped his belt, patting a purse brimming with enough gold and silver to procure a boat to Eston. Any extra would ensure they slept on warm beds with full bellies once they reached the city. The Fjorik-made axe hung from his side, and Krist wore their father's sword across his back. With Braen Braston's weapons nobody would stand in their way. Franque's hand touched the most important of any items they brought, safely hidden from view within his bedroll. A single shot from Sippen's rifle would take down the king.

"There it is," he said to Krist, "Logan City!"

"It's filthy," his brother observed, "just as Mother described."

"It's beautiful," Franque argued. Beyond the tall buildings, he eyed tall masts as dozens of ships lined the harbor. Though he'd never seen them outside of books, he recognized barques, and galleons, merchant traders of all sizes. On a single pier far away from the others, he even spied a pair of Fjorik longboats. Tired of solid ground, the boy yearned to ride the waves of Lake Norton and, soon after, the vast oceans. He found the blue of its expanse alluring, spread out beyond the city as if to go on forever.

"We'll go at once to the docks," he informed his brother. "We'll hire a ship straight away and hopefully leave before Sippen and Cedric even know we're gone."

"Those two probably just woke up," Krist said with a laugh. "They were well sotted when we left."

"Knowing them, they're on their way. And Sippen's steam car will be as fast as horseback."

"Why do you think he did it, Franque?"

"Who? Do what?"

"The king. Why do you think he killed Father?"

"Probably jealousy. I've wondered the same, and I'm certain it was betrayal. Sippen said they were friends working together in the Brother's War, but I'll bet our entire sack of gold he feared Braen would challenge his claim. A Fjorik prince leading all of Pirate's Cove? Surely he wanted Estonia too. Esterling wanted to end his challenge before it was made."

"Yeah, you're probably right," Krist agreed.

They rode in silence for a while, taking in the scenery as they passed through the gates of town. The entire place bustled with activity like they'd never seen. As soon as they entered Logan the sounds of merchant criers reached their ears, followed by laughter, merriment, and bartering.

"I always resented she never brought us here," Krist finally said. "What did she fear? That we'd be kidnapped and hauled away? By not taking us anywhere but home, she only made it seem more alluring."

"I've never seen anything like it," Franque agreed. "I think she knew we didn't fit in at home. Who wants to be a farmer," he asked, "when open seas and adventure call?" He pulled back hard on his reins. Up ahead, a large group had gathered. "Whoa," he comforted his mount.

"What is it?" Krist demanded, standing in his stirrups for a better view.

"I can't tell," he said, "but it looks like pilgrims."

Four constables pushed their way through the crowd, forcing it to part. In the center stood five monks in pure white robes.

"Go back to Fjorik!" someone yelled.

"We don't want your kind here," another citizen shouted, as a piece of rotting fruit struck one of the priests. His once gleaming white vestments dripped with the sticky residue, but he never flinched.

"You may curse and damn us," he proclaimed, "but we will only be judged by the *All Father!*"

"What's an *All Father*?" Krist asked his brother.

"I've no idea. Sippen taught me about the Fjorik Heavenly Host, but said nothing about any particular god."

"Maybe they aren't Northmen," Krist suggested, ignoring the growing crowd that filled in around them.

"I don't know, look at their braided beards." He scratched his own patchy growth. It, like his brother's, struggled to fully come in. He too had not noticed the scores of people pressed close to watch the spectacle.

"Let them preach," one of the constables commanded over the boos and heckles. "The king proclaimed all of Andalon a haven for *any* religion!"

"Theirs is blasphemy!" a local priest argued. "It's worse than the Pescari filth we endure!"

"Ours is peaceful," one of the monks in white countered, "not at all like your heathen gods of nature!"

"Heathen gods?" the Logan priest demanded. "You go against your *own* heathen gods by elevating that... that monster above even *them*!"

"The All Father will judge you all," the monk cried, "when he returns! He watches now, ready to be reborn and come with sword in hand to steer all of Andalon toward a common course!"

"Now you threaten he'll return?" the priest said accusingly. "Constable, do you see our problem? They preach destruction and go against the very peace the king has worked for. Surely to threaten further violence is a crime!"

"The All Father is merciful!" the monk argued. "But only to those who submit and pledge their lives to his holiness!"

"He's a Demon!" screamed the priest. "The Demon from the North! But our gods favored King Esterling, and he triumphed in the end!"

"That's enough," one of the constables finally ordered. "Disperse!" He and the others pushed into the crowd, "Go about your business!"

The boys waited for the street to clear, never taking their eyes from the northern monks. One of them turned. The smear on his robes had not yet dried, but he made no effort to wipe it away. His eyes locked momentarily with Franque's, then down at the axe on his side. After a brief moment, he also scanned Krist.

"Let's go," Franque said as a chill ran down his spine. "I don't like these radicals, nor what they preach." He spurred his horse and the boys turned toward the docks.

The waterfront lost its beauty almost as soon as they arrived. The blue water, once alluring and promising adventure, had faded into a murky brown so close to the city. Instead of fresh and cleansing, they found it foul and stomach wrenching. Everywhere dead fish or gutted entrails floated where flung, including on the dock. Almost immediately, Franque regretted his youthful desire to go to sea, and farm life suddenly beckoned.

"It's disgusting," he said aloud.

"I love it!" Krist said with outstretched arms, breathing in the warm humidity. "I've never felt so *invigorated* as I do now! To think, I've been locked on land my entire life when this beauty existed?"

Franque eyed his brother suspiciously. *Is he mocking me?* he wondered, *for always wanting this?* But Krist truly had a new spark never seen before. *He actually loves this!*

"I'm going to speak with the harbor master," Franque said. "We need to hire a ship. You should stay with the horses."

Krist shrugged. He was more interested in watching a group of sailors braid rope. They used the same technique Cedric had taught the brothers on the farm.

"Well okay, then," Franque said. "I'll be back soon."

Krist had not lied to his brother. The exhilaration he felt upon reaching the waterfront was unlike any he had ever felt. His mind felt clearer, sharper even, then he had ever experienced.

It feels... like what? He mused, then understood. *It feels like I'm finally alive.* The sounds of water splashing the dock and of boats slapping its top filled Krist with desire to dive in and swim around. It called him... beckoned for the boy to get underway and be surrounded. He walked to the edge of the pier and gazed over the side. A school of minnows darted about their endless chase.

He turned his attention to the sailors braiding rope.

"Can I have a go at the splicing?" he asked.

The men grunted, then laughed. "Why toil, Boats," one of them said, "when he offers to do our work?"

"Do you know how?" the boatswain asked.

"Do you want an eye or back splice?"

"It's to tie a snubber to an anchor chain," the boatswain replied with a grin.

"Soft shackle then. That *is* harder," Krist admitted, "but I do remember." He squatted atop a bit and took the line from the men. With a furrowed brow he frowned at the braid, weaving and twisting until it fashioned into eyelet looped over itself and secured by a monkey fist knot on the end. Triumphantly, he held it up for the others. "Got it!" he said with a smile.

The seasoned boatswain took it and scrutinized the work. "Not bad," he finally said. "You lookin' for work, boy?"

"No, sir. My brother and I are here to hire a boat to Eston. We're only passing through."

"That's too bad. You've got talent, and knots like that are hard to teach to landlubbers."

"I had a good teacher," Krist beamed.

"Krist!" an anxious voice called from the pier. "Krist!"

He stood, turning to see Franque racing toward him. "What is it?" he asked, hurrying to meet him halfway. The look on his brother's face screamed worry.

"It's gone!"

"What's gone?"

Franque twisted, showing him two cut leather straps around his belt. "The gold, Krist! It's gone! Someone must've cut it in the crowd!" They both turned, looking dejectedly toward the city. The pickpocket would be long gone, savoring their prize without fear of capture. Then Franque frowned deeper. "Krist," he asked. "Where are the horses?"

"Right there!" he pointed, but the animals were no longer tied where left.

"Everything we owned was on those," Franque said with anger rising. "What were you doing? I told you to watch them!"

"I did!" Krist said, but realized his back had been turned for some while. He looked toward the sailors, about to ask if they'd seen anyone, but they too were gone.

"We're screwed, Krist." Franque pointed out. "Everything's gone!"

CHAPTER ELEVEN

Eusari waited patiently while the constables spoke about her fate. She had been surprised they whisked her so speedily to Logan, expecting instead to have waited several days in her own hamlet. They wasted no time, however, and the bumpy ride nearly shook the life from her. Without cushion nor comfort, every joint hurt. Even her teeth remained rattled.

The floor of her prison cell was no better, with only stone to sit upon. In the corner someone had tossed a pile of blankets, but she wasn't yet desperate enough to risk their fleas and whatever skin diseases they offered. She ignored also the tiny window set high above, with tightly laid bars preventing escape. No, Eusari was confident she would soon find freedom.

After what felt like hours but must have only been minutes, footsteps approached.

"It's about time, Finn Olsen. I was nearly about to give up on you," she said with a sly smile. But when she looked up, the harsh face staring down was not Constable Olsen.

Eusari recognized her at once, despite many years passed since their last encounter. The young woman's hair kept close to her scalp, fiery red and shorn like a man's. Orange freckles once dotted her cheeks, but had now grown together to sweep over her nose. She was dressed like a constable, even wearing breeches like the others. On her chest was the badge of her position.

"I should've known, you'd become a law enforcer," Eusari said.

"You recognize me, then?" the constable asked.

"Of course I do. You're a spittin' image of Maury, and your eyes have the same Thorinson fire the gods gave my brothers."

"I've waited my entire life to see you behind bars," Anne said triumphantly. "Ever since that day, I knew we were destined to meet again. Only, I thought I'd be the one to clamp your irons."

"You wouldn't have been able," Eusari said dismissively.

"You're here now," Anne pointed out. "And easily so, according to Constable Olsen."

"I allowed Finn to bring me in. But don't worry, I won't be here long. In my things is a letter from King Esterling, granting me immunity and pardon for any crimes past, present, or future."

"Oh, yes," Anne said, drawing the folded paper from her back pocket. "Signed oddly by an Amash Horslei, whoever *that* is."

"That *is* King Amash, his name before coronation! Send word to him I'm here, and you'll receive an order for my release."

"No, I don't think I will. You see, the spelling of his previous name assumes either a forgery or, as *you* said, proves it was written before his coronation. Meaning either it's a fraud or he had no power at the time to grant your freedom."

Eusari froze. Neither she nor Amash had considered that technicality when he'd hastily written the order.

Anne smiled as she ripped the page in half, then set one page against the other and ripped a second time. She repeated the action till only small pieces remained, which she casually held next to the candle on the wall. Once the fire had taken hold, she scattered the pieces in the air, allowing them to smolder as they softly fell against the stones.

Eusari watched as all hope for her release—and Robert's absolution—disappeared into smoke.

"You shouldn't have done that," she said calmly. "The king won't be happy when he finds out."

"He won't. You see, you were brought in on a crime against the municipality." She scrunched her face and asked, "What's the name of your little borough?" Before Eusari could answer, Anne added, "That's right. It's unincorporated and nestled just outside of organized territory. As such, and since you were brought here, the high seat of Loganshire presides. Nobody, not even the king, can interfere with the doling of justice for crimes committed outside the territory."

"So, that's it?" Eusari chuckled. "You can't charge me for the crimes you think I deserve, so you'll pin me down for petty assault?"

"Three counts, my dearest Auntie. Three counts add up to a felony, and that allows the magistrate to consider your former crimes when sentencing. You'll *never* see the light of day again, and no one can make it all go away." She turned to go, then smiled over her shoulder. "Then I'm going to find this son who you're covering for and watch him closely until he officially reaches his seventeenth summer. Then I'll make sure he spends that much time or longer behind the same prison bars as you."

"Why?" Eusari demanded. "Why do you hate me so much?"

"It's not just you, Auntie. It's the very thought of you. I remember when my parents died. I was young, but their fates linger with me today. Father broke one law and he paid for it with his life. He was a criminal like you—it was in his blood. But you lived, constantly thumbing your nose at the world while hiding out like a coward."

"You've no idea *what* I experienced. Your grandfather was a constable, but he knew compassion and when to look the other way. If you only knew *half* the reasons I did the things I did, you'd do the same."

"Well, then. It seems Grandaddy was a criminal too. Don't you see? He, Daddy, and you were all cut from the same cloth. I was there when Mother took her own life. I was the one who found her. She killed herself because of grief over hiding my baby brother from the law."

"That law was unnatural—an abomination to all, and she was right to hide him."

"No law should be ignored."

"You tore up the king's letter," Eusari pointed out.

"I tore up either a forgery or an illegal contract."

"It was *my* property, nonetheless."

"You're in *my* custody, and you own no property within these walls. It is well within my office to destroy illegal currency and contracts through which crimes are committed." Anne turned to leave, but paused before shutting the door to the cells. "I pushed back your trial another week, just to give you some time for reflection." She pointed to the filthy blanket in the corner of the cell. "I hope you decide to make yourself comfortable."

Eusari flinched as the door slammed with finality, then examined the rough stone lining the walls and floor. She could leave this place, command the stone to crumble, but then what? Flee to Eston and petition Amash? She didn't even know if she could still trust the king.

Braen did, she thought, *they were close friends.*

But Braen was gone. For seventeen years she had lived without him, even if she never forgot or moved on.

"Captain!" a voice called from the window high above. "Cap'n Eusari, be you in thar?"

"I'm here, Cedric," she called out.

"It's Krill, mum! Ol' Cedric be stowed away till needed, and Gunnery Sergeant Krill be at your service!"

"Who else is here?" she demanded. "Who's looking after the boys?" There was a pause. She hated when Cedric hesitated, it always meant trouble. "Cedric!" she shouted. "Who's protecting the boys?"

"Muh... ma'am," Sippen's voice replied. "We huh... have a pruh... problem in that ruh... regard."

"Spit it out," she growled.

"Suh.... suffice to say we're wuh... working on it."

She stood, walking to the wall standing between them. She removed her gloves, exposing hands deeply scarred with hundreds of tiny cuts, each one hiding a story of her life. With palms touching the stone she took a deep breath.

Limestone, she thought, *full of the remnants of life.* She closed her eyes and focused on the tiny skeletons—tiny creatures now buried within the rock. Sippen had once explained that what once was living leaves behind carbon, the basis of all life. As her mind and body connected with this element, the wall began to shake. With a shove a single brick crushed beneath her hands and fell to the ground as powder. Two very shocked and guilty faces stared back at her.

"Why not the entire wall, Cap'n?" Krill asked. "Why just a brick?"

"Because I have family issues to deal with here," she said dryly. "Where are the boys?"

Krill told the story how Falconers had attacked, then Dreamers arrived demanding Robert. He told how Sebastian helped the boy escape and explained how they may arrive at any time. Skipping over the night of drunken celebration over the *good ol' days,* he told her how they awoke to two missing horses, a good portion of missing gold, and two Fjorik princes, hell-bent on revenge.

"Find them," she growled through the hole in the wall.

The men nodded vigorously.

"Now!" she added, sending them scurrying away.

"Constable Thorinson," she screamed and waited.

After several minutes the young woman opened the door and stood before her cell, eyeing the missing brick and light flooding in with suspicion.

"Whether my charges stem from outside the territory or not, I'm a registered citizen of Brentway, Loganshire. You, as a constable, know this to be true, so to deny me of a speedy trial is a violation of my constitutional right. I demand to go before the magistrate promptly."

Anne eyed the wall, not looking at her aunt. "He's gone for the day, so the best I can offer you is tomorrow."

Eusari nodded curtly. "There seems to be a structural problem within my cell," she added, "and it ruined my blanket."

Anne moved her gaze to the white powder covering the cloth.

"I expect it will get quite chilly in my cell, and I demand a *fresh* replacement."

Anne nodded absently. "Did you just try to escape?"

"I never *try* anything. Now go get my damned blanket."

CHAPTER TWELVE

"We're screwed," Franque said again, staring at his mug of cider. He and Krist had decided to gather their thoughts and chose a small tavern near the waterfront. The sign out front read, *The Mangy Dog,* and so far, it had lived up to that name. His skin crawled like he already caught fleas.

"I've got a little gold here," Krist said, tapping his purse now secure in his breast pocket.

"And how far can we get on it?" Franque asked. "A trip around the pier and back again? No, we're going to have to work our way to Eston, and even when we get there what will we do? How could we even hope to get another rifle?"

"The black market," Krist offered.

"Oh, yeah? And who do you know who has contacts like that? Huh? Think again, Krist! You should've been watching the horses."

"Well *you* should've kept better control over our purse! You lost a fortune! I only lost a bit of food and a rifle."

"We *needed* that rifle!" Franque was ready to come to blows. Had his drink been stronger than cider, he might've already knocked his brother around.

"We *needed* that gold to get to Eston!" From the sounds of him, Krist wanted a fight.

"Excuse me, gentlemen!" an old sailor interrupted. His skin was sun leathered and hair snow white. Though freshly shaved, he missed a few sprigs under his nose and on his neck. He wore a few cuts and nicks, as well. Whoever shaved this man did not have a steady hand. "Did I hear you say you're seeking passage to Eston?"

"Yes," replied Krist.

"No," insisted Franque, shooting his brother a glare.

"Well, I may just have a few contacts who can bill you passage for a bit of work."

"We're not looking for work," Franque said dryly. "Thank you, but no thanks."

"Well, that's too bad," the man said, slipping into a chair at their table. He plopped a small sack of gold on the table.

"What's that?" Franque asked, eyeing it suspiciously.

"It would've been advanced wage," the man said, "for hardy men willing to join the crew."

"What kind of work?" Krist asked, his eyes locked on the purse and coveting its pieces.

"This ship needs sailors, but not too experienced, only willing to learn."

"Is it hard work?" Franque asked.

"Aye, to work upon the sea is to bleed for it and often to feed it with the contents of your stomach," he said with a laugh. His hand moved quickly for an old man, as he pocketed the gold as swiftly as it was presented. "But neither nor both of you are interested." He stood to leave.

"Wait," Franque said, placing a hand on the man's forearm. "How long is an indenture?"

"Six months."

"That's all?" Krist asked with amazement. "I expected a year or more!"

"Where would we go?" Franque asked.

"Eston for sure, then down river to Diaph and beyond. Expect a circle around Andalon, stopping in Middleton, Soston, and Eskera. Then up the Misting River to Weston and back here."

Franque considered. "How long would our stop be in Eston? Would we have leave to see the city?"

"Aye, and wages to enjoy it!" the old man promised.

"What is your name?" Franque asked.

"Peter Longshanks. Who do *I* have the pleasure of meeting?"

"I'm Franque, Franque Thorinson, and this is my brother Krist."

"Well then, Franque and Krist! Will you sign on with the crew?"

"I... We don't know," Franque said truthfully. "Six months is a long time, and we must discuss it, but I believe we're open to the prospect."

"Good! Let's drink to the prospect of a life at sea!"

Krist lifted his tiny purse, jingling the pair of coins within. With a glance at his brother he shook his head and frowned.

"What's this?" Peter asked. "I wouldn't offer a drink without paying for it myself! Barmaid!" he shouted. "Bring a round of ale for my new friends and myself!" He paused, then added, "But not the Estonian brew, it tastes like the waterfront. Bring the strongest you have!"

Both boys smiled. Neither had been allowed strong ale, only ever milled wine and cider.

Peter waited till the boys drank themselves so drunk they could no longer focus on his face. This was the part he hated. The empty promises and lies he spewed were tolerable, at least without a conscience, but this bit condemned his soul to any one of the many hells awaiting his kind. They were big boys, Fjorik stock by the look of it, and the ale worked slowly. After a nod to the tavern keep he cut himself off, pretending to drink the same mug the rest of the night. He had no stomach for what the bartender added to the boys'. Thankfully the drug worked quickly.

You're an awful person, Peter Longshanks. The worst of the worst, his accuser reminded.

There are others worse than me, the old man told himself. He fumbled finding the clasp behind the bench and realized his fingers worked slower each time he doomed young men to their fate. For some reason, this time felt worse than all those others. He swallowed, then looked both ways to ensure no one watched. His fingers ceased shaking just long enough to work the latch, and the back of the booth swung away. With a shove Franque tumbled downward, into the compartment.

"What happened," Krist demanded. "Where's Franque?"

Without answering, Pete condemned Krist next, snatching the boy's purse from his belt as he fell.

Peter did not watch them enter the chute—he never did. He had no stomach for what came next. They were mostly unharmed besides bumps and bruises and would be fine after a short tumble and slide into a hidden cellar beneath the tavern. Soon Jacque's crew would collect them, and, after that, he cared not what happened. The boys now belonged to the Devil, bought and sold into a two-year indenture. Franque and Krist were headed to Pirate's Cove.

"Excuse me!" a loud voice asked from the tavern entrance. "We're looking for two boys about yay tall," a stocky fella said standing on both tiptoes and pegged leg with his arm stretched high. "They're broad across," he stretched his hands to the sides, "and with long blond hair. They're teens who look like men, they do!"

Peter's eyes grew wide and his body trembled. His past had finally caught him.

"Thuh… they don't nuh… know their way uh… around things," a second man added. He was small, frail even, and the years had not aged him well. He pushed his spectacles onto his nose nervously. "There's a ruh…. reward if they're safe."

Longshanks quickly shut the trap door and slid in front of it, hiding the latch with his body. He stared down at his mug of ale, watching the bubbles rise and praying to the gods these men would leave.

So you have a bit of guilt left after all? his accuser asked.

Pete shrank down into his coat, willing them not to recognize him.

"Why! If it ain't Peter Longshanks!" Krill exclaimed. "Where you been all these years, Petey?"

"I'm sorry," the old man said. "Do I know you?"

The pair rushed over and Krill plopped into the booth next to him. "It *is* you! Damn, if the years ain't been good to any of us!"

Pete made a show of studying the men, then feigned happy surprise. "Gunnery Sergeant Krill? Sippen Yurik? You both be a sight fer sore eyes!"

"Wuh… we're looking for tuh… two boys, Peter," Sippen stammered.

"I don't see much of anything these days, but I'll do my best."

"They're big boys, Pete!" Krill added. "You can't miss 'em. They're large and big, and blonde and green behind the gills!"

"Who are they? These boy's you lost. Are they crewmen?" Peter trembled with what they'd say.

"Crewmen?" Krill asked with a laugh. "No, we ain't sailin' no more. These are Eusari's boys. They ran off and she tasked us to bring 'em back."

Peter felt his blood run cold. *Eusari,* he thought, *Thorinson.* Then he remembered Franque's introduction. He opened his mouth to speak, then closed it abruptly. What could he say? Surely it was too late. Of all the reefs he could have run aground against, Eusari's was the least desirable.

His accuser laughed. *It's finally time then,* it said, *to face her wrath.*

He drank the remnants of his mug down with a single gulp, finding courage enough to steady his voice. "Eusari... My goodness. Is she here, then? In Logan?"

"Aye, but she don't be around the waterfront."

Pete let out his held breath without a sigh. "That's a shame," he lied. He was thrilled they wouldn't face off just yet. He had time to leave town, perhaps hop a freighter to Eston and get away. "I've not seen her boys," he lied again, "but I'll keep an eye out for sure!"

"Thuh... thank you, Pete!" Sippen said with a smile. He was always a good man. They both were.

But seeing them brought painful memories Pete could barely stomach.

Perhaps now you have the courage to do it, the accuser suggested, *and the reasons too.*

Do what? Peter demanded from himself.

End your no good, double crossing, back stabbing, cowardly life!

"I would like to see her," Peter said, shutting up his accuser and surprising himself.

"That's nuh... not possible," Sippen said with an air of sadness.

"Why not? Did she hear of my betrayal? Does she hate me like I deserve?"

Krill and Sippen exchanged a look. No, that wasn't it at all.

"Eusari's in jail," Krill finally explained. "She's falsely held and must stand before the magistrate."

"Falsely? So she's not to stand for past crimes?" Peter asked with surprise. He'd been running from his past so long he figured she had as well—otherwise she might have come to seek revenge on him sooner.

"No," Krill answered immediately. "She was pardoned long ago. This is a different matter, a small one even, but one she intends to face."

"That's always been her way," Peter acknowledged. Eusari was a determined woman. "I'm sorry," he said suddenly. "I've something I must attend to. Please excuse me." To his own astonishment, as much as to the others, Peter rose. He took four coins from his own purse, careful not to take those he took from Krist, and placed them on the table. "Have a round on me," he said, then hurried from the tavern.

What are you doing? his accuser demanded.

But he ignored himself.

Peter rushed around the corner and around the building, nearly running down a steep incline that led to the waterfront. The door to the cellar was closed, and he heaved his body against it, swinging the heavy oak inward. He froze. The boys were gone. Turning slowly, he faced the waters of Lake Norton. In the distance, silhouetted by moonlight, he made out a small vessel. The sails and keel were black as the night, but he could easily make out the shape of the bowsprit extended from the growling mouth of a wolf.

She Wolf, the ship was called, the infamous vessel of Devil Jacque. Peter Longshanks fell to his knees and wept. He failed her not only once but now several times over. He had once again betrayed the woman he loved like a daughter, and because of him her children were gone forever.

You're a failure, his accuser said with a laugh.

"No," he argued. "I'll make this right somehow."

CHAPTER THIRTEEN

Tara stood under the lee deck, taking cover from the weather raging above. Their ride down the Misting River had been a storm of emotion, and the lightning striking outside befitted her mood. Her mother had won and she submitted. The Pescari world waited.

The city of New Weston was the youngest in the empire by years, if not historically. Flaya had told the story, that her father had destroyed the walls and homes of those who lived here before, but she never described how. Tara imagined there would still be rubble or traces of the old city, something to blend the two cultures. Sailing past the center of Lake Weston, she realized the old city had entirely disappeared.

"Where are the ruins of the old city?" she finally asked.

"It's beneath us," Flaya explained, "right now."

"Under the lake?" Tara tried to look over the side, but the rain churned the dark waters into a froth. "It's so... the water is so black."

"The old city lies beneath the rock, torched black by the wrath of Felicima."

Did he really wield her power? Tara had long doubted that part of her mother's stories. But how else could he have so completely destroyed the high walls that nature buried it completely?

She gave up trying to imagine, turning her attention to the western shore of the natural harbor. As the lightning flashed above, an eerie reflection mirrored it on the ground.

She leaned forward, peering through the rain, and waited. The next strike lit up tall buildings, each as smooth as glass and solid black. Her eyes followed a reflected image of the lightning, pathing along the sides and tops of buildings just the same as it marked the clouds above.

Tara marveled. "What is it?" she asked her mother. "What material do they use?"

Flaya stood next to her daughter, staring with the same confusion. "I don't know," she admitted. "All this was done after I left Eston with Eusari, but letters from your great uncle spoke of rebuilding using Felicima's power."

Tara stared as two more strikes lit up the city and its splendid rows of smooth black buildings. Each stood taller than five farmhouses. The sight forced her to reconsider Felicima, for surely such marvels come only from a goddess. Filled with excitement, she could not wait until daylight, after the storm had breathed its final word.

"How does the power work?" she asked.

"Felicima fills her agents with power, and they channel her wrath."

"So our goddess only destroys?"

"Look around, she also creates."

"Who wields her power now?" Tara asked.

"Your great uncle is an agent, but I know she has blessed more than he."

"How are her agents chosen?"

"I... I don't know the nature of it. But I know she favors some above others."

"That isn't fair."

"No," Flaya agreed, "but fairness does not mean equality, and gods do not care about wealth or privilege, only faithfulness."

"Especially ours," Tara agreed, "except when we brazenly show strength."

"Especially then."

"I *won't* take a Pescari husband," Tara suddenly blurted out.

"Why do you say this so boldly and with such confidence, child?"

"Isn't that the reason you dragged me downriver? You know I love Robert, yet you seek to force me to marry within our people."

"Eusari and her boys *are* our people. They are not Pescari and do not share our customs, but they are bound to us like family. Eusari is like a sister to me, and I would not care if you married one of her boys as long as you continue to honor Felicima."

"Then why am I here?"

"There are things you must learn about yourself, and you will only gain this knowledge by living among Pescari. After you are ready you may return to him a woman."

Tara frowned. She had not expected options. "One year?"

"One year," her mother promised.

A brilliant flash turned both women's eyes, and both sets grew wide with worry. It struck a stable, or something equally combustible, and an angry inferno met the storm clouds in an instant.

Tara gasped, but Flaya let out a simple, "Hmmm."

"The city will burn!" the girl exclaimed.

"No. Not with Teot around."

They stood there, fixated on the pulsing heat as it throbbed a warning of Felicima's wrath. Then it died, swept into a cyclone that seemed to shrink in an instant. Tara gasped, straining her eyes to watch a solitary figure atop the tallest structure. He seemed to absorb the heat.

"Is that him?"

Flaya grunted, but when her daughter turned she saw her mother wore a smile. A simple thing, but so long missing from the woman's face. "That's him, but you won't meet him tonight. We'll let the storm pass and he'll want rest, of course.

Dawn did not disappoint. As Felicima rose above her people, her image reflected coolly on the black buildings below. They were smooth as glass, but not nearly as delicate. Tara felt her balance waver. With a flutter of her heart and a skipped beat, she feared toppling over the side. The river had felt so... wrong, and she endured its hospitality too long. She hurried, nearly running, across the last steps across the brow, finally breathing once on dry land.

The men who met them were hard, dressed in leather, but not the buckskins she expected. These skins they wore were pressed, layered and thick as armor. She halted abruptly and stared up at them.

"We're here on the shappan's invitation," Flaya told them.

They exchanged a look, then one of them broke a smile.

Tara watched as her mother stepped forward.

"I am Flaya, widow of Shappan Taros and niece to Teot. Take us to him."

"Widow?" one of the warriors asked. "Get to the fireside, and stand not in our way."

Without warning, Flaya answered his insolence with a slap across his face. The fact she did so under the eye of Felicima was not lost on Tara.

"I am the conqueror of Eston, stand not in my way but comply. Let the shappan decide my fate."

Tara blinked, not recognizing the woman speaking for their admittance to the city. Her mother wore a fury she had never seen, with confidence so hot she burned like Felicima. She checked the sky. The goddess shone down with displeasure.

The men laughed again. Without warning Flaya drew a bone handled dagger, placing it to the nearest throat.

"Do not press, nor force me to challenge you in Shapalote. I am a queen, and order you to take us to the shappan. He, not you, decides our fate."

The nearest guard locked eyes with the other, a tinge of red marring his neck. He would have nodded but held his head perfectly still out of fear.

"Comply," he urged. "Let the shappan decide."

The other grunted, then led the women from the docks.

"That was bold," Tara whispered to her mother.

"Felicima understands," Flaya replied with a wink.

They followed in silence after that to a city square. It was abandoned, except for a solitary man standing in the center. His shoulders slumped with exhaustion, facing a row of buildings. These were unlike the others Tara had seen, with stacked rows of rock and sand mortar outlining skeletons of steel.

Steel. She only recognized the substance because of Sippen Yurik. He and Robert had once demonstrated its strength over iron, made stronger by heat—tempered they had explained. *What is it doing here, in a Pescari city?* The beams were perfectly forged, yet the covering simple.

The man entered a dance of flame as fire poured from his body. Even his eyes glowed like golden embers. Tara gasped as she watched the swirling heat form into focused fountains, melting both rock and sand. In moments the simple building components had fused against the steel, and the blackened row of buildings glowed red hot in the night.

"Felicima's wrath?" a stunned girl asked her mother.

"Her gift," Flaya corrected.

Exhausted, the man turned to face the woman and girl. Teot was older and more wizened than Tara imagined, certainly more an elder than a shappan. Had she not just witnessed his use of the goddess' power, she would have guessed a younger man might have challenged long before. It was the Pescari way to follow strength.

When Teot spoke, his words rumbled deeply. "You've returned, Flaya? Why have you come? Does the lady no longer require your counsel?"

"I bring you the daughter of Taros, a girl who does not yet understand her name, but lives as if she does."

The man frowned. "Have you not trained her in our ways? She has been gone from our people her entire life. Why shouldn't I condemn you both to Felicima's fireside?"

Tara stepped forward, full of indignance. "I am *well* trained, and you would not suffer either of us to the fireside. We bear no shame—not our own nor my fathers."

Teot let out a laugh, an odd reaction from a Pescari. "No. Your father did not earn you a shunning, quite the opposite. Come, daughter of Taros. Let me properly greet you."

Tara stepped forward, locking arms in his as her mother taught. They felt surprisingly cooler than expected, with no hint of the warmth they had recently held.

"You are welcome in our city, and to walk freely here, under the eye of Felicima."

"What were you doing, just now?" Tara asked, locking eyes on the smoldering buildings behind Teot.

He let go of her hands and turned. As he did, heat left the molten rock and swirled into a pattern around his body. Tara felt it pass between them and shivered against its searing touch as the air rapidly warmed. The buildings were now identical to the rest of the city, their outer skin encrusted by the same smooth rock. This close to it, she realized it resembled glass.

"Obsidian," Teot explained. "It hides our city from Felicima as she passes over, reflecting her eye and hiding our strength."

"And the steel?" she demanded. "It allows you to build higher, but where does it come from. Do you forge it as well?"

The old shappan raised an eyebrow at her question but did not answer. "Come," he commanded, "make yourself comfortable in New Weston. You will stay with me, in my palace."

"Palace?" Flaya asked with confusion. "Such extravagance is not the Pescari way!"

Teot smiled warmly. "Flaya, granddaughter of Daska and widow of Taros, you've been gone so long you also know little of our ways. We are no longer nomads forced to roam the Steppes of Cinder. We are again blessed by Felicima, gifted many more riches than we ever dreamed."

Tara watched shock form on her mother's face, then took her hand to follow the shappan. Her own resentment had faded, and now felt excitement building inside. Thoughts about Robert would have to wait while she learned all she could about her people and their ways.

CHAPTER FOURTEEN

Robert lay on his side, wrapped tightly in coils of vine and air, watching the wagon and its villainous driver depart. He and Sebastian had acted foolishly to trust him, a stranger and apparently a friend to Falconers. The feathered specters stood over the pair, while their jungle comrades knelt upon the ground and swayed in unison.

What was it Sebastian had called them? He strained to remember, but even breathing was difficult so tightly bound.

One of their jungle cats emerged from the forest, circling their masters to keep guard over their rhythmic dance.

Jaguars. That's what he said.

Robert closed his eyes and tried to focus the way he had been shown, to travel to the Dream World and speak with his friend there. But his effort proved fruitless, feeling somehow cut off from the power. Each time he tried, the caterpillars screeched in his ears.

The ground suddenly shook, rolling Robert over on his other side. His eyes grew wide as the rockface before him opened like a doorway.

They command the rocks! he marveled.

The Falconers waved their hands and he floated upward as if set upon an invisible sled. A moment later he heard Sebastian grunt, then watched him glide by on a shimmering current. He too was wrapped from neck to feet in air and vines, crawling over his skin like snakes writhing to mate. For a brief moment their eyes met.

Robert had never before seen such terror so deeply set in a man's face. Soon he followed Sebastian, gliding a few feet above the ground, drawn by the Falconers leading the way. He was turned just enough to watch the Jaguars and their beasts enter the cave behind him, again kneeling to dance their choreographed sway. The boulders shook, then moved once more into place, plunging everything into darkness.

Abruptly, light flooded the long hallway, glowing from long tubes lining the ceiling. These sputtered, gaining strength to shine brightly. Robert squinted his eyes against their unnatural brightness. Up ahead, a Falconer pushed open a door and pulled Sebastian through.

"What will you do with us?" he asked the specter leading him.

The Falconer did not answer.

Robert, in an attempt to not focus on the lighting overhead, stared at the strangeness of the man-like being beneath the feathered hood. Beneath the sharp beak he wore a black mask that covered half his face. What was it Cedric had said about them? Something about a Jaguar raising a dead one. Seeing one finally up close and well lit, he realized the purpose of their hoods. It looked down at him.

"You're dead, aren't you?" Robert asked. "Or was, once. I see it in your eyes. It was the same when I killed my first buck. Though its eyes were open, there was a hollowness to its stare."

The specter looked away and did not reply. It watched the path ahead, markedly avoiding further eye contact with Robert.

The room they entered was large, filled with dozens of marble slabs. Upon a handful lay stripped bodies, uncovered and fully exposed. Strange tubing, similar to Sippen's copper devices, ran from every orifice of the subjects. As Robert passed an old woman he realized she and the others lived, breathing deeply but soundly asleep. From her back one of these tubes dripped a pale liquid into a waiting collection bottle.

Whatever this is, Robert thought, *that liquid is the reason we're here.*

He grunted as the air supporting his floating body let go, dropping him onto one of the slabs. Nearby he heard Sebastian land on his.

The Falconer drew a strange needle, shoving it directly into his vein. It jolted him more than it hurt, flinching from the unexpected jab. His body slowly went numb. A few moments later, the coils of vines and wisps of air fell away. They were no longer needed, as his own limbs no longer belonged to Robert. He was at the mercy of these specters.

Drowsiness consumed him, and he yearned to sleep.

No, he urged his mind, *resist.* But slumber beckoned.

He felt the first tube enter his nose, sliding deep into his throat. A second, much larger oddity, entered his mouth and slid deep into his chest.

Just like the others, Robert worried, and tried to fight. His body was no longer his to control.

The Falconer standing over him held another tube meant for Robert's more sensitive parts. He abruptly paused, lifting his head and speaking in unison with his comrade. "Intruders have found the entrance," they said.

Somewhere in the cave an explosion echoed.

Robert, unable to move or react, could only listen to his surroundings.

Near the entrance, jungle cats roared then yelped in fear as a more vicious foe entered. The entire place rumbled as if the earth wished to spit out its contents. Another gust of wind followed, then wisps of air passed overhead.

Dreamers? Robert wondered, suddenly thankful for their arrival.

The specter attending him had regained his feet, coming into focus above Robert. He waved his hands and coils of air shot out. Somewhere in the room a woman laughed—no, giggled. The Falconer's eyes grew large with fear, a strange reaction for the dead. While Robert watched him, the specter violently collided with his counterpart. Both feathered hoods crashed together with a thud, then fell to the floor.

"Oooooo! I missed this!" a woman's voice exclaimed.

"Watch out!" another woman warned.

A sickening thud against rock made Robert wince.

"Got him!" the first woman yelled.

"Duck!" shouted the other.

Another thud resounded.

Robert felt sick.

Somewhere an animal roared and a woman yelped.

"Use the trap!" the second woman commanded with a high pitch to her voice.

"I'm trying!" the other replied. "Did you set it?"

"What the hells? Just kill the thing!"

A gust of wind nearly knocked Robert from the table, rolling his body just enough to see.

Two women battled the Falconers in a strange dance of arm movements. Robert focused on their hands, then understanding crept in. He could see the weaves and knots as they formed whips and nets to throw at their foes. Occasionally, one side or the other would attempt to knock the other off balance. An auburn haired woman had the upper hand in this fight, and her face beamed as is if she enjoyed it.

Further, in the entrance to the cave, two Jaguars lay motionless. Their beasts lay piled in the corner. A darkly colored man, presumably from the Southern Continent by his colorful attire, stood beside the dead animals. He held no weapon, but stared at the Falconers as if waiting to rip them to shreds.

"Parumba!" one of the women shouted, "We need their kitties!"

He spun immediately, kneeling and swaying in the exact way Robert had seen the Jaguars. The animals eventually stood and shook off death. They roared in unison, eerily matching Parumba's mood. They charged the hooded specters, leaping into the air and sinking long teeth into delicate throats. All four figures, both man and beast, fell lifeless as one heap.

"Sebastian!" the auburn-haired woman shouted, running to stand by his side on the marble slab. She looked him up and down, noticeably realizing he was in a state of undress. "Well now, Sebastian," the woman said appraisingly. "It seems you've grown a lot in seventeen years."

In a groggy voice, dreamlike and dazed, the man replied. "Hello, Marita," he said then passed out.

Robert, too exhausted to fight off sleep any longer, joined him in slumber.

The world shimmered then came into focus, and Robert blinked his eyes at the brightness of the sun overhead. He lay in a garden, tended and trimmed with fruit-bearing trees all around. The beauty of it soothed his fear as he turned over, groaning as each muscle awakened. He wore clothing, sewn from simple cloth of handspun linen. He found it surprisingly soft and comfortable.

Two figures sat atop stone benches nearby. One of them, a woman with kind yet appraising eyes, watched him closely.

"Good morning, Robert." she said gently.

The other figure turned. He was a man sharing the same age as the woman and with similar enough features the pair could be siblings. "You may be disoriented for a while longer," he explained, "as the drugs given by the Falconers wear off. I'm sorry, but there's not much we can do for you other than the illusion of clothing you wear."

"Where am I?"

"Physically, you are in the Jaguar den in Andalon. Your mind somehow found its way here," the woman said.

"Where is here?"

"The same world your friend Sebastian brought you to visit," the man answered, "but, how you found our home we do not know."

"Who are you?"

"I am Adam and this is Eve. We were the first to find and create the Dream World, and we are the oldest existing memories trapped within its boundaries."

"I don't understand."

"No," Eve agreed. "Visitors rarely do."

"Why am I here?"

"The question is *how,* and the answer is that we don't know," Adam replied. "You somehow bypassed all our protective layers."

"I'm sorry," he said, and tried to stand. His feet held, though he swayed slightly. "I'll leave."

"There's no need," Eve said. "We actually quite enjoy having a worthy visitor for once." She pointed at an empty bench. "Please join us."

Robert sat. "You said you were the first to find the Dream World. You built it?"

"We laid the foundation for what the Dreamers have made, though they have never realized we are even here. We would appreciate that secret be one you keep," Adam insisted.

"So, you get visitors?"

"No. Others randomly find the world, never understand it's real after waking. Their connection is less tangible and leaves no imprint behind."

"Imprint?"

Eve interrupted. "When you arrived with Sebastian, he replaced the version of him tied to the ether. His residual now has updated memories and, if interacted with by those who know him, more closely reflects his true form."

"So, when you visit the Dream World, you leave a bit of yourself behind?"

"No," she corrected, "a copy of you exists in both worlds."

"Is that how I found my way back on my own?"

"Perhaps, but does not explain how you ventured so deeply into our hidden garden," Adam said. Both man and woman paused, cocking their heads oddly, then returned their eyes to Robert. "You must return soon. Sebastian is also awake, and it's time for you to meet your rescuers."

"So that was real?" Robert had wondered.

Eve nodded.

"What about when I used the magic?"

"Craft," she corrected. "None of the abilities are magic. They are the results of a madman's efforts to make himself a god."

"May I return?"

"Of course," Adam agreed. "As long as you keep our existence a secret from the Dreamers."

Robert wore his own clothing when he awakened. Sebastian and the others sat casually around a campfire, and another larger fire burned in the distance. From the smell of it he realized it burned something awful.

"He's awake!" one of the women noticed. She was pretty, with a face full of dark freckles that matched her hair color. She must have been close to thirty years old, nearly the same as Sebastian.

Robert remembered Sebastian calling her Marita. "Hello," he said. "Are you Dreamers?"

Marita scrunched her face. "Hells, no. I'm Marita Pogue, and my sister here is Charleigh." The younger woman nodded, then went back to tinkering on a device. "And this guy," she pointed to Parumba, "is the mighty warrior of the Southern Continent, the fearsome Parumba, slayer of Jaguars."

The dark skinned man smiled, revealing stark white teeth and suddenly appearing less fearsome. "Do not tell lies about me, Marita of Cargia! You have slayed many more than I." His voice rumbled when he spoke. Turning to Robert he held out a hand. "I am new to your land, but Marita taught me a strong handshake is the proper greeting."

Robert took his hand and smiled back. "She's right, that's what Cedric taught me."

"I like him better as Krill," Marita said. "He's much more fun that way."

Robert looked to Sebastian. "They know Cedric? How?" he asked.

Sebastian opened his mouth to speak, but Marita cut him off. "We pirated together, back in the day." In a fake pirate voice, she added, "Arr! We were blackhearted scourges of the sea!"

Sebastian laughed at this, and the two smiled broadly at each other. Robert couldn't help but notice the way their eyes briefly met.

"Is that why you aren't a Dreamer?" Robert asked. "Because they don't like pirates?"

"I'm not a Dreamer," Marita explained, "because I'm not a stuck up bitch like Caroline, or a pompous know-it-all like Cuyler. I'm much happier living on the Southern Continent and solving problems *there*."

"Why are you here, then?" Sebastian asked. "What brought you back?"

Marita pointed a thumb at the bonfire at their backs. "We followed those Jaguars all the way from the port of Cargia. They were up to something, and Charleigh wanted to find their den. Once we got close enough, I picked up on Sebastian's dream pattern and realized he was held captive. We just watched and waited for them to bring you here."

"How did you recognize my pattern?" Sebastian asked, shocked.

"Because, silly, we were closer than the others back then, and you and I dreamed together so many times." She pointed at Robert. "Remember when we found his father? That was you and I, working together. Fun times, those."

Robert noticed Marita blushed a little deeper when reminiscing about Sebastian. "Wait," he asked. "You knew my father?"

"Yep! Prince Robert and Sarai were almost as much fun to hang out with as Alec and Amash! He was so sweet and smart, and she was so... beautiful!" She scrunched her eyes at Robert, looking him up and down. "Come to think about it, I was there when you were born. They kept making me carry you through the entire battle, but I finally passed you off."

"Why didn't my mother carry me?"

Marita paused, losing her smile and realizing she made him sad. "Your mother didn't survive to see you born. I wish she had, because you would have loved her, but she didn't."

Robert yearned to hear more about his parents, but Parumba stood and began dousing the fire.

"We must move on," he said. "These are destroyed, and the others will seek revenge."

"Let them come," Marita said with a smile.

"No," Charleigh argued. "These two are in no shape to fight." She placed the gadget in a satchel and stood. "Besides, I need to get to a work-shop." She patted the satchel. "I've got a lot of work to do."

"What about the people?" Sebastian demanded. "Those being farmed."

"I'll let Cuyler know where to find them. We don't have time for the awakening process, it's too annoying," Marita replied.

"We need to get to Loganshire," Robert asked. "Can you accompany us there?"

"What's there besides fish smells and street urchins?" Marita asked.

"Eusari. Robert needs to get to her," Sebastian explained. "Amash summoned him, but he needs to see her first."

Marita shrugged. "Might as well."

The group broke camp and ventured off into the night. Marita led them, out front and chattering away with Sebastian as if she had no worry in the world. Robert hung back with Parumba and Charleigh, asking dozens of questions about the Southern Continent. He liked this group, though he couldn't explain why, he thought much of it was in the way Sebastian seemed more confident with Marita around.

CHAPTER FIFTEEN

"I want my payout," Collette told the woman. "I've been watching this family for seventeen years, and I deserve a villa!"

Gretchen, the woman *he* always sent, listened without interest. "You'll be rewarded. He promised your family you would."

"Well, half my life has been spent spying and reporting on their goings-on. I'm done. Falconers and Dreamers showed up on the same night, and I *won't* be going back!"

"No, you won't. He said you don't have to." Gretchen drew out a hefty purse and placed it on the table.

Collette eyed it appraisingly. "Too small," she said. "Bring me a wagon full of those, and we have a deal."

"Relax," Gretchen urged. "This is a down payment. "You'll receive an annual stipend deposited into the bank of your choice. This is merely to shut your mouth long enough to hear my questions."

Collette snatched it from the table, hugging it tightly.

"Where are the boys now?" Gretchen asked.

"Robert and Sebastian took off on foot, and Franque and Krist left on horseback. They may even be in Eston by now."

"Why Eston?"

"Something about killing the king."

Gretchen frowned. "That's not likely to happen, but tell me about them. The agreement was that you'd report on *their* lives most of all."

"I don't see *why*," Collette said with a frown. "They're just stupid boys with too much energy. They're nobodies, not like the others."

"You know better than that. Which was born first?"

Collette paused, thinking back to that day seventeen years before. "That's the thing I never understood. Eusari tells everyone that Franque was the first, and even Flaya goes along with it. But I know it was Krist. He suckled from my breast after the queen did what she did."

"Are you certain? It's important which was first."

Collette had never witnessed so much emotion from Gretchen. It was almost like she needed this information to survive. "Yes. A woman always remembers a baby who suckles her milk, and I'm *certain* Robert and Krist were the only ones who did. Franque was born several minutes, maybe a half hour, later."

"Interesting..." Gretchen tossed another purse of gold on the table.

"What's this for?" Collette asked, hiding the purse along with the other.

"Discretion," Gretchen said plainly.

"What if I divulge? I don't know what sway you hold... what power *he* has, but I want more."

"You'll take this and the stipend and nothing more."

Both women sat in silence, staring and sizing each other up.

Finally, Collette offered this, "Krist was first, the son of a queen. Franque came next, and Sippen devised which way we'd remember the event. I don't care. I only want recompense for the time I've spent here. I want gold and lots of it."

"So the son of Braston was second?"

"That's what I said. Wait. Which Braston?"

"The master will be happy to know these as facts." Gretchen tossed a third purse on the table and Collette gathered it hungrily with the others. "Do you want to meet him?" she asked.

"Who?"

"Your benefactor."

Collette paused, suddenly afraid, but also curious. "Is he dangerous?"

"If so, you'd have been dead long ago."

"Oh. Yes, I guess. Where is he?"

A man joined them. He was much older than she'd remembered, but Collette recognized him as the man who visited so many years before.

"So, it's you," Collette demanded.

"Of course it is," he replied. "Who else?"

"I don't know," Collette responded. "Maybe someone with power."

He laughed. "Power isn't what you believe it to be. So you demand gold?"

"Lots."

"That's too bad. All I can offer is death."

Collette stared at her drink, then looked upon his face with fear.

"Yes," he said, "it was quite a terminal contract, I'm afraid."

"So my life," Collette demanded, "was only worth *this*?"

"You can say that, but I see so much more. You kept them safe, and *secret*."

"But that wasn't enough? I'm to die?"

The man frowned. "We *all* die. You get to die so much richer, but sooner than you would have."

"You're cruel."

"I'm fair, and gave you many extra minutes in which we can talk."

"I want to die now, then," Collette begged.

"No. Better that it's gradual. Then I'll take back the gold."

"You're a monster."

"No, I'm a king maker."

"What's the difference?"

"Ambition or, in my case, the lack thereof."

Part II
She Wolf

Krist awoke to a pounding between his ears, most likely from the many rounds of drinks they had consumed in *Mangy Dog*. Images from the night swam in his mind and he groaned slightly, realizing they had spent too much time and probably all of their money at the tavern.

The old man... The face of Peter Longshanks made a particularly long appearance. What was it they had agreed to? *That's right, we signed a contract.*

Krist abruptly sat upright, heart pounding at their foolishness. His head struck something low.

"Ouch!" he cried.

"Well lookie who's up!" a gravelly voice said with a laugh. "Get up and at 'em!"

A foot slammed into Krist's side with what he could only imagine was a kick. His eyes opened with alarm.

He was in a tight space, scarcely tall enough to stand. The walls were lined with wooden planks, sanded and stained quite some time ago. Simple hammocks hung in this room, three rows high and Krist lay atop one in the top row. Beneath him, Franque stirred.

A ragged sailor stood in the middle, finding amusement in Krist's confusion. He grabbed a low rafter and swung again, this time slamming his foot into Franque. "I said get up!" he roared.

Franque rolled out with a vengeful growl, not realizing there was space between him and the ground. He landed hard with a thud.

Krist moved more carefully, easing himself down before standing to full height. He had a full head of height over this man and would not allow himself to be intimidated. "Where are we?" he demanded.

The sailor's hand flashed lightning quick, producing a short wooden cudgel from his belt. It was the perfect weapon in this tight space and met Krist's ear with a sickening crack. He collapsed to his knees, holding his head against the ringing. That was all he could hear for a few seconds, but another sailor's voice soon came into focus.

"Don't kill them, Boats!"

"I dun intend to," the gravelly voice replied.

"Then put away the shillelagh."

"I had to teach 'em a lesson, so they know who to respect. I am the bosun, after all!"

"And I'm the quartermaster, and I'm telling you to leave them be. You probably cracked his skull just now!"

Krist pulled his hand away, marveling at the amount of blood. The man may be right, his head did feel like it had cracked.

The boatswain left with a grunt, pushing past a nicely dressed man holding a log book.

"Where are we?" Franque asked.

"You're on the eastern flow of Lake Norton, about to cross under the Span. But, more precisely, it's more accurate to say aboard the barque *She Wolf*."

"So we *did* sign on? Last night wasn't a dream?"

"Last night? Two days, actually, was when you came aboard."

"I don't remember boarding a ship," Franque replied.

"Well, that's the thing," the quartermaster said, "you wouldn't remember. You were drugged and unconscious when you came aboard." He opened his ledger. "I need to verify your names and their correct spelling for the record. Our boatswain mate didn't know them when he dragged you across the brow."

"Drop us off in Eston," Franque demanded

"That's not advisable. The captain would view an early departure from your contract as desertion. You'd carry the black mark for the rest of your days, earning who ever killed or captured you a hefty reward." Matter of factly he added, "You'd forever be hunted and harassed."

"We're kidnapped?" Krist asked.

"No. You signed the contracts freely."

"Six months..." Franque corrected with quite a bit of irritation.

"Umm, no. I see here it was for two years."

"That's a mistake," Franque argued. "I demand to speak to the captain."

"That won't be possible unless you want to hang from the yard-arm. Names."

"I'm Franque Thorinson, and this is my brother Krist."

"I see. Welcome to the crew, brothers Thorinson. As I said before, I'm the quartermaster. My name's Benjamin Thompson, and you can both call me Ben. I'll handle your wages, which you receive every first of the month. You're each entitled to an advance in order to purchase gear like a marlinspike or a set of sailing clothes. You'll want those, believe me. These things you have on won't last a week of scrubbing or sanding."

Krist touched the tender spot by his ear and asked a very important question. "*Who* do we report to when scrubbing or sanding?"

"That'll be Boats. He pretty much owns the both of you. What he tells you is law, and the captain will uphold it." Ben paused as if he had another thought, then added. "Just so you know, striking an officer onboard a vessel of The Cove is a hanging offense."

The added response quickly dispelled any notions Krist had before.

"Wait," Franque asked quietly. "Did you just say *The Cove?*"

"Aye, that I did. *She Wolf* is captained by none other than Devil Jacque, Pirate King and Guild Leader of Pirate's Cove. Welcome aboard, boys! You picked the finest vessel and best captain to sail under!"

Boats turned out worse than both boys imagined, with a mouth full of vulgarity and insults and a mind packed with meanness. It was as if the gods placed him into the world with the single goal of beating the boys down and ruining their day. Franque eyed him from across the deck, yelling at Krist and forcing him to rearrange the mooring lines.

"Not like that!" the awful man shouted. "Curl it like this! Figure eights around the bits, and push each wrap down before the next. Otherwise they'll tangle and slow departure if we have to leave in a hurry!"

"I'm trying," Krist protested, one hand held to his head. His wound had stopped bleeding, but he still complained to Franque about headaches.

"Try harder!" the boatswain demanded. The man kept a close watch over both boys, rarely letting them work together when topside. Franque thought maybe it was to keep them from planning an escape so close to Eston.

The boy stole a glance at the city, lifting his eyes from his sanding to watch the Span approach overhead. The walls of the city stood high on both sides of the river, and the Span carried its presence over the open harbor. He'd longed for a chance to see it himself and soon would sail directly underneath. If he wasn't working so blasted hard, he might've been excited.

"Will we be getting shore leave in Eston?" Franque called out to Boats.

"Shore leave? For you two?" the sailor laughed so hard his belly shook. "You'll be locked in berthing with guards on your door. No, you won't be runnin' nowhere, so get the thought outta your head!"

"I don't want to run," Franque said truthfully. A contract was a contract and he was coming to grips with the fact. "It's just we've got business in the city." This caused the boatswain to laugh even harder.

"Hey, Smitty!" Boats called toward a group of men tying up the main sails. They didn't need them, not with the lack of wind between the city walls. Instead the ship was pulled along by a system of pulleys along the shoreline. As one set fell slack, they unwrapped it and hauled it in, preparing a cast line and monkey fist for another throw further up river. There, a shore crew hauled it to another pulley.

One of the men hollered down, "What is it, Boats?"

"The rookies say they have business in the city!"

This sparked laughter from the men moving the lines along the port and starboard forecastle.

"*I've* got business in the city, Boats!" Smitty shouted suddenly.

"Oh? What kinda business?"

"Gonna visit your mum!" This made the rest of the crew laugh harder and even the lines crew joined in.

"Man those lines and cease your laughter!" Boats screamed at his men. They stopped, but the damage was done and Smitty had won.

Franque cringed. Boats would probably take it out on him and Krist at first chance, but at least they had weapons. He felt the marlinspike on his hip. It and the clothing set both boys back a month's wage, despite receiving only worn out tools and moth eaten linen. Even if Boats *had* let them leave, they would never be able to purchase what they needed to kill the king.

A rifle. They needed a rifle.

Two years, Franque thought. It would be a long indentureship, and he regretted ever leaving home. He knew Krist felt the same

A hatch opened nearby, and a handsome, older man climbed out. He wore fine clothing, richly embroidered and not suited for sailing. As soon as he emerged, Zane Rogers, the ship's first mate, jogged over and saluted.

"We're nearing the harbor, Captain."

"Good," the older man replied.

So this is Devil Jacque, Franque marveled. This close, he appeared more a gentleman than the scourge of the seas, less a pirate and more gentleman than the boy ever imagined.

"I won't be long in the city, only for the gala. I have to meet with our benefactor but will want to return immediately after. We must shove off by nightfall," the captain explained.

"So there won't be shore leave?"

"No, the men had enough of that in Logan."

"Pardon my pointing out, sir, but this is Eston. It offers much more than Logan, and an evening off is good for morale."

"Midnight, then. Let the men get *some* tension out, but remind them they still have to sail."

"Aye, Captain."

"Zane?"

"Yes, Captain?"

"Just keep the men away from the Span tonight. Security will be tight with the king present, and I won't be bailing anyone out of jail."

The king? Franque watched the man leave, admiring the captain's poise and grace and wondered if the man had spoken true. *I know where the king will be!* He suddenly idolized this man who rubbed elbows with kings, and, if there had ever been a man he wished he could model himself after, they paled to this Devil Jacque. *He's led me to our goal!*

"Francis!" Boats yelled, meaning Franque. He had nicknames for both boys. Krist's was Bleeder after the way his head had split.

Franque jumped to his feet and hurried to join his brother and the boatswain.

"We're almost to the harbor after this last pull," Boats explained. The Span was nearly overhead and he marveled at the size of it.

"We've got a shipment waiting and you two are on the loading crew, so rest up a bit. I need you strong because it's a lot of heavy boxes."

Franque waited till Boats had moved to watch the pulley team then whispered, "I heard the captain talking to the first mate. If we want off, we have an opportunity tonight."

"Do you think we should?" Krist asked. "You heard Ben, we'll be marked and hunted." He rubbed at his skull, pulling his hand away with a muffled yelp.

"Maybe. We don't know how serious desertion really is. Are you okay?" Franque asked. "You seem to be getting worse."

"I'm tired," Krist said with a slight slur, "and I wanna puke, but if I do, Boats and everyone else will make fun of me. I just want off," he added. "I hate it here."

"Yeah, this life is *not* what I expected."

Both boys looked up as the shadow of the Span darkened the deck of the ship. An entire city floated above their heads, a marvelous construction.

"Hey, Bleeder!" Boats called from the bow. "Haul another line to us!"

"I hate when he calls me that," Krist admitted. "I hate him," he whispered to his brother, "and I *am* going to kill him!"

Franque watched his brother trot off to follow Boat's every order. "Not if I get to him first," he muttered.

The shipment turned out to be fifty wooden crates. Boats had been right. They were heavy, but not too much so. Franque hefted them easily, tossing them to his brother. He, in turn, carried them across the brow and onto the ship. There, a group of crewmen waited to stow them away below decks.

Boats watched from the brow and Krist stole a glance at the man. He eyed the boys with suspicion as if daring them to bolt into the city.

I hate him so *much,* the boy thought. It hurt to focus his eyes, and the image of the crusty sailor wavered and blurred momentarily.

"Mind what you're doing with those!" Boats abruptly screamed at someone else, stepping away from the rail and out of sight.

"Pay attention!" Franque called as he handed over a box.

It slipped and Krist tried to catch it, but it fell, striking the pier with a thud and cracking open the wooden lid. He froze, staring at the contents poking out from within.

"Franque," he said, "look!"

His brother saw it too. It was a rifle, though much more advanced than the one stolen with their horses. The two brothers stared wide-eyed. "If they find it," Franque warned, "we'll be killed for seeing it."

Both boys glanced at the brow. Boats was still gone and no one was watching.

"Better they get shorted a delivery," Krist suggested and, working quickly, the pair tucked the crate behind some empty pallets and covered it with burlap sacks they found lying about.

"Wait," Franque demanded. "Arrange them like this, so we'll know if someone disturbs the pile."

Krist nodded dreamily, the pain in his head now a distant throbbing. The numbness had begun to worry him. "What if someone *does* find it?"

"Then all of this is wasted, and the man who killed Father gets away a while longer. Hurry," Franque urged, "let's get these others on board."

Krist nodded. They had little time. The final pallet contained satchels, each filled with what they now assumed were cartridges for the rifles. They were different than Sippen's, tubular and with lead tips at the end. They tucked a bag of these into the hideaway as well. They finished covering it just as Boats returned.

"Hurry up with those sacks!" he commanded." Carry them directly to the armory."

Begrudgingly, the boys did as commanded. Anxious to be finished so he could lie down for the evening, Krist hefted several bags of ammunition at once and hauled them aboard. The armory was below decks, down a hatch and tight ladderwell. His vision swam as he descended and his foot nearly missed a step.

The armorer frowned at the end of the narrow passage. "Hurry up with it," he growled. "I've only got a few hours ashore tonight, and you boys are cuttin' into my time."

Krist pushed past him into the space, dropping the sacks on the counter. He looked around, marveling at the weaponry. Swords, maces, mauls, and cudgels rested in open barrels, and guns and rifles lined the bulkhead. Against one wall rested the latest additions, still packed and stacked neatly. He ignored these, focusing instead on one particular barrel.

In it he recognized the axe Franque took from their mother's footlocker. Next to that was a broadsword, too long for shipboard fighting and exquisitely carved as if it belonged to a king. The pommel depicted a Fjorik crest. Krist gawked as the saber cat devoured the wolf of Loganshire. It was his father's weapon, the royal sword stolen along with his and Franque's horses.

He studied the crest, taking it in and burning the image into his mind. *I want it back,* he brooded.

"What are you gawking at?" the armorer demanded.

"Nothing," he said, but his imagination ran wild and he envisioned himself running the man through. Humbly, he turned and lowered his head and returned to the main deck. The thought of killing the man thrilled him, but the crest most of all called his attention. *I have to sketch it,* he thought, *to remember.*

Their work for the day finally completed, Krist returned to his hammock.

Franque was already in his own bed, sharpening his marlinspike with a stone. "It happens tonight," he suggested. "While the crew is ashore, we'll retrieve the rifle and find the king."

Krist laid back with eyes fixed on the beam holding up his bedding. It was smooth and stained by years of wear. He drew his own spike and began scratching the woodgrain. "We've got business here, too," he said. "This crew is the one that stole our horses."

"How do you know?"

"I saw Father's weapons in the armory."

"Yeah, we'll have to get those back," Franque agreed. "How do you feel? Are you going to be okay for tonight?"

"I have to be," Krist said, wincing against the pain as it throbbed. "We'll get this done."

CHAPTER SEVENTEEN

Eusari walked into the courtroom, iron chains around her wrists and ankles slowing her steps to a shuffle. These weren't necessary; she knew Anne clamped them on to add to her sinister background. A pirate on trial makes a spectacle, and the courtroom was packed with those waiting for a witch hunt. She sighed, then held her head high while approaching the defendant's box.

"Eusari Thorinson, the prosecution charges you with assault by proxy, piracy, and murder. How do you plead?"

She paused, taken aback by the piling of offenses. She stole a glance at Anne, sitting in her booth and looking self-righteous. Niece or not, she knew this girl was trouble the first moment they met. Eusari opened her mouth to speak.

She was interrupted by doors being flung open and the gasp of the crowd. Turning, she saw Cedric and Sippen approaching. She groaned. They looked silly, dressed in the finest silk robes—what they believed lawyers would wear. *Twenty years ago, maybe,* she groaned.

"Your Honor!" Cedric said with the air and articulation like a gentleman. The pegged leg added to his lunacy. "This woman is not guilty on all counts! Her previous record was expunged by the king himself, one Amash Esterling! To try her now is double jeopardy, and she must be released."

The magistrate blinked, then looked to Eusari.

She leaned in close to Cedric and Sippen and whispered, "The little bitch tore up my amnesty proclamation."

Both men blinked and stared silently at the magistrate. Their entire defense was destroyed.

"Your Honor," she finally said. "I plead not guilty."

The room erupted with chatter.

The prosecution went first, laying out the crimes of Eusari Thorinson, the dread captain notorious for various crimes committed while a guild member of The Cove. Anne sat perched in her chair, smugly grinning as they presented the charges she'd prepared.

Cedric stood. "Objection! The only crime my client was arrested for, was assault by proxy. Her alleged past is irrelevant."

Eusari turned to him, surprised and appreciative of his wit and fast thinking. *Maybe I have a chance after all,* she wondered.

"Your Honor," Anne said for the prosecution, "after she was arrested she admitted her identity, and I added the charges based on personal knowledge of her guilt. She admitted to me years ago she was a pirate. Any admission to a constable is admissible."

"Objection! She was not a constable at the time of the alleged conversation."

"Sit down, Mister..."

"Krull, sir! Cedric Krull at your service!"

"Sit down, Mister *Krull*! I haven't even responded to your first objection. Furthermore, who *are* you? Are you even a *licensed* barrister?"

Cedric dug into his pocket and pulled out a folded parchment. It was old, stained—gods knew what with—and wrinkled. He opened it slowly, and stared down at the writing proudly. Eusari caught a quick glance at it before handing it to the bailiff for inspection.

"Is that real or a forgery?" she whispered in his ear.

"It's real."

"How?" she demanded. "When?"

"Correspondence school," he replied proudly. "The University of Lesser Soston."

She had never heard of it, and by the confusion on the bailiff's face, neither had he. But he showed the parchment to the magistrate who shrugged and banged his gavel.

"We'll proceed but, Mister Krull, you may not object to *everything* the prosecution brings or I will hold you in contempt. As for the first objection, I agree she can be charged with other crimes after her arrest.

Regardless of when the information was observed or heard by a constable, that too is admissible."

Eusari looked at Anne who smiled smugly from across the courtroom. Anne had been a child then, still playing with dolls. But she *had* admitted plenty in front of her. Each and every crime ever attributed to her and her crew were laid out bare, earning gasps from the crowd. Gentle women swooned at many of the details, and men stared wide-eyed at the defendant. Despite her lifelong desire to remain in the shadows, Eusari Thorinson had achieved notoriety. Her death would be a spectacle to all of Loganshire.

Sippen leaned in. "You huh... have to tuh... take the stand. Suh... say your side."

She nodded. That would be the toughest part of it by far.

When the time came to swear the oath, her hands trembled, shaking in the iron shackles. Her knees fared no better, and she feared toppling over. Even her chest felt constricted, making breathing shallow and her mind a blur.

"Eusari Thorinson," Anne asked, "are you the same Eusari Thorinson who committed these crimes?"

"No."

The courtroom exploded with conversation. How *dare* she lie under oath!

She went on to explain, "I am a mother, a land owner, and a citizen of the Estonian kingdom. I pay my taxes, obey its laws, and ensure the rest of my family does as well. So no, I am most certainly *not* the same young woman who committed those atrocities."

"I get it," Anne said smugly, "people change. But you *were* the pirate in question, were you not?"

"Yes."

"And your son *did* strike two boys in the schoolhouse?"

"In self-defense. They were bullies, emboldened by the schoolmaster and doing harm to his friend. He tried to protect her, and they interfered."

"So he *did* strike them?"

"I... yes. But like I said, in self-defense."

"And did so in a schoolhouse?"

"Yes."

Turning to the jury, Anne reminded them, "A schoolhouse is always considered a public place, and therefore the crimes bear more punitive measures. Turning to the magistrate she said, "The prosecution has no more questions, Your Honor."

Eusari watched as Krull stood. His jovial demeanor had fled, replaced by worry and concern. This trial was not going well at all. Beside him, Sippen also appeared dejected. His face was drawn and lips pursed. She readied herself for the inevitable.

Sippen watched the constable end her questioning. To the magistrate and entire courtroom, the case was closed. Eusari was done for and would hang. He searched his mind for any way to free her. If only they had Amash's letter. He had granted one to each of them, a pardon for all crimes committed under the black flag of piracy. They had helped him win his throne, and thus rewarded them with peaceful retirement.

Krull approached Eusari. "You once had a letter, one from the king, did you not?"

"Yes," she replied. "I gave it to Constable Thorinson."

"And what did the king say in this letter?"

"He granted me full pardon for past offenses. He forgave me and granted peace to my future years—to ensure trials like *these* never occur."

"Where is this letter now?"

Eusari pointed at the constable. "She tore it up in front of me."

The courtroom again erupted and the magistrate pounded his gavel for quiet.

Cedric turned to the magistrate and waited for the room to quiet down. "If that is true, then the constable is guilty of a crime herself, one punishable by only the king."

"Constable?" the magistrate demanded. "Is this true?"

"She showed me a letter that was most certainly a forgery. It wasn't even signed using the king's ruling name. There was no seal either, to prove authenticity. It was within my right to destroy a forgery with those recognizable flaws."

The magistrate turned to Cedric. "Without further proof the king intended her amnesty, then we must strike the existence of the letter from these proceedings."

Sippen felt a rush of nerves inside. His heart palpitated while he searched his mind for a way to free his friend. Without Amash's seal she had no way to prove her amnesty and, even if they could, she would be guilty of Robert's crime. *Assault in a public place,* he wondered, *what an odd charge.* Anne was cruel to up the charge and, since the scuffle occurred in a school, would indeed ensure a stricter sentence if piracy was thrown out.

He froze, suddenly confident what to do, and began rifling through the various parchments he brought along in case they needed anything.

Meanwhile, Cedric continued the questioning. "Where were you during the Battle of Eston?"

"I was there, in Eston, fighting in the streets alongside Amash Horslei."

"Objection," Anne called out. "She's twisting the facts. As a pirate she would have been fighting alongside the Demon from the North! I want this part thrown out on the grounds it uses conjecture and assumptions."

"The constable is right," the magistrate agreed. "There's no way to prove what side she fought for."

Sippen's hand found a parchment with a raised seal. It trembled as he drew it forth from the satchel, reading it over several times to be certain of what it meant.

"Mister Krull, unless you have a reasonable line of questioning that pertains strictly to the charges at hand, or can prove her amnesty letter was valid, I'm afraid you will have to step down. I'm ready to make my decision."

"Wuh... wait!" Sippen shouted.

The courtroom fell silent, watching as he hurried to Cedric and thrust the parchment into his hand.

"What is this?" Cedric asked and Sippen whispered into his ear.

"Well?" the magistrate demanded. "Do you have evidence or not?"

Sippen stepped back and watched as realization filled Cedric's face. He nodded, and Sippen smiled broadly while walking slowly to his seat.

He couldn't wait to see the look on Anne Thorinson's face—or Eusari's, for that matter.

Eusari watched as Sippen took his seat, scanning his face for any clue of his plan.

Anne stood. "Objection! No new evidence can be entered into the court without first being viewed by the prosecution!"

"I have not entered evidence," Cedric said flatly. "So I demand the prosecution sit down and shut her mouth from again interrupting my time on the floor."

The magistrate nodded, waving his hand at Anne. She sat angrily, waiting along with everyone in the courtroom for Cedric to continue.

"Eusari," he asked, "what else did the king grant you for aiding in the Battle of Eston?"

"Land," she said, confused how that had bearing on the case.

"How much land? A parcel? A full farm? How much?"

"Objection!" the constable again shouted. "Relevance?"

Before the magistrate could rule, Cedric turned and spoke directly to Anne. "Oh, it has relevance! A sizable bequeathal would certainly prove intent to grant amnesty!"

The magistrate actually chuckled. "It would have to be sizable indeed. By Estonian land laws, anyone can own parcels up to five hundred acres— even convicted felons. It would *have* to be bigger than that!"

Cedric strolled over to Anne and slammed the parchment on her table. When he turned, he made a show of it, twirling flamboyantly like an exaggerated actor on stage. "Miss Thorinson, Eusari, how much land did king Amash grant you to settle the unorganized lands northwest of Logan, bringing them under his control as king?"

Eusari froze, she finally understood the relevance. "Ten thousand acres," she said with confidence.

"Essentially the land between the river and the mountains and everything in between, am I wrong?"

"You are correct."

The courtroom again fell quiet with one collective gasp. Everyone in attendance waited to learn what it meant.

"Your Honor," Cedric said to the magistrate, "I enter into evidence a *Tenure of Barony,* signed by the king and bearing his seal—inscribed and granted for *heroic actions to benefit the crown.* Eusari Thorinson is a *Land Baron*!"

All eyes, even Anne's and Eusari's, turned to the magistrate. "Show me the tenure!" he demanded. Anne silently gave it over to the bailiff, who passed it along. "This is indeed in order," he finally said. "Miss Thorinson, this court throws out all charges regarding piracy, murder, and mayhem. We shall now decide on the remaining charge of assault in a public place by proxy."

Eusari felt her mind spin and let out the breath she had held. *Thank you, Sippen,* she mouthed to her friend. He only nodded and pointed to Cedric with a broad smile. She followed the gesture and saw their faces wore matching jubilation.

"Your Honor, the defense asks you to toss out that charge as well," the awkward looking barrister demanded.

"On what grounds?"

"On the grounds it did not occur on public property after all. The schoolhouse, the town, *all* of it belongs to Eusari... *Lady* Thorinson. Her son defended his friend on *private* property."

Eusari, Cedric, and Sippen all turned to watch the constable. Her mouth dangled open and her eyes were open wide with shock. The pirates had beaten her soundly.

The magistrate spoke. "Lady Thorinson, I find you clear of all charges, and beg your forgiveness for the rash behavior by the prosecution. This court prides itself on thorough execution of the law, and your case was certainly not conducted properly. I also grant you reimbursement as recompense for your detainment and confinement. This court is dismissed." He banged the gavel a single time, then fled quickly from the eruption of dozens of people speaking at once.

CHAPTER EIGHTEEN

Eusari followed Krill and Sippen from the courthouse, leaving Cedric's gentleman persona behind. Back in his favorite skin and again wearing his eyepatch, the pirate beamed at Sippen's praise. She owed so much to these men who called her friend, and loved them beyond measure. But Krill said one thing that brought her sadness—when he suggested this moment felt like their *good ol' days.*

Those days were indeed grand but had contained something this adventure did not—Braen Braston. She never recovered either from his loss or how he departed. No man would ever be good enough to make her love him more, or even the same as Braen, but these, his best of friends, helped her believe he could still be around. At least his boys filled some of the gap he left in her heart, and her first order of business as a free woman was to find them.

"Mother!" a voice called from the street and she turned, recognizing Robert's voice. He rushed to hug her tightly.

Behind him, Sebastian beamed proudly at the reunion. She would have to thank him profoundly for keeping her son safe.

She paused.

Three other figures followed the pair, travelling as their companions. She recognized the freckled woman with auburn hair at once, with her cheery smile that almost seemed exaggerated. The dark skinned man and the other woman she did not know.

"Marita?" she asked, surprised to see her. The last time she had, the woman had been a cheery teen bound for the Southern Continent with Alec Pogue. Marita's smile grew larger, and she offered two thumbs upward toward the sky. This made Eusari laugh. "And who are your friends?"

The young woman stepped forward. She was a pretty thing, still in her twenties. Her spectacles made her appear studious, and the eyes behind them held wisdom. "You may not remember me," she said shyly, but you saved my life, once... you and..."

"Gelert," Eusari blurted. Sudden recognition brought forth a torrent of memories. "Of course I remember you, Charleigh. But Gelert saved you... He *found* you, not I."

"I always understood you two were one and the same," the woman said with tears in her eyes. She also retained memories from that fateful day long ago, and lost her parents not long after. Had it not been for Alec Pogue, neither she nor Marita would have ever had a family to love them into adulthood. Eusari hugged both women and Robert tightly. She was thankful they and Sebastian accompanied her son's journey and was certain a grand story awaited their telling.

But he isn't really my son, she mused, *and he knows that now.*

She pulled back and placed a hand on each of his shoulders. "Sippen tells me you've learned the truth about your parents. What else has Sebastian told you?"

"Most of it, I think," he replied. He chuckled. "That I'm the son of Robert Esterling and heir to Eston. That I was born during the Battle of Eston, and the king is searching for me."

"I'm sorry you learned it this way," she said, "and that I failed to tell you sooner. I meant to, on the day of your seventeenth summer. But it's true, all of it and more, and it's time for you to meet your uncle."

"Uncle?"

"Amash Esterling was once Amash Horslei. His sister was Sarai, your mother, and he charged me with keeping you safe until old enough to name as his heir."

Robert's eyes grew wide. "That's why the king never took a wife or produced an heir? He always meant it for me?"

Eusari nodded. "You can trust him. I did, and so did your father and mother."

Marita added, "I spent a lot of time with him as well. Amash is the greatest kind of man. He's compassionate and loving, an intellectual as well as a man of honor. He *will* keep his promise."

"I don't want it, Mother. I'm not ready to leave you or the farm," Robert admitted.

"None of us wanted to leave, but look where we are," Eusari said with a laugh. "This adventure found us all, and sadly there's more to do."

"What do you mean?" Robert looked around, finally seeing Sippen and Krill. "Where are Franque and Krist?" he demanded.

"We don't know. They may have travelled on to Eston or even be here in the city. I'm about to begin a search."

"We'll help," Marita promised.

"Thank you. They were last seen on the waterfront, so we'll begin there."

"Excuse me, ma'am, for overhearing." A drunk sauntered up on a weathered pegleg. His face was grimy, old and wrinkled, and his stomach bloated from years of addiction. Every pore reeked of spirits, and his breath might've turned to fire had open flame been nearby. "I know where your boys are."

Eusari let the words settle in, at first thinking this was a new approach to begging coin. Then she recognized him. "Peter Longshanks?"

He nodded his head, never allowing his eyes to meet hers.

What shame does he hold? she wondered, *that he can't look me in the eye?* "Peter," she asked, "how did you get into this condition? What went so wrong with your life you went down this path?"

"I'm sorry," he said with tears flowing. His knee buckled and he fell to the ground, laying on the steps and sobbing.

Eusari knelt beside him. "Peter, what are you sorry for?"

"So much," he sobbed. "I betrayed you without knowing... I let you down."

"How, Peter? How did you betray me?"

"I let *him* take her. I should have died aboard *She Wolf,* but he killed so many of your crew. I was your first mate and my obligation was to shed my blood upon her boards, but I fled. I jumped like a coward over the side and swam away. I *gave* Devil Jacque your ship, Captain. I'm so sorry."

"*Your* ship?" Robert asked, his eyes large with shock.

Eusari met his stare. "I didn't want you to learn that about me, ever," she told him. "But yes, I lived a different life once." Turning her attention back to Peter, she said, "You did not betray me, and I'm glad you lived. *She Wolf* was only a ship—planks of wood and yards of canvas. Her loss meant less to me over the years than the loss of my men, but especially my loss of you."

"No," Peter shook his head. "I don't deserve pity. I'm a horrible man, I never deserved to live at all. I should have died."

"I thought you *had* died and mourned you along with the others. But most of all I regretted I would never again hear your advice or heed your counsel. I lost my best friend, one of the first men I ever trusted, when I lost you. I forgive you for whatever you need me to. I... I love you, Peter. I love you like a father."

This caused Peter to sob even harder. "There's more, and you won't forgive this."

"What is it, Peter. Say it and let's be done with it."

"I didn't know they were your boys."

"What?" Eusari flinched as if punched. "Where are they? What happened to my sons?"

"I didn't know they were yours," Peter admitted, "when I sold them to Devil Jacque."

Eusari leapt to her feet.

A feeling grew inside, one she had not felt in many years, not since Braen had come into her life. Inside, an animal howled and her eyes burned with fiery hatred. She did not realize, but her hand reached inside her clothes for a hidden knife that was not there, meaning to plunge it into the heart of a certain man. Hatred and vengeance found its way into Eusari for the first time in nearly seventeen years. For a brief moment, the true she-wolf replaced the woman.

"Sippen, Krill," she commanded, "clean up my first mate and dry him out. Then get to the docks and buy me a ship. Recruit the best crew you can. I don't care how dark-hearted these men might be. Find me killers."

"Wuh... where are we guh... going?" Sippen asked.

"I'm going to find Devil Jacque and split him from bow to stern. Get guns and cannons, the best you can find, and Sippen?"

"Yuh... yes?"

"Find me a ship that's fast!"

She turned on her heel and strode off, leaving behind a collection of stunned and staring faces among her friends. One more difficult conversation was needed, and with the unlikeliest of people.

Anne Thorinson sat at her desk, chewing on a quill and studying *Common Law and Trial,* the book that had for so long been her guide. Not accepting she had lost and her pirate aunt had prevailed, she searched for a way to appeal. That fateful error had been her first and allowed the lawbreaker to go free. She would never make that mistake again. Losing one case was more than enough for this constable.

The door to her office burst open and she leapt to her feet, feeling for the gun at her side.

"Stay your hand," Eusari growled from the doorway, "I'm not here to fight."

Anne studied the woman carefully and, after ensuring she carried no weapon, allowed herself to sit. "What do *you* want?" she demanded. "Are you here to gloat?"

"That's not my style," Eusari replied. "I'm here to beg."

"Well now, you have an odd way of doing it. I may have to repair that door."

Eusari took a seat without being offered one.

"I'll pay for damages."

"Why *are* you here?" Anne demanded. "I've nothing for you and hope we never meet again."

"I want to strike a bargain, a trade, if you will."

"You've nothing I want."

"Earlier today you thought you'd be hanging a pirate, and I'm here to give you one. Devil Jacque has two of my sons illegally pressed into his crew. I aim to get them back and settle an old score along the way."

"Pirate hunting is illegal, especially if they're guilded. You have to catch them in the midst of committing a crime and, even then, only a constable can arrest them."

"That's why I'm here. I want you to deputize my entire crew and me, then I'll deliver the most dangerous thug who ever lived."

Anne stared at her aunt without blinking. This *was* a surprise indeed. "I'll agree," she heard herself say, "but I'm coming with you to ensure everything's done within the law."

CHAPTER NINETEEN

"Wake up!"

Tara groaned, closing her eyes against the intrusion upon her rest. The journey had been long, and she deserved this sleep. Besides, the bed she lay upon felt so... there was no word either in Andalonian or Pescari for the comfort she experienced. Her people may have lived a life of poverty upon the Steppes of Cinder but lived extravagantly in New Weston. She pulled her pillow closer and began to doze more deeply.

"I said wake up!" the voice commanded.

She opened her eyes drowsily, focusing slowly on her mother looming over her bed, holding a lantern and looking very stern. "How early is it?" Tara demanded. No light flooded the room.

"Felicima will rise soon, and we've work to do as Pescari."

Tara rolled over, turning her back on the disruption. "Nice try," she said, "Pescari only work under sight of your goddess. Even *I* know that!"

"You have much more to learn of our ways," Flaya insisted, "and today is your first lesson. Arise, and demonstrate to Felicima your subservience!"

Tara breathed deeply, then let it out with a huff. This was her mother's world, not hers, but she had made a promise. Tossing the blanket, she swung her feet over the side. "Leave so I may dress," she demanded.

"I've seen you many times. Just dress modestly so Felicima is honored." Flaya stormed from her room.

"Modestly?" Tara muttered. "I've been modest my entire life." She rose, pulling on the buckskins she'd always worn. No matter her desire to be more Andalonian, she obeyed her mother. She loved her, even if they disagreed.

Flaya waited downstairs with two leather satchels, thrusting the heavier of the two into her daughter's hand before leading her outside. The girl followed without checking its contents.

The humidity clung to the night, and the women could almost taste the moisture. The stars had not yet faded, and Tara noticed how the night sky was the exact same as it had been over her home in Loganshire. Only, there was more of it without mountains. Off in the far distance, she noticed a faint glow on the western horizon.

"That's the caldera," Flaya explained, "where Felicima descends each night for slumber. When I was a girl living on the steppes, and before we crossed the Forbidden Waste, it was close enough I could feel the heat of her fire. It's also where we interred our warriors."

"But not anymore?"

"The journey is still made across the Forbidden Waste, but only the bravest make it. It takes several days and there is little food and no water."

"What of my father? Where was he laid to rest?"

"Taros' body was carried to the caldera by your great uncle, carrying only a single waterskin and surviving on whatever he could find along the way."

"So, Father was honored," Tara observed. "Are all shappans honored so?"

"No. If a shappan falls in Shapalote, the new shappan decides."

"What of his family?"

"They are shunned and their wives sent to the fireside, only their children can return to the village, but that is only after their naming ritual. Taros was like that. His father fell in Shapalote to Cornin, a cruel warrior who decreed the body lay upon the steppes to be consumed by carrion."

"How awful."

"It was to prove a point, but even then, Taros showed defiance. He eventually retrieved his father's body and committed it to the caldera."

"On his own?" Tara was shocked. "How old was he?"

"At the time he had not yet had his ceremony and only knew thirteen summers. He earned his name then and knew its meaning till the day he died."

"What did it mean?"

"Each Pescari name holds different meaning for the bearer," Flaya explained. "Yours *I* know, but it shall not be revealed until you are ready."

"How do you know mine, if it has not been revealed to me?"

"It is my duty as your family to tell you when the time comes, or your great uncle's if I do not survive to see the day."

"So, he knows as well?"

"Yes, and also Eusari and two others who were present when it was earned."

Tara fell silent then, wondering how and when she may have had time to earn her name. Her life so far had always been uneventful, boring, and even stifling dull at times.

The pair walked until they reached the far eastern edge of the city. Without a city wall, Tara expected the buildings to merely end and the prairie begin. But strangely, it withered instead. The tall buildings, sleek and smoothly black, lowered by an entire story each row until finally only tiny hovels remained. Beyond those, simple structures of animal skins stretched over tent poles. This village beyond the city was already awake, with women and children drawing water from a well and some baking bread in massive ovens. A middle aged man on crutches limped by, dragging a mishappen foot along the reddish dirt of the street.

"Where are we?" Tara demanded. "Why does Teot allow poverty when the rest of the city stands strong?"

"This is the fireside, where the shunned, lame, and lazy are sent. They are the first Felicima looks upon, fooling her into believing we are all wretched in hopes she turns her attention away before passing over the strongest."

"So the western side of the city..." Tara remembered the magnificent structures along the shoreline and the tremendous harbor, "is where the wealthy like Teot reside. That's why the entire city seemed so splendid!"

"Yes. Our strength resides there, while our weakest remains here. The rest are in between. That is the way of it, and how it must be."

"Mother," Tara asked quietly, "why are *we* here? Have we been shunned?"

"Though my husband was a shappan, he died honorably in battle so that others would live. I am one of the few widows to walk the city freely. No, we are here to meet with another whose father faced a different fate. Wait here." Flaya stepped away, conversing quietly with a woman lugging waterskins. Her eyes never met Tara's mother's and stared at the ground while they talked. After a brief exchange, a finger pointed down the way toward a single home.

"Come," Flaya commanded, and Tara hurried to catch up. The tent flap was closed, but the soft scent of a cooking fire wafted out from within. "Open and attend to visitors," she told the occupants.

"Who demands this?" an older woman demanded from the other side.

"Flaya, wife of Taros, the slayer of Cornin."

Shuffling and movement signaled someone hurrying to open the flap. It flew aside and a young man not much older than Tara stared out with wide eyes. Beyond him an old woman lay upon furs while a young girl fed her porridge.

"Forgive me for not standing and bowing, but I've struggled to do either for many years, granddaughter of Daska," the elder said smugly.

"I am not here for homage, Kailani, I am here with gifts." Flaya took the satchel from Tara and handed both to the young man.

"And you journeyed under cover of nighttime so as not to offend Felicima. Such a consummate believer, even when I lay condemned to die in poverty for the disgrace of my husband. What is it you want with a firesider, Flaya, wife of Taros? Will gifts of rich foods and clean water clear your conscience enough to sleep as soundly as Felicima? Why do you pity me?"

Flaya stood her ground stoically. The insults, if they bothered her at all, flew by without even a flinch.

"Well?" Kailani demanded. "Why are you here? Hurry, before Felicima sees you among the weak and discarded."

"If you shut your ancient mouth long enough for me to speak, you will know!" Flaya finally snapped.

"Ah, your temper's as fiery as your husband's, I see," Kailani said with smiling victory.

"I said I bring you gifts. The gift I bring you is also a favor to me."

"Why would I grant you any favor?"

Flaya placed a hand on Tara's back and shoved her forward. "This is my daughter, Tara, who knows nothing of Pescari ways."

"The daughter of Taros?" Kailani laughed hysterically. "How is *she* a gift?"

"*She* is not my gift. I bring you both her ignorance and also some insolence. I think you will enjoy both with equal measure, as it is a reflection upon my failure as a mother. Succeed where I did not by teaching her what it truly is to be Pescari, and how one outcome can topple a queen."

Kailani paused, nodding and considering. "Your gift is humility, coming to me with this task. You honor me, offering an old woman the opportunity to be seen and heard by more than just Felicima. I understand this task and will do it willingly."

"Wait," Tara exclaimed, filling with understanding and suddenly resenting her mother. "You won't train me yourself?" she demanded of Flaya.

"No. Soon your great uncle will test you, so you may discover the meaning of your name. Learn what you can from Kailani. I will return for you in a few weeks to test you myself." With that, Flaya turned from the room and departed, hurrying down the dirt road toward the waiting stone of the city.

"Come here," Kailani said with a voice reeking of command. "My eyes are weak and I do not wish to strain."

Tara complied, stepping forward and closer to the old woman, trembling slightly under appraising eyes and feeling her skin crawl with a mixture of anger and fear.

"Do you know who I am?"

"No. I do not," Tara admitted.

"I am the widow of the shappan your father murdered. Do you know how he did it? What weapon he used to kill my husband?"

"No."

"It was an ordinary day. The goddess had risen, the air had not yet warmed, and none of us suspected her wrath would unleash." The old woman paused, wincing at some distant memory. "Have you ever seen a fumarole form or even its fire and steam belch from the ground?" she finally asked.

Tara shook her head that she had not.

"Pray you never do," the woman snapped, then collected her anger and proceeded. "It rose up in the middle of the village, just at the division between us and the firesiders. Many perished that day under Felicima's wrath, but we never understood the reason for her anger. That is, until your father returned from his morning hunt." The woman paused in telling the story, groaning as she sat up. The girl attending her placed a rolled fur behind her back. "Taros defied Cornin and ran into the flames to find his mother. Lynette had earned her shunning and was to be left to die on the fireside as our custom prescribes. But he soon emerged with her in his arms, stepping out of the flame, untouched and unaffected by the heat. I watched as tongues of flame licked at his skin, but it did not blister or peel as it should."

"He drew the heat?" Tara asked with amazement. "I saw Teot absorb the same way."

"He *stole* it!" the woman wailed. "It did not belong to him! He robbed the goddess of her power, tricking my husband into Shapalote. Had Cornin known your father would cheat, he would have demanded a different set of rules. But how could he have? The battle ended as soon as it began with my husband, the most powerful warrior among the Pescari, burned to ashes and left to blow across the Steppes of Cinder."

"I..." Tara stammered. She had no way of knowing any of this. Flaya had certainly left out many details. "I'm sorry. I didn't know."

"He marched us here, nearly destroying us with his anger, then later melted the Andalonian city into molten rock."

Tara tried to open her mouth, but the multitude of questions dueled in her mind. She did not know which she should ask first if any. Kailani spared her from trying.

"What *do* you know of our ways?" the old woman demanded.

"Not much."

"Then your training begins today. Go fill those waterskins in full view of the rising Felicima, so she may know you as a firesider and begin her full judgement."

The young man handed her four waterskins, his eyes, once friendly and welcoming, were now filled with anger and avoided her own. Tara pushed the tent flap and scurried toward the well she had passed along the way. By the length of her shadow, she knew Felicima stared at her back appraisingly. The girl inside the budding woman wept.

CHAPTER TWENTY

Eusari stood on the Logan pier for the first time in seventeen years, a place she long believed she would die before ever setting eyes upon once more. Much more she stared up at *her* ship. It was a four-masted frigate, fast and full of firepower. The outer hull was dressed in copper plating, much in the same design as another ship she had sailed with long ago. Sippen promised the low draft would give her speed, even after the extra deck space was filled with guns. She wanted lots of firepower.

"It looks brand new," she told Sippen.

"It uh... is. Is thuh... that a pruh... problem?"

"No. It's perfect," she said. This man really knew his ships and how to pick them. "What's its name?"

"It's nuh... not christened." He pulled out a dusty old bottle from his satchel, carefully wrapped in burlap so as not to break prematurely.

Eusari eyed the bottle suspiciously. "I thought all that vintage was gone," she said.

"There's nuh... not much left, and thu... then it's guh... gone like us."

"Shame to waste a bottle like that on a ship."

"He wuh... would uh... approve."

"Yes, he would. You guys always ran through this stuff like it would last forever, but I guess wine, like people, isn't meant to collect dust on shelves. Braen knew that, didn't he?"

"He duh... did."

"So, what do I do? There's no rope. Do I just throw it at the keel? What if I miss?"

"Don't muh... miss," Sippen replied with a smile.

Eusari reared her arm back, grasping the bottle by the neck. She heaved it forward, sending it smashing against the hull.

"What's huh... her name?"

"*Reprisal.*"

"Why nuh... not vengeance?"

"Because I'm taking back what's mine." She led Sippen up the brow, stepping onto the deck. The first thing she noticed was the smell. "The lacquer hasn't cured," she observed, "that means we're vulnerable to fire."

"Don't luh.... let it catch fire, then," he said with a grin.

Peter and Krill noticed they'd arrived and hobbled over.

"She's nearly seaworthy, ma'am," her first mate informed. "Once we reach the lake, you should shake her down and run some paces."

"I agree. You look better, Peter," she lied. He looked like all the hells in one, but at least he smelled better.

"Thank you, but I feel awful. The tremors finally stopped, though, so I'm nearly seaworthy as well."

She looked around. "The crew?"

"The blackheartiest band of misfit killers you've ever met, ma'am, but each knows their way around a sail, a grommet, or a braided line of hemp."

She turned to Krill. "And the weapons, Gunnery Sergeant?"

"Ready to blow our foes into whale kibble, Cap'n!"

"Need I remind you my boys are with our foes, Krill?" she snapped. "I don't want to hit the powder storage by mistake."

"Aw, you hurt me feelings, mum! You know right well I can sight guns as well as I can count all ten of me fingers."

"You only have eight."

He held up two fists with grin, invisibly showing her is missing middle two. "Just wanted you to recount them, Cap'n!" With a laugh, he hobbled away.

"I forgot how irritating he gets underway," she muttered.

"I thuh... thought it was fuh... funny," Sippen admitted.

"You always do. I swear though, this mission had better be a short one. What are the captain's quarters like?" she asked.

He said nothing, only grinned like he had a secret.

After years living aboard *She Wolf,* she wasn't prepared for the spacious cabin aboard *Reprisal.* The room itself seemed carved from a single piece of dark wood stained smooth and the floor covered in thick rugs.

"Seems like most of this could've been storage," she said upon entering.

"If we nuh... need the space, we'll yuh... use it."

"It's beautiful. After we no longer need it, we should get full value when we sell." Eusari noticed a dark form hanging in the corner. Turning slowly, she recognized a black fur cloak, terminating as a wolf's head for a hood. She raised an eyebrow and Sippen nodded. Neatly folded and placed on a chair nearby, she found leather armor and a brace of knives. "Out of retirement, then?" she asked.

"Out of ruh... retirement," he agreed. "Duh... don't worry. I luh... let out the seams. It will fuh... fit."

She raised an eyebrow and shot him a look. She needed it of course, but how dare he point it out.

Sippen departed quietly, and she stripped, catching a glimpse of her naked self in a long mirror. *Am I ready for this?* she thought. *I'm so out of shape, what if I have to fight?* She slipped on the leather breeches, sucking in to pull them over her belly. *They'll fit better as the journey progresses,* she thought, pulling on the jerkin and thankful for the extra room. She placed the knives in their homes, pausing and frowning as she counted. One in particular was missing. She felt the inside of her wrist and the pocket it fit. *This will be a problem,* she knew. She had always depended on that one the most.

Eusari stared again at the cloak. It seemed silly now looking at it, and she wondered why she chose such a symbol when she was younger. *To strike fear,* she knew, but there must have been more. Gelert had taught her that. *Gelert.* Her wolf companion for such a brief, but needed, time. After his death, she swore she would never bond with another. She lifted it from the hook and pulled it over her head, setting the breakaway clasps to her shoulders. Turning, she took one more look at herself in the mirror. The woman staring back was older and more tired than she remembered, but the she-wolf had returned.

Robert stood on deck, waiting for his mother to return topside. *Reprisal,* she had named it, an odd name from a woman who preached calm forgiveness his entire life. Sippen had already returned, so she shouldn't be too long. He wondered if he'd have the nerve to ask her about the name.

Sippen noticed Charleigh tinkering with the same box Robert had noticed before. He moved closer to hear their conversation.

"Wuh... what is it?"

"This?" she replied. "It's supposed to be a trap, but I can't quite get it to work."

"Let me see," he said, turning it over in his hands, examining its workings and clicking his tongue as he did. Giving up, he handed it over. "I can't figure out how it opens."

Robert noticed he hadn't stuttered. Sippen was in his zone.

Charleigh smiled and said to Robert, "Set it on the deck, then send in a current of air."

Frowning, he dispatched a thin tendril. It poked and prodded, finally finding a way in. The gadget popped open, sending out dozens of caltrops and marbles onto the wood.

Sippen's eyes grew wide. "It's marvelous!"

"It doesn't work," Charleigh said, defeated.

"It looks like it works fine to me," Robert said.

"Oh, it works, but not how I intended. No one else should be able to open it but Marita, and we can't use it in a fight until they can't use it against *us*."

"I see," Sippen said thoughtfully. Now that it was open, he could see the inner workings and studied them closely. "It's like puh... picking a luh... lock?"

"Yes."

"That's your problem, then," Robert suggested. "Lockpicking is simple and orderly, too easy to crack. You need to rearrange the pins, adding a hinge that drops them all again if the wrong order is tapped."

Charleigh nodded. "I hadn't thought of that."

"When were you going to tell me?" Eusari asked from behind Robert.

He looked up, surprised to see his mother wearing fighting leathers, knives, and a wolf fur cloak. "Tell you what?"

"How long have you been able to do that?"

"Only in the past couple of days. I guess I figured some things out by accident, and Sebastian has been helping me learn more."

"I see."

"But not surprised?" he asked.

"No, not surprised given who your father was. I only hoped you'd be spared."

"Spared? I don't understand."

"For seventeen years I've prayed the gods kept this power from you. It comes with responsibility, doesn't it Sebastian?"

The man nodded gravely.

"I *do* want to learn more about it," Robert admitted.

"You'll get your chance. I'm sure he'll guide you further in training once you arrive in Eston." Turning to the farmhand, she added, "A pirate vessel going into war is no place for you, Sebastian, and I will feel better knowing you are there to protect my boy."

"Eston?" Robert asked. "I can't go there now, not with Franque and Krist in trouble."

"I'll find the boys, but not until after I introduce you to Amash. You have a lot to learn that only Sebastian, and now also the Dreamers, can teach. Learn as much from them as you can, and I promise to visit after we return."

"Okay." Robert agreed.

All eyes on deck turned as a woman walked across the brow. "Who's that?" Robert asked.

"Your cousin, Anne. She's a constable and here to make this a legal pirate hunt," his mother said. "Now, if you all don't mind, I have work to do. This is a rough crew and many of the men may not respect my first mate. They remember him only as the town drunk, and so I've got to bear the burden of leadership."

As Eusari walked away, Sippen stared after her. "She luh... learned that fruh... from Braen. He was a luh... leader and his cruh... crew loved him."

"I still can't believe she's a pirate, much less a captain," Robert said.

"Thuh... the best." Sippen agreed.

"That's the last of the crew," Peter Longshanks shouted upon Anne's arrival. On his command the lines crew pulled away the brow and tossed off lines. The ship immediately began to drift. "Sailing master! Take control!"

At mention of her new title, Marita stepped forward with a grin. "Just like the good ol' days," she said with a wink to Sippen. "Triple the lashings and add storm lines!" she shouted to the crew.

The grumblings began at once.

"Triple lashings?" someone asked.

"Storm lines?" demanded another.

Her face grew dark, suddenly serious and quite determined if not angry. "I'll give an order once," she growled, "but remember I've been pirating since many of you were suckling your mother's teets!" Several wisps of air sprang outward at once, smacking each crew member on the butt with a loud snap. "I don't *have* to explain myself, but when I blow wind in those sails, prepare to be blown over the side, or hanging from a yardarm to secure a flapping canvas! Either way is fine with me, as long as you do as I say!"

Every hand snapped to, tying off storm lines and lashing grommets with an extra wrap. Robert could tell by their faces none of them had sailed with an emotant. As soon as *Reprisal* had turned toward the harbor entrance, each man grabbed ahold of a storm line.

Sippen stood hurriedly. "I nuh… know her," he said. "Gruh… grab on."

"You're right," Charleigh agreed, wrapping her forearms to the rail. "She's about to show off."

All at once every sail filled with air, so much of it all three masts groaned against the strain. The ship, much to the chagrin of the harbor master, abruptly lurched and shot through the entrance. In a heartbeat, *Reprisal* sailed Lake Norton.

Robert looked at Eusari, standing next to Marita as the woman's arms conducted a silent orchestra. His mother, usually melancholy, beamed underneath the hood. She grinned and stared straight ahead, loving every minute of her renewed time at sea.

CHAPTER TWENTY-ONE

Krist squeezed his eyes together, wincing against pain. His entire head throbbed with relentless pulses, with pressure building and threatening to push the eyes from his head. Where Boats had struck him felt tender and palpable to the touch, and the boy swore he felt a dent in the bone. He had worked all day through nausea and dizzying head spins, trying not to let the sailors see how much agony he was really in. The time had come to reveal how bad it was to his brother.

Franque crouched by the door, listening and waiting for a break in the topside laughter, hoping for a moment in which they could both exit the room. They had to be careful if they were to sneak across the brow.

"I can't go," Krist finally admitted. "My head's bad, Franque. I'm not well."

"Are you sure?" His brother seemed deeply worried at the news, and Krist regretted telling him right away.

"It's awful."

"That's it," Franque decided. "I'll stay here with you."

"No, go on alone and come back. You've only a few hours. Besides, how do you know you can even get into the palace, much less kill the king?" Krist laughed, but winced at the pain it brought.

"I know where he'll be. He's going to the same gala as Captain Jacque, so all I have to do is make the shot and get back before the crew. I have till midnight."

"Get off the shot?" Uttering the words took great effort, and they came out slurred. "You've never fired one of those. You'll miss and he'll get away."

"I won't!" Franque was insistent.

Krist said nothing else. He was too tired to argue, and the pain... it was too much to bear and growing worse. *I'm going to die,* he thought.

"It can't be too difficult. I'll line it up and take a breath to steady my nerves. I'll shoot him, then run like hell back to the boat."

"If you don't make it back, don't worry about me."

"I'll make it back," Franque promised. "Krist, are you sure you're okay?"

Krist managed a nod, then closed his eyes. He was not okay, not even close. He was going to die.

Franque watched his brother. The wound was bad, he could tell that from here, and it wasn't like Krist to want to stay in bed and miss out on the action. After a while he turned his eyes toward the door, thinking of the lock and how difficult it would be to pick. His hand moved to the marlinspike on his hip. Not hard, not with the right tool.

Once he was certain no one lurked in the passage, he placed the tip of the spike in the lock and punched it through with his right hand. It made some noise, but not much. He turned the knob and the door opened easily. The locks on a ship weren't meant to be difficult, he had realized, only strong enough to keep doors from swinging open on rough seas. A brig, he knew, would be more difficult to escape.

After one more glance at Krist he slipped into the passage.

The ship turned out deserted. Boats had lied, and no one watched at all. Other than a bored officer of the deck and an equally asleep messenger, nobody stirred. Franque slipped past both of these two men without even a challenge. Sailors, it seemed, loved their shore leave and those left behind resented their duty. He hoped to be as lucky with the city guard.

Thankfully, moonlight lit the pier, though not as well as he would have hoped. The shadows were plentiful, and it took a lot of time for his eyes to adjust to the darkness between ships, but he eventually found the place. Half feeling around where they had left the pallet, he eventually found it beneath the satchels. He paused, trying to remember if they were the way he and Krist had left them. Nothing appeared out of sorts. Franque breathed a sigh of relief and moved the sacks aside, tossing them quickly as fear of discovery grew into anxiety. With a heave he lifted the pallet, shoving it aside to find the crate hidden below.

For a moment in the darkness, anxiety grew into panic and he hoped the rifle would be gone, saving him from doing the deed. The boy inside yearned to chicken out, to run back to the ship and grab his brother from his hammock. Once free, they could hop a merchant vessel headed for home.

But it was there, just as the man inside wanted, the man yearning for justice and revenge over the father he never knew. He reached into the broken crate and touched the polished wood and smooth barrel of the killing machine. It felt so right and wrong at the same time. It felt like power.

His eyes turned upward, focusing in the dark yet unseeing. His mind imagined what eyes could not reflect in the darkness. The Span waited. Somewhere upon the stones high above, the central most part of the city waited with a party held for a king—a king who must die. Clutching the rifle to his chest, Franque made his departure from the docks, climbing steps and praying the gods would lead him to the correct destination.

Gretchen's eyes flickered as she slumbered, not deeply as with real sleep, but lightly and aware as was the way of the bead. She had mildly attained what the ancient oracles had called Da'ash'mael, careful not to progress further. To do so could bring death. She had consumed the bead several hours earlier, so this vision had mostly faded. But he drew nearer, the boy she had been sent to deal with, and her wits were needed to convey the master's message.

The boy fumbled around in the dark, unsure of his destination and certainly not mastered with the weapon he carried. Determination and stubbornness drove him, this product of fated lineage. Gretchen's natural thoughts returned to the conversation with Collette. Franque was born second, even if Eusari and Sippen decreed otherwise. *But can her words be trusted?* The former nursemaid was dead and gone, so there was no way to be certain.

He reached the overlook, by chance and luck more than any skill, and set up the firearm as if he truly believed in his chances to succeed.

Gretchen stepped out from the shadows, now fully alert and anchored more in reality than the Dream World. Of course, not being an emotant, she could never fully touch that plane, only glimpse it briefly and share in the secrets it told. "You will miss," she warned.

The boy jumped, unsuspecting anyone watched, much less know his motives.

"Who are you?" he asked, training the rifle in her direction with finger dangerously close to the trigger.

"Put it down. I'm no threat. And neither are you to the king."

"What did you say?" he demanded. "You don't even know what I'm doing!"

"I said you will miss the king with your rifle, high and to either the right or left because you never control the trigger in any rendition I've seen."

He paled, even in the darkness it was obvious, and the moonlight above the Span betrayed wide eyes filled with both fear and surprise.

"He's not my target."

"You're a pitiful liar, Franque Thorinson."

"How do you know me?"

"I know many things like your name, but your motives I have seen, witnessed with my mind's eye. You try to kill King Esterling, but miss wildly in every vision I have seen. Once, I even saw it from your own point of view. You're finger trembled terribly like it is now, and you pulled the tip of the weapon just enough to hit a bystander. No, believe me when I say you do not have the *slimmest* chance of succeeding."

"I... I have to try," the boy insisted, though doubt now clouded his face. "This is a good rifle, better built than the old one Sippen uses. He's nearly blind, and if he can hit his target so can I!"

"You've never fired this weapon or any like it, and you have no concept of factors affecting a shot from this distance."

"It can't be too difficult. I simply point and shoot."

"Wind is a factor, and so is elevation. Have you no concept of how fast a bullet will fall or drift away on the breeze?"

"Surely it's not that complicated," the boy argued. She found his confidence irritating.

"Fire it and see, but you will not kill the king," she said with a shrug. "Rather, the city will go into a panic and lock down the streets. You will never return to your ship."

The boy turned his head, focusing on the arrival of a grand procession onto the Span. At its center a carriage rolled with a magnificent escort. Flags and banners waved, each with the king's crest of a single crimson rose. As he approached the center platform, trumpets announced the arrival of a king. Franque ignored the woman, took aim, and waited.

Gretchen tried another approach, one not tried in any of the scenarios she envisioned. She told him the truth. "Either you or your brother is the son of a king, destined for power over the sea. Wouldn't you like to know which one?"

"Nice try. We already know we're the sons of Braen Braston, the exiled prince who never attained the throne. He chose piracy instead." Franque leaned his cheek against the wooden stock and breathed deeply to steady his nerves. "Neither of us will ever be a king."

"Half right," she admitted, "but close. One of you is the son of Braen, the other is the unwanted spawn of his brother Skander."

"I don't know much about *him*," Franque admitted disinterested. But then the wording gave him pause. "Wait," he said, "we're twins, so how can we have two separate fathers?"

"Because Eusari is only mother to one of you." This troubled the boy, and Gretchen could see she struck a nerve. She went on. "Eusari bore one child on the night you were born. Several minutes after, the Queen of Fjorik bore another."

The boy stated squinted his eye and stared death down upon the king in the carriage.

"Nine months before one of you were born, the queen arrived on my mother's doorstep. She pounded on the oak and cried out until I answered. I was only a child, younger than you are now."

"What did she want?" Franque asked quietly. His right forefinger had relaxed, extended past the trigger and waited for more.

"She demanded a way to end pregnancy, but it was too late. Either you or your brother had taken hold in her uterus, and motherhood was certain. She was advised to convince Braen the child was his and left Fjorik on the early tide."

"So what? Are you suggesting my mother had her killed after birthing a prince, and claimed that child as her own?"

"No. Eusari recognized Braen's claim over Skander's as it hatched from her own womb, and placed you above your brother."

"Why?"

"Skander had his... well, problems. We won't get into those."

"I love my brother. I won't interfere if he's the heir to Fjorik."

"That's just it. He isn't. But the throne doesn't matter. What's important is which of you is the true son of Esterling, and which is the son of Andalon. The question is which of you is actually latent with the power over water."

Franque gripped the rifle angrily, staring down the sights and trembling as he aimed the barrel at a crown. "You speak riddles, and I'm tired of the delay. I'm here to avenge him, no matter which he truly fathered."

"One of you is a prophesied child who could destroy a continent. No... *will* destroy one. My father saw that clearly."

"Neither Krist nor I have that much power." Franque began to squeeze, breathing out his anxiety and steadying his finger.

Gretchen panicked. She had led him to certain success. "One or both of you craves a life at sea. It draws you, calling you away from the continent and out over deeper waters. It's an obsession, and that's part of the Braston curse."

Franque released the trigger, thankfully in time to change fate.

"It's you, isn't it?" she demanded.

"No, I... I don't know," he admitted with a gasp.

"Both Braston brothers commanded the seas, walked upon them, drew them forth, and rained storms upon dry land. One of you is the destroyer and, no matter which it is, he must not succeed."

"You speak of witchcraft. What good is any of this speculation? One of us is of Braen? The other from this Skander? So what? Leave Krist and me out of this. Neither of us knows the truth, so Eusari is our mother! We care not about fate, and both of us are agreed this king shall die!"

"For what? Killing Braen Braston? What if Skander was the prophesied, and Amash knew it? That alone suggests you cannot interfere."

Franque laid down the rifle. His pause gave Gretchen time to breathe.

"What shall we look for?" the boy finally asked. "What traits will this prophesied possess?"

Gretchen drew another breath; it had been many years since her father forced her to recite the lines. He had been convinced at the time the prophecy was fulfilled, but learned later it wasn't so. In his haste, conclusion was forced, but true prophecy cannot be rushed.

She spoke slowly and deliberately.

"From the corners of Andalon children awaken,
Remembering not their past nor the powers that slumber.
The pain of their suffering increases with numbers.
Come, witness the birth of their salvation!
Rise the Kraken from the depths,
Dealing destruction and slaughter.
Watch him destroy our legacy.
On land the monster roars and walks.
Death surrounds in light and shadow,
Destroy the seed before it roots.
All forces of nature have awakened,
Chaos sown without distinction.
No longer controlled by boundaries,
Siblings consume each other.
Emotions of water but born of land,
Lord of beast and friend of man.
Pain and suffering early known,
Raised a King without a crown.
Life of Misery, Death not binding."

Franque listened, but let out a laugh after her recitation had finished.

"That? You offer *that* as a reason not to kill my father's murderer?"

Gretchen faltered. The words had meant so much to her, were a *part* of her as she entered womanhood, maybe even before. That this boy simply laughed them off lifted a veil she never knew clouded her mind. Suddenly the prophecy felt silly, any meaning behind it forced.

Franque again focused on the forward sight of the weapon. After a brief moment he let out a sigh and tossed his rifle aside. "The opportunity is missed," he cursed.

Gretchen leaned over the side and watched as the king and his entourage disappeared around a corner. She let out all the air she had held during this definitive night. The fight was over, ended by distraction.

"Tell me more about this Skander," Franque said, "and what to look for. What does it mean, this Kraken?"

"The brothers Braston each wielded power over water. The sea fueled their rage into uncontrollable anger that eventually consumed their minds with madness. One or both of you may have inherited this curse of destruction. It may begin simply as a desire to be around water, or grow into an ambition to sail upon the ocean, but will eventually grow into a deeper connection with the life teeming below the surface and eventually the water itself."

Worry entered Franque's face, lining it deeply in the moonlight. "Well," he suddenly said, shaking off imaginary cold. "None of that applies to him or me. Neither asked to be forced into this crew and, so far, the trip has done nothing but fuel an insatiable yearning for home."

"Braen and Skander brooded as well," she said, watching for more reaction.

"I've got to go," the boy decided, standing without even a glance toward the rifle. He left it and Gretchen behind, hurrying toward the stairs leading downward to the city below the Span.

I saw it, though, she thought as he pushed his way past. *He's frightened one of them indeed will turn out like their fathers.* She had come no closer to certainty in determining which brother had the power, but the king had survived to fulfill his final duties to her master.

Franque nearly stumbled in his rush to the waterfront. Midnight was nigh and there was no way to know how angry Boats would be if he returned to *She Wolf* first. Thoughts raced as he made his way downward, thinking about all the times the brothers played in the river as boys and of how he had craved a life at sea.

She was testing me, he knew, *watching for a reaction and suspecting I'm the one!*

He paused as a crowd of men joyfully swayed and sang a chanty up ahead. Were they part of his crew? He could not tell in the darkness but decided to press close and use them for cover. None of them seemed to know or care he trailed behind, lost in their merriment and relishing their few hours ashore.

One of them finally noticed, turning a pair of appraising eyes toward the newcomer. Franque recognized they belonged to Ben Thompson, the quartermaster. The officer raised an eyebrow and Franque shrugged.

"What were you doing in town?" Ben demanded quietly. "If Boats finds out, he'll skin your back across the keel."

"Looking for a doctor," Franque lied. "My brother's worse."

"Bad enough to risk Boats' wrath? In that case you should have told me sooner. We're setting sail within the hour."

"Boats locked us in berthing, and everyone was gone by the time I got free."

"I see," Ben muttered.

"Francis!" a voice screamed from the forecastle waiting up ahead. "Where's that blimey Francis?" Boats demanded. "I swear he's jumped ship and deserted!"

"Quick!" Ben commanded. "Smitty, play drunk!"

"But I dun hafta play at it, Ben! I'm toasted!"

"Grab Smitty under the arms, Franque, and sweep that leg," Ben explained. "We'll give you a ride up the brow, Smitty!"

Franque did as he was told, and they lifted the carpenter into the air.

"Look at me!" Smitty cried out as he suddenly floated into the air on their arms, "I'm the King of Andalon!"

The men all turned and laughed except Boats who peered over the side angrily. "What's he doing with you?" he demanded of the quartermaster.

"I needed a sober hand to help round up the drunks, and he was the only able body onboard. Interesting how I found him locked and left behind, isn't it?"

"He was where *I* wanted him!" the boatswain growled. "Don't ever take one of my hands again, not without my permission!" Turning to Franque he roared, "Drop that fool and heave to! We're casting off soon!"

"Aye, Boats," Franque looked around. Krist was on the lee deck hauling a basket of rat guards. He swayed unsteadily, but managed a nod for his brother. "Right away," he said again, passing along his own nod of thanks to the quartermaster. Ben only frowned and walked away.

After a thorough muster, *She Wolf* shoved off and headed down river toward Diaph and, eventually, the open sea.

CHAPTER TWENTY-TWO

Eusari swore she'd never return to Eston, yet that dreaded Span loomed just ahead. It reeked with the vile filth of a city piled on top of itself and stood high above the rest of the empire, flaunting its sense of superiority. Money, politics, thievery, corruption, and pain lived in this place, and she wanted nothing to do with it. But beneath its shadow of greed, a sign of absolute freedom rested—tied off to piers and awaiting their crews to set them free upon the waters of the world. She missed sailing, had forgotten how strong the ocean called, no matter her strong connection to nature and dry land.

She scanned the scores of sailing vessels for a single ship, the one she'd lost so long ago. *He stole it,* she recalled, though never really cared until now. She had shrugged off the mutiny then, focused on her mission to protect the world her son was about to be born into. What Jacque had done then was a blessing, ending the chapter of her life upon the sea. It had begun when she was very young, barely a teen and stolen from her family by those cursed raiders from the north. *He* was there at the time, that man who deserved her vengeance. He earned it here, in this city, but not in the way she had planned. Braen had stayed her hand.

"She isn't here," she told her first mate.

"No. Several days ahead of us, their business here was swift."

"So on to Diaph after presenting Robert? I spend a night and we'll be on our way."

Peter nodded.

It felt good to stand beside him once more. He was beating the addiction, reeking less of the rum every day and trembling less.

"I never thought I'd return here," she admitted.

"I never thought I'd be beside you again."

"You never left."

He turned at this, a slight tear forming as he met her gaze. "You mean that?" he asked.

"You were the closest thing to a father I'd ever found since losing my own, and love for a man like that never dies."

"I loved you the same, you're the child I never raised."

"You don't raise children upon the sea," she noted. "For that you must step upon dry land."

"Dry. I'm dryer now than I've been in my life, thanks to you."

It was her turn to nod. It was the least she could do for her first mate and closest friend besides Braen. "I miss him," she said. "This is where it happened."

"I'm sorry I wasn't here to step in front."

"I would never have forgiven you that, isn't it strange?"

"No. That's the thing with love and family. Forgiveness *must* come or else it's wasted."

"You always provided me wisdom. I wish you had been there, all these years."

"I won't be around many more, let's cherish what we have."

Eusari nodded. She cherished this moment already. "Find us a good berth," she commanded, "one with ready egress but easy to reach if pursued."

"You don't trust the king?"

"I trust him as much as any other man I've met, save you and him and one other." But there *was* another, once, the betrayer, the despicable. If she'd ever run across his face again, she'd know it, and would mark him for the gods. "You have the helm, Peter. I'm going below to prepare."

Robert was surprised his mother chose a carriage to ride to the palace. He'd always assumed she'd avoid such extravagance given a choice, but she proved him wrong. Dressed in a stunning gown, she starkly appeared a different side of the coin from the woman who commanded her ship. *Reprisal* and Eusari bore death and destruction, but the woman in the evening gown carried deceit far worse than her blades. She even smiled as they approached the rose garden.

"Your grandmother planted these," she explained. "I was quite busy the first time I saw them, too much so to appreciate what she did for this city. Despite her faults she loved this city, if not the people."

Robert took more notice of the roses here and all around the city. The vines crawled upward on nearly every building, blooming with color that seemed to offer brightness and hope where most would expect decay and poverty. The presence of so much beauty truly changed the mood of the people walking around when compared to Logan and home. "Was she a good woman? My grandmother?" he asked.

"Good woman? No, not at all. Excellent queen, from what I've gathered, but, from our brief encounter I wouldn't venture to say she was good. She doted on the wrong son and certainly overlooked your father. He was Andalon's best bet for success, but she found him... weaker than she would have preferred. She never truly understood Robert."

"Did you know him?"

"Only for a brief time during the war, but Amash knew him intimately and will tell you more."

"Can I trust him, this king?"

"I think so. I did, and so did someone very special to me. He was a wonderful judge of character. But Robert, your life is about to become very confusing rather quickly. You are my son, despite not giving birth to you, and, as your mother, I offer you counsel as a future king. Heed it as the most important truth regarding your role."

"I love you too, Mother, of course. What is it you'll have me know?"

"Never trust a politician. If one is speaking, they've already schemed behind some grimy door concealing their motives. Each deal benefits them directly or those around them supporting a different purpose than for the people they represent."

"Can't we simply weed out the corrupt and replace them with honest men and women who care?"

"I wish it were that simple. Power breeds corruption, and there's no way around that. Your role must always be to find balance, mitigate their impact upon any large swing of the pendulum, and always consider the needs and wants of your people as *they* see it, not these schemers wearing sheep's clothing."

"So, basically trust no one?"

"You will eventually build your cadre of trust, and then keep it *very* close. Trust your heart when you cannot believe your ears. You've already lost if you forget this advice."

"Lost what, exactly?"

"Freedom of the people to live and, along with it, their liberty. Once those ideals are muddied for political gain, they soon depart from the people entirely and you have lost their trust."

"Thank you, Mother."

"I love you, Robert, with all my heart. You *will* make a wonderful king and certainly not because I raised you for the role."

"You raised me well."

"I made mistakes with each of you, just as Flaya did with Tara."

His face betrayed sadness and loss at mention of her name. "I miss her so much. Should I give up pursuing her?"

"Follow your path and let her follow hers. If it's meant to be, you will find each other again."

"Her mother's strict, and her path may not be her own."

"I knew nothing about parenting, Robert, when I became mother over all of you children. My own childhood was wonderful but sheltered. My father was a constable and well-off, so my mother was home with us all the time. But that ended at the worst of times for me, just as I became a woman. I was thirteen summers when raiders stripped away my childhood. Taken and destroyed, I no longer remembered my past because the present was too terrifying."

Eusari held up her hands, so deeply scarred in patterns of tight rows and angles. Whatever had harmed the skin between fingers, upon her palms, wrists, and forearms must have been painful both physically and emotionally to endure. The children had rarely asked her about them, and when they did she would simply explain them as a part of her she had decided to set free from captivity.

"Robert, there's an age old question regarding humanity and why people behave the way they do. The answer, some say, pertains to the role of a child's nature by birth, that they are a product of who their parents were. In that regard failure or success is inescapable, predetermined and creating an endless cycle of both good and bad."

"But children don't always act like their parents. Tara, for instance, is *nothing* like her mother," he argued.

"Yet, her mother claims she's *exactly* like her father," Eusari pointed out.

"I see," Robert still had doubts, "but doesn't situation play a role? Tara wasn't raised around the same culture as Flaya."

"That's very true and presents the other side of the argument. How children are nurtured also plays a role. I once knew two men, bred by the same parents and raised in exactly the same manner in nearly every regard except one. For some reason the mother favored one over the other and punished the younger harshly, raising him with constant criticism and fierce reprimand. Both men inherited her anger, but one had learned to manage it while the other gave in to the point it grew into madness."

"How awful." Robert tried to imagine if his father, King Robert, had experienced the same, if she spoke now of him and his brother Marcus. Their feud was the reason for the Brother's War.

"I just told you my childhood was ripped from me, but that's not entirely true. The truth is *I* was stolen, sold to cruel men, and forced to endure trauma no young person ever should. While I had once been on a path toward success, and living out the values of my parents, I took a sharp turn and sought darkness in the forms of hatred, resentment, and revenge. I no longer remembered my past because I chose not to. I ripped it out and hid it away, buried it deeply in a feeble attempt to preserve the only part of me I viewed as good. I essentially became the darkness, and it surrounded me always."

"But not now. You're good, a wonderful mother to us who taught us love and forgiveness."

"Those are values I relearned along the way with the help of a very special man, the one who had learned to understand and control his own anger and hatred—the brother *not* consumed by madness. Without him

I never would have found the seed my parents had planted, and he taught me how to find it in my heart and nurture its growth. I tried to instill those values in you, Franque, and Krist, to aid you on your own paths wherever they led."

Robert laughed at the thought of his brothers. "Who was their father? Was it this man you speak of?"

"Yes, Braen was nothing at all like the monster the legends have painted. They blurred his bad in with the good, then confused facts surrounding his brother."

"Is it true the king killed him?"

"The person Amash killed was *not* my Braen. That man had died long before."

Robert thought long for a moment, then understood her meaning for telling him this. "I'm neither my father nor my mother, but may resemble one or both at times. I'm also not you, but have those seeds you planted to guide me. I'm about to begin a path that's darker than any I've ever ventured, even considering what I've experienced this past week. If I forget those values you taught me, I will bury them deep and become something I never intended."

"You have always been so wise, Robert, and that truly comes from your father, the true king. Hold onto that sweet compassion, but do not trust everyone so easily. That was his biggest flaw. Eventually it overshadowed his strengths and led to his death."

"I'll remember, Mother."

"Good. Now let's hope Franque and Krist remember those values as well. I've some idea what they're going through, and I intend to put an end to their suffering before it gets too far. They each have a lot of their father in them, the darkest, most dangerous aspects of him, but they too trust too easily."

"During the voyage, I noticed you changed, Mother. You're different than the woman who raised me, I see a fighter in you now, and it terrifies me."

"That was intentional. If I'm to rescue your brothers, I must find the woman I was before I met Braen. I must be the darkness and wield revenge with impunity. But I feel I've forgotten what that woman was like. It's been so long."

"Is that why you're dressed like this now? Elegant and like a lady of nobility, instead of leather and fur?"

"Yes. I need a break from those memories the voyage shook loose. Also I must to present myself to this court to help boost the king's advisor's confidence in *you*. They must see you are of noble upbringing as well as birth."

Robert smiled, a small chuckle leaking out as he thought of Krill and Sippen back on the ship. "If they only knew how I was raised and by whom," he said, sharing a laugh with his mother.

Charleigh, riding alongside the driver with Marita and Sebastian, interrupted their brief moment. "The Dreamers know he's here," she explained. "They're sending a cadre to lead us into the palace. Amash insisted their escort will give Robert more legitimacy."

"Caroline's part of it," Marita added with a huff.

Robert watched as Sebastian patted her hand supportively. To both his and Sebastian's surprise, the woman grabbed it eagerly and held it tight. This turned the farmhand's face red with embarrassment behind the biggest smile Robert had ever seen.

Eusari nodded. "Are you okay with that?" she asked Marita. "I know you and Caroline never got along."

"I never got along with *any* of them. They were always so cruel."

"Because you were different than them, in a way they never understood."

"I was odd as a child," Marita retorted, "and even you rejected me."

"I did not reject you. I feared your power because I recognized how dangerous it was, and I feared what taking you on the most dangerous of missions would do to your mind. Besides," she added, "that's how you and Alec bonded so well. He was the perfect adult to attach you to."

"We needed each other," Marita said with a firm nod of her head.

Up ahead, a contingent of palace horses approached. They carried the banners of the Dreamers alongside those of the king. Robert stared up at the rose and his heart fluttered as the flag flapped in the breeze, yearning to share those wings and to fly.

"Why did King Amash change the banner?" he asked.

"Every ruler gets to choose their own. The rose often stays, only the eagle seems to come and go. Amash felt it belonged more to your father and left it off," Eusari explained.

"Lady Eusari," Caroline said as she approached, "the king welcomes you to Eston."

"Hello, Caroline," Marita sang dreamily, smiling and fluttering her eyes. "I heard you got tied up for a bit."

Caroline scowled and turned to Robert. "You bested us back there but don't let it go to your head. Cuyler will humble you soon, if you are to train."

Robert merely shrugged.

"There will be a ball in your honor, Lady Eusari," Bearnard added, "and the king hopes you will attend, despite the urgency with which you must leave."

"I will remain here through the night, so I will attend," Eusari answered kindly. She motioned toward Charleigh and Marita. "But my friends and I do not have ball gowns or accessories for such a splendid occasion. Might the palace provide?"

Caroline sneered at Marita, "Don't worry, I think we can find something to match their *station*."

"I doubt it," Marita said to Charleigh and they both snorted with laughter. To Caroline she added, "But the best efforts of the palace will do nicely. Thank you." This sent the woman and Bearnard quickly away, to the front of the procession.

"They really do hate you?" Robert asked Marita.

"Yep, always have."

"Why?"

"Jealousy," Eusari said, and flashed Marita a smile and two thumbs up.

"That," Marita replied giving the same gesture, "and the fact Caroline's nothing but a skanky tavern turner."

CHAPTER TWENTY-THREE

Tara folded the dough, kneading it with a pounding fist as she beat her muffled frustrations into the hearth beneath. With each punch she imagined her mother, cursing the day she dumped her in the fireside with the old woman. Every day since had been the same, wasted cooking, cleaning, or doting on the hag as if she were a maid. She scooped up the flattened mixture and sprinkled leaven, folded, and beat it once more.

"You'll waste energy like that," the girl warned.

Lina, Tara remembered. *Her name is Lina and her brother is Adsil.* "I don't care. It helps me pass the time." A kind hand touched her arm and Tara froze, suddenly regretting her anger toward her mother. She looked up, meeting the girl's eyes and trembled beneath their kindness. Her breath shook as it left her breast and the tears fell at once. "How could she leave me here?" she demanded. "With people who hate me?"

"I don't hate you," Lina offered.

"No. You pity me, the daughter of a shappan sent as a slave to your grandmother."

"You're mistaken."

Tara opened her mouth to argue, but the girl's sincerity deflected any accusation she could offer.

"I'm sure your mother has a reason, to send you to the fireside."

"She hates me."

"No. She wants you to become Pescari."

"I *am* Pescari!"

"Pescari is earned by more than just birth."

Tara paused, considering.

"Felicima did not choose us as her people because we are born under her eye," the girl explained. "She observes our actions, appraises, and decides our worthiness of the name."

"I don't know..." Tara began.

"What don't you know?" the girl asked gently. "Are you unsure whether you believe?"

"Yes."

"That is normal. As a child I saw her as nothing but a fire in the sky. Every child disbelieves until they witness her miracles."

"I am not a child," Tara protested.

"In the eyes of Felicima we *all* are children."

"I... I do not know her. Felicima is my mother's goddess, not mine. To me she is just that, a fire in the sky that warms us and greens the crops."

Lina took her hands in hers, placing them atop the mound of dough. "Do you feel her warmth?"

"No. Only cold."

"Come." The girl led her to the window, where several mounds rose in the sunlight. "Have you ever wondered why bread rises in the heat?"

"It's a process. Robert said it's because the yeast becomes more active and gives off gasses to fluff the mixture."

"But why rise better under the eye of Felicima, and not in cool darkness?"

"I... I don't know."

Lina pounded one of the rising loaves, flattening the center.

Tara flinched, not expecting the ferocity with which the girl had struck.

"This bread will rise, just like the others. But if I place it in a cooler place, away from the gaze of Felicima, it will rise slowly. Even the dough yearns to please her, rising triumphant beneath her eye."

Tara paused. She gingerly touched the risen mounds on either side, feeling the heat emanating from within. "Nonsense," she said. "They absorb the heat and rise, but that does not mean the sky fire is a goddess. The Andalonians call it the sun. It gives off heat, not power."

"Come." Lina, still holding Tara's hand, led her outside. "See the flowers," she commanded, sounding much like her grandmother. "See which direction they face?"

Tara gasped. Each bloom faced Felicima, basking in her glory.

"I once turned a pot," the girl admitted, "to see if the bloom would continue to grow facing away. By the next day it had turned, straining to bathe beneath the eye of our goddess. Felicima is real, Tara, daughter of Taros, and she is present in every aspect of our world. She leaves her favor upon us. Even in the winter our faces feel warm beneath her gaze. Only when offended does she hide."

Tara was not convinced. "I don't know. I don't think I ever will believe like a Pescari."

"Come." Lina again grabbed her hand, leading her away toward a kiln. "What do you see here?"

"A fire in an oven, a kiln to bake pottery instead of bread."

"And where does that heat come from?"

"The wood, it burns and gives it off."

"No. All heat comes from the Goddess," Lina corrected. "Watch." She set a pile of leaves and small branches to the side, then held a prism above the pile.

"I see nothing."

"I said watch," the girl snapped, again reflecting the command of Kailani. She surely was her granddaughter.

Tara stared and waited. Soon a spark ignited the leaves, and the kindling flamed. "That means nothing to prove your goddess," she protested. "Headmaster taught us the sun gives off heat that can be magnified by glass."

"Then I've nothing to teach you," Lina said sadly. "Perhaps my brother may succeed where I have failed."

Tara turned to find the girl's brother watching from the entrance of their hovel. His eyes still burned with anger, and his tightly set mouth prevented any comment.

"Go with Adsil," Lina offered, "and learn from him what you will not from me."

Adsil, it turned out, was the grandson of a former shappan named Cornin. From what Tara gathered, her father had killed the shappan, sending his progeny into exile on the fireside.

Though Lina had been kind and instructive, Adsil was hard and cruel.

"Why are you with me?" he demanded.

"Lina thinks I can learn more from you," she explained atop horseback. This was a skill she knew, riding bareback, as Flaya had forced it upon her from youth.

The man dismounted without comment, checking a trap and frowning at the way it had collapsed without snaring prey. His irritation was obvious, both at her and the lack of meat for the day.

"I'm sorry my father killed your grandfather," she offered. "I did not know either of them, so I cannot speak as to which was most righteous."

Adsil froze. "How dare you dishonor your father in such a way," he accused.

"I'm sorry. I did not know either of them," she admitted. "My father died before I was born, so I don't consider my doubts as dishonor."

"It does not matter who or which you knew," he pointed upward as he added, "the fact your father won Shapalote is enough to say beneath the eye of Felicima!"

"But your grandmother believes my father cheated."

"An old woman's ramblings does not make a case against Felicima true!" the young man snapped. "Whether or not he cheated or stole the power of the goddess is irrelevant!" Adsil added. "Taros won and Cornin lost. That was the will of Felicima."

Tara could not believe her ears. "You don't question whether the fight was fair?"

"No! I question whether we can question the goddess!" Adsil fumed for a moment, grinding his teeth and searching for words. When he finally answered, the anger had subsided. "I heard you admit to Lina you disbelieve."

"I don't disbelieve, I doubt."

"Grandmother once taught me it is better to believe in Felicima and die, only to learn she is *not* real, than to live like she does not and later learn she truly *is* the goddess. Vengeance belongs to her, and ignorance is the only chance a soul has at forgiveness. Once you are taught, and doubt fully becomes disbelief, she will deny her warmth and cast you into eternal cold."

"The Andalonians teach that fire is the opposite fate, that sinful souls are cast into brimstone."

"The Andalonians are stupid and so are the immigrants from Fjorik."

Tara stiffened. "You have them here? In New Weston? I don't trust anyone from Fjorik," she said, thinking of Greta.

Adsil nodded. "Rightfully so. They are a plague upon this entire continent, preaching about their All Father. They speak warped philosophy and witches walk among them."

"Witches? How so?"

"Have you seen the Dreamers? The northern snowcats have access to the same magic, only they use it indiscriminately to torture and force conversion to their religion."

"That can't be true," Tara protested, "the king and the Dreamers would not allow it!" But she *had* learned of the snowcats from Headmaster and how they aided the pirate Braston during the Brother's War.

"They're a cult, worshipping their *All Father* in darkness and making sacrifices to his memory. Whenever a child or young girl goes missing in the city, it is rumored they've been snatched by these Fjorik demons."

"Adsil?" Tara asked, hoping to both forget the fight with Greta and change the subject from cults and demons. "Will you teach me more about Felicima? I want to believe. I think your grandmother's words are full of wisdom."

"I will," the young man promised, "but first I must teach you how to snare game. Your test will include knowledge of these skills."

"Will there really be a test? What will it be like?"

"It's different for everyone, but I had mine last summer. I know the meaning behind my name."

"What is it?"

"If you do not know, I cannot tell you."

Tara watched the young man as he carefully retied the trap, bating it carefully so as not to disturb the outer ring. "Why do you live in the fireside, Adsil? Surely every generation of your family is not to be punished."

"No, we are not. In fact, my father followed yours into war with the Andalonians. He was there, when your father died and spoke often of the shappan's unrivaled bravery. But he too died not long after, during a collapse in one of the mines. My mother soon followed, a victim of Andalon and their endless supply of fermented spirits. She drank herself first into a stupor, then into weakness before the goddess."

"I'm so sorry, Adsil. How did she die?"

"She stripped herself naked and walked out of the camp, straight toward the Caldera of Cinder. We all assume she hurled herself in to join my father in the flames. Grandmother raised Lina and me, after that, but she is very old and will not last long beneath Felicima. We chose to remain in the fireside after our naming ceremonies until she no longer needs our care."

"You defy Felicima?"

"How so?"

"Weakness belongs in the fireside, the first visage the goddess views in her rising. Pescari hide our strength on the western edge of the camp, or, in this case the city. You defy her by hiding among the weak."

"How do you know I am not *also* of the weak?"

"Because I see you, Adsil. I saw the defiance behind your eyes when you defended my father, going against even your own grandmother who curses the name of Taros. But you are different, speaking with me honestly and aiding me even now."

"I *must* aid you to prepare for the test."

"Only at your grandmother's command, but even then I think you would refuse if given choice. Adsil, I believe I know the meaning of your name."

The young man laughed and waited expectantly with amused eyes.

"Your name means strength, both of heart and mind, but especially of duty."

Adsil's smile faded, and he again stared through the girl atop the horse. "Come," he finally said, "we've much to do and you a lot to learn. But as for being Pescari, you certainly are on your way if not there already." He climbed atop his horse and gently urged it forward with his heels.

Tara followed, certain she had guessed correctly.

CHAPTER TWENTY-FOUR

The past few days had been good for King Esterling. His mind felt clearer, and the voice left him mostly alone. Except for a few nudges, like the night on the Span when it told him when to move out of range of the sniper, it had stayed out of his head. He was thankful for that, even if it had refused to offer details like who the assassin may be.

He stood taller, with excitement adding a bounce to his feet and urgency in his mood. His friends were nearby, in his palace—dear comrades he had not laid eyes upon in seventeen years. Eusari had arrived, and so did Sippen and Krill. Seeing them would stir memories of card games, fine wine, and adventure. But most of all Marita was there, that sweet but odd child had grown up and he couldn't wait to hear her stories. No doubt they would entertain him for hours.

"Hurry," he commanded his body servants. Their meticulous actions needed speed if he were to make the most of the only night he had to reminisce. Tonight was for him, and he would arrive earlier than normal. This may be his final celebration if the voice were to be believed.

Of course I'm to be believed, it replied, wiping the smile from his face in an instant. The ringing laughter it left behind caused his body to flinch, pulling is arm away from a servant.

"I wasn't finished, Your Highness."

"What?" he asked, surprised to hear an actual person speak. "Oh." He presented his arm to receive cufflinks.

The door to his chamber opened and Percy Roan entered.

"Ah! Your Highness! I see you've already dressed!"

"No affairs of state tonight, Percy, unless war is on our doorstep or something else equally dire is imminent. I've a party to attend."

"Yes, my lord! The entire nobility is present and excited to learn why you announced a ball with two days' notice. The palace staff pulled it off, though, and the great hall is magnificent!"

"Wonderful!" Amash beamed. Though he hated extravagance, he had ordered none of it be spared for this gala.

"Sire?" Percy pressed, "when will you be sharing the reason you ordered such an event? You don't ever keep me in the dark, and I must say I'm perplexed."

"You will learn tonight, along with the others." The attendants finished fluffing his finery, and he stepped forward, holding his arm out for his chancellor. "Lead me to my party, Percy!"

Robert stood beside his mother, awestruck by her beauty inside the ball gown. Black and flowing, it matched her raven hair now washed and teased to gracefully curve around and accentuate the roundness of her face. It was magnificent, resplendent with sparkling emeralds that perfectly matched the hue of her eyes. She glowed with nobility, despite living her entire life either at sea or upon her modest farm.

"Relax," she told him.

"How?" he asked. "I'm shaking in my shoes. This is all too much." He fiddled with his ascot and she smacked his hand playfully.

"At least learn to look the part like me. Be in control no matter what. Speak very little, and remember your best defense against conversation is boredom." She paused, then smiled devilishly. "And no matter what, do *not* attempt to dance tonight, no matter how beautiful the asker. You must remain an enigma to these nobles, and each of their approaches will be to size you up. Give them nothing."

"That's tougher than it sounds."

"I know, but it's all you must do tonight. Don't give them anything about you, no matter what."

The line stepped forward as the doormen announced the Duke and Lady Winston of Eston. They were a proud house, one of the richest in attendance, or so Marita explained.

"How would *you* know?" Caroline demanded from behind her.

Marita and Charleigh both turned and gave her looks of exaggerated pity before yawning simultaneously and fanning their bosoms. Robert tried so hard not to stare at those, but, being a young man celebrating his seventeenth summer, failed miserably.

Both women were strikingly beautiful and were, in his opinion, the best dressed in attendance. Though the gowns were cut entirely differently, they appeared to come from the same bolt of royal purple silk. How they had come upon such expensive gowns in a single day baffled him since they appeared to be sewn into them. These were certainly custom designs and they each appeared to be true royalty.

Caroline, in her simply cut sky blue gown with gold trim matching a ruby set necklace, attempted to gain ground on the women. "Where did you steal that jewelry, anyway? There's no way either of you were given permission to borrow it... Oh, I understand, they're costume designs. I should have realized by the gaudiness."

Robert had also wondered how they were trusted to borrow such expensive jewels. Marita wore a tiara of diamonds weighing at least fifty carats. Charleigh's, though daintier to match her shorter frame, had that many as well as a perfectly set stone the same purple as her gown.

Eusari stood next to go in with Robert, but Marita, ignoring Caroline, tapped his mother on the shoulder. "I'm sorry, Lady Eusari, but we *must* be announced before Robert. Our station demands it."

Eusari stepped aside with a smile and waved them ahead while Caroline snickered.

Marita, with a wave of flair, handed her calling card to the doorman. He read it several times and scanned both women with wide eyed appraisal before cueing up the fanfare. Everyone in attendance turned as if the king himself had arrived.

"Noble ladies and gentlemen, please bow and curtsy in Andalonian acceptance of the *official* arrival and presentation of the eligible Princesses Marita and Charleigh Pogue, the youngest daughters of his royal highness, *King* Alec Pogue, the Supreme Ruler of Cargia and Emperor of the Unified Southern Continent."

Robert watched as the women each turned and winked at a shocked and disbelieving Caroline before gliding into the room with every eye fixated upon them. They glided. By every meaning of the word, Marita bore them upon a cushion of air and they flew upon it several inches above the ground. Every person in the room gasped and then cheered the spectacle.

"No!" Caroline protested. "That must be a lie! And that's not really flying! It's a trick!"

"Actually no, Caroline, it's not a lie," Eusari explained casually. "Emperor Pogue recently expanded his holdings to the cascading islands in the furthest reaches of the south. Also, with their older sisters all married, this really is their official presentation of their eligibility for Andalonian suitors." Eusari beckoned Robert forward. "You will enter before me, as you are the last announcement of the night. The rest of us will enter as minor nobles and merchants. The only presentation after you shall be the king."

"What do I do?"

Eusari handed his card to the doorman and whispered, "Walk to the back of the room as if you own it, then find a prominent spot to stand and await me. I will be right behind you."

He nodded, then flinched when the fanfare erupted once more. The stare given him by the doorman brought alarming uneasiness, afraid now of what the card would read.

"My ladies and gentlemen of Andalon and the gathered nobility of Eston, please kneel for the presentation of Prince Robert Esterling, the son of Robert and Sarai Esterling, and grandson of Emperor Charles and Lady Crestal Esterling."

The room fell immediately silent and every person in attendance froze in place. From the center of the ballroom, Marita and Charleigh spun in unison and genuflected deeply before Robert, sending the entire room into a wave as every knee followed suit. He strolled in just as his mother instructed, as if owning the room and focused on a particular spot in the back of it.

Hushed whispers followed in his wake, "The true heir!" some said.

"The imposter!" others exclaimed.

Robert ignored these and other utterings, following his path just as instructed. But he was soon mortified to learn the path he had picked took him directly beside a grand dais with two thrones set atop. He turned and stood awkwardly while simultaneously trying to appear casual. Unfortunately, he had ended up standing directly next to a very surprised nobleman.

The man appraised him, staring him up and down, before stating simply, "My, but aren't you a spitting image of your father but with your mother's eyes. It's as if I only saw them yesterday."

"And you are?" Robert asked indifferently, hoping to appear bored like Eusari instructed.

"I'm Percy Roan, of Weston, the Royal Chancellor of the Estonian Kingdom."

Robert panicked when he realized he spoke with the second most important man in the kingdom. *Act bored,* he told himself, yawning and looking away. He then waited like all the others for the king's imminent arrival. He felt the man's eyes burning into the side of his head but refused to speak with the chancellor. Thankfully, the monarch appeared quickly, breaking the nobleman's waiting stare.

The fanfare eclipsed the combined symphony that greeted both the prince and princesses, and the room once more fell into full genuflection as King Esterling arrived. He walked into the room exactly as Robert had, with purpose and direction as if the room belonged to him, which, in this case, it actually did. To Robert's horror, the ruler was headed his way.

The king appraised him, grinned, then placed an arm around the boy as he turned to face the stunned crowd. Every eye in the ballroom blinked as the king and chancellor stood with a disinherited son of a revolutionary prince.

"Hello, Prince Robert," the king whispered.

Prince? Robert wondered. *I'm really just a farm boy who yearns to be an engineer.* He, like every person in the room, waited for the monarch to speak.

Eusari watched as Amash began his speech. Years ago he was an eloquent speaker, schooled in rhetoric as well as knowledgeable about law and discord. Unfortunately, the last speech she had heard him utter had landed upon a tone-deaf audience. She prayed tonight's would resonate big with the nobility.

"Tonight is an occasion I've awaited my entire reign to announce," Amash began. "I accepted my lot in life with zero ambition, a bit of resentment, and confusion over how I had been elevated to lead the Estonian Kingdom much less all of Andalon." With his arm around a worried but composed Robert, he went on. "Some of you have wondered why I've not taken a bride since my ascension or why I have not produced an heir by other means..."

Eusari knew. That detail only she figured out, as not even Braen had realized his friend had died and was controlled by another. After the final battle had ended, the controlling voice had revealed himself to her. Sickened and horrified she had listened to his plan, but agreed, and promised him Robert. She cringed at the memory Amash would never share with her, dreading the moment she would hear that voice again.

The Deceiver, she thought unfondly of the man, the voice who puppeteered the king's movements and mind whenever it chose. She had heard his voice many times before and never worried, until it proclaimed itself from inside another before Braen's echo was struck down.

The voice speaking was indeed Amash's, and she relaxed.

"My announcement is the chastity I chose for myself as king," he said, "a burden sure, but a guarantee Andalon would never be denied its true ruler when he came of age. I am truly an Esterling, the son of Charles but not the heir you deserve. That heir is this young man, Robert, the son of Robert and my half-sister Sarai."

The crowd murmured and Eusari heard mention of madness or senility.

"It's true that I am the son of Charles, his bastard with the Lady Horslei, but not the heir promised to his true wife Crestal. No, that child married my sister and I vowed to abdicate my rule once the true heir reached his age."

The crowd muttered again, this time of blasphemy and betrayal. Eusari felt panic rise and reached for the knives she'd so cleverly hidden among various places in her gown.

"But I am a man of my word, a true Esterling in the sense I've kept my promise. Through my own valiant efforts at the conclusion of the Brother's War, I present to you the son of Charles' true heir, the lineage to supersede his bastard. I present Robert, son of Robert my half-brother, as my heir and successor. He will be crowned Robert I of Eston, the true Emperor of Andalon. He *is* my sole remaining relative and therefore already entitled to my fortune. He *will* become the King of Estonia upon my death or abdication upon the celebration of his seventeenth summer, whichever comes first. I decree that Percy Roan shall serve as regent for one year until the witan agrees Robert is ready."

The voice, Eusari recognized, lurked beneath Amash's own, and she remembered the man whom Braen respected but she barely knew. Though she hated to peer into a human aura, a gift she discovered later in life and sheerly by accident, Eusari intruded upon the king. Sadness filled her at once. Oh, that she had this ability when it mattered most, to recognize the animated husks that wreaked havoc upon the revolution. They, like this one, had set Andalon upon a path to this very moment. One that ensured the future of Robert.

Amash won't last much longer than summer, she knew. His offer of abdication would not matter; the Deceiver would ensure he died shortly after Robert officially came of age. *You almost fooled me,* she told the voice in case he listened to her. Of course he couldn't. She was very much alive and well cutoff from his link to Astia.

Amash finished speaking to the room and turned to Robert. "Surprised?" he asked.

"I am," the boy admitted shyly, "but the emotion of it has already passed. Mother prepared me for this moment during our talks upon the voyage. She instructed me how to act when you announced it. It still feels weird, though." He cocked his head, as if a thought had only just reached him. "Why would you abdicate so soon? I'm nearly seventeen already, and that's not nearly enough time."

"I'm dying," the king confessed in a whisper so low the chancellor would not hear. He quickly put a finger to his lips to keep that fact a secret even from Roan.

Dead already, you mean, the voice corrected.

"I'm sorry," Robert said, reminding Amash of Sarai, his sister and the boy's mother. Losing her would have broken him had he not passed first.

"Don't be..." The king slapped the boy on the shoulder encouragingly. "Rest assured, you will be instructed properly. Cuyler will draw out the abilities you'll need, and Percy here will teach you how to rule. He did a good enough job on me, so I'm certain he'll do well with you."

"My lord," Percy Roan said, feigning modesty. "You were already well-schooled in the finer points before I dedicated my aid." Leaning in, he ignored Robert and whispered scolds to Amash as if the boy were not even there. "What is *this*?" he demanded. "You're healthy enough to continue ruling! He is a boy, not ready at all!"

"Train him, Percy." the king commanded in a low voice. "He's yours to groom, as long as it's for Andalon and not your other schemes."

"Schemes? My lord! I swear I have none!" the chancellor protested quietly.

Amash left the two to converse alone, explaining before striding off, "I've been waiting seventeen years to complete a conversation with Eusari, please excuse me while I do."

Eusari watched Amash approach with that faraway look. She had seen it before, many years ago when the dead rose and walked among them.

The Deceiver addressed her directly.

"Hello, Eusari," the voice said pleasantly. It had not changed, still full of his self-righteous arrogance and a bit of boredom.

"Hmm," she replied indifferently. "So you deny me a conversation with my old friend?"

"You will speak with me and Amash will remember a wonderful conversation afterward, one full of memories of his adventures you never actually discussed."

"How long has he been a husk? That part I never understood."

"Since that day he died upon the pier."

"Sippen told me you were behind everything, but part of me found it difficult to believe. You deceived us, making us believe our work was for Andalon."

"It was *all* for Andalon, which is out of reach now from Astia. Their Falconers are gone and have no means by which to make more."

"Robert encountered Falconers."

"Those were not from Astia. Well, not directly."

"So Astia is not returning? You can promise me that?"

"Their ruling council fears your emotants enough not to try open attack but, eventually they *will* try again. Just not in the way they did before and not for a very long time. When they come it will be after Robert's reign, I've taken precautions to ensure that."

"For now."

"For now," the voice speaking from Amash agreed.

"So this isn't about how you plan to control Andalon?"

"This is not about *my* ambition, for I will be gone from this world soon. I will cease to exist the moment Amash does, too. No, it was always about Andalon, especially for the children. Thank you for ensuring all of them survived."

"So you include Braen's as well? Even if that child could be the destroyer of Astia?"

"Of course I mean Braen's, but especially Robert's, Taros', and even *Skander's*," the voice replied.

Eusari froze, silenced by the news. She had long wondered, wanting to trust Braen had not laid with his former queen, but always doubted.

"You loved Braen so much despite believing he laid with her," the voice said, edged with amusement, "and I was certain that belief would ensure the child's survival, so I said nothing to correct your beliefs. She had tricked him, made him believe they had, but your lover never betrayed you. Eusari, you trusted Braen in every *other* way, why did you never trust him in that regard?"

"In my heart I wanted to," she admitted, "but that's too much for a woman to believe about her man..." Though he had professed his love, Braen had loved Hester far longer than she. Also, he had never denied the two had reconnected. "Why did you allow me to think otherwise if you knew?"

"Nature versus nurture. I knew you'd raise the child as your own if you believed him Braen's."

"You're full of evil."

"What will you do with this knowledge now, Eusari?"

"Nothing at all. A mother loves her children equally."

"But *he's* not yours."

"Of course he is."

"Until he threatens your own," the voice explained.

"I love them both, because of your deceit. Is that why you used Amash to kill him?"

"You know better than that. Amash did *not* kill your lover."

"No," she agreed. "It wasn't him Amash killed."

"I ask you again, what will you do with this knowledge?"

"Nothing, you bastard!" she spat. "I'll love him as my own son, as I always have."

"He needs you now, yet you are here."

"I leave in the morning."

"Better you left tonight."

"I cannot."

"Then it's too late for *your* son. He will never be the same by the time you reach them..."

The husk of Amash turned as Marita and Charleigh approached. Both women knelt with broad smiles across their faces. The husk changed instantly into the man, filling with his own lifeforce and addressing the women.

"Marita! I was just talking with Eusari about our travels to Eskera! My goodness, you and Charleigh have grown into women!"

"Charleigh is quite the engineer," Robert said, joining them after leaving a sulky Percy Roan across the room. "She's contrived traps and weapons only Marita can use when fighting."

"Quite interesting," either Amash or the voice answered. "I would love to know more. Marita, do you still practice the way of the swordsman?"

"Of course, don't be silly," the woman replied. "Alec and I run a school in Cargia. I've elevated five masters who currently instruct twenty adepts."

"I'm proud," the king beamed with a smile, "and quite jealous." He patted his over-sized belly. "I've not been able to maintain proficiency with so many distractions." He looked around the room. "Where are Sippen and Krill? Did they come?"

"They are with the ship. We could not find the weapons we needed in Loganshire," Robert explained.

"Weapons? We're not in a war, and you're not a pirate any longer, Eusari. Why in the name of Cinder do you need weapons?"

"Devil Jacque," Marita sneered. "He pressed Franque and Krist into his crew unwillingly."

"Pirate hunting is unsanctioned," Amash warned. "I cannot condone..."

"I've a constable aboard, and we're all deputized," Eusari snapped quickly, eager to end the conversation. "And that's the reason we cannot remain another night."

"I completely understand," the king replied sadly, "but please visit again soon. And bring Sippen and Krill!"

"We will. And Amash? I have one more favor to ask."

"Of course! Anything for you!"

"I trust your Dreamers and your guardsmen to protect Robert, but he is alone without friends. Sebastian has been like an older brother to him his entire life. I ask that he be assigned as his personal attendant and concierge."

"Sebastian..." Amash stared unblinking into the room. "The boy, of course! He rode with Braen and protected Charleigh and the youngest Dreamers!"

"The same." Eusari nodded.

"I will instruct Percy to make it so."

As if on cue the man approached. "Make *what* so, sire?"

"Prince Robert has arrived with a personal concierge. He is to remain in that role exclusively. No one has direct access to him except through Sebastian."

The chancellor bowed deeply. "It is done, sire."

The women curtsied and Robert bowed his thanks as the king departed, aiming to settle the curiosity shared by every noble in the room. Eusari watched him leave, this shadow of a man who was once Braen's friend.

A husk, she corrected her thoughts, *not even a shadow. Braen was the shadow, but this man is only a glimmer.* A shudder ran down her spine as she added, *and I'm leaving Robert in his care.*

CHAPTER TWENTY-FIVE

The fog hung thicker this far east, lingering long into the morning and filtering a flickering sun. The orb shone cooler to Franque since they had departed Eston, and he yearned for the promise of its warmth against his skin once the bank finally lifted. Once a marvel, the heavy clouds had long lost its allure on the boy, complicating his work as a sailor and stressing him as it had the entire crew over rocks and sandbars threatening *She Wolf's* hull.

Taking soundings through the night, he had barely glimpsed Diaph over their portside rail as they passed. Without the many lanterns, he would never have noticed it at all through the mist. The entire city was built up from its harbor, a river town fully reliant upon passersby and visitors seeking respite before striking upriver for the capital. Of course, this captain and crew had no intention of stopping, pressing toward open waters and the bounty it offered pirates.

Franque yawned deeply as he leaned over the side, arms weak with exhaustion and powered by a mind as foggy as the river. The brackish spray caused him to shiver, feeling colder as it splashed against his face and hinted of a vast ocean waiting further downriver. Once they reached open water, all chance for escape would be gone.

We're broken, he thought, *a part of this crew forever without a chance for escape.* But not both of them. Franque's mind returned to his brother, asleep in his hammock. The headaches had worsened since leaving Eston, and Boats bragged about what he would do if the boy proved a malingerer. *Krist won't make it,* he knew. *He's going to die soon, but he's the lucky one to be off this ship.*

"Francis!" Boats screamed from the helm. "What's our draft?"

Franque shook free of his thoughts, staring up at the boatswain and not understanding.

"Gods damn it, boy! How much do we draw?"

"I don't..." he stammered, "is it different?"

"We're brackish, you idiot! There's salt in the water and growing denser! I need to know how deep we draw as we approach the delta!"

Franque stared at the painted stripes on the hull, blinking and counting as the boat bobbed with speed. He counted eleven stripes above waterline, trying to remember what Boats had taught him. Fifty stripes total.

"Thirty-nine!" he shouted, hoping and praying to the gods he was right.

"Aye, we're near max salinity, then," the cur of a sailor muttered. "How many burbles?"

Franque froze. That wasn't a term he knew.

"I... I don't know!" the boy screamed.

The men on the yardarms and deck broke out in laughter, forcing Franque's eyes to the deck. He wished for more time to learn the calculations and terms.

"How friggin deep is the frothy water, you imbecile!"

"Deep enough to drown your insistent arse!" Franque finally yelled, sparking the crew's laughter into a frenzied roar. No one had ever spoken to Boats that way, and each hand loved it.

Franque smiled to himself as he held the sounding line steady, hoping for a reading that could satisfy the master sailor commanding him.

Footsteps pounded as the seasoned sailor made his approach. A fist met Franque's chin, sending his breath and eyesight into a gasp.

"When I give you orders," the officer yelled, "you give an answer that's exact. Don't ad lib!"

Franque didn't mean to, but years of fighting his brothers and over exhaustion won out. He stood, hand reaching for the marlinspike at his side, brandishing it like a knife and growling challenge. "Hit me again," he shouted. "Come on!"

Boats stared back, well aware of the audience watching the display. "I don't have to *hit* you to force you to comply, boy!" he finally said, stepping away and moving toward the hatch leading to berthing.

Franque looked around, smiling at the cheering and jeering faces urging him on. Some hung from the spires and masts, while others were paused mid-work and waited. He felt like a hero for taking on the bully, and the fact the man fled below decks was proof enough the bullying days were over. He returned the weapon to his belt and soaked in the cheers. For the first time since leaving home, Franque felt invigorated by the prospect of going to sea.

It will eventually grow into a deeper connection, the girl, Gretchen, had said of the sea. Perhaps it was him possessing the gift shared between the Braston brothers. At this moment it felt like it.

The hatch leading below threw open with a loud crash and Boats emerged, trailing a pile of clothing behind him.

No, not clothing. Franque stared with unblinking disbelief, shocked by the image of his brother's limp and barely conscious body dragged behind the boatswain.

"Like I said," the lead sailor growled with a smile, "I don't have to hit *you* to force compliance." His foot met Krist in the ribs, and the slight groan did little to prove the boy clung to any life. He pulled back and delivered a second blow.

"Stop!" Franque growled, then rushed to his brother's side and knelt, shielding him from the attack. He did not feel the marlinspike leave his hip, too focused on Boats' rough hands on his lapel. Hauled to his feet, the sailor delivered a stunning punch that met Franque's temple. The ship and every face looking on abruptly blurred as the boy staggered.

Boats suddenly roared with anger.

As Franque's eyes refocused he gasped as Krist's hand held the marlin-spike, now stabbed deep in the sailor's leg.

"Boatswain!" a voice shouted from aft and all eyes turned. A very irritated or annoyed Devil Jacque stood before his quarters. Beside the captain was Ben Thompson and another man Franque did not know. He was dressed simply but smart, carrying a leather satchel and bearing the air of a gentleman.

Boats paused mid stride as he delivered another kick.

"What are you doing?" Jacque demanded.

"I'm disciplining the new recruits, Cap'n. One of them's a malingerer and the other spews insolence!"

"Is that the boy you mentioned?" the captain asked Ben.

"Yes, sir, his head was injured when he arrived."

"How?"

"I did it!" Boats growled. "It was in my right as their better to beat a little submission into him."

The captain nodded to the gentleman who stepped forward. Kneeling beside Krist he opened his satchel and drew out an instrument. Franque recognized it right away, the town doctor always carried one around his neck. This man used it to listen to Krist's breathing, then frowned. He pulled out another device, a sort of magnifying glass, and examined the boy's head.

"He's got a cracked skull," the ship's surgeon finally explained, "and has an internal edema."

"What's that mean?" Boats demanded.

"It means he's bleeding inside his brain," the captain replied, "and that you struck him too hard." Turning to the doctor he asked, "Will he live?"

"Probably not," the gentleman replied.

"What about *me*?" Boats demanded. He pointed to the metal protruding from his leg. "This cur just stabbed me, his superior officer, in full view of the crew! I want justice!"

"It's deep," Doc agreed, "and will heal, but there's a small threat of lockjaw setting in if it was rusty."

"Captain," Boats argued, "small threat or not, that means I *could* die and makes this an attempt on my life! I want him dealt with!"

Ben Thompson whispered counsel into the captain's ear.

Jacque stared at Krist the entire time as he listened, nodding and weighing his options. When he finally spoke, the words wrenched Franque's gut. "Striking an officer alone is an offense, one I'll never tolerate, but boatswain used excessive force and inflicted far too much damage on this boy. I can excuse the desire and need for these brothers to seek revenge. But stabbing him with a weapon is beyond justified, and *that* act will be punished. To which does the marlinspike belong?"

"It's mine," Franque admitted.

"Then you will both receive discipline in kind. Boats?"

"Yes, Cap'n?"

"How would you best extort recompense from these offenders?"

"They deserve death," Boats muttered, "but I'd be satisfied with a dunking."

Devil Jacque nodded then gave the order. "Bind their hands and feet and find two lines each the length of the ship from bow to stern. We're nearly to open ocean, and dunking these offenders will mark the occasion as one to remember! Square away the sails for full speed! I want a rooster tail for them to ride upon!"

The crew rejoiced at this, whooping and hollering their excitement.

Franque tried to resist, but the other deckhands overpowered him, binding and lashing his hands in front. Krist was barely conscious, and merely groaned as they easily tied him to the line then dragged him to the stern. Franque followed, receiving shoves, slaps and insults. The water behind the speeding vessel frothed and sprayed as the captain described, a rooster tail growing taller as the vessel gained speed and left the river mouth behind.

"They'll each drag three times," Devil Jacque explained, raising the ire of the crew. "Cast them full slack each time, then linesmen will haul each aboard. It'll be a race, see? The lines crew to win two out of three will earn a double ration of grog with dinner and a full ration of mead!"

This brought forth a cheer that raised dread within Franque. Terrified, he turned to check on his brother. He was awake and staring up, with tears in his eyes that pleaded for mercy. "I love you," Franque told Krist, who tried and failed to reply.

After both crews stood ready, the captain gave the order. Eager hands shoved Franque from behind and he tumbled helplessly through the air, down into the salty abyss below. Though his mouth remained firmly closed, salt found its way in, forcing him to gag and sputter more than breathe. *Krist won't survive this,* he knew, and prayed to the gods above his death would be swift and painless.

Krist gasped, his limp body striking icy water. Every nerve in his body reacted, forcing him fully alert. If he had the energy he would struggle, but having none proved a blessing. Without the strength to writhe and fight against the current, he bobbed like a cork set to soak before being laid out by the vintner to dry. With hands pulled outstretched by the mooring line, he dragged along his back with mouth open to the blue sky above.

He drew a breath, holding it as his shoulders rotated. There was a rhythm to the movement, and he recognized it from watching the line crews pulling *She Wolf* into Eston. When they heaved, he surged ahead, upward and breaching briefly before settling beneath the wave once more.

Gasp. Hold. Exhale. The pattern of it became natural and his mind focused on his watery surroundings.

He slowly rolled over amid an exhale, watching through the bubbles as a school of fish darted between him and the rocky ocean bed below. He yearned to join them, to be free of the pain and stresses of life on the surface. Everything up there amounted to loss, an emotion not shared by these carefree lifeforms. He envied the way they gathered for protection, huddled like a ball to appear larger to predators and moving as a single body this way and that.

He and Franque had always been like that, fatherless and dependent upon each other to learn their role in the world. Despite the chiding by Headmaster, they had learned to grow into men on their own.

Mother had tried, but she always stressed the same values over brute strength—forgiveness, tolerance, and compassion. *Like she ever knew what it felt like to be angry,* truly *angry enough to lose control.* No, Eusari was a saintly woman full of patience and always finding another way that excluded violence. *But she loved a pirate, the Demon from the North, Braen Braston.* She was a hypocrite, teaching compassion while attached to a brutal man of masculinity.

Krist breached once more and breathed deeply in, but lost that breath unexpectedly. He had crashed into a large form, solid and muscular, and following the same course along the ship's wake. *It had to be Franque,* he reasoned, and returned to his thoughts. *What* is *a man?* he wondered, if not strength and leadership? What good was a man who could not topple another with determination, wits, or brute power. Tolerance and patience would do nothing for him in a fight.

But he knew better. In this weakened state he lacked strength in every form, unable to defend himself or Franque and barely able to plunge that marlinspike into Boat's leg. He smiled at that memory, relishing how his wits had won an opportunity to properly insult the man.

He abruptly emerged from the water, hoisted into the air and dripping while gasping and spinning slowly around. Beneath him and further portside, Franque emerged in the same state of breathless shock. Above them, the crew hoisting his line cheered with victory, having won the first contest. But the true win belonged to the brothers, they had both survived the first of three dunkings.

The captain gave them each two minutes of respite, then ordered them cast over the side once again.

Franque briefly glimpsed his brother lying in a heap on the deck beside him. His eyes were open, that was good, but they were very far away. Distant or lifeless he could not tell. They did not focus or settle on him before strong hands bore both boys into the air and cast them once more over the side, laughing and jeering while offering advice on how to survive. He wished they would all one day go to the hells and prayed the gods would grant him the strength and opportunity to send them.

The cold water, now less surprising than before, sucked his breath and sent his muscles into spasm. This time, like the last, enraged the teen.

I'll kill them, he promised, and cursed each of their names. *Boats, Zane Rogers, Devil Jacque, Ben Thompson...*

He surged upward, gasping and exhaling simultaneously. This angered him more, yearning for revenge.

I hate them.

He sputtered and gagged, barely breathing between trips to the surface.

I'll kill them.

Franque thought about his mother, then about the words the woman named Gretchen had said. One of them, Krist or him, was special like their father.

But she suggested two *fathers, brothers who sired children with two women Eusari had raised.* Franque fought against this, just as he fought to breathe. *I cannot be of another,* he believed, *and neither can he!*

The line tied to his hands surged once more, dragging him gasping and wheezing atop whitecaps. Finally, the waves won and sent him spiraling down once more, barely sucking air before descending beneath the depths.

The lines crew dragged him onto the deck, celebrating their victory, but Franque's eyes focused on the emergence of Krist. It wasn't long, but delayed enough to tie up their contest. He held his breath as both boys were cast over the side once more. The next dunk would be the tie-breaker.

CHAPTER TWENTY-SIX

Robert rose before dawn, a habit from farm life made easier by anxiety and apprehension. He dreaded this day. Except for Sebastian as his concierge, he was alone. His mother would have already departed before his rising, eager to give chase after Franque and Krist. He understood the urgency but resented the timing. He wasn't ready for her to go, leaving him to political wolves and knives forever aimed at his back.

A soft knock at the door let him know it didn't matter whether he was ready for it or not.

"Come in," he answered.

With a creak the heavy plank eased open and a timid Sebastian peered in. "I think I'm supposed to help you get ready," said the former farmhand.

Robert shrugged. "What in Cinder's Crack is a concierge, anyway? By the way, I don't think you have to knock. You're supposed to be able to come and go as you please, you know, in case I need my butt wiped in the middle of the night."

Sebastian laughed. "That's where I'll draw the line." He pulled out a small parchment, studied it, then frowned. "You've got a full day scheduled," he warned.

"Is any of it mine?"

"Doesn't appear so. Seems you've a meeting with the chancellor in an hour, followed by training with the Dreamers. They even scheduled in your bath before dressing again for dinner with the king."

Robert grimaced. "I'm doomed to a life of politics and wealth. Dressing? I've no formal finery."

Sebastian nodded. "They scheduled that, too. After dinner you're to be fitted by tailors, so as... and it's written here... never to again cause offense to the royal chefs by failing to arrive in proper eating attire."

"Wonderful." His skin crawled at the thought of all the poking, prodding, and scrutiny he would endure the rest of his life. "Sebastian?" he asked solemnly.

"Yes?"

"You *do* know this isn't what I want, right?"

"I know."

"I wish I could leave it all behind, catch a boat to New Weston and spring Tara from the clutches of her goddess."

"Where would you go?"

"Anywhere," Robert said but thought of their friend Marita. "Maybe we can work in the vineyards of Cargia. No one would ever think to seek us there."

"I knew a man who tried that once," Sebastian said sadly.

"And?"

"It didn't work out for *him*, either. Duty brought him back."

"I think fate's inescapable," Robert agreed. "Sebastian?" he pleaded, suddenly feeling very small but a little less isolated. "Please don't leave me alone with either the chancellor or Cuyler. I'm not ready to do this on my own. Promise that, no matter what, even if we're separated, you'll find a way to be by my side."

The concierge nodded, suddenly fitting into his role. "I promise."

The meeting with the chancellor, it turned out, took place at the Dreamer Academy. The school itself was bigger than the palace, constructed across the Span. The chancellor had set up a carriage to carry Robert the distance, and he and Sebastian watched wide-eyed out the window while their escort chirped incessantly about the history of the new building.

"It's not very old," the man prattled, "only been open fifteen years. They built it right after the Brother's War, when King Esterling defeated the combined forces of Fjorik and Pirate's Cove."

Robert exchanged a look with Sebastian who shook his head at the man's ignorance. It seems very few people actually knew the truth about the king's ascension and even less details about who actually fought who the war.

"Every stone was mined from the same quarry they used for the Span, that's why it matches so perfectly." They were passing the center of the bridge, a place called *Unity Square*, according to the tour guide. "Right here is where I saw the Queen Regent Crestal Esterling bless every harvest from Logan, and also where the pretender king sentenced the former chancellor to die." He placed a hand beside his mouth like he intended to whisper, but added with a full voice, "The peasants tore him into pieces!"

Both driver and escort bowed their heads at mention of the incident, one neither Robert nor Sebastian had heard tell.

"The Academy actually serves as a bit of a war memorial since it was constructed on the site where the Dreamers and King Esterling defeated The Fjorik invaders. They say Braen Braston also killed his own brother at the very spot where the training grounds currently stand, though that detail is unconfirmed. Most of those buildings on the western side are dormitories and dining facilities, while those on the east and south are classrooms."

The space in the center, Robert could easily tell, was a green lawn serving as the training ground. He and Sebastian looked on as five apprentices practiced their craft. One, a young girl, lost control for a brief moment and several others blew outward from their circle. Teachers blew whistles and rushed to the spot, tending to wounded and consoling the visibly emotional child.

"They're mostly children," Robert observed, sharing his thoughts with Sebastian. "Why is that?"

"So were we when Eusari's crew rescued us. I think I once heard something about puberty affecting how and when it emerges."

"But I'm nearly seventeen, I'm long past puberty. Why didn't my ability emerge sooner?"

Sebastian shook his head. "You'll have to ask Cuyler."

Robert sat quietly the rest of the way, barely listening to the escort who now talked about the significance of each timber used in construction and how they were harvested from some place called Estowen's Landing.

Apparently the Dreamers had fought a battle there, as well. Sebastian knew of it, but refused to talk about it.

The carriage pulled to a stop in front of a large building, the tallest overlooking the training grounds. Robert recognized Chancellor Roan, not as elegantly dressed as the night before, but just as bald. The wisps of hair upon his head danced in the wind. He stood outside the building with a much younger man by his side, dressed in the robes of a Dreamer.

"That's Cuyler," Sebastian whispered, a mixture of fear and awe.

"Is he the most powerful? Is that why he leads the Dreamers?"

"He's the second most powerful emotant I've ever met," Sebastian replied.

Robert thought about this a moment, then asked. "Marita?"

His concierge nodded, smiling as if he thought of her currently sailing with Eusari. "She's always been the strongest. I once witnessed Marita splitting her mind twenty times."

"Is that a lot? How many can you?"

"It's a lot, but emotants shouldn't discuss such things in public. It's dangerous and tells the enemy how many are needed to defeat each one of us."

"I see," Robert replied.

Sebastian sat silent for a moment, then whispered in his ear, "Nine for me, ten for Cuyler."

Robert paused, then looked up with amazement. "So you're nearly as strong as he?"

The concierge nodded, grinning away with pride. "I was, but that's not to say he's not found a way to become stronger. But I think it's set. I've always been stuck at my limit."

"I wonder how strong my father was," Robert mused. He had hoped the man had been the strongest of them all.

Sebastian only shrugged as the carriage slowed to a stop in front of two men.

An attendant hurried to place a stool and swung open the door. Robert steadied himself with a hand on the frame as he stepped down, not as much for balance as to reassure his rapidly beating heart.

"Ah, Prince Robert," the chancellor greeted with a bow. "I hope you slept well and that your short ride was pleasurable."

Prince Robert, the title felt so odd. "I did," he lied. It had been a night fraught with dread. "And I found the ride informative, thanks to a wise and knowledgeable escort," he added with his best princely air. The man beamed with pride at the approval.

"Excellent! It's my pleasure to introduce Master Cuyler, Lead Dreamer." The younger man bowed to Robert, then gave a nod to Sebastian.

Good, Robert thought. *The respect between these two is mutual.*

"Prince Robert," Cuyler spoke calmly and with steady purpose, "I know you've been told you're to be trained, but I must insist that you'll never be elevated to Dreamer." There was a sharpness to his words, but also a bit of compassion.

"I don't know if that's good or bad, Master Cuyler. I sincerely want to train but never gave thought to becoming a Dreamer." The doors to the large building opened and Bearnard and Caroline emerged. Robert couldn't help himself and added, "To be honest, I've not seen any reason I'd *need* nor *want* that title."

The point was made and the lead Dreamer stepped away, swirling in his robes and making his way up the steps. "This way then," he commanded. "I'll show you to the conference hall."

The chancellor turned to follow and beckoned for Robert to follow.

Sebastian leaned in close. "Don't gall him, he's a good person despite ambition."

"Sippen says ambition is a sign of a *poor* leader." Nonetheless, he followed the man into the building.

Sebastian hated that Robert had chided Cuyler. Of all the Dreamers he was one to look up to. That's how he emerged as leader over the others besides his age. They all admired him, that is except for Marita. She never respected any of them.

I did too, she said in his mind, startling him out of his wits, *I respected you!*

Stop that! he demanded.

Stop what? she asked.

Reading my thoughts. It's not nice.

It is when you think about me. *You did that a lot when we were children.*

I most certainly did not!

Well, I thought about you, *and it's nice to feel this connection again.*

Her sudden arrival had distracted him, even if her words did not. He lagged behind the other men, nearly running to catch up, arriving just as two adepts pulled open two heavy doors. Cuyler led Percy Roan and Robert inside, but the guards put up a hand when Sebastian tried to follow.

"I'm concierge to the prince!" he explained loudly, hoping Robert would hear.

The prince turned and started to speak but the chancellor cut him off. "This is a highly privileged briefing," he explained, "and certainly no place for a mere *concierge*. You may wait in the kitchens, um... Esteban."

"Sebastian," the prince corrected. "His name is Sebastian and he *will* accompany me."

"Then this meeting is over," Cuyler said with power. He did not scream but spoke the words calmly and with enough confidence all three men silenced at once. "I have information to share that can only be heard by the royal family and higher statesmen. You choose if you want to hear it, Prince Robert."

Sebastian waited one heartbeat then two. Finally, Robert answered. "It's okay Sebastian. I'm sure you'll find something else to busy yourself with while we meet."

That was it, the signal. He *did* know what else to busy himself with, by keeping his promise to stand by his friend. Sebastian bowed, turned, then followed two other guards to the kitchens. They shut the doors behind him. This was to be expected, a fear Robert had earlier in the day and he knew what to do. As soon as he was alone he cloaked himself with the craft, disappearing into thin air. Then he waited.

Soon a host of servers scurried through a servant's door, scooping up platters of fancy breakfast dishes, juices, and at least six kinds of toast. Sebastian followed close to their procession, praying to every god of Andalon that Cuyler would not see him through the shroud. It was possible this man was a seer, though he did not have that ability when last they knew each other. Just to be safe, he hugged the wall and chose the corner directly behind the lead Dreamer.

The conversation halted the moment the servants arrived. The men talking to Robert smiled at the interruption, but irritation lurked behind their eyes. The prince seemed deeply upset by whatever they had said before, and his face burned red. As quickly as they had arrived, the staff departed and the doors slammed shut behind them.

"That's preposterous," Robert said angrily.

"It's the way it is," the chancellor replied. "You're training is merely symbolic. There cannot be a sitting king with the title of Dreamer!"

A side door into the room opened, and King Esterling entered. "I'm afraid he's right," he said, taking a seat and loading a plate to join them. "When Cuyler and I created the Dreamers, we vowed to separate them completely from the state. Could you imagine what would happen if citizens believed their king ruled his people with mind control, illusion, and forceful terror? If Astia did one thing right, they kept us from ever sitting an emotant on the throne."

"If that's what you want," Robert said, unable to hide his anger, "why did you force me here? I never wanted it. Don't want it now!"

"We believed you might be an emotant, true," the king explained, "but knowing and believing are not the same. We had already agreed years ago your training, if any, would be limited in nature. You may do parlor tricks, but nothing more. Think rationally—power corrupts, and *that* much power would ensure destruction of our empire."

Sebastian watched as Robert sulked, taking in the words but finally understanding. "I'd be a despot," he said.

"The worst of them," the king agreed. "I beg you not to pursue any more of your craft. What you've done already is enough."

Robert chewed his food, thinking and weighing his options before finally replying, "Okay. I'll limit my training."

"Good lad," the king said. "What else is on the agenda?"

"Sire," Percy Roan begged, "we must address the Fjorik refugee problem."

"It's *not* a problem. They are guests in our kingdom, and their presence has been mostly peaceful."

"It *is* a problem, Your Highness. Simply put, the entire country seems to be flooding across our borders and you're allowing them passage. They're dangerous—a cult full of zealots committed to their blasphemous *All Father*!"

"Oh, Percy. Have you forgotten the day the Pescari won Weston?"

The chancellor froze mid bite, setting down his fork and staring at his meal with a sudden loss of interest. "Of course I haven't."

"Yes, you have. You were there when a tyrant abused his authority. And how did Taros respond?"

"With anger..." the chancellor replied.

"No! With wrath!" the king abruptly screamed, slamming his fist on the table. The silverware and plates jumped as high as the four others in the room. It was quite out of character for the man, at least from what Sebastian remembered of him. "Taros razed the city and filled the crater with a lake! As long as I'm ruler, I'll treat immigrants with love and compassion, entreating them to sup beside us. We'll honor and learn their customs and they ours. Robert, do well to treat them the same, after I'm gone."

"They mean us harm, your highness," Percy argued. "Have you forgotten the Snow Cats?"

"Hmm. Now *they* were a cult, I agree." The king had noticeably calmed, but still appeared a raging tempest compared to the steady Cuyler. "But the Snow Cats were defeated, a distant memory to the people of Fjorik. They do not trouble us here, no matter how much you disagree." Turning to Robert, the king added, "This conversation only strengthens the reason you cannot train in emotancy."

"How so?" the prince asked.

"Skander Braston and his brood are the perfect examples. That man built an army of emotants, controlling and bending them to his will through fear and propaganda. Emotancy *must* be kept far away from the throne, Robert."

"I... I understand," the boy promised, "but what about the Dreamers? You have your own army."

"I lead the Dreamers," Cuyler explained. "I am their master, commander, and their law. We do not blindly obey the king and can only act on a joint vote of the nobles, the representatives of the commoners, the chancellor who leads the combined assembly, and also the king. Though each vote is weighted differently, the checks and balances remain intact. Amash or I can veto, though the assembly and the chancellor can override if they have enough unity."

"What would stop the Dreamers, or you, from taking control of that assembly?" Robert demanded. "With your power you could sway that vote or simply destroy their army and take it for yourself."

"We have our own government within the Dreamers. No tyrant can take control, not with each sharing an equal vote."

"See, Prince Robert?" the chancellor added, "You've got a lot to learn before you're ready to rule."

"That's why I called this breakfast," the king interrupted. "I want to discuss the regency after I'm gone." He pulled out a collection of papers. "This is what you've long been after, Percy, my last will and testament."

"Sire, I..."

"Save it, Percy. I've long known how it's galled you not knowing my plan. I'm sorry I had to keep it from you, and it wasn't out of mistrust. I had to protect Robert at all costs."

"Did you know?" Percy Roan demanded from Cuyler.

"Of course I knew. We were tasked with keeping tabs on all four children."

"Four?" the chancellor's eyes darkened. "So, the Pescari queen remained with Eusari after all? She did not return to her people as I was led to believe?"

Cuyler and Amash exchanged a worried glance.

"We agreed that you were *too close* to Old Weston to trust with the child's location."

"But I'm the chancellor!"

"You weren't at the time. Lord Philip was, and that decision was made in a meeting very much like this one," the king explained. "It was not voted on by the Assembly."

"Then tell me this, *sire,* did the shappan's bride birth him a boy or a girl?"

"A girl," Robert replied before the others, "and her name is Tara."

"What's she like? Is she quick to anger like her father was? Does she throw tantrums of fire and fart firebolts when she's in mourning? What's her mental state?"

"Tara is even-tempered, though she does have a rebellious nature. She is independent, not at all like the Pescari people in New Weston. She is kind, beautiful, and enigmatic."

"Beautiful?" the chancellor frowned. "So you're in love with her, this Pescari princess? Well you certainly can't marry *her*, I insist upon that!"

"Why not?" Robert demanded.

"She's not suitable," Roan argued. "No Pescari is!"

"Robert," Amash said quietly, "this is where I agree with the chancellor. The queen of Andalon cannot be of Pescari blood. In fact, I've been working on a more... suitable match."

"I don't want to be matched!"

"Kings don't choose their brides, and the decision must be made based on the unification it brings. In this case, restoring Andalon to its full strength."

Percy sat straighter. "Yes, King Pogue of Cargia has several daughters but no son heir. His eldest daughter is married well in the Southern Nobility. I believe they have a daughter as well, and she's only a year or two younger than you."

"I was thinking farther... um, north," the king explained. "There are several noble houses in Fjorik. Their civil war rages, and a warlord has yet to emerge and fill the void left by the fall of the Braston sigil."

Percy tapped his finger to his lips, deep in thought. "No, I strongly disagree. You've been following all four children, including Braston's sons. Robert should marry in the south, and those boys should marry in the north."

"And risk another Kraken King retaking the Fjorik throne?" Cuyler was no longer as calm as before. He seemed deeply troubled, thrown off by something he feared very much. "Just a single winter emotant is too powerful, difficult to control without a unified effort by Spring and Autumn."

"Robert," the king asked softly, "do either of your brother's show affinity for a craft?"

"Franque and Krist?" Robert chuckled. "Neither of them do. They fight with their fists, not with any element."

"Then I think we're all in agreement," the king said, pushing back his plate and whatever remained upon it. He had barely touched it. "Robert will marry a Fjorik nobleman's daughter, unifying the kingdoms and breaking the balance between Andalon and the Southern Continent?"

"Yes, your highness," Cuyler replied.

"Of course, sire," Percy agreed, albeit reluctantly.

"No!" Robert protested. "We're not in agreement at all!"

"Good!" The king proclaimed, ignoring the princely protests. "I've business to attend to, and then I'm off to plan my abdication."

Roan sat up, aghast at the king's insistence. "So you mean to? So soon?"

"I do," Amash replied, the relief heavy in his voice. "My time is done. But Robert will need a regent for a time, and that's why I've left him to *you,* Percy. You have one year to shape him into a military commander, a statesman, and a lawmaker. Cuyler will aid you, of course." With that he stood, strode toward his private door and left without another word.

Cuyler was the first to speak after the king departed. "Your Royal Highness, it's time for your lessons." A sudden gust of wind knocked three times on the heavy doors, nearly knocking them free of their hinges. In an instant the guards entered the conference room. "Please escort Prince Robert to the Autumn hall," he commanded. "His instructors await."

They bowed and Robert stood, eager to leave the room. Sebastian tried to leave on their heels but heard a whisper and paused.

"This won't do!" he heard Percy Roan complain. "It goes against everything we've worked for!"

"I know," Cuyler agreed, "and so we'll have to ensure a Fjorik noblewoman *never* shares his throne!"

Sebastian swallowed hard and hurried from the room, reaching the open door to the kitchens. He entered and threw off his camouflage just in time before Cuyler himself entered.

"I'm sorry we could not include you, Sebastian."

"No need to apologize," the concierge said, trying to keep his legs from crumbling beneath him. What he overheard bordered on subterfuge. With a smile he added, "I understood."

"Good. Then you'll also understand you're not welcome in these halls at all. You failed to be recognized as a full Dreamer and are banned from the campus. From now on, whenever the prince comes here to train, you will return to the palace to plan his schedule and lay out his clothing." Without another word Cuyler spun on his heel and departed, leaving behind a shocked Sebastian.

CHAPTER TWENTY-SEVEN

Tara rose before Felicima, eyes blinking against darkness. After weeks of practice, the routine had worked its way into her body. She stood, yawned and stretched, then slipped on moccasins before venturing into the predawn coolness of morning. Her arms bore waterskins and her feet carried a firesider toward the well.

I've become one of them, she realized, thinking of the woman her mother had pointed out on their first visit. The emptiness behind that woman's eyes must match Tara's, and she quickly filled the bladders, then hurried to begin her day.

Toil was the ancient way of the Pescari. While the city dwellers may have forgotten its meaning, the firesiders had not. There was meat to hunt and bread to bake, lariats to braid, baskets to weave, and so forth. Work ensured survival and, though firesiders were forbidden from selling openly in the market, trading men would visit at midday to shop for wares. These go-betweens sought impeccable quality. If Tara hoped to make some coin, she would also need to finish her baskets. Four sat completed against the wall of Kailani's hovel beside three more yet to weave.

But first she had to light the fire, check her traps, and prepare breakfast for the family. The brick oven waited as Tara unloaded her burden beside the unfinished baskets. She filled the hungry mouth with a blend of oak and birch, then built a nest of kindling in the center. Thinking of how Lina had lit a flame using Felicima's eye, Tara frowned at the darkness. She had to use the other method she'd learned and carefully struck a dull blade against flint. After several attempts and a bruised finger, she succeeded.

Tara eyed the horizon, taking relief in its darkness. There was so much more to do, and the work must be completed before the goddess emerged. She still had doubts regarding the deity, but she had learned to keep those to herself. She asked questions when she could, seeking to further understand the culture of her people.

The fireside tradition, it turned out, was more than mere doling out of punishment and instead served as the source of daily blessing for the tribe. When Felicima finally awakened from her slumber, she would witness the wretchedness of her people first thing. The widows, lame, and indebted would always be hard at work when the goddess rose, just like Tara did now. She earned for all the people a daily dose of mercy instead of wrath.

After ensuring the fire had roared to life and would continue to burn, Tara ventured out once more down the southern road following the river. In the dark, she found it difficult to spot the specific boulder she sought, but she eventually recognized the signal to turn eastward. This road, Adsil said, led toward the mines. He had been proud to point out this crossroad, well shaded and with parts overgrown, describing it as the perfect place to snare quail.

Tara scanned the horizon, finding the first glow of Felicima beginning to rise. She quickened her pace, checking the traps laid the night before and finding two birds struggling against imprisonment. Snapping their necks for mercy, the girl thanked Felicima for the nourishing heat they would provide Kailani and her wards.

A melodious cry interrupted the silence of morning, reaching Tara's ears and mournfully condemning the loss of tiny lives. She turned, expecting another quail, but found a surprising creature watched on. As large as an eagle, a different sort of raptor perched on a rock, cocking its head and measuring the girl with fierce eyes that nearly glowed the yellow of fire. Its feathers, layers of red and orange, lay flat against a skin that matched the appraising orbs.

"What sort of bird are you?" Tara asked softly, careful not to send it flying away or raging toward human prey.

It silently fanned its plume, revealing splendid colors. With a screech and a powerful beating of wings it rose up into the air, a spectacle of ascending grace. Tara marveled how the light reflected off the beast, shimmering and flaring under the rising eye of Felicima. The bird almost appeared to burn with inner flame as it surged into the sky, eastward to warn the awakening goddess of the human it had encountered.

Tara thought instantly of Robert, her sweet love who desired to soar with eagles. She finally understood his desire now, yearning to join this bird rising into the sky. If only it could have carried her off to her love, she would find happiness and rekindle the spark they shared with their first kiss.

No. She told herself, putting aside selfish thoughts. *I must first honor Felicima by learning my people's ways.* Flaya had been right after all. *Robert* will *have to wait.*

She quickly lashed the quail and tied them to her belt, hurrying toward New Weston and the waiting fireside. As she approached, an angry Kailani stood on her crutch next to a cold oven.

"Why didn't you light the fire?" the old woman demanded.

"I did." Tara peered inside. The wood, once roaring with flames, had completely burned to ash. "That's impossible," she protested. "I was only gone for a few moments, only long enough to check my traps. There's no way the fire burned all the wood!"

"More likely, you failed to sweep yesterday's ashes and forgot entirely to light it today!" Kailani scolded, placing a feeble hand against the stones. "It's obviously cold! If you had lit it I would have burned myself, or at least felt warmth." She pointed a finger to the rising light in the sky. "Felicima witnesses your lies, and so you are unclean. Do not leave the house again until nightfall."

"No." Tara did not mean to speak the word, and it's utterance surprised her as much as Kailani.

"Excuse me?" The old woman stood straighter, as tall as her curved spine would allow. It had been ages since she had felt such emotion, and she stared up at the girl with unbridled anger. "Do you openly display defiance as well? Here, on the fireside, and beneath the eye of Felicima? Your mother did well to bring you to me and, were I younger, I would beat this arrogance from you."

"I do not defy the goddess," Tara explained, but her defiance continued.

She would never be a true Pescari and Kailani knew it. She watched as the girl's jaw clenched and cheeks danced with anger. "So you defy *me*, then? Either way it's an affront to our goddess. Go now, serve your penance away from her gaze and maybe she won't curse you further."

"Curse *me*?" The girl let out a laugh, but the words which followed were laced with anger. "I've done nothing wrong," she said. "I'm dutiful under Felicima's eye, and your correction of *me* offends *her*! You forget I'm no firesider and don't belong here with you!"

Kailani froze in place, watching the girl as she scolded. *Her eyes,* she observed, *I've seen those before!* Every muscle in her body abruptly trembled with fear as she remembered. Once a dull brown, they had changed color to golden, burning like embers with her fury.

"You must leave my home," the old woman commanded, "now and never to return."

"No," the girl said again, defying the elder.

"Twice blasphemed is thrice punished, child," Kailani warned. "Be off with you, and make haste in your departure."

"So you cast me out of the fireside?" Tara spat upon Kailani's hovel. "I leave on my own accord."

Kailani smoothed her buckskins and watched the girl depart. She would be trouble, just as her father before her. Looking up to the goddess she said a prayer for blessing, pleading for mercy and forgiveness. Her people's troubles had not ended with Taros' death, and the daughter may be worse than the father.

"Kailani banned you from the fireside?" Flaya spoke the words as accusation, not with disbelief. She had expected this outcome. The girl knelt before her, begging forgiveness and spouting nonsense about how she had *tried* to honor the goddess. "You're an embarrassment to our people," the mother scolded.

"Then send me to Robert," Tara quipped, earning a backhanded slap across her mouth.

"The prince won't have you!"

"Prince?"

"That's right! Your sweet love is the Prince of Andalon, no doubt matched to an eligible arrangement by now. What? You really thought he'd choose a Pescari wife? No, Tara, women like us are only passing dalliances to Andalonian men. They mean to lure us, defile us, then leave us with bastard children."

"Robert's not like that!" Tara shouted.

Flaya turned away as the door to her apartment opened. Teot stood in the entrance, waiting.

"She won't take her back," the shappan said sadly. "We must move up her test, whether she's ready or not."

"So be it," Flaya agreed, "I am through with her insolence. Take her, whether she returns a Pescari or dies in the wilderness makes no difference to me. May Felicima judge her worthiness!" She turned her back on Tara. "I'm finished raising her."

Teot nodded and helped his great-niece into a standing position. Her muscles trembled at his touch, but her skin felt normal. That was good, with all the yelling he half expected her to burn feverishly.

"Come," he commanded and she obeyed. He led her outside where two horses waited, tied to hitch, nervously snorting at their bridles. To saddle was an Andalonian custom, not Pescari, but they needed supplies and also to move quickly. The Pescari custom would not do for this journey.

Tara took the reins immediately, eager to be gone. "Where are we going?" she asked.

"To find a goddess."

CHAPTER TWENTY-EIGHT

The river, though swift, ran slower than Eusari wanted. Even with Marita's wind filling the sails, the journey downriver proved treacherous, with many twists and turns along the way. They slowed for each of these, losing precious time in chasing after the boys, and the captain and her crew each yearned for open water. As the river curved around a cliffside, it widened to reveal a large harbor. On the northern bank perched a city.

"Diaph," Eusari muttered to Peter Longshanks. "Do you remember when last we sailed this harbor?"

"Aye, mum, it was at night under a full moon. You left me with Gelert, and he wasn't too fond of your leaving."

"Gelert…" the name left her lips dipped in sadness. "I miss him. Part of me died with him."

"I know, dearie, but it wouldn't be improper to bond another."

"I can't."

"You may need to. Your craft is worthless at sea, and it will not protect you. Marita is extremely strong as far as emotants go, as well as a blade master, but cannot protect you in every moment of the fight."

Eusari tapped one of her hidden knives. "I'm a fighter as well."

"Your blades are oiled, but pardon me for pointing out that you, as a weapon, are covered in rust. You've lived to see fifty summers, and, though farm life has kept you busy, you've not drawn those blades in nearly twenty."

"I hate it when you speak honestly."

"It's the only way I've *ever* spoken to you, mum. I will not choose now to stop, not when I've knowledge you must face directly."

Eusari nodded. "I appreciate that candor more than I'll ever resent the words, and that's the reason you're my first mate." She looked his face over closely. Much of the redness and puffiness had left him during the week, a sign the alcohol had departed even if the addiction had not. "How do you feel?" she asked.

"Less bloody awful than before and more optimistic as well." He slapped his chest. "I just hope the ticker holds up with all the exercise I'm getting. It's been a strain hauling lines with the younger men."

"Then don't do it."

"I have to. I'm first mate and must handle the burden in every sense, despite my age."

Eusari paused. She loved him like a father and hadn't considered how old that would make him. "Good gods," she realized. "You're near eighty summers?"

Peter nodded. "Well beyond retirement age."

"Peter?"

"Yes, mum?"

"I know a secret, and I don't know whether it's good or bad."

"Does it involve your boys?"

"I think it involves all of us."

"Are you asking me if I want to know the details?"

"No, only seeking your counsel as usual."

"That's why I'm here."

"Do you remember when we fought the Brother's War? When I told you there was another force driving the Falconers and Jaguars?"

"Yes, I do. You told me they were from a place called Astia."

"Amash told me Astia is no longer a threat, but Robert fought against Falconers *and* Jaguars."

Peter shuddered at their mention. Those memories were something everyone who fought the war would like to forget.

"Also, I'm worried about the others, those Skander freed. I fear Robert faces a war after Amash abdicates."

"He has advisors," Peter offered.

"He has Percy Roan," she countered, "a politician so well-versed in corruption he evades its stench."

"So this secret, dearie? How does it come into play?"

"The king isn't really in charge of his kingdom."

"Are they ever really?" Peter asked with a chuckle.

"No, I suppose not, but this time it affects Robert. You know I never wanted to be anywhere but the shadows. It took Braen to drag me out before and Franque and Krist now."

"You wish to go back?"

"Part of me does, but part also enjoys adventure. I think I'm happy to be out again. I think something bigger than us is about to happen, and I believe I'm finally ready to be a part of it."

"And after you've found your boys, now that your duty to Robert has ended? Then what? Once they've tasted the sea, they may not wish to return to the farm. Worse still, they may not survive this journey they're on."

"If anything happens to my boys, I would most definitely return to The Cove."

"Piracy, mum?"

"In the most malfeasant of terms."

"My, but that *is* a secret, and I shall hold it dearly in confidence."

"I don't know. I may feel differently after dealing with Devil Jacque. But, either way, that destination lies ahead." She turned to the sailing master and called out, "Marita, point us to open water and give us wind, lots of it—as much as this ship can handle. We've a stop to make before we find *She Wolf.*"

The woman nodded and the ship lurched as sails squared by her winds.

"What's our destination, Captain?" Peter Longshanks called out so the men would hear.

"Estowen's Landing," Eusari replied loudly. "I've business there, before heading south to Pirate's Cove!"

The crew let out cheers of approval and went right away to work.

"It's good you have business there," Peter whispered to his captain with a grin, then hurried off to trim lines with the crew.

"Let's only hope we still find my boys in time," she muttered, shuddering at the urgency in the voice controlling the king. *He will never be the same by the time you reach them...,* it had warned. "Be strong, boys, I'm coming," she whispered.

"All hands topside!" the voice commanded.

"That's us," Franque said to his brother, lying unmoving on the hammock.

"Drown them all," Krist finally muttered, barely forming the words but meaning every bit of the effort to say it. "I'm staying here. Doc said I can."

"Well, I have to go." Franque stood, inspected his brother, and thanked the gods he lived. Doc had called it a true miracle, and no one argued. Even the captain agreed Krist could rest for a few weeks, said he earned it by surviving the dunking.

Franque made his way up the ladder, emerging to see the entire crew manning the rails and staring off into the distance. Boats was with them. The boys were square with him, all apparently forgiven after emerging from the water alive—even if none of it would ever be forgotten. Krist was out of his reach under the care of Doc, but that didn't mean the boatswain would let up on Franque.

"Where's Francis?" he shouted from the deck.

"I'm here," said Franque, not bothering to correct the boatswain any longer.

"I've got to figure out how to use you during the fight."

"Fight?" Confusion fogged Franque's thoughts. "Who's going to fight?"

"We are," Boats said, pointing to the horizon. Two masts and the sleek body of a longboat stood out against the clouds. "It's one of those immigrant boats from Fjorik."

"Why would we fight immigrants? What do they matter?"

Boats shrugged. "The captain is guilded, so he attacks whoever he wants as long as the insurance pays the merchants and nobles. First mate said they're our target, so we hit 'em."

"Women and children?"

"Oh, there's fightin' men, too! Along with all their belongings and gold to start their new life with! It's a bountiful garden ripe for harvest," Boats countered.

Franque stared at the ship. Its occupants no doubt were doing the same as him, praying to their northern gods the sails they saw weren't hoisting a flag of piracy. *I don't like it,* he told himself, but there was nothing he could do. He was about to be part of murder and mayhem.

"Look at it this way, Francis," Boats sounded less irritated, and almost seemed to have respect for him after the dunking. "Those people and their ancestors made war against us and ours for centuries. They're no-good raiders and rapists during wartime and even worse now that they came over legally."

"How so?"

"Do you know how people like those no-good northerners will conquer our kingdom? They'll infiltrate it slowly without assimilating our culture into theirs. Once they're strong enough, they'll change the mindset of our children, planting seeds of rebellion against parents, the government, and even the gods themselves. They'll demand *we* respect their culture, all the while spittin' on ours. It'll take years, but they'll wait it out until the timing's right. Then they'll change the laws—little by little if they want or all at once in a single swoop. Next thing we know, just less than half the kingdom will be left staring dumbfounded and wondering why we can't eat nothing but plants or carry weapons to protect ourselves or our property. That's when Fjorik will let loose the true reason they came, and that's to rob us blind and erase our culture because our way was always better and they resented they never beat us."

Franque had never heard Boats say so much in a single sitting. He blinked at him, taking it all in and stunned at the simplicity of the man's rationale. It was true, Fjorik always hated and resented the rest of Andalon, but he always assumed it was the government instead of the people who wanted to destroy the Estonian control over the continent.

"Look, you fought against me pretty well the other day," Boats admitted. "I've still never been bested, but you came close. If it hadn't been in front of the crew, and hadn't been over insolence, I might've bought you a round to drink away our differences on the road to friendship." He pointed to the other ship. "Now we've got a fight coming soon, and it's time you serve our captain, this ship, and your crewmates with loyalty. You'll be part of the raiding party, those who grapple and cross over in the first wave."

Franque laughed. "Fight with what? You kept my marlinspike."

Boats shrugged. "You ain't gettin' that back till I'm ready, just to prove the point further, but you'll be issued a weapon by the armorer once we get closer. If you survive, you'll check it back in and maybe I'll give you the spike then. Now, go help the others prepare the cannons. There's a lot of work to do before the battle."

"Seaman Thorinson," a voice called from behind.

Franque turned to see Zane Rogers standing with Ben Thompson.

"Well, now," Boats exclaimed, "what does the first mate want with the likes of you?"

Franque shrugged. He had no guesses. He strolled over to face the two men. "Yes, sir?"

"The captain wants a word with you."

"Me?"

"Yes, you! Go now and make it fast, he's a busy man!"

Franque hurried away, nearly running to the door to the captain's quarters. He raised a fist and paused, suddenly afraid to knock in case this was a prank or set up. *From Boats, maybe, or the rest of the crew, but not the first mate and the quartermaster.* With a deep breath and a swallow, he knocked.

"Enter," came the single command from within.

The quarters were not elaborate, not like Franque imagined. The dark wood was worn, but not as badly as in berthing, and decorative. Tall bookcases lined one wall, with doors to hold items fast on turbulent seas. There was a bed, a desk, and a table upon which the captain could dine and another covered with charts and a sextant. The captain stood there, frowning down at a particular map.

"You sent for me, sir?"

Jacque looked up, and narrowed his eyes as if sizing the boy up or appraising his worth. "You lost me a hefty sum to the quartermaster."

"Sir? I don't understand."

"You lived. The sure bet was that your brother would perish in the dunking, but I took the risk. I said you would both die. Ben Thompson bet you would both survive. He won the ship's pot," he let out a laugh, "and is probably richer than me now!"

"I'm sorry sir, I didn't mean to..."

"None of that," the captain said with a smile, "I don't give a damn about gold. Gods know I have enough of it stashed in banks."

"Why did you send for me, sir?"

"How's your brother? Besides still living, I mean. Doc said he's certain to perish at some point, he's as shocked as me he made it through the dunk."

"He's determined."

"That's often a good thing. So your last name's Thorinson? I knew a few of them in my time. What part of Loganshire are you from?"

"Brentway," Franque lied.

"I see. There's plenty of your kin around there, for sure. I knew one in particular back in my prime. She was a beauty."

"What happened to her?"

"I've no idea, nor do I care. I used her to get what I wanted, that's all, but it's nice to reminisce about girls, isn't it?

"I don't know."

"Surely you left a gal behind, or at least rolled in the hay a few times!"

"I really never struck a fancy to one. I never wanted to stay near home and planned to hop a ship for as long as I can remember. My brother, too."

"I see." The captain returned his eyes to the chart. Whatever it was he wanted to talk about seemed unimportant now.

"Is that all, sir? Am I excused?"

"Do you have my leave."

"Sir?"

"You ask to be excused from a dinner table. You ask your captain if you have his leave to depart."

"I'm sorry, sir. Do I have your leave to go?"

"No. I'm not finished."

Franque paused, the darkness in the captain's tone had overshadowed his jovial and easy-going demeanor. Even Jacque's eyes had changed. They were darker with sinister undertones of danger the likes of which the boy had never seen.

"How did you both survive? Your brother, at the very least, should have died," the captain accused.

"I don't... I don't know!"

"Your name is Franque *Thorinson*?"

"Yes."

"But your brother is *Krist* Thorinson?" Devil Jacque pronounced the name as if it were bitter herbs or rancid meat on his tongue.

"Yes."

"A Fjorik name!"

"What? I don't understand..." Franque had no idea. His brother's name was unusual, sure, but he never thought of its origin.

"I know of one other Krist, a Krist Braston! The father of Braen and Skander Braston."

"I..." Franque stammered, hearing his father's name uttered by this man.

"Who is your mother?" Devil Jacque suddenly demanded.

Franque froze. Why did this man care who is mother was? *Is there harm in telling?* He rose to full height, a full two heads above the captain. *I won't tell him!*

"It's Eusari Thorinson, isn't it?"

Franque felt bile form in his throat and the urge to vomit overwhelmed his ability to think. *How does he know of Mother?* he wondered.

"Answer me!" the captain barked.

"No. I've never heard that name," Franque lied. The tip of the cutlass moved fast, slicing through air as it found its home against the boy's neck. A tiny drop of blood ran down his collar and onto his chest.

"The truth. Now!" Devil Jacque demanded, backing him against the wall. "Is Eusari Thorinson your mother?"

"Yes."

"Why are you on *my* ship? Is this her plot for revenge? She baited me with her two brats, the whelps of Braen Braston?"

"She doesn't know we're here," Franque tried the truth as he stared down cold steel into the captain's rabid eyes. He finally understood the nickname and why he was called *Devil Jacque*.

"Tell me more. Why did you volunteer for my crew?"

"We ran away to kill the king. We found out he killed our father and just wanted to get to Eston, but we were robbed in Loganshire. Our horses and gear stolen. Then we ran into this guy Peter Longshanks in a tavern. He tricked us into signing up for years instead of months, and pushed us down a trap door. We *woke up* on *She Wolf,* we didn't choose her!"

The tip of the cutlass faltered, quivering in what was once a steady hand. The man's eyes grew wide with what Franque recognized as passing fear.

"Peg-legged Pete?" The captain suddenly recovered, breaking out with honest laughter. "He placed you on *my* crew?" His laughter stopped abruptly. The fear returned. "That son of a bitch meant to gall me... but now this means *she* knows!" The cutlass returned to its scabbard. "If she knows," he muttered, "she's on her way here!"

"She doesn't even know where we are! She was arrested, probably still in jail in Loganshire!"

"Loganshire... She was that close to me, then? Hot on my heels?"

"She doesn't even *know* about you! I swear, Captain! She has no idea where we are!"

"If Peter Longshanks kidnapped you, and she finds him, then she knows."

"I swear, she doesn't!"

"Prove to me you were headed to Eston to kill the king!"

"I saw you there, atop the Span. I held a rifle, one of the fifty you had brought aboard *She Wolf,* and pointed it at the man's head."

"But you didn't fire?"

"No. I saw you there, not far away talking to a man with only wisps of hair atop his head. He was dressed in finery, *scarlet* threads that spoke wealth and influence!"

"Hmmm." Jacque considered his story. "But you didn't pull the trigger? Why not?"

Franque wanted to tell him of Gretchen and the horrifying things she foretold, but lied once more, this time more convincingly. "I realized that man, dressed in red robes, was more powerful than the king. He must have been an advisor, but the fact you spoke to him and not the monarch convinced me that *he* runs the kingdom! I think it's him who gave you the rifles to take to The Cove and who asked you to start a war with Fjorik."

The cutlass drew once more, this time jabbed against Franque's breast.

"My," the captain remarked, "aren't you a smart one! But wrong about one thing. The rifles were headed to Ataraxia, to sell to arms dealers who will smuggle them into Fjorik. We attack the immigrants enough, supply the government with guns, and *then* we get our war. Now, what will you *do* with this information?"

"Do? What *can* I do? We're part of your crew, hundreds of miles from home, and about to attack a Fjorik vessel. Boats told me I'm to swing across the lanyards as part of the boarding team. What will *I* do? I'll fight and kill my first man or men before *they* kill *me*!"

Jacque considered his words. This time they were truthful, and even the captain knew it. He had a job to do, the entire crew did. No matter what this captain's history was with his mother, they would fight alongside each other. The cutlass dropped. "Really? You'll fight with loyalty for me, my ship, and the crew? No matter what squabble I had with your mother?"

"Yes," Franque promised. "But Krist isn't healthy, not at all, so I'll fight for the pair of us."

"I... I believe you," Devil Jacque replied, laughing and again returning the blade to its sheath. "Tell me this, first. Has anything *odd* ever happen when either of you are around water?"

"Like what?"

"I don't know... just oddness."

Franque remembered Gretchen's warning, that one or both of them may hold an affinity for the sea—that their father... *Fathers, she had said...* may have shared that ability. "No. Neither of us. Other than the dunking, we've never even swam in it."

"How *did* you survive?" Jacque demanded once more.

"By sheer determination not to let Boats defeat us."

The captain laughed. "Then you really are like your mother, in more ways than you could ever know. Welcome to *She Wolf*," he said. "Choose any weapon you want from the armory, and bleed it well!"

Dusk set on *She Wolf,* the sky overcast and threatening rain, while she raced toward the slower Fjorik vessel. They had chased it all day and were finally in reach of their prey. The slower ship beat drums and blew whistles, a futile attempt to ready its fighting men to repel an onslaught. Franque Thorinson was a part of that threat, and he gripped his father's axe with a tightness that offered promise—one of victory.

The water between the ships grew frothy, agitated by the coming storm of steel, gunpowder, and screams. Franque watched as it swirled and spun against the vessels.

"Ready portside guns!" the captain ordered.

Every man on the gunner's crew ran to and fro, hauling powder and shot. The entire evening felt surreal, a thrilling reminder to Franque he would fight alongside pirates. As awful as that should be, he found it alluring, a promise of everything the sea offered. He felt alive.

"Fire!" The command came suddenly, and the retort deafened every hand. *She Wolf* rocked starboard with the concussion, smashing hard into the waves and sending a violent volley toward the bigger vessel.

Franque paled. The four pounders did more damage than he expected, tearing splinters free and hurtling their sharpest points toward the huddled mass of people watching topside.

They hadn't realized we meant to attack! The boy understood at once, as women and children rushed below decks to hide. All men left above deck were dressed in the heavy fur-clad armor the Fjorik people wore. Five of these warriors stood far away from the others, painted with dark hues of crimson and blue. They beat their swords and axes against their shields, while some savagely growled and bit until their teeth and gums bled with anticipation of battle.

Berserkers! Franque had heard of these. Krill had spilled the beans once, around a campfire, telling heinous stories about the most dangerous warriors Fjorik offered. *But on an immigrant ship?* Their presence made no sense at all.

"Grapplers!" the first mate roared. "Away!"

Franque gripped a tool with his right hand, sweating with fear as he let it slip downward to slacken the attached line. He spun it slowly the way Boats had taught. In his left he held the end of a long rope, with the coil held loosely by only two fingers. Once he felt enough momentum for the toss, he heaved the metal and loosed the line. Most of the others failed and had to haul theirs wet and limp over the side to try again, losing precious minutes in the effort. But Franque's found the rail, and he pulled it taut.

Now came the hard part, the maneuver requiring a bit of luck, a lot of danger, and tremendous foolishness. He stood, gripping the rope tightly and waited for Boats' command.

"Heave!" he shouted, and the grappling crew pulled hard until the ships closed the gap. With each heave the tempest between them shrank, until both vessels crashed together.

Franque stepped onto the rail then leapt, boots crashing hard onto the enemy's deck. He swayed, but soon the timbers felt right beneath the treads of his boots. A sword swung down and he moved, the blade arching mere inches past his ear. Thankfully the attacker missed, striking the wooden beam instead.

Franque grabbed his father's axe from his hip. It felt so right. He swung the head of it, sharp and heavy toward the fool who challenged. It met a shield with a crack, as fifteen years of chopping wood paid off, and splinters dug into a Fjorik forearm. The startled warrior stepped backward, eyes full of anger as she again raised her sword.

Franque steadied his feet for another blow. *She?* He wavered, marveling at a woman dressed in Fjorik furs and wielding an instrument of death. She charged.

Franque stepped aside, he would never fight a woman, from any man he would accept a challenge, even his brother—a stranger more easily.

She lurched, furious at his feint, and frothing at the mouth. He stepped aside again, but the tip of her steel met his ribs, slicing a line around his body. The salt spray entered immediately, sending a burning scream of panic into his heart. Thankfully it wasn't deep. Anger suddenly burned within, furious over his precious blood now dripping on the deck of a foreign vessel. He lunged.

Franque was a good boy, loving and loyal to family—especially his mother and even Tara whom he loved like a sister. He had sworn once, in a grandiose display of chivalry before his brothers, never to raise arms or fists to a woman. That pledge disappeared in an instant as the anger overtook him.

Never had he lost his temper so, ramming his shoulder into the berserker's breast and knocking free her wind. They stood so close, it loosed near his mouth like a lover's pant. Driving his left boot into the deck for balance, he raised his father's axe. The weapon, already blooded decades before by his father, yearned for more as Franque brought it down. The blade of it cleaved the slender bit where the woman's shoulder met neck. The blood sprayed, there was so much of it. Her body bled out any fury she once held for battle and useless legs crumbled beneath her dying body.

His rage now reigned supreme, pulling the axe free just in time to block an angry sword thrust. From whom? Her husband? A lover? Whatever connection this new attacker shared with the deceased it did not matter, their boldness to challenge fueled his demon wrath. Their life would be devoured as well, and Franque roared at the man's arrival. The blunt of his axe handle crushed a Fjorik nose, smashing the tender parts into his brains. The second movement finished the job.

In a matter of moments Franque Thorinson had killed not only once but twice, and the feeling thrilled his soul. His father was certainly one of them, either Skander or Braen, the sons of Braston and princes of hell. He roared challenge to another Fjorik target who backed away with fear. They all now feared the axe of their former sovereign. They, like many more that evening, felled against its blow. The Demon of the North lived, and it controlled Franque's every move.

CHAPTER TWENTY-NINE

Robert listened to every word the professor said. She was a tall woman named Adairia, graceful in her Dreamer's robes and wearing her hair in a tight bun. Her face was stern but very pretty. Her voice, on the other hand, galled his patience and threatened to pierce the prince's eardrums. He preferred nails on a chalkboard. Worst of all, she droned on and on with every topic. Unfortunately, what she had to say was important, and he listened through the nasally contrived cacophony.

"The history of emotancy is ancient, from a time long before our own. Though records are limited, we have determined humans once desired to improve upon their minds while seeking ways to communicate—essentially creating what we discovered waiting for us in the Dream World."

Robert wondered about that possibility, how humans could essentially change their bodies to adapt or become different over time. But Sippen had taught him basic evolution. "It's like farming," he said aloud.

Adairia did not welcome the interruption and glared at him as he went on.

"When a farmer discovers a plant has produced better than average yield or more desirable fruit, he chooses those seeds for the next year. Eventually his crops become bountiful and more resilient."

"Crude to compare humans to farming, but I guess that's all you've known before now," she replied through her nose. She wasn't intentionally trying to be mean, only stating facts as she saw them.

Robert wasn't offended. "Well, animals then. Husbandry has long bred qualities into all domesticated beasts—for speed, greater quantities of milk or fatted meat, or even for strength at pulling a plow. It takes longer with animals than plants to achieve the traits you desire, but not at all impossible."

"This level of class is not a seminar, Prince Robert. Please listen to the lectures without interrupting."

He shrugged and made no promises.

"Since the great awakening nearly eighteen years ago, we've learned much more about controlling our craft, how to wield it, so to speak."

"What caused that, do you think?" Robert asked abruptly. "The great awakening, I mean."

"We know atmosphere plays a part, but also the Caldera of Cinder. There's radiation left over in the crater from a catastrophic event that occurred more than twelve hundred years ago. When the caldera belches out a large scale eruption, it charges the air in much the same way a thunderstorm creates lightning. This stimulates the abilities existing in a latent—a person sensitive to a craft, and it eventually awakens in some uncontrollable fashion. We first Dreamers, many of whom were children during the great awakening, discovered our craft accidentally, usually during times of great anger or sadness."

"So trauma plays a part in it?" Robert asked directly. "I heard many of you were from a town along the coastline leading to Fjorik. I heard about northern raiders who kickstarted your abilities. Where was it... oh yes, Ataraxia!"

"Very astute of you, and yes. Thank you for conjuring thoughts of my parents brutally murdered in their beds and us hiding in the forest, shivering, and whimpering."

"Wait!" Robert thought of Cuyler, and how similarly stoic Adairia seemed. "You've mastered control over your emotions! That's what's changed and how you can modify and change your outcomes! I first felt my powers..."

"Craft. It is a craft."

"When I first felt the craft, I was terrified. We were being hunted and I had no idea why. I sort of panicked, and there it was! But as I controlled my breathing and refocused, I could *see* the tendrils of air. I could almost touch the braids with my mind and so I did."

"Yes. What you are describing is called Basal Abilities Manifestation. But you jumped into an intermediate level when you understood the need to focus."

"Like when I travelled to the Dream World!" he blurted out. "I didn't know what I was doing, but BAM! There I was!" He laughed at the acronym.

"What?" The look on Adairia's face was anything but stoic, offense and even resentment seemed to radiate from her face.

"I've travelled to the Dream World twice now. Once with help, but the second time on my own."

"Prove it. Describe our meeting place."

Robert did, down to every last detail. He described the castle and its moat that curved around and entered a wondrous forest. He took care to describe the mountains and even the most prevalent flowers. It seems someone had a great love for tulips at some point, but the blooms were predominately wildflowers. He was about to mention the garden where he encountered Adam and Eve but clamped his mouth shut to keep his promise.

"I'm sorry," Robert said, "I found it an amazing place."

"You're forbidden from travelling there," Adairia suddenly scolded, "and will not travel there again uninvited. Even after you ascend to the monarchy, you will not be welcome in our private world, but especially uninvited."

"I'm sorry, I..." But then Robert remembered what Adam and Eve had said. The Dreamers did not know everything about that world, and there's many places for visitors to hide. "Yes, professor."

"Swear it! I shall also report that you've been warned to Master Cuyler. He won't be happy with this news."

"I swear!" he lied. He had every intention of returning.

His second professor was much more tolerable to listen to, even if the information was less eye-opening. He was a small man, slender and unassuming with large spectacles. His name was Galayn and his topic was Relational Emotancy.

"The crafts are divided by season. Autumn is the most prevalent found in Andalon, granting its wielders control over air. Spring is next common, though half, if not more, as likely to occur at all. The Springs can tap into living things or anything organic in nature."

"What about rock?" Robert asked.

"It depends. Granite, no. Obsidian, no. But limestone and other sedimentary stones like sandstone and shale can be manipulated. On a cellular level they very much remember how they formed."

"What about organic stones, like coal?"

"That is favored by the Summer Emotants."

"The Pescari…"

"Yes, that craft has so far been found exclusively in the Pescari people. Their history forbade intermingling with outsiders and, until recently, no known unions occurred. Besides, it is the rarest chance of occurrence, roughly one in one hundred thousand latents."

"But it's possible an Andalonian and a Pescari could produce offspring of the Summer craft?"

"Yes," Galayn agreed. "But highly unlikely. Even then, we don't know which would be dominant."

"What about the Winter Emotants?"

"Those with affinity for water are as rare as fire. There have only been a handful discovered since the awakening, and we have only one currently working within the Dreamers."

"I've heard they're quite dangerous," Robert said, thinking of the legendary Braen Braston and what Cuyler had said, discouraging a possible marriage with Fjorik.

"It is. A single Winter Emotant can take on a squad of any of the others and win without effort."

"Do you ever combine crafts? Blend your teams to unite an effort?"

"That's a question I will not answer," Galayn replied.

"Oh, so that's the higher level training Cuyler promised I *won't* receive." Robert's mind went to work at once, charting out possible combinations of Air + Fire, Organic + Water, and Air + Organic. The outcomes were endlessly stimulating and he found himself running scenarios in his mind. He almost missed the professor mention familiars.

"... a bonding can be forced or natural, the strongest being when the animal is drawn to and chooses you."

Robert snapped out of his musings. "I'm sorry, professor. Did you say we can bond animals?" His mind went at once to the Falconers and Jaguars he and Sebastian had encountered. "I thought Falconers and Jaguars practiced a different craft."

Galayn shook his head. "Not at all. The Falconers of old mimicked our craft by digesting a substance derived from our bodies and were capable, if not much weaker, of every ability we might possess. Your father bonded an eagle."

Robert froze. "So, any Falconers encountered now also draw that substance from emotants?" He thought again of the large room with strange lights and weird tubing, and how he and Sebastian had been stripped and laid upon stone slabs. "They meant to farm us?"

"I beg your pardon?" the confused professor demanded.

"Cuyler. I need to speak to Master Cuyler right away!"

"I'm very busy, Prince Robert. What's so important that it interrupted your first day of lessons? Did you find it so dry and boring you needed to distract me as well as you?"

"No, not at all," Robert protested. "I enjoyed it very much. Cuyler, there's ..."

"Master Dreamer. I'd prefer you address me by my title and not my given name."

"I'm sorry, Master Dreamer. There's something you need to know. I've been so sidetracked by becoming a prince and all, I never thought to tell you what happened to me in the forest."

"Marita told me. You were taken by a small band of Falconers and Jaguars and she and her South Continent friend rescued you. I know all about it. We already freed the captives and are reintroducing them to society. Some of the latents may even attend the Academy soon."

"Well, yes, but..."

"See?" the lead Dreamer pointed out dryly, "you did wish to distract me after all. There's nothing you can tell me I don't already know."

Robert felt his stomach churn, the result of anxiety wringing his heart. But then he paused. *This man is separate of the government, but he is* not *elevated higher than me.* Sitting straighter in his chair the prince spoke with newfound authority. "You are arrogant, Master Dreamer, but I hope that lack of respect is not displayed openly in the throne room or behind my back once I'm king."

Cuyler's eyes snapped toward him, less with anger and more filled with curiosity. "So, you have a backbone as well? I'd wondered if I'd be able to force it out of you."

"You've done nothing to bring it forth, I'm simply tired of your arrogance. Sebastian earlier raved about how great of a leader you are, but I've seen no evidence to agree."

"Sebastian would look up to a sand flea if it treated him nicely."

"Sebastian is a greater man than you and a stronger emotant as well."

"Please. He cannot even split his mind more times than me."

"I've seen him do it eleven times," Robert lied, watching close for a reaction. It worked. The stoicism wavered and a bit of shock worked into Cuyler's face.

"He's a coward."

"No. He's a protector. Though he shies away from direct combat, he does so because he can't stand to watch people he loves die around him. He saw enough of that sailing with Braen Braston."

"He's never fought in any battle, much less sparring."

"Not true. He valiantly defended me against both Falconers *and* Jaguars."

"They *took* you despite his efforts otherwise," Cuyler argued.

"They had help. You said Marita told you of our rescue, but she did not know details of our taking."

The lead Dreamer sat taller, listening with curiosity.

So, Robert thought. *I've information he needs after all.*

"Tell me," Cuyler demanded, trying hard to regain his stoic demeanor. "Tell me everything you know."

"First, catch me up on these new Falconers. I know you believed them defeated after the war, but they're obviously back."

After weighing the benefit of the trade, Cuyler finally agreed. "I'll tell you everything that's public record. We've only had a few encounters with the Falconers themselves, but people have been going missing across Andalon. At first, it was a problem for constables but, as the numbers increased, we realized a large number of Academy dropouts had joined the list of disappearances. That's when I sent out several teams to investigate, and two Dreamers reported encounters with Falconers."

"But none with Jaguars?"

"No," Cuyler agreed. "Not until yours."

"Where do they come from, these new Falconers. Marita said they all died at the end of the war."

"Falconers are not bound by death, they are born from it," the lead Dreamer explained. "When you fought the Jaguars, you watched Parumba resurrect the fallen beasts and turn them on their masters?"

"I did."

"That is an unnatural resurrection, part of the Spring Emotant craft, one that leaves the subject under complete control of whoever raised them. They may feel normal, even have their own thoughts now and again, but they are never truly self-motivated. Everything about them is compromised."

"How long does the connection last?" Robert asked.

"For as long as the controlling emotant lives. Upon their death, all subjects they control die with them."

"But the Falconers wield emotancy…"

"*Stolen* emotancy. Those beads they make from our bodies fuel their powers."

"Powers? Not craft?"

"What they do is no craft."

"So someone is killing people and raising them again as Falconers."

"No," Cuyler corrected, "someone is killing people sensitive to the beads made from our bodies and raising them. Then they're stealing emotants to farm more beads."

"And you're looking for the source? The single person responsible for building an army capable of defeating your Dreamers."

"Yes. Now tell me what you know."

"The source is a man who calls himself *Camp*. He told us his full name was Campton."

Cuyler's eyes grew wide with surprise and all pretense of his stoic nature fled.

"You know that name? Who is he?" Robert demanded.

"Campton Shol is the former Chancellor of Eston, your grandmother's chief advisor and your uncle's after her. He fueled the war against your father."

Robert and Cuyler discussed Campton long into the afternoon, even bringing a sketch artist up from the constabulary to draw his likeness. Robert described everything, how he walked, the pitch of his voice, his build, and even habits while he ate.

"Thank you, Prince Robert," Cuyler finally said. "You've been most helpful in our investigation.

Robert stood and reached to shake hands, but the Master Dreamer surprised him with a respectful bow.

"How was your first day?" Sebastian asked.

"Remarkable," Robert replied, slumping into his chair exhausted. He filled Sebastian in on every detail of his lessons and his conversation with Master Cuyler.

"I don't trust him," Sebastian admitted, revealing what he had overheard.

Robert sat up straight. "They conspire against the king? Even after agreeing to his decree?"

Sebastian nodded. "They seem to hate Fjorik, even more than the Pescari."

"I don't know. Percy *really* despises them. Could you imagine how much it would gall him if Tara and I managed to elope?" Robert let out a laugh.

"Robert," Sebastian warned, "be careful talking like that. Galling Percy Roan is one thing, but you have to think how many more in your kingdom think like him or worse. If you married the wrong type of woman, you could anger thousands of your people, losing their support and even prompting a revolution."

Robert paused. He hadn't thought of the effect on the people. "My life isn't my own, anymore, is it?"

"No," his concierge agreed, "it most certainly isn't."

CHAPTER THIRTY

Reprisal moored inside a tranquil inlet, a once thriving harbor, but left abandoned as the ship found it now. A single pier survived war and the elements, while rotting posts told a different tale of a grand waterfront. Buildings caved in or collapsed upon themselves, and weeds had overgrown most of the town. Bushes sprouted between cobblestones, and young trees dotted a clearing that once produced food.

Eusari walked alone, climbing a high embankment overlooking the ghost town and reminiscing about past visits. Some were wrought with loss and dark sadness while others provided laughter and love. Looking down upon the ship in the harbor, she thought about another time when she learned about forgiveness and friendship. All of those memories revolved around a single man, her forever love, Braen Braston.

Once certain no one could overhear, she spoke to him. "It's funny how my life has come full circle, bringing me back here to the place I'd sworn I never would. It's humorous, isn't it? You opened my eyes in this place, illuminated my soul and filled it with light where only darkness existed."

Down below, waves crashed against rock and foamed his answer. The sea could be angry or calm depending upon its mood, much like the man she loved.

"I'll find them, Braen. I'll find them and bring them home only... They've seen the world now, and I fear they're changed—boys grown into men surrounded by the evils of the world. Oh Braen," she sobbed, "I tried so hard to protect them, to keep them pure and innocent. Why did he take them?"

Deep in the forest, beyond the town, a wolf brayed. Eusari wiped her eyes and turned to follow.

As she did, the light of morning reflected off the rock facing beside her. Curious, Eusari moved in closer. Though mostly worn by time, scratches in the rock revealed a memory, an inscription that must have endured centuries of weather. Had the sun not been just right over the water, she would have missed the carvings entirely. She gasped as she read.

Estowen's Landing

Every Ending is a Beginning ...

-Andalon

She leaned in, placing a scarred hand on the limestone and felt the emotion planted therein. A man had taken great care to carve this message, one of hope regarding his own future. A rush of feelings overcame her, loss, grief, fear, hope, and resentment. Everything she had experienced for herself in this place, the man had left here as well. For a brief moment, the man and Eusari were combined as one and neither felt alone.

You are Andalon? she asked, not expecting an answer.

I am.

What does that mean? You are this place or you visited here?

I visited once, many centuries ago upon my return.

How is it we communicate now?

This spot is for us, emotants of shared organic affinity, just as the Dream World is for those of air. Though not elaborate a setting, we can still connect in places like this. Here, like there, a piece of us is imprinted on the earth.

What is earth?

Nothing but a name, it seems.

But how? How are we imprinted here?

I'm not sure, the man said, *but you and I must have a very deep connection indeed. It's been many centuries since anyone has spoken with me. I hope you do so again.* His existence faded into silence.

Eusari removed her hand, stepping back and staring at the stone. When she turned around again, she jumped, startled to find six large forms lying at her feet.

Sippen stood on the forecastle, gazing out over Estowen's Landing and wondering how long Eusari would be gone. She did not tell him the reason for her visit here, but he had an idea. The look on Peter Longshanks said he knew as well and, if both of them were right, the crew was in for a surprise. The only problem was mariners did not like surprises.

Marita, Charleigh, and Parumba sat perched on some barrels nearby, discussing strategies and how to incorporate their new traps. The young engineer had appreciated Sippen's suggestions, and now they were working out how to make similar contraptions for use by Parumba. Their talk was fascinating, but the little man returned his eyes to the town, scanning the streets for Eusari's return.

"Where's Eusari?" Constable Thorinson demanded, approaching from the lee deck. "What's her business here? I won't tolerate any smuggling or secret deals with outlaws. This is, and has always been a den for both."

"She's nuh... not meeting anyone."

"You're certain?"

"I uh... am."

The intolerable woman strode off, frowning at various crewmen and sizing them up as pirates themselves.

"Aye, but this be a cursed place," Krill said from behind, making Sippen turn.

"I dih ... disagree! It ruh... reminds me of Braen."

"Perhaps, but the place never stays settled long, besides," Krill knocked on his wooden leg, "this be where I lost me favorite toenail!"

"You luh... lost muh... more than a toenail. You luh... lost five."

"Aye, but the green one wuz me favorite."

"Do yuh... you think we'll find the buh... boys?" Sippen asked his friend.

"Aye, sooner than later and with a lot of fanfare."

"You're nuh... not worried about buh... battle?"

"Nah, I'm worried about the... great mother mackerel of the seas!" Krill pointed toward shore and Sippen spun to see what shocked his friend.

Eusari, dressed in her black leathers and with the wolf head hood hiding her eyes, made a menacing sight. Every topside hand had seen her, dropping their arms uselessly to their sides to watch their captain. Ropes fell slack, tools hit the deck, and jaws opened to catch flies while they stared. Behind the woman followed six large animals, beasts of the forest with foaming jowls dripping hungrily for flesh.

As she crossed the brow and stepped onto the deck they followed, growling low at the humans standing around. These wolves, unlike Gelert who had always seemed more like a dog unless defending his master, appeared rabid and wild and ready to rip apart friends as likely as foes. Every hand stepped backward, all except Marita.

With a shriek of joy that made every crewman jump, she lunged forward, dropping to her knees and wrapping her arms around the largest, most ferocious of beasts. She hugged him around the neck, squeezing and giggling with merriment for several moments. Then, letting go and leaning back, she looked up at her captain.

"Great choice, Eusari!"

The animal licked the sailing master's face and lay across her lap. As if on cue, the other five beasts lay down at the feet of the true she-wolf, the bringer of revenge and devastation.

"Peter Longshanks," Eusari called to the gathered crew.

"Aye, mum?" he stepped out of the crowd grinning wildly.

"Shove off the lines and set sail for Pirate's Cove. I got what I came after, and now it's time to hunt."

Part III
Eagle Reborn

CHAPTER THIRTY-ONE

The sounds of battle raged overhead, with cannons and rifles shaking the hammock that held a once dying man. Shouts met his ears, followed by screams and more explosions. The creaking beams of the hull threatened to flood the compartment without notice, but none of that woke Krist Thorinson. His body lay deep in slumber, swinging like a babe in a rocker. His mind journeyed elsewhere.

What began as a nightmare, cruel in the way it forced him to relive the dunking, dragged him through the sea and finally under. The ropes binding both his wrists and soul snapped, sending him sinking deeper into the abyss. He neither floated nor sank for a time, wondering why he had not drowned. He was part of the ocean, at one with its bounty, and the desire to fill his empty stomach proved ravenous.

A shark, long and grey, blinked its eyes and flexed a mouth full of razor sharp teeth. It seemed to resent his intrusion into the watery depths. Its home. Its hunting grounds. Biting and thrashing, the beast swam quickly away for space. The predator circled, no longer king of its domain. Krist, now desperate to fill his belly, gave a kick with all eight of his legs. His longest appendage reached out, ready to snag the beast and hold it tightly. He glided through the water, now frothy and bubbling with pursuit, and gave one more thrust forward.

The shark writhed within his grasp, snapping and biting, but Krist wound his arms tighter and drew it closer to his mouth. Large and sharp, his beak snapped and tore into flesh, spinning and creating a vortex of tiny bubbles and bodily fluids. There was so much blood, the taste of it fueled him to bite faster, devouring his prey and spreading the blurry substance now spinning like a painted cyclone in the water. Despite the danger he posed, others would come, and these he'd devour as well.

Franque sat atop the deck of *She Wolf,* fully spent and trembling from the violence he wrought upon the immigrant ship. He had sought out this spot to be alone, to escape the blood. But it was everywhere, staining his clothing, his hands, his arms, and even his face by the coppery taste of his sweat. The color of it made him sick, yearning to leap over the side and bathe until it was gone. But the sharks had arrived early during battle, smelling the blood of the first injured and unable to resist an easy meal.

"Francis!" Boats called from the forecastle.

Franque refused to look up.

"Francis! I know you hear me!"

Franque responded with a single raised finger. The man deserved nothing more from him.

Boats just laughed at the slight, strolling over and squatting down beside him. "First kill, eh? I know that's a toughie and have been there me self, but don't fret long over it. You moved on from that one *real* quick and racked up several more shortly after! I swear! I named you and your brother wrong! *You* should've been bleeder by the way you swung that axe!" He reached out to take it.

"No." Franque gripped it tighter, unwilling to let go.

"It belongs in the armory, mate. I'm gathering them all. Trust me, it'll be there again when you need it. After what you did here today, ain't nobody gonna keep this weapon from you!"

Franque's hand let go even if his mind did not. Boats was right. He bled so many people, innocents as well as those defending, and it would serve him best to let go of the instrument. It had played him, more than he it, during the concert of death.

"Franque," a voice called softly.

Leave me be, he thought.

"Franque!" the voice called again. "Brother!"

Brother? He looked up, confused to find Krist standing beside him. "You should be in bed," he told him. "How are you able to walk?"

"I don't know. I woke up only a bit ago, weak but feeling stronger. My head doesn't hurt as bad as it did." He touched the site of his wound, pressing it gingerly. "It doesn't feel soft, either, and my vision isn't doubled."

Franque froze, remembering the warnings by the girl Gretchen. *She called it a curse,* descending from either of the Braston brothers. Captain Jacque had even asked, *Has anything odd ever happened when either of you are around water?* Franque remembered the stories, of how their father and his crazed brother terrorized Andalon wielding the power of the sea. *How odd did the captain mean?* Krist should have died. *Could the water have saved him?*

"I killed," Franque finally admitted. "Man, woman, it didn't matter. I lost myself during the raid."

"Were any of them trying to kill you back?" Krist asked gently.

"Some. Not all." The image of a cowering old man came to mind, he lamented that one the most. "They were immigrants, headed to Andalon to start a new life, and we murdered them."

"Not all," Krist disagreed, "look."

Ben Thompson addressed a small group of men being led to *She Wolf.* "After we've taken anything of value, we'll scuttle your ship. If any of you wish to be spared a few hours treading water with sharks, we'll be happy to sign you aboard. We had a few job openings today, and this chance won't come around again."

Not surprising, they all stepped forward, six in all, to join the crew. Most appeared able bodied, suited for life at sea, but one in particular seemed runtish—an oddity from Fjorik.

"What's your name?" the quartermaster demanded.

"Sven Nielson," the man sputtered with a shaky voice. He was afraid, but smart enough to choose life.

"Occupation?"

"Carpenter. But I could work as a cooper, if needed. I'm not picky, sir!"

"Carpenter job is filled, so is cooper. You'll work under the boatswain until we have need for you elsewhere." Thompson looked around. "Where's Boats?"

No one seemed to know.

"Boats?"

"He's in the armory, Mr. Thompson," Franque replied.

"Nielson, go with Franque Thorinson. He'll find you a bunk. If you need clothing and tools you can purchase them from me on credit, and we'll deduct it from your first pay. Next!"

The little man walked up to Franque, eyeing the blood on his face and body. Terror filled this carpenter from the north, the kind of horror one would expect when first laying eyes on a demon.

"He'll sell you clothing and tools," Krist told the newcomer. "But it's not new, comes overpriced, and it'll cost you more than your first wages. Franque here and I can lend you tools as you need them to help save you money." He put out his hand. "I'm Krist."

"Sven." The little man eyed Franque once more.

"Like he said, I'm Franque. I'd shake your hand but," he absently tried to wipe the blood on his pants, "I'm covered in your kinfolk." Not wanting anymore conversation, he left his brother alone to settle in the newcomer.

He walked toward a rain barrel and plunged his entire head inside, scrubbing as much as he could to remove his sins. He yearned to hold it there and drown them all, along with himself, forever. It turned out he was better at killing others than himself and raised his head up again to breathe.

"Good job today," a voice said from behind.

Franque turned and found the captain standing beside the first mate and watching him wash away the blood. "I'm sorry, Captain. I'd salute, but my hands are a bit occupied. Is there something I can do for you, sir?"

Devil Jacque smiled broadly. "No, Thorinson, I think you did enough for one day. You handled yourself like a true pirate and fought with valor!"

"Valor, sir? Killing innocents was valorous?"

Devil Jacque's smile disappeared abruptly. "I don't like your tone, seaman!"

"No, sir, I don't suppose you do. But I know you appreciated my actions today, so let's agree now isn't the time for us to chat."

"You're exactly like your father, Thorinson, or should I say Braston?"

"Call me what you will, Captain, but just don't do it when your enemy's blood is still in my mouth." With that, Franque dunked his head once more, holding it under as long as he could. When he again surfaced, he found himself alone. With no one watching, the son of Braen Braston wept.

Krist liked Sven. He was a young man, the sort who easily make friends. He reminded him a lot of their brother Robert. He found him smart, one of those types who could work his way out of any problem with ease. That was good. He would pick up the job easily and not upset Boats too much.

"I've just reported to duty, myself," Krist told him. "I got my head bashed a couple of weeks ago, and it's only just healed." He pointed at the wound. It had fully closed and already showed a pink scar. "You'll work with me and Franque, and we all report to Boats. That's short for boatswain mate. You'll do well to keep on his good side, 'cause he's got a temper. Don't ever strike an officer, say 'yes, sir—no, sir,' and work as hard as you can all the time. Got all that?"

"I think so."

"Good. Got any questions?" Krist asked.

"Just one," Sven said. "You're name, is that from Fjorik?"

"It sure is. I'm named for my grandfather, Krist Braston. There's an empty hammock with me and Franque, so you're welcome to bunk with us."

Sven Neilson said nothing, only nodded and stared back at the grandson of his beloved former king.

CHAPTER THIRTY-TWO

Robert eyed the general with awe. He exceeded all expectations of what a military man should look like, despite the prince had never seen a real soldier. They were a rarity in the empire, unnecessary in a time when the cities more easily relied on local constables and deputies to keep peace. Of course, each governor could raise their own guard if needed, but Logan, the largest city Robert had seen before Eston, never had taken the trouble. Unlike Eston, Middleton, or Soston, it lay so deep inland its leaders saw no need and the threat there came from thieves and pickpockets, not outlaws or invaders.

Percy Roan introduced this man as General Murdock Kelly. Tall, hardened, and standing with a bearing more regal than any noble in the assembly could hope for, the commander of Eston's army was magnificent. When he spoke, it was with confidence.

"I can root him out, my lords. If Campton Shol still hides within our borders, then I will find him."

"And how would you deal with his abominations?" Cuyler laughed, breaking his stoic character and sending a rumble of whispers within the chamber. "He's protected by Falconers and Jaguars at the very least! My dear General, Campton Shol, and the entire affair for that matter, is above you. If he truly *is* alive and scheming against the crown, then this falls in *my* jurisdiction. I've already dispatched four contingents of Dreamers to Loganshire, each armed with seekers. Your assistance is unnecessary."

"You forget I fought my own share of emotants in the Battle of Eston, Master Dreamer, and I don't recall you even being in the city at the time!"

"Your war record is not in question, General Kelly, and neither is mine. But, if you need my resume, then I'll point out my service in Estowen's

Landing when I fought against the main force of Campton Shol's abominations. *This* task is a job for Dreamers. Not the Estonian army."

"I suggest a combined force!" the General pressed, addressing the assemblage. "Grant me emergency powers to raise armies in each of the cities, and I'll root out the revolutionary!" Turning to Cuyler he added, "And I'll be happy to utilize your Dreamers into my army to aid my efforts."

Cheers went up amongst the common house, their distrust for emotants running deeper than with the nobles, although more than a handful of the upper house offered their approval as well.

Amash, as Robert had come to know his uncle the king, chose this moment to stand and address the assembly. A hush came upon both houses as their king made his thoughts known. "My reign has lasted seventeen years and, in all this time I never believed I'd again hear the name Campton Shol. But here it is and with it comes memories of our tumultuous past. But we are not yet at war, despite what the hawks among you or even the general suggests. We *are* threatened. But only by fear. Fear is the true enemy that works its way into our hearts and minds, relieving us of our higher thinking."

Every eye fell upon the king, just as every ear took in his words.

"General Kelly is eager, but Master Cuyler is wiser in this matter. Subterfuge is what we fight against, not open hostility. My advice as your monarch is to allow the Dreamers to handle this matter, and save our army."

Cheers and jeers intermingled, but both eventually died down.

Robert could not believe his eyes and ears watching this spectacle called an assembly. It all seemed a waste of time and effort. A controlled shouting match was all it was, but final arguments were made, votes were cast and tallied, and a decision was soon announced. The army would not be dispatched and the Dreamers would handle the affair.

Robert watched the dejected military commander as he honorably accepted defeat. *That's a man to look up to,* he thought, *stalwart and strong. Even in defeat he's confident.*

"When you are king, I hope you have more open-mindedness," the general whispered to Robert.

"Meet me later," Robert whispered back. "I wish to pick your brain."

The general's eyes grew large, appreciative at the opportunity to be heard. He bowed before the king-to-be then stepped back.

Robert observed the relief in both Percy Roan and Cuyler at the outcome. They each seemed invested in the venture, as if more was riding on bringing in a revolutionary. But still, their relief seemed a combination of worry. Robert also observed the king. Amash appeared dejected. Despite the effect his words had on the outcome, his energy had fled him the moment he finished speaking. Something wasn't right with the man.

A few more petitions were heard, but the king finally waved off the approach of the merchant's guild. "I'm sorry," he said to the assembly, "I'm not feeling well at all." He stood, whispered something to Roan, then fled the room.

The chancellor's face markedly changed at the king's words, whatever those had been. He stood, called a recess, and hurriedly approached the prince. "Go to him," Percy commanded under his breath. "He asked for you... alone."

Robert approached the king's chamber and two guards stepped aside, pushing the heavy doors open.

"He's expecting you," one of them muttered.

The king lay atop the covers of his bed. *Uncle Amash instead of king? This has all happened so fast,* Robert thought, unsure how to address him in private. Finally, he asked, "Are you okay, Uncle?"

"No," the monarch admitted. His voice sounded different. It was the same voice, only the inflection and tone had changed. He sounded more... arrogant. "I told you before I am dying, only it seems I've less time than I thought."

"I'll fetch a doctor."

"No. This body is not the problem. Robert, and your mother will confirm this on her return, but I am not really Amash Esterling."

"I know," the prince admitted. "Your real name was Horslei. King Charles sired you out of wedlock."

Amash laughed, grasping his head with both hands at the abrupt pain it caused. "Rest assured both Charles and Amash's mother were wed, only not to each other. No, what I mean is that I am not Amash at all. Your mother knows who I am, and I don't care if she tells you, as long as you keep the truth from everyone else, especially Cuyler and Percy."

"I don't understand. Is this delirium?"

"Don't I wish? No. Amash Horslei died eighteen years ago and I claimed his body. It wasn't planned, nor did I know who he was at the time, but I capitalized on that windfall nonetheless."

Robert thought about his few lessons with the Dreamers. "You're a *Spring* Emotant?"

"No, only an imposter who can steal the essence of one."

"The beads?" Robert asked. "You are one of those able to digest the beads?"

"Exactly. I can consume and tolerate all four types, though I'm only well practiced at two."

"Why did you take over the king?"

"Like I said, I pitied a dying man once and did not know at the time he was to be king."

"So none of his, not any of his achievements, were him?"

"No. Amash did well and I tried not to interfere with any of his governance unless it affected the grander situation."

"So the king is dead."

"Yes. Long live King Robert," the voice said with a rasping laugh. "We have time. His heart won't stop beating until mine does."

"When?"

"Soon. I'm struggling to hold on, and when I do let go, I'm afraid all hell will break loose. Right now I'm a dam, a thin barrier holding back a deluge of chaos."

"How will it affect Andalon once I'm king?"

"Hopefully not at all in your lifetime, but it will most certainly will affect your heirs."

"Tell me," Robert pleaded, "what I have to fear."

"Andalon and is not the only continent."

"I know, there's the Southern."

"They are actually two of seven. The most important is Astia, a land far to the east, a combination of two of the remaining five—it's vast. I control the governing body there as well as here. That's kept you safe, but they will come again. I don't know when."

"We'll fight them," Robert vowed.

"No. You aren't ready. Their technology far exceeds yours, even if they are a shadow of what their civilization once was. You must expand the Dreamers as well as your army, increase your technology, and give your descendants a fighting chance."

"I don't know that I trust Cuyler," Robert admitted. "Sebastian told me he and Percy Roan scheme against you."

The voice laughed again, this time breaking out with a coughing fit. After it subsided, it added, "Of course they do. Percy Roan is a snake in the grass and Cuyler an arrogant prick. They're both ambitious, and that's their Achilles' heel."

"Achilles? What's that?"

"Only a man from long ago. A man blessed by the gods. Call him a hero, if you will, but do so knowing all heroes have their weaknesses. His was his heel, the only part of him which could be harmed."

"I don't know mine," Robert admitted. "But I'm certain it's my ignorance in politics. I don't know anything about running a government, leading men, or even fighting another civilization," the prince complained. "How will I succeed?"

"I can't promise you success, but you've no choice but to try your best. You've great counsel, as long as you both heed it and keep it in balance."

"Meaning I must balance both Cuyler and Percy's schemes, keeping my eyes and ears open at all times."

"Yes, and a pair of eyes watching your back for knives. Sebastian will do fine, I'm sure."

"What of this Campton Shol? Is he as much of a danger as the others say? Is he a greater threat than this Astia?"

"Campton Shol *is* Astia, or will be after I'm gone. But thankfully he's stuck here, unable to return home."

"He could commission a ship and sail across, couldn't he?"

"If only it were that easy. Did you ever wonder why no one has ventured east? Why the government never sanctioned an expedition in more than eight hundred years?"

"They would have discovered Astia," Robert mused. "So, every Esterling king has known of them and discouraged discovery?"

"Known *and* collaborated. Amash was the first king not working directly for them, at least not to his own knowledge. You will be the first to rule without interference."

"I'm really not ready," Robert protested again. "Maybe Percy should be regent longer than a year."

"No. A year may even be too much, but it's set. Use this time to prepare yourself thoroughly."

"I'll try," Robert promised.

"Also know this. Amash was very wrong about one thing in regard to you. He tried to prevent you from ruling as a fully trained emotant, citing conflict of interest with the Dreamers."

"Yes, he was adamant."

"He was dead wrong. You *must* learn to control and use your powers. Most of all, bond with an animal if you can, and learn to extend your sight."

"Cuyler and Percy won't like that."

"No, I don't suppose they will, but you must insist… at least upon the bonding of an animal. The eagle was part of your family emblem for a reason. Use it to build the love of your people. Make them revere you like a god."

"I don't want to be a god," Robert protested, aghast by the suggestion. "I don't want *any* of this, actually."

"Then you are truly the best suited for the job. Now go, let me rest. I've got others to speak with elsewhere."

Robert left the room feeling oddly alone. The entire conversation felt surreal and he walked the palace halls with more questions than before. But through it all, he'd forgotten to ask the voice the most important question. Who were they, really? *He told me my mother would know.*

"Prince Robert," a voice called from the hallway, startling him free of his thoughts.

He looked up to find Cuyler standing beside Percy Roan and General Murdock Kelly. "Yes, Chancellor?" he asked.

"What did he want? What did he say?"

"His words were for me, but he told me to bond with an eagle."

"Out of the question," Cuyler protested.

"The way I understand it," Robert quickly addressed the lead Dreamer, "you may have no say in the matter. If able, I'll eventually bond one on my own. Amash—the king—told me to bond one before my coronation." That added part was a lie, but apparently an effective one.

"What really would the harm be if he did?" Percy asked the Dreamer.

"I guess none."

"Good. I want to venture out tomorrow."

"I will go with you, Your Highness, to give you protection," the general offered.

"Nonsense," Cuyler argued, "I'll send Dreamers."

"I'll take both, actually," Robert replied with confidence. If he were to be king then he had to sell his regality now, rather than later. "Thank you both for volunteering assistance. And Percy," he said to the chancellor, "I'm looking forward to our own studies. Amash told me to heed your lessons, that they were instrumental to his success. I'm glad to have you as well."

"Of course, Your Highness!"

"Now, if you'll excuse me," Robert said with finality. "I've had a long day and have much reading to catch up on. Amash insisted I read *Common Law and Trial* as soon as possible." He kept his head held high as he walked away, leaving the three men to further quibble and argue amongst themselves. Inside, however, he burned with anxiety at how fast things were changing. *I'm not ready! Not even close!*

Sebastian looked up as the door to Robert's chamber opened. He opened his mouth to speak, excited to hear about the prince's day, but snapped it shut when he recognized the look on the boy's face.

"It didn't go well?"

"No, it went *very* well, until the king died."

"What? He's dead?"

"Yes and no," Robert explained. He started with the strange story the voice had told him, and, despite it swore him to secrecy, held nothing back from Sebastian.

"I... I think I understand," was all he could tell Robert. He knew who the voice was, of course. He hadn't until this moment, but it all fit perfectly with the events leading up to Eston. This man, wherever he was hiding at this point, had disappeared at a crucial point during the Brothers' War. It was up to Eusari to tell Robert, if she ever chose to. "What now?"

"He said I have to train, no matter what Cuyler says. He also told me to bond an animal."

"That's not guaranteed," Sebastian explained. "Even Marita, as strong as she is, never figured out how. She can see differently, but even that's limited."

"What about Cuyler. Can he?"

"He never did, not that I know of. It's weird how it works, easy for some and impossible for others. I once knew a girl named Beth who bonded an owl so easily she hadn't even tried. It just followed her, inching closer until she had no choice but to accept its offering to bind itself."

"What happened to her?" Robert asked.

"The war. It devoured her like so many others, in the most awful of ways."

"Sebastian?"

"Yes, Robert?"

"I think I *have* to. I can't explain it, but I've always felt like I had to soar. I want to try tomorrow."

"I'll go with you."

"Thank you, I want you there."

Sebastian abruptly picked up the clothes he'd left out and carried them to the wardrobe.

"What are you doing?"

"Trust your concierge. These won't do for a ride in the forest. Get some sleep," he said pointing to the bed, "and I'll prepare everything."

CHAPTER THIRTY-THREE

The land beyond the Misting River Valley proved worse than uninhabitable, tormenting the pair of riders passing through the angry landscape. Dry and hot, it scalded the horse's hooves and the sweat of man and beast provided the only moisture to grace the ground. The Forbidden Waste yearned for rain, and the obvious lack of it prevented anything but spiny cactus to grow in the packed crust. Rocky and barren, the upper layer would break the plow of any fool who tried to till.

Tara, like Teot leading the way, had tied a scarf to protect her face from steamy southern winds that relentlessly blasted their skin with tiny particles of sand. She yearned to make it across, but the shappan made no mention of how much longer their trek would last. They had travelled five days so far, following the dry bed of an ancient river that led them westward. As Felicima settled into her bed before them, the girl prayed for respite and a good night's sleep.

As if reading her thoughts, Teot called over his shoulder, pointing toward a stony ridge. "We'll make camp against those rocks. The caldera is only a few hours walk from here, and it's best to approach the sacred site in morning, when the air is coolest."

"You know this area well," Tara noted. "You carried my father's body this way, didn't you?"

The shappan shook his head. "No. I brought him from the northeast, bearing him across our previous homeland, the Steppes of Cinder."

"What are they like?" she asked. "Mother never talked about them except to say life in the grasslands was difficult."

"Some would argue it was better than the way we live now," Teot countered. "I, myself, miss the tall grasses full of game and teeming with edible roots and berries."

"Mother said horses ran wild on the steppes."

"They did, along with the bison and longhorn cattle, but, when I crossed them last, the Steppes of Cinder offered no more hospitality than the Forbidden Waste."

"What changed?" she asked. "Mother said you were forced to flee toward Weston but said nothing of why."

"Felicima grew angry and fumaroles rose from beneath our feet. Steamy geysers emerged, cracking the ground we once farmed for grain and forcing us either south toward the wastes or north into the tundra. But your father's name meant brave, and he led us eastward to defy the Andalonians. Taros changed our lives forever, and we survived because he did."

Tara fell silent at the mention of her father, wishing she could picture his face or hear his voice. She longed to know the man who won her mother's heart.

Having reached the natural shelter, Teot dismounted and swept the area for snakes and stinging insects. Once confident the place would suffice, he ordered her down as well. "Start the fire," he commanded.

Tara drew out her tinder pouch and flint, unsheathing her blade to strike against the rock for sparks.

"No," he interrupted, "do it our traditional way. Our meal tonight will be in honor of our past. It's best to approach the home of the goddess with humility." He handed her a shard of volcanic glass.

The girl took it, aiming toward the goddess and praying her eye would be hot enough to ignite the flame. Several minutes passed in which Tara anxiously stole glances toward the shappan. Though he was not watching, she knew he judged her knowledge of their people's ways. Finally, after what felt an eternity, flames sprang up and she added branches. He reached out immediately for his glass, and she handed it over.

"I used to think Pescari ways were old fashioned," she offered, "unnecessary in this new world of luxury."

"And now?" Teot asked.

"I see they are important to hold onto, because luxuries can be taken away by both man and Felicima. Learning the old ways have taught me how to survive with nothing."

"You speak with respect but come across boastful while Felicima has not yet settled."

Tara flinched. The rebuke came unexpected. "I'm sorry. I only mean I have been wrong and am grateful for what I've learned."

"Come tomorrow," Teot said without expression, "ask yourself how much you've really learned." He pulled a clay pot from his saddle bag and mixed water and herbs, placing it near the fire to warm.

"What is that?" she asked.

"Felicima will be settled soon for the night, and it's time for your ritual."

"What does it entail?" she demanded, suddenly fearful as all confidence fled. "What must I prove?"

"You must prove you are Pescari, and in doing so reveal the meaning of your name." The water had begun to steam and Teot pulled it away from the fire while the pot was still cool enough to touch. "Drink this," he commanded, "and awake ready to meet Felicima."

Tara awoke clearheaded, alert, and ready for the new day. She yawned and stretched, looking around. The smooth rock walls of the outcropping had not cooled at all, radiating Felicima's heat as if it were just past midday. Curious, she turned her eyes upward, confused why the highest rocks still shone with Felicima's gaze. The goddess herself had only just began her descension high overhead. It was late afternoon.

The girl sat upright and looked around. There was no sign of Teot, the horses, or even a trace of the campfire she had lit the night before. Everything they brought had vanished along with him—her knife, tinder pouch, and rations. She scrambled to her feet and panicked, searching for anything that would reveal where her great uncle had gone. Looking down she spied a full waterskin lying beside an arrow drawn in the dirt. It pointed westward.

Has he gone on before me then? she wondered. He may have, but why take her horse as well as his own? Why also would he remove all traces of their camp? *This must be part of the ritual,* she realized and tried to reason out what to do next.

She remembered Flaya's final words to Teot before they departed for the trip. *Whether she dies in the wilderness or returns,* she had said.

This must be the way of it then. When a child was ready for their ritual, they were taken into the wilderness to meet their goddess. She looked around, not finding any food or tools in sight. *And this is why they trained me in the traditional ways,* she thought. *If I'm to find my way home, I must do so only with what I was taught.*

But the arrow pointed westward toward the Caldera of Cinder, so he may have left a challenge for her there.

Tara looked upward, frowning at her goddess. When they made camp, Teot mentioned it best to arrive at the caldera in the morning, when the air was cooler, he had said. But she had slept through the morning and much of the afternoon. With no desire to waste another night and half a day, she would venture out and get this part of the ritual over with.

But was she ready? She was unsure. A quick inventory reminded Tara she wasn't. *I have a full waterskin,* she thought, *that's all. A waterskin and the clothes on my back.* She surveyed her surroundings. She also had shelter. *A waterskin, my clothes, and rocks,* she corrected. The rock outcropping would protect her from all elements except rain, and that scenario seemed highly unlikely. *Food, then.* She had nothing with which to snare game and no knife to fashion a spear.

Tara tugged at the rawhide fringes hanging from her buckskins, searching her mind for a solution when one abruptly hit her. Looking down, she held a handful of the strips and worked out a plan. Grabbing the sharpest rock she could find, she sawed at the fringes, pulling them off and making a pile until she had enough. Though she hated to waste her precious drinking water, she carefully doused the pieces of leather and began braiding and pulling them tightly into a long rope.

After a few minutes she held her creation triumphantly. The snare was thicker than others she had used, but it would do the trick. She quickly found a perfect spot atop the outcropping, a well-worn path beneath the cacti with bits of fur left behind from a rabbit who recently passed by.

"Felicima," she said aloud, "by your grace please fill this snare by morning." But praying to her goddess reminded Tara of the arrow drawn in the dirt, and she gathered her waterskin and headed west, toward the caldera.

She had heard stories about it, of course, but her mother had only described it as a place where the world fell in upon itself. That had always seemed simple enough explanation to the girl, but Adsil had laughed off any description at all.

"It's indescribable," he had said. "A place where the goddess cools her fires for the night."

So close to it now, Tara felt excitement boiling and put off her worries over survival. This was it, she was so near to the moment of her ritual—the revelation of her name. She finally felt Pescari, which was odd because she walked alone without tribesmen.

The trek across the Forbidden Waste was way worse on foot than on horseback, but thankfully, as Teot promised, she only had to pick her way across the barren ground for a few hours before approaching the caldera. Felicima had descended quickly by the time Tara felt the heat of the place, her skin itching from the dryness and flushing red as if it would burst into flames. As she topped the final ridge she let out a gasp, awed by the vastness of the crater.

Adsil proved correct, the Caldera of Cinder was indescribable. Stretching far in every direction, beyond even the horizon, it did appear as if the edge of the world had fallen in upon itself, but it was more than that. Here and there tall mountains had crumbled on all sides, leaving only jagged pillars reaching toward the sky. Each rocky surface had been scorched darker than the charred leavings inside the ovens, and she struggled to focus her eyes now confused by a sea of blackness stretching beyond every horizon. It was leagues across, certain death to anyone who dared to cross.

She found the lack of vegetation startling. Everything had burned away and nothing tried to regrow. The only color was the occasional pool of red and orange molten rock, bubbling to the surface and cooling slowly as a new layer of blackness. She wondered how quickly the surface would melt her moccasins if foolish enough to venture forth.

A gasp bellowed nearby, followed by a hissing escape of gasses and steam as a geyser erupted, belching sulfur-laced foulness into the sky. Startled by the sudden eruption, she jumped, losing footing and slipping from the ledge. To her horror, she slid into the pit itself. Tara landed hard, knocking her wind and rattling her ribcage. Here, so close to the burning pool, she listened to the sounds of ripping and tinkling as molten rock tore itself apart. The air around her had changed as well, filled with fumes that burned both nostrils and chest. She panted to breathe, scrambling to her knees and doubling over against the pain now raging throughout her body.

High overhead a bird screeched displeasure, a welcome sound above the brimstone hell around the girl. She raised her eyes, welcoming the flash of color as the creature plumed radiant feathers against a sky of soft blue. Such oddity, to find herself on all fours in such a horrific place on what should have been a beautiful evening. The muscles of her arms gave out and she crashed hard once more against the black surface, able only to raise her eyes. Ahead, Felicima neared the horizon with her cooling fires. Tara imagined the goddess laughing at the mortal lying prostrate before her grandeur.

So close to the ground, the symphony from the molten pools vibrated, sparking emotions deep within the girl. Tara, so lonely, so lost, so confused. Who was she? Why was she doomed to fall in love with a boy her people would never accept? The sounds dared the child to leave her mother's house and venture out a woman—to find her way in the world and truly know destiny.

She detected a humming, faint at first but growing, and listened while catching her breath. The rhythmic sounds blended with this new resonance and her vision, fogged by the gasses all around, blurred on the edges until it darkened nearly the same shade as the rock all around. In that darkness she found a light, brightly shining and no longer intolerable to look upon.

"Why must we fear you?" Tara demanded of the light. "Do you hate us so much you scorn our very faces? Must we cower in fear of your wrath forever, or will your people ever find favor?"

You include yourself with my people? a voice spoke within her mind.

"I… I have no one else, but I feel neither Pescari nor Andalonian."

Yet here you are. Praying.

"Who else *would* I pray to? Who else do I have? I don't know *what* to believe in, but you're all I've known!"

The voice did not answer.

"Why do you hate us?" she demanded again. "Why won't you allow us to enjoy prosperity under your gaze?"

Once again her question was met with silence.

Suddenly, a girl appeared before Tara, dressed in Andalonian fashion with white flowers tied into raven black hair. She found her beautiful, the kind of highborn beauty she yearned to be, and was about to address her before abruptly swallowing her greeting.

She's me, Tara realized, *free from these buckskins and Mother's control.*

I'm who you want *to become,* the girl explained, *after you run off with Robert.* As soon as she spoke, a swarm of high-class society surrounded and harassed her, tearing out flowers and ripping the lace from her dress, leaving behind a wretched, unhappy Tara.

Another Tara immediately appeared beside her, this one adorned in the finely decorated buckskins of a shappan, with hair pulled back in a warrior's braid. Tara gasped. Her hair was multi-colored, a blend of red, orange, and yellow—such boldness from a Pescari. Upon her back was a quiver, and stood with bow in hand. On her hip was a warrior's blade. This Tara's eyes glowed golden with the goddess' power, burning with internal fire.

Is this the form you fear? the newcomer demanded, her voice filled with wrath.

"I... I don't know what I'm supposed to say," the real Tara stammered, "that can *never* be me!"

Because wrath is mine *to wield!* the voice screamed into the darkness, echoing through Tara's body. Every inch of her skin now burned with invisible fire, unbearable and causing her to cry out with pain. The other Taras disappeared abruptly.

"Her power is not ours to keep," a man's voice whispered from the darkness. "I held it, just as Teot does now, and you have used it as well."

"No," Tara whimpered, the fire consuming her skin, "I don't want it! I won't have it!"

"You do not desire to become the agent of Felicima?" the man asked with concern. "Think of the great things you could do for our people.

You could lead them, create a new kingdom of Pescari that spreads from Weston, across the Steppes of Cinder, and north to the tundra."

"I don't... I can't..."

"You can but you *won't*," the man accused, suddenly appearing beside her. With the wave of his hand the pain left her body, though skin seared and the flame remained, she no longer felt its bite. "Flaya kept you safe, but raising you among the Andalonians was not what I desired for my daughter. If you desire to be full Pescari then you must forget about the boy. He has a different destiny than you."

The voice spoke again, *Listen to your father, Tara, son of Taros. I will only ever grant my gift to a Pescari.*

"Are you truly my goddess?" Tara demanded.

"Only *you* know the answer to that," Taros said, gathering his daughter into his arms and lifting her from the hot surface of the caldera.

She felt her body raise up then float as he carried her up the ridge. As she stared over his shoulder at Felicima, descending into her nighttime slumber, rain began to fall from the sky.

CHAPTER THIRTY-FOUR

Eusari stared out over the vast open water, scanning the horizon for ships and relying upon Marita to scan farther. That woman used a different method than her captain, an aspect of the craft she had perfected in youth. While most Autumn Emotants bonded birds for extended sight, the heiress experienced extended viewing upon the air itself.

She did so now, resting comfortably on a chair brought up from the captain's quarters. With eyes tightly shut, her mind wandered along the breeze as many tendrils reached out to find *She Wolf*. To the crew, however, the sailing master appeared only to be asleep on the job while they toiled. The grumblings had reached Eusari, but she saw no reason to address or put them straight. This would not be her crew for long—as soon as she found her boys she would return home and live out her remaining days there.

Nonetheless, *Reprisal* had wasted weeks sailing in circles, even pulling into the massive harbor of Middleton, only to double back and search open water once more. The entire affair felt wrong, as if her captain chased a ghost. That pushed Eusari's crew even further away from her trust and closer to mutiny. She was certain the pack of wolves laying at her feet were the only deterrent to that end. That, and the presence of Marita.

"Are you certain Devil Jacque headed south, dearie?" Peter Longshanks finally asked his captain, stepping over the animals on the deck.

"No, not any longer. But where else would he take them? Middleton made most sense if he sought plunder, but he must have pressed on to The Cove without delay."

The first mate gestured to the crew. "You've got a problem brewing, as I'm certain you're aware. Even if you don't find *She Wolf,* they only see weakness in our lack of action. They want loot, doesn't matter where they find it. That's the price for hiring pirates to do your hunting."

"How hot is their ire?"

"Downright seditious—calling this voyage a waste of their talents. Mutiny won't be far behind their list of demands, which I soon expect."

"They'll be compensated whether there's loot or not."

"Aye, but it's high time we find some."

Eusari shook her head. "Our good constable would never agree to taking a ship for sport. She'd arrest the lot of us."

"She could disappear over the side," Peter suggested jokingly. "A good keelhauling would cure the crew's grumblings and provide ample entertainment for the rest of us."

"As tempting as that sounds, we need her onboard. Besides, any ship we take must be part of the Pirate's Guild."

Marita spoke dreamily without opening her eyes. "I think I found one. There's a ship just east and beyond eyesight. It's keeping outside the shipping lanes, Eusari."

"But it's not *She Wolf*?" Eusari asked, the frustration in her voice.

"No, not her. This one appears to be a Fjorik hybrid. It reminds me of *Ice Prince*, actually, not a longboat but not a frigate neither. It may be one of the constructs Sippen built before *Malfeasance*."

"You're certain it's not a transport?" Peter asked. "There're plenty of Fjorik immigrants flooding to every port. This one may be headed for Soston."

"No, this one's acting funny," Marita explained, "like it's going out of its way not to be seen by ships in the main channel."

"So it's either a pirate or a smuggler, either way that would befit our hunting license," Eusari decided. "I'll take it. Summon Constable *Goody Two Shoes* and let her know."

"There's no need," a woman's voice said from behind, "I'm here, heard it all, and won't sanction any attack except on *She Wolf*."

Eusari turned to face her niece. "The men are restless. They came for pirate hunting and crave some action."

"Look around," Anne said with an *I-told-you-so* smile. "There're no pirates around to hunt."

"There," Eusari handed over a spyglass and pointed. "Marita found a ship on the eastern horizon, between us and the shipping lanes."

Anne made a show of straining to see, then gave up in an exaggerated huff. "I see a ship, not a pirate. You've no evidence a crime is committed and no authority to randomly search vessels."

"You see, dear constable," Eusari said with the same air as her niece, also making a show but of a different sort, "this is where it *takes* a pirate to *find* a pirate. You see a *ship* but outside of the shipping lanes, avoiding commercial routes, and you don't ask yourself *why*?"

Anne raised the glass and looked again. "I still see a ship, and not yet a pirate. I don't care what your gut tells you, unless it runs a black flag up its mast, I will *only* see a ship."

"The men will mutiny if we don't investigate. I'm coming about," Eusari decided.

"If you attack or board that ship without cause, I'll deputize your crew and lead the mutiny myself."

A low rumble caused Anne to look down, finding herself staring at several snarling wolves.

"Good luck with that," Eusari told her niece. "Peter, set a course and bring us close."

"Right away, mum," the first mate said with a salute. "I'll also get a line ready in case you decide to floss the keel after all," he added with a wink.

The ship in question, it turned out, was indeed one built under Sippen's direction. A three master, the hybrid enjoyed a shallow draft providing both speed and easy egress into shallow waters. Whoever captained it upon *Reprisal's* approach, however, seemed unaware or uncaring of its advantages. They kept to deep water, unable to flee due to a heavily ladened hold. Whatever they carried was heavier than Sippen designed it to carry.

"It cuh... could be *Perdition*," he stammered, "or muh... maybe *Elysium*. It's huh.... hard to tell."

Marita and Parumba stood nearby with Charleigh. The younger woman was placing bandoliers over their heads and affixing several of her gadgets. This boarding seemed the best opportunity to test them out.

"The guns are ready, Captain!" Krill called from the forecastle.

"We've got the wind," Longshanks called out, "and the approach!"

"Raise our colors!" Eusari commanded. The official flag of Eston hoisted swiftly to the top of the mast while another, with a black background emblazoned with a red wolf, unfurled from the jackstaff. "Now fire a warning shot across her bow," she added.

Krill gave the signal and a deafening retort cracked the howling wind powering the sails. It sailed true, directly over the other vessel, low enough to buzz the crew but true enough to miss canvas, wood, and flesh.

Abruptly, a white flag raised to the top of the other vessel.

"They struck their colors, Captain!" Longshanks announced.

"Definitely not Pirate's Guild, then," Anne warned. It was common knowledge all members of the guild refused to strike colors on principle, mutually regarding the practice as cowardly.

"Or it's a trap," Eusari snapped back at her niece. "Approach with caution!"

"No movement on deck," Longshanks said from behind his spyglass.

As *Reprisal* neared her quarry, Marita scanned the ship with her tendrils of air. "Something's off, Eusari. The crew's all gone below decks." She commanded the air to caress the wooden deck, feeling it out and listening for conversation within. Neither whisper nor warning was uttered.

She then felt along the planked timbers making up the hull. The soft vibration of water pounding alongside relaxed her further, a sound she'd loved since her first voyage as a young girl. Both her adopted father and Amash Horslei had been along on that journey, and she smiled at the memory of the now king puking his guts over the rail. She ran the tendrils upward, toward the rail of this vessel, passing by the row of twelve pound cannons. Each protruded from the darkness, still and ready though eerily quiet.

A pair of eyes behind each cannon stared out toward *Reprisal*.

"Guns are manned!" Marita shouted, eyes snapping open just before a deafening boom roared out over the water.

"Hard port!" Eusari screamed, hoping to turn the ship under the broadside.

Everything topside seemed to move in slow motion, as ten projectiles raced above the water. Crewmen shouted, and over these Marita heard the voice of Krill.

"Lash yourselves, laddies!" he cried, "or we'll be fishing you out later!"

Marita shoved Parumba and Charleigh down hard on the deck, lashing them to the deck with tendrils of air. She threw out as many of these as she could to secure any crew member too far from the rails or masts and unable to do so on their own. Then she tried to shift the winds, intent on blowing the cannonballs off course but failing to manage even a breeze in time. The impact proved horrific and, despite her efforts, several of *Reprisal's* crew flew over the side.

"My turn," Marita shouted at the enemy vessel, enraged by the cowardly afront. She ran across the deck, screaming obscenities like a true pirate, and leaped over the side.

"Give her cover!" Eusari's voice cried from *Reprisal*.

Just before splashing into the sea, Marita created a cushion of air between her and the water, landing hard with one hand and a knee seemingly hovering just above the waves. She lifted her head, trained her eyes on the vessel ahead, and took off running, moving the cushion to stay beneath her feet.

With a part of her mind still focused on the cannoneers, she watched as they loaded. One of them noticed her sprinting toward them and shouted, alerting his shipmates to the emotant. Five rifle barrels poked out beside the cannon. Marita plugged each one with a wad of air and waited, smiling as she ran. Each rifle breeched one after another, taking a portion of each shooter's face in the explosions. It took another round of dead sharpshooters for the crew to realize the crazed woman running across the water had caused their deaths.

For good measure, she stuffed each of the ship's port cannons in the same fashion. Surely they wouldn't be stupid enough to fire those. Much to her surprised amusement they were. The portside hull ripped open with a deafening roar, splintering the sea and opening the vessel like a half opened can of tuna.

A can of tuna sounds nice after the fight, she mused, *that and a cocktail. Maybe a mimosa?* With a mighty leap she jumped onto the first exposed level of the ruined ship. Only the top portion was missing, it would hold out the water and not sink before Eusari's men could plunder its hold.

Marita drew her swords and settled into the first of her stances, Calm the Waters, hoping there was a skilled swordsman onboard who could put her through a good workout. The first men to charge certainly were not and fell simultaneously to her dance.

"Hi, boys!" she said, flowing in and out of the gunners, some raising either cutlass or knife while others stood armed but with dumfounded expressions. The former felled as easily as the latter, and she worked her way through the crew.

Occasionally a rifle or pistol would point her direction and she'd giggle, wadding air into its muzzle and dancing through her attackers, making her way toward the main deck. Up a ladder she climbed, running through two men at once who dared race downward while she desired to move up. Soon she stood on what remained of the deck, facing down seven men—each dazed and confused by the blood covered woman standing before them. By now her laughter bordered on hysterical.

Behind her, *Reprisal* had come alongside and grapples pulled the ships together. With a shrug she sheathed her swords just as Eusari and her wolves leapt aboard, deciding at last to leave some killing for the others. Marita hopped on an intact barrel and sat cross-legged while the two captains squared off.

Eusari landed on the splintered deck. Most of it had ripped away during the explosion, exposing several levels of carnage wrought by Marita. Every bulkhead was splattered, sprayed, or pooling with blood as dying or dead men stared up at the sky or at each other. The young woman, it seemed, had only grown more efficient at her craft when it called for killing.

Only seven men remained on the entire crew. These held their swords with arms extended, terrified by the emotant now resting casually on a barrel and cleaning her nails. None of them approached or charged, imprisoned by their fear. Eusari, angered by the false flag of peace, reached out to her bonded beasts and sent them forward to free six crewmen of their lives. The captain watched as wolves ripped out the throats of his men. Alone, and without looking at Eusari, he addressed her.

"If I'd known you had an emotant onboard, I wouldn't have fired the broadside."

"But you still wouldn't have honored the stricken colors?"

"Of course not, Captain Eusari."

The sound of her name caused her pause, examining his face more closely. He and she were close in age, so he may have been around The Cove around the same time as her and Braen. "You know me?"

"Who doesn't know either the flag on your jackstaff or the woman standing before me. Why do you think I lured you in to fire upon? As soon as I saw that wolf I realized you'd left retirement."

"I don't know you," she admitted.

"I am Captain Tiberius Schott, a lifetime guilded member and resident of Pirate's Cove. I was away when you overthrew the legitimate Pirate King and returned right after your northern lover attacked the island. You may have forgotten *me,* Eusari, but I'll never forget the she-bitch who destroyed The Cove from within, broke our codes, changed our government, and then left us all to deal with the return of your lackey, Devil Jacque." He reared back and spit, sending a lump of wet mucus on her cheek.

Eusari's knife was in her hand in a flash, ready to arc toward his throat when a woman's voice screamed, "Stay your hand, Eusari!" She missed just barely and spun to find Constable Thorinson standing on deck.

"Stay my hand?" Eusari asked. "How about you stay the hell out of this!"

"The fight is over and, while I can look the other way from the death of the crew as self-defense, killing this captain would be an act of murder."

"Well, crap!" Marita exclaimed, drawing every eye on board. "I broke a damn nail!" She stood, crossed over to Eusari and placed a hand on her shoulder. "And I just had them done!" She leaned in close and said loud enough so all could hear, "If the fluffed up do-goody doesn't want you to kill him, then don't." After a wink she spun around, drawing both blades and crossing them against Captain Schott's throat. "Ever sailed down a river, Captain?" she spat in his eye then drew both blades across his neck in a single motion.

Captain Schott dropped to his knees then toppled over, sent down the crimson river by a master blades-woman.

"That's murder!" Constable Thorinson accused.

"I'm an ambassador from Cargia with a broken nail. I've got diplomatic immunity, bitch." As she walked away, returning to *Reprisal,* Marita held up the broken middle fingernail to prove her point to the constable.

CHAPTER THIRTY-FIVE

The expedition set out early, led by an overexuberant general and accompanied by a grumbling and irritated Caroline and Bearnard. The Dreamers seemed put out from the get-go, lagging behind and whispering often to themselves while Murdock Kelly rambled on to anyone who would listen how excited he was to join Robert on his quest. Sebastian frowned at the rest of those tagging along; so many extras who should have been left behind. There was a royal chef, a dozen or so attendants, a chronicler, sixteen riflemen, and an expert birdwatcher—all overkill, and likely to impede the prince's chances of actually bonding a bird.

"Think he's truly an expert?" Robert asked Sebastian.

"Who?"

"The birdwatcher. I mean, he *could* be useful, but if he starts tasting bird scat I'm turning back and headed to the palace."

The prince's joke caught Sebastian mid-swallow from his canteen, and he spit water all over his horse.

"And why's Amash's chef here? He cooks eggs or poultry with every meal. Isn't that a bit counter-intuitive? Seems he'd chase off every bird for a hundred miles with his menu."

"I think he's here on Cuyler's behest, in case you actually find a bird," Sebastian said with a laugh.

"Yes, that seems right." Robert spurred his horse to catch up with the general. Sebastian followed.

"Ah! Prince Robert!" The general seemed more than pleased to finally have a chance to visit with the heir. "Perhaps we can have that chat you wanted?"

"That was my hope, General. I was wondering, did you fight in the war?"

"I most certainly did! Valiantly so, that's how I earned my commission."

"Where did you fight? And for which side?"

The general's face turned thoughtful, as if choosing his next words carefully. "I fought in Eston," he said under a cloud of dark memories, "and fought evils unimaginable. As for which side? It wasn't for your father, nor was it for King Marcus. No, I fought against more than northern invaders during that battle. I defended humanity itself."

"I don't understand, wasn't the Battle of Eston a fight between Braen Braston and my uncle?"

"It wasn't as simple as you describe, and nothing we fought against was human. Even the northern marauders fought like demons! As for your uncle? He's another story altogether. I curse the day he put on that crown! No, The Battle of Eston was a shit show! We fought against all kinds of unholy terrors that night. I was on the western wall when a massive wall of water crashed against our gates, killing half our army in a single surge. And that was only the beginning!"

"Why isn't any of this in the history books?"

"King Amash didn't want the full story recorded, fearing the general public would panic. Said the people weren't ready for the truth."

"I think the people deserve the truth."

"Mighty noble of you, Your Highness, but trust me... they weren't, and still aren't, ready for *this* truth!"

Robert pondered the general's words for a while, then changed the subject. "You're awfully young for a general, aren't you?"

"I'm old enough."

"But you can't be forty summers!"

"I'm not, and that's all you need to know," Kelly said with a wink. "I joined up early. Two years early, to be honest, and I proved age doesn't matter. Take you, for instance. I'm sure you're worried how you'll be received, taking over as king soon, and barely seventeen summers. I was leading men by the time I was your age, leading them into all kinds of scrapes and situations. But I led most of them out again, and that's what matters. Do the best you can, and I'll follow you."

Robert couldn't believe his ears. This man earned more of his respect each time he spoke. "Thank you. I'm sure will speak much more on many topics."

"Many more times than you'll want, Your Highness." They rode quietly for a moment but the general, who Robert now realized hated silence, changed the subject. "How are you going to deal with the problem your uncle created?"

Robert froze, unsure how to answer and caught off guard by the question. It had come so abruptly, slipping into conversation without the jovialness normally carried upon Kelly's words. *So the man's a politician, as well.* He looked up at the young general, now waiting patiently for an answer and not allowing the prince a retreat. "What problem is that?" he asked.

"King Amash is a wonderful man, one I've admired during my ascension to this position, and I consider him a friend. But he and I—and many others, for that matter—disagree on a single policy. While Master Cuyler, Percy Roan, and I caution him against trusting the northerners, he has welcomed them into every city with open arms."

"My uncle sees good in people, it seems. Why should we judge a group of people for the actions of a few?"

"That's been almost *exactly* his words to us, but he sees trees when there's an entire forest." the general agreed. "If only he could see the bigger picture!"

"And what's that?" Robert asked cautiously.

"There's no such thing as a good northerner. The entire Kingdom of Fjorik is tainted, full of covetous spite fueled by centuries of raiding instead of proper farming! They have always taken what they want instead of earning or building it for themselves."

"They haven't raided in *my* lifetime," Robert corrected, "and their immigrants are mostly peaceful." As soon as he uttered the words he thought of Greta Greenbriar, the northern girl who bullied Tara in the schoolhouse, and of Peta Grenwich, the northern blacksmith's son. Neither of the teens had proved peaceful, revealing themselves eventually as liars and troublemakers who took what they wanted at the expense of others.

"You have a lot of experience with Fjorikan migrants?"

"I do, actually. Many have settled Loganshire over the years."

"Well, I can't speak for those choosing the countryside as well as I can the ones who chose city life, but trust me when I tell you there's no such thing as a good Fjorikan. Theft and violent crime in Eston alone has doubled in the past five summers."

"That doesn't mean they all crave bloodletting," Robert insisted. "They don't walk around murdering and pillaging every day."

"Nonetheless, many of them have berserker blood. It fuels their anger, burning like lamp oil and just waiting to be kicked over to ignite the entire barn. No, the only good northerner's the one who stayed home to cool their flame in ice and snow."

Robert stared blankly at the general, once a man he thought of as high caliber—brave and righteous. Now he viewed him differently, as a narrow-minded bigot. Another thought crossed his thoughts and he blurted out, "How do you feel about Pescari?"

Murdock Kelly's response surprised the prince. "I don't give two shits about them; I've never fought one. Think of me however you will now, Your Highness, but know this—once a group of people attack your home and slaughter your mates, a soldier may forgive but never forgets. I don't hate just to hate. I speak from experience. There's *no* good Fjorikan!"

Sebastian, who had listened quietly until this point, spoke his mind. "You're wrong, General. I knew a Northman who I respected and loved like a father. He was fair, true, and worked only to unite instead of destroy."

"Is that so?" Murdock Kelly asked with amusement. "And he never let you down in the end? Never turned so violent in your presence that you feared for your life or lost others around you?"

Sebastian opened his mouth to reply but paused mid-response, silently gagging on a memory while his mouth worked out the words he'd suddenly lost.

"That's not fair, General Kelly," Robert chastised. "Sebastian is a wonderful judge of character and I, like him, choose to believe there's good in everyone."

"Then you're doomed to failure, Prince Robert, destined to fall victim to the whims of those more ruthless and worldly than you."

Robert felt a sudden urge to challenge the man, to demand he reveal his own intentions in regard to the crown. *How* dare *he speak to me that way!* he thought. *I'm...* He was about to remind himself of his title but froze. *I'm not a prince,* he realized. *I'm a farm boy from Loganshire with a title, but I know nothing about thinking or acting like a future ruler.* He swallowed anger and spoke as calmly as he could. "General Kelly, I'm certain you have your reasons to distrust the northern people of Fjorik, but we must agree to disagree about how they should be treated as a whole."

Abruptly, Caroline and Bearnard spurred their horses and raced to the front of the procession.

"General Kelly and Prince Robert," Caroline exclaimed breathlessly, "there are outlaws in a clearing nearby."

"Where?" the general demanded, sitting higher in his saddle and waving over one of his junior officers.

"Half a league to the north."

"So close..." he mused. "How many?"

"At least twenty, all fighting age and well-armed," Bearnard answered. "They know we're here and are gearing up."

"How do you know this?" Robert demanded. "Neither of you have bonded birds!"

Caroline snapped, "Be quiet, Your *Highness*, and let us figure out a way to get you out of here."

"But how?" Robert insisted

"We have other ways to see across distances," Bearnard explained.

"We need to get the prince and the civilians to safety," Caroline insisted.

The general frowned at her words. "I think it's too dangerous to egress the prince, Dreamer. If they know we're here, then they have scouts watching our flank already. No, at this point we should keep him protected and close by while we deal with the camp. Surely my riflemen and you two Dreamers can handle twenty outlaws."

"Arm me," Robert insisted. "I can fight."

"No," the general refused. "Can you hide the civilians with your magic, Caroline?"

She nodded.

"I can do that," Sebastian offered, trembling slightly at the thought of danger so near.

Bearnard frowned and Caroline snickered. "Coward," she muttered.

"Gather the civilians," Kelly commanded his officer, "and the prince's man will camouflage them. Stay with the prince and keep him safe."

The soldier saluted and went to work gathering the entourage.

"I assure you I can fight," Robert insisted.

"No need," the general snapped. "The battle will be over quickly. Your Highness, please gather with the others."

Reluctantly, Robert allowed Sebastian to lead him away. They dismounted and huddled between the chef and the birdwatcher while the general and Dreamers planned strategy.

"I don't like this," the prince muttered to his friend.

"They're right," Sebastian whispered. "We have to protect you." With the wave of his hand, a web of air formed around the gathered civilians, reflecting the light around them while hiding the entire group from view.

CHAPTER THIRTY-SIX

The northern sun felt cooler, more tolerable the further north *She Wolf* travelled. The wind carried a briskness that forced both Franque and Krist to purchase a heavy coat from the quartermaster. The newcomer, Sven Nielson, found himself hopelessly indebted to Ben Thompson, the thieving bastard, as well. The trio wondered but never discussed with each other whether his price on jackets had gone up closer to Fjorik.

Franque watched from his task of patching sails while Krist scrubbed boards with Sven. The pair seemed to be enthusiastically enjoying their newfound friendship. Krist's desire to learn more about his roots proved insatiable, while Sven equally enjoyed teaching about his homeland. It all bothered Franque immensely, especially considering Krist told Sven who their grandfather was.

"I swore him to secrecy!" Krist promised after his brother called him out.

"It doesn't matter. It was a mistake! What if the rest of the crew finds out? Or worse, Boats? They'd flay us!" Franque had argued.

But so far the man had kept his agreement, but that hadn't curbed his eagerness to teach Krist all about the northern kingdom. Unfortunately, he also brimmed with stories about the *All Father*. Headmaster and the other historians of Andalon had their story wrong, it seems. Skander Braston, the younger of the two princes, had been the one to invade the cities united under Estonian rule. He had discovered a dark secret kept close by the Esterling family and committed to righting their wrongs.

"He was a liberator," Sven said of the King of Fjorik. "He discovered rooms in each of the cities he invaded, each filled with emotants who the crown had been farming to steal power for Falconers."

"You make this Skander sound like a good guy," Franque said without looking up from his sewing.

"He most certainly was! He became a father to those he rescued, not like his brother, Braen, who ripped ships apart with his mind," Sven insisted.

This version of events caused Franque to cringe, thinking of how he would have done the same to the immigrant vessel. *Braen really is my father, then. I would have ripped that ship apart, too, if I could have. Like father like son, I guess.*

"How did the younger brother become king, then?" Krist asked.

He's got no idea the king was his father, Franque thought angrily, sticking himself with a needle.

"Braen Braston could not wait to be crowned, and Krist Braston stood in his way. So he murdered his father in his sleep, barring him entrance to the Heavenly Hall. Skander tried to catch him, but Braen fled like a coward."

Wonderful, Franque thought, *my father was a lunatic, a murderer, and a coward!*

"Well, coward or not, Braen is our father and I wish I could have known him," Krist admitted.

"Which of you is oldest?" Sven asked.

"Franque is," Krist said, "by only a few minutes."

"Well, Franque, that makes you the king of Fjorik."

"Quiet!" Franque set down his mending. "Both of you shut up right now! Someone will overhear!"

"C'mon, Franque," Krist urged, "don't you *want* to be king?"

"Absolutely not!"

"Well I *do*! Sven, take me to Fjorik and crown me!" Krist said with a laugh.

Franque suddenly had a thought. "Who *is* in charge of Fjorik?"

Sven turned thoughtful and a bit sad. "It's provincial, really. Each noble family has a claim, but none can replace the All Father. They bicker and fight among themselves, but the priests know the All Father will return."

"Return?" Krist wondered.

"His second coming will be his permanent reign," Sven agreed.

"Second coming," Franque laughed out loud. "What are the signs of this second coming?"

Sven grew very serious, leaned in, and whispered. "He'll perform miracles. Our All Father will bring down lightning from the heavens, rain, and snow from the clouds, and even walk on water! The beasts of the sea will answer his call and, best of all, he will be dead and dying, and reborn by water!"

Franque felt a knot form in his stomach and watched his brother for any reaction. Thankfully, Krist only watched with as much interest as he would any other folk story. *He doesn't know,* Franque thought, *or doesn't realize.*

"That's enough!" the older brother decided. "We're Andalonian and don't believe in *any* of that superstition!"

"Yet, you have Dreamers," Sven pointed out.

"I don't care much for them."

"Neither do I," Krist agreed.

"Yet, you believe in superstition, as long as it's approved by your government," Sven pointed out.

"I... you're twisting my words!" Franque protested. "I just told you I don't care for Dreamers!"

"Have you ever met one?"

"Yes," Krist replied, "two. They came for our brother Robert a few weeks back."

"Came for him? What's his crime?" Sven asked with a knowing smile.

"Okay," Franque tried a different argument. "So maybe your *All Father* is a water emotant. That doesn't mean he's a god!"

"It proves he is. Water makes up nearly everything in our world. We breathe air that holds humidity, we drink lakes, rivers, streams, and brooks. Our bodies bleed with it when punctured."

"The Pescari would use similar arguments to suggest the sun is their goddess of fire," Krist agreed with his brother.

"Yet, you were healed after being dunked in seawater," Sven countered.

"I wasn't," Krist argued.

"Prove you weren't!"

"I... I can't."

"So goes it with religion," Sven said. "I say you're reborn by water, yet you disagree. Regardless, you were near death when pirates plunged you into the briny abyss, and you emerged whole. Your heart beats, your mind functions, yet you call it by chance. Krist, you *are* the grandson of a king, you told me so, yourself..."

"I'm not the *All Father*," Krist snapped. I'm a man, nothing more!"

"Brother," Franque admitted, "I think you might be... I'm not sure, but I think you *are* more than a normal man." Then he told them about his night ashore in Eston, and his encounter with Gretchen.

CHAPTER THIRTY-SEVEN

The thrum of fire inside Tara subsided to gentle warmness. She lay motionless, feeling the rain cool her skin while an inferno of conflict burned her thoughts. She felt defeated, scorned by a goddess. But the experience... Felicima herself... and the man... Taros, he claimed to be during the vision—or was it real? Her father, the shappan who died in battle according to Tara's mother and uncle, had saved her from certain death—if he had been there at all.

Tara opened her eyes. The rain poured down like nothing she had ever seen, much less expected, upon the Forbidden Waste. Water had nowhere to go, here in the world of sand and dust, and it rushed downward toward a watershed unseen except in times of flood. It found it, now, just to the north, in the ancient riverbed. There it gathered and collected before rushing downstream toward freedom and a better climate.

"Father," Tara called out for a ghost who never existed, her voice raspy and strained, "are you there?" She scrambled to sit up and searched her body for wounds, finding only eight punctures—four on her left leg and four more on her left arm. They were strange wounds to discover when searching for burns. No fire had seemed to have damaged her skin, smooth and of normal coloring as seen through singed and ruined buckskins.

The wind howled and the rain seemed to pick up, falling heavier than before. Unable to see the night sky through the storm, she could no longer judge direction. Tara scanned the desert for a familiar landmark. A screech made her turn. Twenty feet away she spied the same sort of raptor as seen before. It rose from the ground just as a lightning flashed, revealing a plume of red, orange, and yellow feathers fanning out. The bird made for an outcropping a short distance away. Tara ran as fast as she could toward the shelter it offered.

She collapsed, panting on the ground and the bird landed a few paces away. It screeched again, waddling toward something struggling above the rocks. Tara recognized where she had left her snare. Realizing she had caught food, her stomach roared to life with a rumble that reminded the girl she had not eaten for several hours. Finding the strength to stand, she investigated the trap. The bird merely watched, inclining its head as the human walked by, making no effort to move out of her way.

"You're an odd bird," Tara said, and it made no attempt to argue.

The crude trap had snared a rabbit, one of the longer types with tall ears found in both the waste and on the steppes. Though lean, it would feed her well if she could manage fire. She cursed Teot for taking her tinder pouch, flint and steel, unable to replace any of them for a long time. The tinder alone would be difficult to gather until everything dried again after the storm. She forcibly held the animal down and broke its neck. This time the colorful bird did not complain.

Returning to the campsite with the hare now tied to her belt, she watched the raptor as it seemed to celebrate her kill. It hopped around on the exact spot she had lit a fire before, spreading its wings as if miming the flames. It cawed and crackled its voice as well, sounding oddly like sparks.

"I can't," Tara told it. "I've nothing to light one with."

Without warning, the bird rose up into the air and disappeared for a few minutes, returning with a fallen branch gripped in its talons. The limb appeared heavy, certainly found miles away, but the bird carried it effortlessly.

Tara rubbed at the puncture marks on her arm and an idea struck her. "Did you carry me from the caldera?" she asked.

The bird replied with a higher pitched screech, one less alarming this time.

"I should have known better to believe a ghost carried me out. The entire experience must have been in my head, then." With a heavy sigh, she thought again of the conversation with Felicima and her other selves.

She opened her mouth to speak, ready to add something about how she should have known the goddess wasn't real, but caught herself. *I've no way to know what's real or not now.* Either way, she had experienced a vision and faced choices.

"I've got to give him up, you know," she said to the bird. It cocked its head as if listening. "The boy I love," she explained. "His named Robert, and I'm to choose between life as a Pescari or be with him."

The bird waddled closer and gently nudged the rabbit with its beak, then backed up and again imitated the fire.

"I said I can't do it. I don't have the tools."

The bird gave up, waddling to a dry spot in the cleft of two rocks and nestled inside to rest.

"I guess you need a name," Tara offered.

The bird perked up its head.

"You seem to like fire, so I should call you Blaze." The resulting screech was deafening, and Tara had to cover her ears. "I'm sorry," she screamed. "How about *Ember*?"

The bird immediately settled down.

"Okay, then. Ember it is." Finding the sharp rock she had used once before, Tara cleaned and skinned the rabbit while Ember napped in the corner. Adsil had taught her the importance of cleaning game, and she now could wait up to half a day before finding a way to cook or dry the meat. Unable to sleep, she busied herself by breaking branches off the larger limb and making a pile. Luckily, the rain hadn't fully soaked into the wood, and it was dryer than she believed.

The rabbit fur was mostly dry as well, and she pulled several handfuls to use as tinder. Placing it among the smaller, driest branches, she tried rubbing two larger sticks together. She had seen Adsil do this once, but he admitted at the time it wasn't the best way. The goal was to generate heat by the rubbing. All it did for Tara was frustrate and fuel hidden anger. Neither of the sticks heated up at all during the process, and she threw them down and cursed.

She felt a nudging on her arm and looked over to see Ember had awakened, coming close enough to touch.

"What is it?" she asked. The bird pointed its beak at the pile of tinder. "You want me to keep trying?" the girl asked, picking up the sticks. Ember let out a screech, the one Tara now associated with *no*. "What, then?"

This time, the bird nudged her arm where the puncture marks had been. Tara looked down and gasped. All four on her arm had fully healed. To be certain, she also checked her leg and found the same condition.

"How?" she asked, then understood. The second Tara in the vision, the girl whose eyes burned with fire, could wield it.

Her father's words echoed in her mind. *You have used it as well.*

"Certainly not!" she whispered, then placed both hands on the tinder. She focused her mind on this single goal, to give off enough heat to spark a tiny flame. But she had absorbed so much without knowing; first at the schoolhouse during her fight with Greta Greenbriar, then from Kailani's oven, and most recently she absorbed directly from the caldera.

The flame that poured out was unfettered, uncontrolled, and lit everything flammable under the outcropping. Ember leapt up, rejoicing, dancing in the flames as they rose into the sky, swirling with plumed feathers unharmed and made brighter by the heat. Even Tara, who recoiled expecting the fire to burn her skin, found it cool to the touch. She stood and, like her new feathered friend, danced in the fire and laughed with joy.

Tara had made her choice and had become Felicima's chosen agent.

CHAPTER THIRTY-EIGHT

Sebastian held the shroud in place with trembling hands, determined not to let Robert or the others see him worry. He imagined all eyes judging him, the cowardly failure who never obtained the status of Dreamer and silently begged the gods to make him better than he was—to keep them all safe. He hated being so close to the action; a battle was about to wage less than half a league away. Sickness claimed his stomach, and he fought to hold it down.

"Can you hear what they're saying?" Robert demanded.

He nodded. Of course he could. The conversation of war carried silently along the hidden airwaves and pounded like death upon his terrified ears.

"They're Fjorikan after all, not normal outlaws," Sebastian whispered back. "Murdock Kelly said so."

"A war party? *Here*? This far upriver?" Robert exclaimed. "Surely they couldn't have moved behind Eston's defenses!"

"Caroline just said they've been disguised among the immigrants and Murdock Kelly agreed," Sebastian explained. "I guess he's had real reason to distrust them. He just cursed Amash and spat, saying he and Percy Roan both warned him against letting so many across the border—that the real threat is more organized than the king wanted to admit!"

"Organized? It's only twenty men!" Robert insisted.

"Caroline spotted three more camps, each a league or more away. There's easily a hundred or more... probably more."

"So the general's right? They intend to attack Estonia from within our borders?"

"Seems so," Sebastian agreed. "Hang on," he said, holding up a finger and focusing his mind. Caroline was saying something he could barely make out.

"Percy Roan suspected this," she told the general, her voice now an echo in Sebastian's mind, brought softly along the wind. "Just last month he authorized the seizure of immigrant ships north of Estowen's Landing."

"Surely not? He has no authority to raise a navy without notifying me first!" Murdock Kelly protested.

"Not a navy," Bearnard explained. "He presented the Pirate's Guild with a new Letter of Marque, granting them pillage rights in the north in return for finding any evidence Fjorik intends war."

"The Pirate's Guild?" The general had grown angry at the news, but seemed pleased at the same time. "This gives me the war I wanted for sure," he admitted, "but he and Cuyler shouldn't have left me out of the plan! What did he pay them with? The pirates?"

"Firearms, to sell on the black market," Bearnard revealed.

"No! They'll find their way into Fjorik and fuel their war machine! So many will die!" the general argued.

"Nonetheless," Caroline explained, "Fjorik plans war, and Devil Jacque and his pirates are off their coast as we speak—too far to get this news back to the chancellor in a timely manner. We must clear these camps and bring the evidence back ourselves."

Sebastian bolted to his feet, suddenly determined to take action.

"What is it?" Robert demanded. "What did they say?"

"Devil Jacque... He's not sailing to Pirate's Cove! Eusari's gone in the wrong direction!"

Eusari waited on deck, watching as her crew brought forth crate after crate of the cursed instruments of death.

"Rifles," Anne said to Sippen. "Do you see what you and Braen Braston *did* to this world we're in?"

"Thuh... these are nuh... not my design," the little man protested, but his eyes betrayed his guilt. Every ranged weapon since those he'd first invented traced to him. Every death they brought linked him closer to hell, including that of his best friend long passed.

Eusari, reading the guilt on his face placed a hand around his shoulders. "The devil doesn't live in the steel, nor does the steel deserve fault," she told him. "The evil that takes innocent lives resides in the hearts of mankind, those who pull the trigger. Your invention is not to blame, but the weakness of those who wield it. We are all weak, that's our nature, but some among us are more prone to the lies whispered in our minds when weakest. The blame does not reside with you, Sippen, but within those who ignored the signs of those abusing your design."

"Where were these weapons going?" Marita asked Eusari.

"We don't know, because you killed the captain who could tell us that answer!" the Constable spat.

Marita again showed her the broken nail.

"That's not the question, Marita," Eusari insisted. "To *whom* were they going? That's the question we must answer. Who would use these weapons if we hadn't intervened? They certainly weren't headed for The Cove, that's clear, but perhaps to Soston? Middleton?"

Marita suddenly stood taller, taken over by some invisible force. Her eyes remained opened, but her jaw slackened wider. "Captain," she whispered.

"What? What do you see?" Eusari demanded.

"See? Not what I see, but what I was just told," the woman argued.

"Spit it out, then!" Constable Thorinson shouted. Her patience with Marita had waned thin.

"Sebastian... Robert... They're in trouble!" Marita exclaimed. "But they know where to find Devil Jacque!"

Eusari paused, her mind torn in two directions at this news. Robert, her charge, and Sebastian, her friend and faithful hand, needed her help. But Devil Jacque, that personification of evil she wished to extinguish, had her sons. "Where is he?" she demanded, making her choice.

"He's north," Marita gasped, "off the coast of Fjorik!"

"Hurry!" Eusari ordered her men. "Get these crates aboard *Reprisal*! Mr. Longshanks! Set a course to Fjorik!"

"I'll find them," Marita swore to her captain. "I'll find your boys!"

Caroline and Bearnard separated, each moving behind a line of General Kelly's dragoons. The enemy camp was alerted to their arrival, but only just in time to man their measly pickets. Even their fires and torches still burned near each line, caught without time to douse any at all. The northern soldiers hid behind their fences and berms like they had a chance to win this outcome—against the dragoons, maybe, but not against two Dreamers. This battle would be more of a rout than a fight, and she'd be back in the University by dinner.

"Company, halt!" the general shouted, no longer hiding his unit's presence in the forest. "Scatter ranks!" On his command the dragoons fanned out, found their own cover, and formed a wide arc around the camp. There was only one way to flee, and that would be straight into the river at the enemies backs. "Hold fire," he cautioned, "until we can see the blues of their scheming northern eyes!"

Caroline stole a glance in Bearnard's direction. He, like her, waited to see how the general planned to use their help. So far this was his fight alone until they needed to step in.

Why isn't the enemy firing yet? she asked her partner. *It's almost like they* wanted *the dragoons to form their snare.*

I'm wondering that as well, the broad shouldered Dreamer replied. *Something's off, for sure.*

Caroline turned to address the general, to warn him of a trap, when she noticed the slightest shimmering of air just beyond Bearnard. It had been a subtle shift of light that gave it away, and she would have missed it had it not been for the angle. She'd never seen anything like this weave— no, not a weave, more like a compressed ball of air hovering just at the Dreamer's feet.

Bearnard! she quickly warned. *Look to your left!*

Where? he asked, confused and now scanning the woods beside him.

No! By your feet! Look down!

I see nothing! he replied.

Caroline wildly turned her head left and right, scanning for more and finding one off to her own right. This one she could see more clearly, certainly a compressed ball of air—no, the purest portion of it humans needed to survive. Somehow, someone had separated the particles and chose only this gas to remain as a floating ball hidden among the ferns and leaves.

"It's a trap!" she yelled to the general.

But her warning came too late, as several enemy soldiers touched tiny fuses against their torches.

Of course! she realized how the trap would spring, but it was a moment too late. "Get down!" she commanded, and some of the lucky dragoons listened. The grenades flew through the air, each in a different direction and not necessarily into the line of dragoons. Each path was predetermined, and Caroline watched as one of the bombs flew just to Bearnard's left and another landed just to her own right.

The explosions were violent and immediate. Each ball of compressed gas erupted with roaring flame as the traps expanded, a phenomenon the Dreamers had witnessed once before—on a battlefield so far distanced by time she'd nearly forgotten. The backdraft roared with heat and flame, flinging men in every direction, scattering both their screams and limbs into the forest.

Caroline gasped when she again lifted her head, the ringing thrumming a constant tone drowning out gunfire. All around her, dragoons recovered and fired upon the now advancing enemy and pushed them back behind their pickets. She tried to stand but the world around her swayed. The Dreamer fell hard to the forest floor. With panic controlling the pace of her heart, she noticed Bearnard no longer stood where he had. Only a blackened crater remained.

Slowly her mind settled and sound returned, drowning out the ringing tone and replacing it with soft moans of the wounded.

"Hold steady, men!" the unfocused image of General Kelly commanded, having picked up a rifle from a dead dragoon. He took aim while leading the defense. "Hold them back!"

Caroline managed to find her knees and pulled them under her belly, righting her view of the battlefield with eyes straining to understand the images as they cleared.

"Emotants!" she spat in the direction of the general. "They have emotants!"

"Find them!" he insisted.

She tried to, reaching out with tendrils to see upon the air, but abruptly let go with a puff of futility when several binding whisps wrapped like pythons around her body. *There,* she thought as she followed the braided strands to their source—two men and a woman dressed in northern attire, all snow white like their homeland. Upon their backs and heads the trio wore the hooded fur cloaks of their order. *Snow Cats!* She recognized from the war, the zealot cultists from the north.

Caroline tried to rise up and fight, but their grip tightened—there were too many to fight off. These were not Falconers, nor were they as limited in their use of the craft, they were true wielders of power—emotants destined to become Dreamers had their fates not locked them in the madness of fervent religion. They controlled her now, overwhelmed by combined strength greater than her own. With Bearnard she might have had a chance, maybe still could if the coward joined in. She struggled to free herself.

Helpless to aid, she knelt on the forest floor and watched as a gust of wind blew back General Kelly's dragoons. Very soon they would be overrun and Prince Robert captured or killed, and all Caroline could do was watch.

CHAPTER THIRTY-NINE

Sebastian maintained the shroud, hiding the civilians the best he could despite the explosions all around. They belonged neither to General Kelly nor the Dreamers, and reeked of ambush. The sudden, ferocious fireballs posed a threat he had never seen, a new way to inflict mass casualty. Fear forced its way into his body, forcing his heart to pump faster and his hands to tremble. He hated death. Yet, it harassed him since childhood.

Beside him, Robert winced. Sebastian could tell the young prince felt compelled to do something other than cower. He tried to rise but Sebastian grabbed his shoulder and shoved him down.

"Let me go," the prince demanded, "I'm better than this!"

"No!" Sebastian urged. "You're not trained! You'll get yourself killed!"

"I have to try," Robert insisted, again scrambling to his feet for a better look. A gust of wind sent him sprawling backward, and he hit the ground hard, knocking out his breath. Sebastian waved his hand, and a stream of air rushed into the boy's lungs, filling them with a gasp.

"That blast wasn't aimed at you," Sebastian encouraged. "I don't think they can see us."

"Who are they?" Robert panted. "Are they Falconers?"

"Worse," Sebastian replied dryly. "I think they're Snow Cats."

Robert had never heard of these, but the former Dreamer filled him in quickly. Religious zealots from the north with emotant abilities.

"So General Kelly fights Fjorik?"

"I'm afraid so."

"I haven't seen Bearnard since the first blast!" Robert worried. "And Caroline's tied down by two of them!"

The Dreamers were not his friends and had never been good to him, but something within Sebastian changed. The fear seemed to dissipate, replaced by concern for others. "Stay here," he commanded Robert and the others, "and I'll keep you hidden."

"I'm coming," Robert argued.

"Then stay behind me and only try to unwind their weaves. You're not strong offensively yet, and they're well trained in killing."

"Okay," Robert agreed, but obviously yearned to do more. "But that means it's up to you! Are you sure you can fight?"

Sebastian wavered at the question, but his feet continued moving forward. He found Caroline just as Robert described, pinned down and tied by six wispy tentacles of air. Two Snow Cats stood over the woman, wearing their signature attire—white hooded furs of the north. With surprise on his side, he unraveled all six at once, maintaining a constant parry as each emotant tried to quickly replace them.

Seven divisions of his mind. He had never attempted so many since boyhood, yet it felt so casual.

Caroline tried to stand but two more Snow Cats stepped out of the woods on her flank. They quickly sealed her in an intricate bubble—the kind that robbed the victim of air. They meant to kill not capture.

"Unravel their bubble," Sebastian told Robert, and sent six blasts of air in rapid succession. Thirteen divisions. Each struck the pair in their chests, pounding hard upon their sternums. One of them fell lifeless, her heart unable to withstand the force. Sebastian stumbled, saddened by the loss of human life, but noticed Caroline collapsed to her knees and struggling to breathe.

Robert hadn't figured out the weave.

It had weakened with one of the emotants down, and Sebastian parried the other's attack, holding it at bay while Caroline gasped for air as her prison evaporated. Eight Divisions. He had to keep track, or he may over extend.

The first Snow Cats turned their attack toward Robert, hoping to distract Sebastian but he had found a zone of concentration. With a wave of his hand he threw up two shields around the prince, holding those in place while sending out a bubble of his own. Eleven divisions. It wrapped around the pair and slowly contracted, squeezing the northern attackers together. He added an extra layer to hold them tight in case they unraveled his attack. Twelve.

"Charge those two!" Sebastian called out to General Kelly.

The military commander glanced their way, but replied, "I can't! We're pinned down by riflemen!"

Without looking, Sebastian send a concussive blast that pushed back the line of northern soldiers. Thirteen. He repeated that attack while Kelly sent two dragoons charging the Snow Cats with bayonets. Out of nowhere the third Snow Cat hurled five air bombs toward Sebastian. Robert waved his hands, working out their structure, and three of them dissipated. That left two for Sebastian.

He immediately saw what Robert had discovered. They weren't woven the same as the bubbles but rather were an inverted version that worked from within. He reached out and untied the hold in the center, working it like the catch of a lock. The air harmlessly puffed out from each.

Fifteen divisions of his mind. Sebastian fell to his knees, dizzied by the effort.

Thankfully Caroline had regained her feet just as the dragoons pierced the hearts of the captured pair. She wove and intricate pattern and cast a strong net over the remaining emotant.

Sebastian passed out cold.

Robert, helpless in the fight except to defuse the three air bombs, watched as his friend slumped unmoving to the ground. He knelt to help, but Caroline shouted for attention.

"He'll be fine!" she yelled. "Form a layer of bubbles around this net! Hold her tight!"

"I... I don't know how!" he admitted.

"Like this!" She traced the pattern and Robert nodded, copying her movement and channeling the air within his hands to match. It obeyed, shimmering and forming around the woman wearing white furs.

Robert shivered with an invisible chill, noticing how much colder the forest air had become. His eyes remained locked on the woman laying at his feet. She was old, at least eighty summers, but her eyes pierced his with hatred, shouting for him to kill her and send her to someone called the All Father.

Robert diverted his eyes elsewhere. General Kelly and his dragoons had chased away the attackers, sending them deep into the forest. Caroline knelt above an unmoving Bearnard.

"He's alive," she said with a breath of relief, "but burned badly." She sent tiny currents of rich air around his body, nourishing his skin where it had singed and melted away.

"Get him on the wagon," Murdock Kelly commanded his men. "I'm sorry, Your Highness," he added, "but your expedition to find a bird is ended. We must return at once."

To his surprise, Caroline placed a kind hand on Robert's shoulder. "You did well."

"I did very little at all."

"But you showed courage and adeptness. I'll talk to Cuyler about your training. Even if you can't be a Dreamer, you need to learn to defend yourself and others."

"What about him?" He pointed at Sebastian, recovered and sitting up, but dazed and confused.

Caroline knelt beside the man and looked him in the eyes. "Sebastian," she said. "Can you understand me?"

He nodded. He was mostly alert.

She wrapped her arms around him as tears fell slowly down her cheeks. "I've been... No, *we've* been so awful to you for too many years. I'm so sorry for everything I've said or done to you. You are *not* a coward, and I see you now for who you are. You saved us, all of us, today, and I owe my life to you."

"I..." Sebastian stammered, not expecting such kindness from Caroline. "I forgive you," he finally said.

Robert watched as the dragoons loaded first Bearnard and then the Snow Cat into the wagon. Caroline and Sebastian explained to him how to maintain his bubble during the ride to Eston. He nodded quietly, sobered by the events of the day.

Suddenly feeling very homesick and alone, the young prince yearned for the company of Eusari, Franque, Krist, Sippen, and Cedric. But, he realized, even though they were off on their own adventures, he was vastly blessed by the gods to have Sebastian. In this moment he missed someone else, yearning for another friend more deeply than he ever understood possible.

Tara, he mourned, sending his thoughts to her, wherever she may be. *I love you, and I need you with me. I don't want to be alone without you,* he told her. Even if she couldn't hear him, the effort gave him strength.

He turned, just as Caroline whispered to General Kelly. The man stood with wide eyes, staring up at Robert, then abruptly knelt. Caroline, Sebastian, and the dragoons did the same.

"What?" the prince demanded. "What are you doing?"

"King Esterling is dead," Caroline explained. "Cuyler just informed me that Amash collapsed during breakfast."

A mournful screech caught his ear from above and Robert looked up. Perched atop the highest tree he spotted an eagle. It fanned its wings and shook, sending another sad cry echoing through the forest. It leapt upward and circled.

"Reach out to him, Your Highness," Caroline persuaded gently. "He's invited you to bond."

Robert Esterling trembled with both fear and excitement, then closed his eyes. He reached out, just as he had so many times before, yearning to sail above the treetops and glide upon the wind. When he opened them, he spotted himself standing so tiny on the forest floor. The eagle screeched again, but this time it was with joyful laughter—the last boyish dream fulfilled before celebrating his seventeenth summer as a king.

CHAPTER FORTY

Krist stood with Sven in their quarters, staring down at a bucket of water. So far it had done nothing except slosh back and forth in tempo with the rocking ship. What they had hoped to achieve with it, was yet to be decided.

"Stir it," Sven suggested.

"I'm trying."

"Try harder."

"*You* do it if it's so easy!" Krist snapped.

"Give it up," Franque muttered from his bunk. "If you had powers you'd have figured them out by now."

"Maybe you have to be under duress to use them," Sven offered.

"What does that mean?" Krist asked wide-eyed.

"I don't know, maybe sick or injured," the Northman suggested.

Franque swiftly kicked his foot, connecting hard with Krist's ear.

"Ow! What in Cinder's Crack was *that* for?"

Franque shrugged and asked Sven. "Did the water stir?"

"Nope, not a bit."

"Well, that's as duress as I dare put him under."

Krist turned and punched his brother in the gut, causing Franque to double over in a mixture of laughter and pain.

Sven picked up the bucket. "Let's try something else. Maybe his power isn't over the water itself, but the sea life. Let's go topside."

"Just steer clear of Boats," Franque suggested. "He's been in a fouler mood than normal, and might not care you two are off duty right now. If he sees you with a bucket, he may have you swab or dump the piss pots." He closed his eyes and tried once more to nap—the activity the others had interrupted with their experiment.

After the pair had gone, he drew in a deep breath and held it, letting it out slowly. His mind quickly caught pace with the ship's rocking and started to drift. This, he had discovered, was the best part of being at sea—the deepest, most restful, sleep he had ever experienced. He dreamily thought of home, their farm, and how many secrets their mother had managed to keep from them all. Had he not loved her so deeply, he may have resented her lies.

Soon he dozed restfully, dreaming no longer of home but again at sea. He stood on the forecastle of a copper sided frigate, much larger than *She Wolf* and faster by several knots. The winds behind him howled with fury and fed a steady stream into the sails. Atop the mast flew a banner of a wolf. He looked up and found his mother standing beside him, dressed in black leather, and wearing a hooded cloak. The hood, he realized, was the head of a wolf.

"They're near Ataraxia," the drunk from Loganshire said, stepping up to look out over the sea. "We're close now, and she said she can see the ship but only one of the boys is topside. She has no idea which of the twins it is."

"Can she push us faster?" Eusari asked.

"No, mum, not without risking structural damage, she said. "But don't worry, it'll all be over soon."

A stern looking woman approached with hands on hips, demanding both time and attention from Eusari. Annoyed, she turned her eyes from the sea and met hers.

"Have you given thought to how you'll force his surrender?" the woman asked. "It won't do to kill him like the other. I may not be able to charge *her*, but I can surely make a case for premeditated murder for you."

"I promise to take him alive," Eusari insisted, but Franque doubted her sincerity. He could smell the anger rising up from her pores. It seethed and boiled, and tasted like murder. He licked his long tongue over his sharp teeth and savored the flavor of blood.

"They're just over the horizon!" a third woman's voice shouted over the howling wind.

"Soon, then," Eusari said, taking a deep breath to steady her nerves. Now she gave off a new scent, a mixture of fear, excitement, and revenge.

Franque felt her tug at their connection, but he resisted, growling slightly at the intrusion. His mother's eyes met his at once, deeply disturbed by the sudden insubordination. They reflected back a black wolf, not her son. The next feeling was more than a tug; it was a forceful shove.

His eyes snapped open immediately, once again laying in his bunk and feeling the rocking of *She Wolf* upon the waves. The dream—it *had* to be a dream—had felt wrong. He swung his feet over the side and slipped on his boots to head topside.

Krist and Sven leaned over the rail, watching the water splash against the hull. A pod of dolphins swam merrily in the ship's wake, jumping and sunning before splashing deep to repeat their fun. So far, every attempt to connect with the creatures failed, and Krist felt ready to give up.

"It's useless," he said.

"Keep trying," suggested Sven.

Footsteps approached and the boys turned to find Zane Rogers and Devil Jacque nearby.

"When we offload the crates in Ataraxia, insist we get a signed bill of lading. Our benefactor said we only get paid the second half after delivery," Devil Jacque explained.

"Aye, Captain," Zane said with a swift salute and then hurried off.

"What are you slackers doing?" Devil Jacque demanded of Krist and Sven. "Boats!" he shouted, "Haven't you any work for these slugs!"

Krist froze, of all people to catch him skylarking, it *had* to be the captain. He was about to open his mouth to protest, when Franque approached, saving them both with his timely arrival.

"They're watching for sails, Captain," he said. "This close to Fjorik they wanted to win Boat's bounty. He said he'd give five days light duty to the person who spots the next one."

"Is that true, Boats?" Jacque asked the man as he approached to chastise his slackers. "Did you offer a bounty on the next sail spotted?"

"Aye, I thought it'd be a good way to sharpen eyes this far north, but I never dreamed they'd use it as an excuse to skip their bunks when off duty."

"Seems like they need *extra* duty, then."

Boats saluted as the captain strolled away. Turning to the trio he growled over his shoulder, "You heard the man, grab your marlinspikes and go splice more line."

Krist and Sven both groaned, but Franque waited calmly till the boatswain mate left them alone. "Mother's coming," he said.

"What? How do you know?"

"I can't describe it, but it's more than a feeling," Franque explained. "I think she's close. I had a dream."

Krist and Sven said nothing, only stared back, perturbed.

"What?" he asked, meeting their faces.

"Is this a joke?" Krist demanded, suddenly angry with his brother.

"No, why?"

"I've been trying for weeks to find my powers if I have any. But here you are, pretending to have a prophetic dream." With two hands he shoved Franque backward, causing him to stagger. "Don't even joke about it being *you* because guess what? It's *not* you! If it's either of us with powers, it's me!"

"I'm not joking, and I'm not trying to take *anything* from you," Franque replied, returning the shove hard enough Krist slammed into the rail, nearly falling overboard.

Krist recovered, his right hook catching Franque across the chin.

The blows flooded in thereafter, with each boy forgetting the other was his brother. Sven yelled for them to stop, but the punches showed no sign of stopping. Boats tried to intervene, and a huge left uppercut from Krist sent him sprawling to the deck. Ben Thompson stepped in where the boatswain had failed, and a headbutt from Franque hurled the quartermaster to the deck. The entire crew gathered around, too speechless by the display to cheer or jeer or try to stop it.

Devil Jacque finally stepped in, hell-bent on bringing order to his vessel, but Krist missed a wild right cross that connected with the captain's nose, crushing the tiny bones that held it upright. The blood that flowed spilled unstoppable on the deck, even after Franque missed his brother with a headbutt that crushed the captain's upper lip as well. No one else dared to intervene, except for Sven who kept screaming for the brothers to stop.

Why should we? thought Franque. With all the brothers had put up with, they deserved this chance to box things out, and who cared if their mother came soon or not. But Krist took advantage of Franque's slow left parry and met his temple with another solid right cross. Franque roared, but Krist met his brother's challenge with an elbow to the eye and a knee to the groin. All was fair in war and family, and Franque would forgive him later... but not in this moment.

Cookie stepped in, hoping to stop the fray, but Franque gripped his neck with fingers ten. Krist, realizing the crew had set upon his brother, pulled out his marlinspike and turned to meet Boats now steady on his feet. The man roared and charged, but Krist was faster, sinking it deep into the man's temple. It was a mistake, a reaction almost, but the deed was done and the boatswain fell to the deck with upstaring eyes.

"Sails!" screamed the lookout, breaking Franque from his bloodlust. Sven stood beside the brothers, staring down at the brained boatswain and strangled cook. Two men had fallen to their rage, but neither terrified the Northman as much as the weather.

"Look!" he cried, pointing at the sky once blue and serene.

Franque followed his finger and his eyes grew wide with wonder at the storm now raging above. Even the sea had turned angry, tossing and swirling the ship in circles. Then he noticed his brother, angry and panting several paces away with intent to charge. *He'll kill me,* Franque realized, *brother or not.*

But the sails on the horizon had closed in quickly, and Franque pointed them out to his brother. "She's here," he pleaded, "to deal with the captain."

"Battle stations!" someone roared from topside. "They sail a flag of no quarter!"

"I know that banner," Devil Jacque shouted with disbelief. "All hands topside! Load cannons and prepare to fight!"

He pointed at Franque and Krist. "Bind these two! I need them as barter against the she-wolf!"

"What in Cinder's Crack is happening over there?" Eusari demanded of Marita.

"Your boys," the woman, always confident and laughing off danger, replied with a tremor in her voice and horror reflected in her eyes, "are fighting and the sea is angry."

"No!" Eusari picked up a spy glass and watched as *She Wolf* swirled around in circles, caught in a maelstrom and pounded from above by a powerful tempest. The rest of the sea around her remained calm, a serenity surrounding her son's rage. *But which controls the water?* she wondered. "Get us there now! We don't have time to waste!"

Marita pushed the ship to near breaking point while Longshanks and Krill readied the guns and crew.

"This isn't how I wanted it!" Eusari said to Marita. "I wanted more time to prepare. He'll kill them before we get there!"

The constable interrupted. "Just a reminder that you have to capture Devil Jacque alive," she said.

"Shut up," Eusari screamed, the anger inside growing with her panic.

"We had a deal!" Anne shouted, stepping up to face her aunt. "We do this honorably!"

"The deal hasn't changed, but you *will* shut up while I do it!" Turning to address the crew, the captain added, "Only fire at those who shoot at us first! I won't risk either of my boys getting killed by mistake. Parumba! You're with Marita and me on the landing party. The rest of you stay aboard until I know the boys are secured. Longshanks, you have command."

"Aye, mum!" the first mate replied. The others readied themselves with rifles while Krill sighted only the smaller cannons. Parumba stepped forward.

"Take three of the wolves," she told him, handing those three over. "Marita and I will deal with the crew while you separate the captain. Whatever happens, don't let the coward take the easy way out, and no matter what don't let him take my boys!"

Parumba nodded, turning to Charleigh and taking a handful of her tiny contraptions.

"What are those?" Eusari demanded as the woman shoved several in her hands as well.

"Sippen thought of them. They're untested, but he thinks they'll work. Throw them on the ground hard enough to break open, then tap into the seedlings inside."

"Seedlings? I don't understand."

"Make them grow," Parumba told Eusari with a smile. "Use them to fight!"

A wide grin filled the captain's face and she winked at Sippen standing beside Krill. He nodded and went back to work helping his friend.

"We're almost there, Captain!" Marita warned.

A volley rang out from *She Wolf*. At close range there was no way to counter maneuver. Thankfully their gunners sighted in haste and only half their cannons struck *Reprisal*. The entire ship trembled with impact, but the waterline held and no one appeared injured.

"She wasted her shot!" Eusari exclaimed. Turning to Longshanks, she added, "Get the grappling hooks ready!"

Marita abruptly cut off the wind to the sails, sending them limp and dangling from their masts. *Reprisal* turned and came alongside the smaller vessel. Momentarily catching wind, the sails fluttered and threatened to send the ship into a wild spin. It lurched and the grappling crew tumbled to the deck.

"Cut the lines!" Longshanks shouted, "Let the sails fly!"

Krill was the closest and scrambled up the mast with a knife in his teeth, his arms pulling his body weight as his pegged-leg dangled uselessly. Eusari marveled for a moment at the speed at which the man moved when most needed. He sliced the tether to the mains, sending the canvas ripping off into the storm.

The grapple team stood to cast their lines, but riflemen on the other ship were ready and fired immediately. Four men fell to the deck and the rest of the team scrambled for cover. Krill gave a command, screaming from atop the barren mast, and a volley from his sharpshooters sent the enemy ducking.

Eusari stole a look over the side, watching as Jacque's crew handed out weapons.

"They weren't ready for us at all," Eusari observed. "The boy's fight made a good distraction."

The grappling team finally tossed their lines. Nearly all the hooks caught and the crew began heaving the vessels together. Eusari nodded to Parumba and Marita. It was time to save her boys.

Franque never looked up at the ship pulled alongside. He knew his mother was on it, was glad she came, but his entire focus remained on Krist. His brother was now fully enveloped in his rage, his mood matching the storm raging overhead and churning the seas below. He was incoherent, babbling about the Fjorik All Father with hands wrapped around Zane Roger's throat. Spit sprayed the man's face as he muttered something about being a god.

Several crewmen had heeded their captain and circled the boys, fearful like rounding up rabid dogs.

"Krist," Franque pleaded, "please calm down. Mother's here." He looked around to find Sven to help, finding the man cowering behind a barrel with eyes locked on his friend and shocked by his madness. "Help me!" Franque shouted, tackling his brother and wrapping his arms and legs tightly around him to subdue the rage. Sven rushed over and helped pry relentless fingers from the dead man's throat.

Franque had a good hold on him, finally, and lay there on the deck with his brother while a battle ensued. He watched as Devil Jacque, the man once earning his respect, trembled, broke, and ran to his quarters like a coward. Eusari had arrived.

Franque watched as several figures leaped over the rail. A dark skinned man and a woman appeared first, followed by his mother. She was dressed just as she had in Franque's dream, in black leathers and wearing a black wolf cloak. They were followed by six beasts, snarling and savagely attacking the crewmen who stood to repel boarders.

The dark skinned man and Eusari took a moment to throw several small objects on the deck. Almost immediately, dozens of growing vines sprang to life all around the ship. These twisted and crawled as they matured to full size right before everyone's eyes, grabbing for necks, arms, and legs to hold onto. A dozen crewmen rushed the three invaders and Franque wondered why his mother had not brought actual soldiers aboard. Then he found out.

The woman beside her drew dual swords and sat back into a blades-man's stance, one of the legendary sword fighters and martial artists Franque had only heard stories of. She danced before the attackers and felled each one by one as they charged. To Franque's surprise, his mother had entered her own form of dance, a blur among the crew, a creature of shadows forced into daylight, but ready to dole out death.

Eusari pulled knives from hidden sheaths and pockets. If she left one inside a man, she would deftly pull a second, then quickly retrieve the first and fling it mercilessly toward another victim. She was a killing machine. Franque continued to watch, wide-eyed and bewildered, marveling at the calmness in the way she killed. When she and the other woman finished, and the counterattack lay defeated, fifteen men had fallen dead while the remainder of the crew lay bound with vines writhing like snakes about their bodies.

The dark skinned man and three of the wolves made their way to the captain's quarters. He knelt, studying the lock as a vine wriggled its way into the mechanism. He then stepped to the side and turned the knob, pushing it open while the wolves raced inside. Two shots rang out in succession, both high expecting a human to enter, followed by shouts and screams for mercy.

"He's disarmed," the man said to Eusari without even looking inside.

"That was fast," she said with a nod, and the remaining three wolves slowly entered the cabin to join the others. The mother knelt beside her sons. In a gentle voice, she explained to Franque, "Krist entered a berserker rage, and it will take some more time for it to wear off. When it finally does he will be weak and need to eat—sugar would be best for the energy he'll need."

"I know," Franque admitted weakly. "I've experienced it too."

"I always feared one or both of you would," she admitted, "your father was a berserker."

"We know our fathers are different," Franque admitted. "We've learned much on this voyage."

Eusari paused, sorrow filling her face at the thought of losing a son. "I know we've much to discuss," she admitted. "I'm sorry I've kept so many secrets from you all."

Franque nodded. Though this moment was not the time, he asked, "Which one of us is really your son? Do you even know?"

"I know," she said. "I've always known, even if I've only recently learned the truth." Bending down, she gently kissed his forehead and whispered into his ear. "Because you much more resemble your father's gentler mood."

"I've killed," Franque blurted out. "Women, even."

"So have I, but what's important is that it matters now to you." She stood, eyes darting to business she must attend in the captain's quarters. "I promise we'll discuss everything later—after Krist has recovered."

Franque watched her go, a woman he had known his entire life, just realizing he knew nothing about her at all.

CHAPTER FORTY-ONE

The trip to Eston took only two days. The most amazing part of the voyage was watching Marita fill the sails of two vessels at once. She reclined on the forecastle of *Reprisal*, sunning her body while she worked. Adorned in the bathing attire of the Southern Continent, she wore only the bottom half, her top exposed to the world. Somehow she avoided stares, gawks, and leers, the crew either finally respecting or fearing for their own lives if accidentally gazing upon their sailing master. She could have laid out naked and they wouldn't have cared or noticed.

Next to her lay Krill doing the same and wearing only his skivvies while telling her stories about fights he'd been in *back in the good ol' days*, as he put it. The two laughed and joked about how much better those days had been.

The rest of the crew and passengers seemed oddly muted in their feelings toward a mission complete, and most seemed sad to have this one come to an end. Sippen hadn't been feeling well since the fight, and he spent most of the voyage home resting in *Reprisal*'s sick bay. Parumba and Charleigh worked out kinks in their inventions. Peter Longshanks appeared to relish his renewed spirit for sailing, leading the crew and smiling all the way as temporary captain.

Aboard *She Wolf*, Franque and Krist, were ordered by their mother to do nothing. Though promised a return trip without labor, but both chose to pitch in and helped the crew any way possible. They had each grown into adept sailors and actually seemed to enjoy the work. Only Eusari and Anne seemed burdened during the voyage as they sat inside *She Wolf's* brig with six actual wolves standing guard over Devil Jacque.

"What about the rifles and ammunition?" Anne demanded. She led the interrogation while Eusari mostly sat and listened.

"I know nothing about rifles and ammunition," the prisoner lied.

"I have witnesses, even your former quartermaster, who swear you were taking them to Ataraxia for smuggling into Fjorik. Why were you both attacking immigrants and also providing arms to their government?"

"I know nothing about rifles and ammunition," Jacque repeated, sticking to the code of the Pirate's Guild.

"He won't talk," Eusari finally said, frustrated. "He's bound by an oath." She stood, fed up with the entire exchange. "Besides, it's obvious someone wants him to start a war by attacking innocents and arming those who would want revenge. He won't give up the *who* no matter what you ask without torture."

"Well I *won't* torture him!" Anne exclaimed.

Eusari shrugged, "Then he won't talk." Without another word she left the room and ascended the tall ladder. Once topside she strolled toward the captain's cabin, *her* old cabin. Franque and Krist sat outside its door, happily whistling and splicing line. "Follow me, boys. It's time to talk," she said, leading them inside.

The cabin had retained its familiarity, despite she hadn't slept in these quarters in seventeen years. The wood seemed more worn than she remembered, and more boards creaked than before, but it hadn't changed a bit. She ran her fingers along a smooth table in the corner and sat down, urging the boys to sit across from her. She had once sat across from Braen Braston in this very spot. She nearly wept at that sudden memory and pushed it aside.

"I know you've got questions," she said, "so ask."

"The girl I met," Franque began, "who said her name was Gretchen, said Krist's mother was a queen."

"You met Gretchen?"

Franque nodded.

"It seems Samani found a way to mettle from beyond the grave," she muttered angrily. "What did Gretchen tell you?"

"She said the Queen of Fjorik demanded from her a way to end pregnancy, to kill Skander's child, but it was too late. She tried to convince Braen the child was his, she said. Is this true?"

"I only learned this recently myself, but I believe it so," she admitted.

Krist appeared downtrodden by the news. "So we aren't… we aren't brothers? You aren't my mother?"

"No matter what, you *are* my son. Don't you feel like brothers?"

"Well, yeah," he replied honestly.

"Then you're brothers *and* cousins. But either way, you're both *my* sons."

"Who *was* my mother, then? What was she like?" Krist asked.

"She was a strong and beautiful woman," Eusari said truthfully, "and, like Gretchen said, she was a queen. I admired her in some ways and envied her for many more."

"And this Skander? He was a king so I'm a prince?"

Eusari fell quiet, choosing her next words carefully. "Braen was the eldest son and Skander was the youngest, but Braen never sat upon the throne nor wore the crown."

Franque interrupted. "I remember Headmaster saying Braen killed the real king."

"No," Eusari corrected, "that act was committed by Skander and blamed on Braen."

"Great," complained Krist. "My father was a murderer *and* a thief."

"He suffered from illness," Eusari explained, though it pained her to speak kindly or without detail about Krist's father, "an illness that affected his mind. He lost it completely in the end, and his death became a mercy."

"Is that what I have to look forward to?" Krist demanded. "I lost my mind on the ship! Am I crazy too?" he demanded.

"I lost mine in battle," Franque admitted to his brother. "I think this is something else."

"You are both descended from a line of berserkers, like those you described fighting on the Fjorik ship, Franque. That is a different thing entirely and something you can learn to control most of the time. No, the illness was far worse, more dangerous, and neither of you show any signs of it."

"You know this? How?" Krist demanded.

"I know because we've been watching you both very closely for signs since the day you both were born. Sippen, Sebastian, Krill, Collette, and

I, all of us knew what to look for. You are both strong, well balanced boys—albeit rough around the edges. Neither of you have anything to fear."

"Why did Devil Jacque hate Braen Braston so badly?" Franque asked.

"Because Braen possessed the one thing Jacque could never have—my heart."

"So you loved him?" Franque asked. "You loved my father and he loved you?"

"Very deeply. My greatest loss throughout the years was losing him. He was the only man I've *ever* loved. He taught me *how* to love. He taught me how to..." She fell quiet, choking back a small sob and wiping away tears. "He taught me how to trust and show compassion. He truly was the most compassionate person I've ever met."

"But he also had a dark side?" Franque pressed.

"Yes. He also had a darker side and learned to balance the two. Boys," Eusari urged, "war is coming with Fjorik. Promise me, both of you, not to investigate your roots. Have nothing to do with Fjorik and its zealots, especially them."

"What about Sven?" Krist asked. "He's my friend and is now part of this crew."

"I'm sure a single friendship, especially one formed at sea would be fine. As far as the crew, we've no longer need of ships. I intend to sell both *Reprisal* and *She Wolf* in Eston."

"I would like to keep one," Franque admitted. "I've decided I like the ship life very much and, if you were to sponsor the crew and a new captain, I'd like to remain a crewman."

"Absolutely not," Eusari protested. This life was no place for her boys. Or was it? She softened, mulling it over. She would not have to sail them herself but legally own two ships. She trusted Peter Longshanks to captain one, and she could commission the other. "We'll see," she finally said. "What about the quartermaster we captured. Ben Thompson? Can we trust him? What if I kept him onboard? He offered his services."

"He's fair," Franque explained. "Wise and experienced in business and able to work one gold piece into several with only a ledger."

"So, practical?"

"Yes," Krist agreed. "I trust him."

"As do I," added Franque.

"Then I'll hire him on *if* I decide to sponsor merchants." She decided it was time for the big surprise. "There's more that's happened, boys, since you've been away on this adventure. Your brother, Robert, is a prince in his own right. He was my ward, you knew I wasn't his mother."

"Yes, the Dreamers said he was the true heir to the kingdom."

"Well, he's no longer the heir. King Amash died while we were looking for you, and Robert is now officially the king, although the chancellor will rule the kingdom as regent for one year."

Both boys grew wide-eyed and their mouths dropped open.

"We should just make it back for his coronation and the balls that will follow."

"Balls?" Franque's earlier excitement diminished. "Certainly we're not expected to dance?"

"You are and you will, and those lessons begin today. Krill will be your dance instructor and you must learn the basic waltz at the very least."

"Krill?" questioned Krist. "Don't you mean Cedric?"

"We're out to sea, so we deal with Krill," she said, rolling her eyes. "Now go prepare to bring both ships alongside. This is *one* school I won't *let* you skip out on!"

The boys rose, dejectedly, and departed, leaving Eusari alone with her thoughts. After a few moments a knock shook her door.

"Come in," she commanded.

The door opened and Ben Thompson entered, with head down and offering a plea.

"Captain," he begged, "Your sons told me you haven't made your decision, but I wanted to speak with you plainly."

"Go on," she said, interested in his offer.

"I know who Devil Jacque's benefactor is—who sent us raiding and commissioned him to deliver the firearms."

"So do I," she said. "It was Percy Roan."

"How?" he asked, surprised.

"He's always been a schemer, and this is just the sort of thing he'd do. He wanted a war, even when his king did not. Why do you tell me now, when your captain won't even break his code?"

"Because I'm not at all like the pirates. I, too, was captured during a raid many years ago. I was put to work on *She Wolf* and worked my way up from seaman. I was learned, so Jacque assigned me to the books, never realizing how much I resented both him and the crooked ledger he forced me to keep."

"So you'll turn him over?"

"Of course I will."

"I may be in need of a man like you," she said, "to run legitimate merchant business once I fully retire. Are you interested?"

"I.. why, yes, ma'am!"

"If I decide to do so, I will let you know. As for any evidence against Devil Jacque, will you step ashore and testify against him?"

"Ma'am," the quartermaster said sadly, "I'm not suited to life ashore. My sea legs wouldn't do me any good past the pier. I'll give you my ledgers and the knowledge to put away Devil Jacque, but do not ask me something as foolish as to walk on dry land."

"But you have it, the evidence we'll need to put him away for crimes outside his charter as a guilded pirate?"

"I have it," the quartermaster promised, "and more."

"Then welcome aboard, Captain Thompson, you can have whichever vessel Captain Longshanks refuses."

CHAPTER FORTY-TWO

The entire populace filled the Span, lining the streets from palace to Unification Square. Many more perched atop buildings for a view. Engineers had worked for weeks erecting a grand review platform, with two thrones set atop a high stairwell. Only the nobles and merchant class were allowed within the safety perimeter, and even they had arrived early for the best vantage point for watching the ceremony. Since it was now officially summer, the city of Eston was awash in color, with crimson roses in full bloom along every building, street, and walkway. There were no banners, of course, as these were furled for the great revelation of the king's chosen crest.

Robert's legs trembled as he climbed into the carriage, ready to make the processional into a display of its own. Percy would not ride with him, as regent it would be too presumptuous, but neither could Eusari or his brothers—even as nobles, they were too low-born. Sebastian couldn't even ride with him and sat perched atop the carriage with the driver. Only General Murdoch Kelly was on hand to keep him company and, given their recent adventure, made a welcome companion.

"I'm terrified," Robert admitted.

"I bet you are," the general said with a laugh. "Just remember to smile and wave like you aren't, though."

With great fanfare the carriage began to roll, easing forward and churning the young king's stomach even more than it was. A great cheer went up from the crowd, a thunderous one as the joyful chants and cries made their way toward the Span.

"Your Highness," the general said, suddenly very serious with his tone. "I don't want to spoil this day, but I have some concerns to share with you, and this was the only place to truly speak alone without the rest of your counsel."

Robert's face dropped, suddenly worried by the covert nature of this conversation. "What's wrong?" he asked.

"Nothing yet, but I fear it's coming soon."

"Why the secrecy? Why not wait until Percy and Cuyler are gathered as well?"

"Because, though Percy is the regent, you are, or will be in a few minutes, the king. This matter is between a general and his monarch."

"What worries you, General?"

"This war, the one Percy Roan is about to declare, was of his making. I believe *he* commissioned the pirate attacks against Fjorikan immigrants, and worse, may have been engaged with the arms trafficking."

"Do you have proof?" Robert demanded. These were serious accusations, but echoed Eusari's and Anne's speculations. That the general was willing to risk his life to speak these aloud spoke volume over his loyalty to Eston.

"No, sire. Only a hunch so far. Devil Jacque won't talk, and the quartermaster's testimony only went so far. With the first mate's death, I'm afraid no one but the pirate captain himself knows the truth. Well, him and whoever supplied those arms."

"Then why tell me?" Robert asked.

"Because I believe this may be a difficult year for you, and I want you to get through it with open eyes."

Robert laughed. "The best advice I was given when I arrived was to trust no one."

"Do you trust the person who told you that?"

"Well... No, I guess I shouldn't."

"Then take what I've told you with an open mind. Just know that, if Roan is the war hawk, he's in league with the Master Dreamer. I don't want you to feel outnumbered."

"So you're against war like the king was?"

"Against war? To my dying day."

"That sounds strange coming from a general."

"I'm against it but sworn to win whichever the politicians throw me into."

"Good to hear," the young king said. He admitted, "I'm thankful you're on our side, General."

"I'm thankful to be standing on it, sire."

The carriage rolled to a stop and a footman rushed to open the door. Using the stool because he feared tripping over the heavy robes, Robert eased down and began the trek upward. At the base of the platform he was instructed to genuflect for the ministrations by the priests, enduring a separate ritual for each of the seven heavens. By the time they finished, a flock of attendants helped him rise to his feet and Percy Roan joined him at his side.

"This is a grand day, Your Highness," the chancellor said with a smile.

"A terrifying one," Robert agreed.

Together the pair made their way up the tall staircase to the side by side thrones.

"And... turn... smile!" Percy said as practiced. "And... sit." They sat in unison, again as planned. "That's it, Your Highness! You're officially King of Estonia and the empire it controls."

"It feels odd, but I'm glad you're by my side, Percy," Robert lied. This was the *last* man in Andalon he trusted.

A blast of fanfare trumpeted, echoing through the streets and one by one the banners unfurled, revealing an eagle with a single red rose clutched in its talons.

Percy raised an eyebrow; the crest had been kept secret even from him. "You chose your grandfather's emblem? The eagle and the rose?

"It seemed fitting," Robert said with a smile, then did something not planned at all. He was instructed to remain sitting until the event had concluded, but stood defiantly as king and raised his arm straight up into the air.

A great screech roared from the clouds and an eagle descended wearing a circlet of roses around its neck and clutching a single long-stemmed bloom in its talons. The crowd erupted much louder than before as the raptor circled slowly downward, perching on Robert's arm. Only then did he retake his seat.

"Let's hope that's your last surprise, Your Highness," Percy Roan advised through a clenched smile.

"Then you'd better bring none of your own, Chancellor," the king warned in return. The day had finally come, Robert Esterling's seventeenth summer, his passage into adulthood, and his coronation as King of Eston.

Flaya watched the harbor from her balcony, waiting and praying to Felicima her daughter would return soon to Weston. The ritual was not difficult for Pescari-raised children, but Tara would certainly struggle. A month had passed since Teot returned alone, and even he felt concern for his great niece, remarking just that morning she should have long returned.

What if she lays dead in the caldera, Flaya worried, *or dehydrated and starved in the Forbidden Waste?*

She chewed her lip and scanned every ferry, hoping each contained her daughter.

"If she does not return soon," Teot said from the doorway, "I will journey out to retrieve what I find."

"So you think she's dead?" Flaya said, tears welling up at his suggestion.

"Pescari do not die during their ritual. If she is dead, then she was more Andalonian than you feared. Either way, it may simply be she chose not to return."

"I should never have allowed her to test. She wasn't ready."

"She was, I quizzed her along the way to the caldera."

Flaya watched as one ferry unloaded. Two Andalonian merchants disembarked, and a Pescari boy led a horse by braided rawhide. She frowned. His hair was odd, cut short and wild—full of various shades of red, orange, and yellow. His buckskin breeches and shirt were traditionally cut, but intricately adorned with braided rawhide and painted animal bones to matched his hair. On his back he carried a traditional bow and quiver, the latter dyed to match his adornments.

"That's disgusting," Teot said of the boy. "How dare this youth defy Felicima by drawing attention to his appearance. I swear to Felicima the Andalonian influence will be the destruction of our ways."

"Wait," Flaya gasped. "She wears buckskin pants, but that *is* a girl!" She strained her eyes and exclaimed, "It's her! It's Tara!" The joyful mother pushed past the shappan and rushed outside to greet her.

Tara disembarked, leading Nightfire through the waterfront. She carried a handmade bow across her shoulders, the way she had upon the Steppes of Cinder, absently touching the flint knife on her side. It was crude, not nearly as good as steel, but it had saved her life many times in the wilderness. That month, she guessed it was a month by the risings and settings of Felicima, had taught her many things about what it truly meant to be Pescari.

She patted Nightfire, urging him through the sea of people crowding the street. He had been wild when she found him, the reason she had sewn breeches instead of a dress—easier to break a horse bareback if you aren't rubbing the inside of your thighs raw. She was proud of the cleverness it took to fashion sewing needles from cactus and the way she felled her first deer to harvest the skins.

Ignoring the onlooking stares, she touched her hair. That had been a surprise, that first night she and Ember had danced in the flames, when she emerged laughing and joyful at her newfound ability. She shook her braid into a frazzle, noticing the colors when attempting to braid it anew. The shortness of it was a necessity, as she had burned up her snare and needed to weave another in a hurry. She smiled at the memory of cooked rabbit that night—her first meal as a Pescari woman.

"Tara!" Flaya's voice shouted up ahead.

As the crowd parted she spied her mother and Teot approaching with wide smiles. Tara waved, overjoyed to find her mother smiling at her return. The forcefulness of the running embrace nearly knocked her wind free.

"Oh, Daughter, I worried so! I had begun to fear you would not return."

"Pescari *always* return from their ritual," Tara said with a grin.

"And so you are finally Pescari?" Teot asked.

"Yes, Uncle. I know my place among Felicima's people. I have learned our ways, left alone in the wilderness but returned rich with its bounty."

She pulled a pile of skins from atop Nightfire and tossed them to Teot. "I offer these hides as hope and a direction for our people."

Teot appeared confused. "I don't understand. How did you find so many hides in the waste?"

"I didn't. The first night after my vision, a storm cleansed the waste. By morning, the desert was awash with color, splendid flowers and fauna once hidden were revealed for a single moment. Like my hair, Felicima painted the desert as a sign of her covenant. She wants us to expand our people west and north to the land we once farmed."

"That's impossible," Teot disagreed. "The Steppes of Cinder are uninhabitable, made so by her wrath on the day your father became shappan."

"It's healed and awaits us, Uncle. Felicima has filled it once more with tall grasses and trees, and it teems with food and water as it once did." She patted her horse. "That is where I found Nightfire."

"A splendid Pescari name," Flaya remarked. "Tell us again of your hair, Daughter. You say Felicima has painted you? Have you discovered her then, received your blessing?"

"That I'm her agent? Yes, Mother. That was revealed to me in my vision. Only, I was told I had wielded her gift once before. How come you never told me. How young was I, Mother?"

Flaya touched her own belly and frowned at the memory. "That was nearly seventeen summers ago, when I carried you here. You cleansed the world of evil and fulfilled your father's destiny."

"Mother, I have another blessing from our goddess." Tara raised her arm and a screech from above turned every head upward. In a spectacular display of plumage, Ember slowly descended like a flame falling downward. With a final beat of his wings he landed beside mother and daughter, cocking his head and curiously eyeing Flaya.

"A phoenix!" Flaya gasped.

"Is that what he is?" Tara finally knew what kind of bird he was, but the name was odd—certainly not originated from the Pescari language. "How do you know of his kind?"

"I encountered them once, long ago, when I fought alongside Eusari. It was the night Robert was born, actually, and phoenix was the name given to them by the Andalonians. They die but are reborn endlessly. How? How did you find one? They are not from our continent!"

"Mother, he found me, saved me from the fumes of the caldera, and we are bonded. I can see with his eyes when we hunt, and he and I sometimes share a single mind."

"What is his name?" Teot asked, curious.

"I call him Ember," Tara explained, "but you both knew him by a different name before his return. You called him Taros."

Flaya teared up immediately, praising Felicima's miracle. She bowed and the bird bowed in return. Then she faced her daughter and quietly said, "You are truly Pescari, Tara, daughter of Taros, and your name means *reborn*. You entered the wasteland confused of your place in the world, but the child died there. You emerged reborn as a Pescari woman."

"I have so much more to tell you, Mother, and you too, Uncle. Felicima has not stopped speaking to me since my first vision, and has laid out a plan for her people. It's time for us to shed our cloak of shame and emerge empowered by strength. It's time for a new Andalon."

If you enjoyed *Andalon Legacy,* please take a moment to leave stars
or a review.
Please also visit my store at <u>andalonstudios.com</u> where autographed
copies are always available.

From T.B. Phillips...

The *Andalon® Saga* is a chain of independent series. It is a speculative
future of our world following an apocalyptic event. Spanning twelve centuries of evolution traced to a single genetic scientist, each standalone series
offers fresh characters and unique surroundings. Every journey along the
timeline explores how the world of Andalon changes over time.

The concept sprang from difficult conversations between me, a single
father, and my three teenagers, as well as talks with my students. As an
educator working in the most difficult of environments, I knew not every
situation has a happy ending, and the world affects all of us in different
ways. In *Dreamers of Andalon*, my debut series, I tried to teach all my
children and students about the world they lived in, and how trauma and
circumstance are equally impactful. Most of all I wanted them to know
situations could eventually be overcome through tenacity and resilience.
Essential a tragedy, I wrote about raw and emotional characters that reflect
real readers bruised by life.

In the entirety of Andalon, the heroes and villains are separated by
a thin moral line. All actions stemming from their choices are based on
experiences unique to them, and we cannot judge them equally. Nor can
we silence their difference of opinions. I guess you can say my characters
are as perfectly flawed as each of us.

I hope that you will visit my other works while waiting for book two
of *Children of Andalon*!

ANDALON® SAGA

Andalon Origins
Andalon Project (April 2022)
Andalon Paradox (Expected Spring 2023)

Dreamers of Andalon
Andalon Awakens (June 2019)
Andalon Arises (July 2020)
Andalon Attacks (December 2020)

Children of Andalon
Andalon Legacy (September 2022)

OTHER REALMS

Blossom of the Fae
Wailing Tempest (April 2021)
Howling Shadow (September 2021)

CHILLING CREATIONS
Spine-Tingling Collaborations

Don't Pay the Ferryman (Expected Fall 2022)